HUNGER IN HER BONES

CLARE C. MARSHALL

Enjoy!! :)

BOOK THREE

THE SPARKSTONE SAGA

Hunger In Her Bones
Book Three of the Sparkstone Saga

Editing by Jessica Corra

FAERY INK PRESS
faeryinkpress.com
Calgary, Alberta
clare@faeryinkpress.com

Printed in Canada by Webcom.

Library and Archives Canada Cataloguing in Publication
Marshall, Clare author
Hunger in her bones / Clare C. Marshall. -- Offset edition.
(The Sparkstone saga ; book three)
Issued in print and electronic formats.
ISBN 978-1-988110-01-1 (softcover).--ISBN 978-1-988110-03-5 (EPUB).--
ISBN 978-1-988110-04-2 (Kindle)
I. Title.
PS8626.A76675H86 2017 jC813'.6 C2017-902371-3
C2017-902372-1

MIX
Paper from
responsible sources
FSC® C004071

Other books by Clare C. Marshall:

The Violet Fox Series:

The Violet Fox

The Silver Spear

The Emerald Cloth

The Sparkstone Saga:

Stars In Her Eyes

Dreams In Her Head

Hunger In Her Bones

Darkness In Her Reach

Other Titles:

Within

PART ONE

Music is a powerful weapon in the right hands.

—J.G.C., *Campbell's Multiple Verses*

PROLOGUE

Sunni and I stroll across the quad towards the town of Sparkstone. It's approaching midnight, and the glittering Milky Way splashes across the sky. The air is thick and stuffy, with no fresh breeze to alleviate the heat. My arm moves lazily at my side, swimming through the air as I note the vivid green of the grass and the stark navy blue of the sky. The Milky Way stars appear cartoonishly yellow, as if we are walking beneath a painted curtain of sky, and the Northern Star, the moon, Venus, and the faint light of Mars are also absent.

"That's funny," I say, "I don't remember the news saying there would be no regular stars out tonight. Do you think that's why we're here?"

I expect the surroundings to fill in the gap in my memory. Sparkstone campus. The old buildings behind us that aren't really old, and the orderly suburb town before us was built for the servants of the Collective. A small university town to the naked eye, but within those white-and-grey shingled homes, people from another world, spying on us, waiting for our powers to emerge so they can ...

I'm tugged in that direction, but remain anchored by Sunni's firm grip on my arm. She gestures in the other direction, towards the isolated structure of Conrod Building.

A running figure moves swiftly toward us. I draw back instinctively. It doesn't look like any of my friends—it can't be Jia, she'd probably opt to travel invisibly even in the dark. The figure pants with effort, glancing over her shoulder every few seconds as she attempts to put more space between herself and whoever she thinks is chasing her. In the dim lighting, I strain to make out her features and move towards her. The more I focus on her face, the slower I move, as if the air has transmuted into molasses.

Her white sneakers snag something in the grass and she falls face-first to the ground. I run towards her to help but she takes no notice of me. She groans, struggling to climb to her elbows.

"Are you all right?" I ask, kneeling before her.

She fixes a fearful stare at me, squints, and then looks past my right shoulder. She sobs, and then clamps her mouth shut. Her wide cheekbones and olive green eyes remind me of a friend I had in elementary school. She had a similar haircut when we were young: a thick, messy bob and heavy bangs that covered her eyebrows.

And as I think of my old, forgotten friend, the girl's image wavers for a brief moment, twisting to accommodate my thoughts.

"Focus on the present," Sunni says.

Sunni's sharp voice rips the old memory from me as the true image of the girl comes back into focus. Her dark coffee-brown hair is short and curled in the autumn climate. Freckles dot the bridge of her nose and her sharp chin juts upward as she peers at the sky. Her lips move; I think she's praying.

I look frantically around for help, but it's just me and Sunni here. Mostly just me, though. I don't think Sunni has the physical presence to help. I climb to my feet and offer a hand. "C'mon. You can come back to my dorm. I have friends that can protect you. You don't have to be afraid."

Again, she ignores me, but this time for a good reason. As if conjured by the darkness, two figures come soundlessly from either side of me and grab the girl under her arms. Whether from surprise or an unknown force, I am knocked backward onto the cold grass.

"Hey!" I shout at the strangers, scrambling to my feet. My butt should hurt from the fall, yet the grass is strangely pillowy.

The two humanoids hover over the girl. Heavy, navy robes hide their true form. Their moves are calculated and cold as one holds her against the grass, and the other fumbles with a leather pouch around his waist. Their hands look human, but I wouldn't be surprised if they are hafelglob, gross alien shapeshifters who take human form and make up the majority of the security here at Sparkstone. Their faces are obscured by darkness, the hoods, and my fear of seeing their features.

One man holds the girl down as the other injects a transparent liquid via a large syringe into the crook of her elbow. She kicks and screams, and calls for help. No one is here, but me and Sunni, and Sunni isn't really here at all.

As if I am captaining a dingy on a turbulent sea, I buck and swerve to maintain my balance in the face of hopelessness.

The Collective are so much stronger than us.

They're more advanced.

They can manipulate us, and bring harm to those we love if we resist them. I know because they've hurt my family before.

And yet...

This ocean is mine. I can still the waters.

I can change the rules because I have superpowers. I *can* fight this.

"You could," says Sunni, next to me. "Won't do much good, since you're not really here."

The first dose does little to subdue the girl. She is strong. The would-be captor deftly retrieves another vial of the bright liquid from his pouch and inserts it into the needle, tests it, and forcefully gives the girl another dose. She screams. Dull pain surges up my left arm, as if I am the victim and not the witness in this crime.

"But this is really happening, isn't it?" I push to my feet, aided by dream physics. The grass feels like nothing on my toes. Blankets surround me; they are the air. I am close to opening my eyes—my real eyes—and seeing my dorm room, feeling the dread that accompanies the morning.

"I'm going to wake up. I'm going to run outside and stop this."

"I used to think I could do that too," Sunni admits.

"I'm different. I'm special."

Sunni shrugs. "Maybe."

My Sunni wouldn't have said that. She told me that I was

meant to do something great here—that my coming heralded a change. Hopefully one for the better. Me and the Sparks, we were meant to lead our peers out of this sick experiment and destroy the Collective's attempts to harvest our DNA in the name of progress. No, this Sunni is just a shadow, pieced together from my twenty-four hours of knowing her and watching her die.

The girl has quieted now. She lays limp in one of the attacker's arms as he drags her across the grass toward Conrod Building. Beneath that building, there's a secret launch bay where the Collective keeps its shuttles. They must not have the teleportation arm bands like the other hafelglob.

Maybe they didn't take the precaution because they thought this would be easy.

Well. They shouldn't have underestimated us humans.

Time to be a hero.

I launch into a run, yet once again, the air is as thick as molasses. The kidnappers move at a good clip as if a thicker atmosphere is normal for them—maybe it is. Damn dream physics.

"I can move faster than this," I mumble. My lips are cracked and dry, and again, the world of sleep and wakefulness thins. But I can't afford to leave yet. Dream or not, I won't wake up in the dorm knowing that I failed to prevent yet another kidnapping of a Sparkstone student.

Sunni, in a blur of colour and light, dashes in front of me and blocks my way. She throws her head back and screams, and gripping my arm tightly, together we leap into the sky. I lean away from her—I have to save the girl—but Sunni's in control now.

We're no longer outside: we're in what feels like a cabin living room, if the cabin owners were into the occult. Several women sit around a Ouija board resting on a table near the far wall. Shelves filled with crystals and candles line the walls; a purple cloth banner displaying a pentagram hangs next to a beaded doorway. I squint, trying to peer through the obscured grey beyond, yet my unconscious tells me that I'm still in Sparkstone. The room is stuffy; my legs writhe in the sheets, and in the dream realm, I try to wriggle from Sunni's strong grip. She holds me in place as a heavy mist descends upon the women. They're chanting in unison, eyes closed, as they grip each other tightly.

"I'm going back to save that girl," I tell Sunni.

Sunni's grip tightens. The faces of the missing students—including Sunni's own smiling visage—swirl in the mist. The women stare indifferently at them.

"Don't you know who they are?" I ask them. "The Collective has taken them. We want justice. What do you know?"

A thick, warm gust of wind gathers the crisp cabin and occult colours and peels them away, revealing the vibrant quad once more. The shock of being outside in the cold, even if it's still just a dream, hits me hard. The kidnappers and the girl are almost to Conrod Building. I could make it.

Sunni's outstretched hand now presses firmly against my chest. Heat radiates from her in a way that I couldn't feel from the kidnapped girl. She is more real in this moment than in any other.

Her eyes glow faintly as she utters her usual request.

"Open... "

"The door. I know. But I don't know which—" My words are sluggish. I can taste the sleep in my mouth. In the distance, the attackers and the girl are fading black dots as they approach the hidden shuttle bay. "I can't do this now."

"This is more important than just one girl," she says insistently. Her fingertips dig into my skin as her other hand moves up to my neck. The hand is cold, scaled, and familiar.

"You're not Sunni. You never are."

"Trying... " For a moment, it really does look like she's trying to resist possession. Her hand stiffens, yet the dream doesn't allow me to back away. My body is lead and trapped on the hard mattress in real life, preventing me from escaping her grasp.

Sunni loses the battle. Her green eyes darken and transform, possessed by my memory of the alien Professor Jadore, when she threatened our lives. I gulp in air as she clamps her grip around me. While one hand chokes, the other whips out a knife from behind her back. She stabs me in the chest. It's a dull, muted pain, made more intense as she twists the blade clockwise, as if trying to turn a sound dial on a radio.

This is the part where I can usually force myself to wake up.

Fog rolls in from my peripheral vision, though it could be me slowly dying. I choke out a plea for Sunni-Jadore to stop, but with each wasted utterance, she becomes more and more like Jadore. Green-skinned, black eyes, and taller. Even if I wanted to comply with their request, there's no door to be seen. My eyes roll upward. Just let the dream be over already.

The Sunni-Jadore form dissipates and becomes one with the fog, and for a moment, my dream mind wonders if she was really there in the first place. Only my hands hold the knife stuck in my chest. It doesn't hurt anymore. There's no blood, only the sense of something foreign stuck inside me. I slide the blade out, and breathe a little easier.

In the sky, misty cloud nebulas swirl at a stand-still pace into a black hole. I'm still on Earth, and still at Sparkstone, yet the fog has devoured it all: the campus, the never-ending stretch of prairie, and Canadian Rockies.

The further away an object, the slower it appears to move. Standing alone on the barren planet as white mist rises and envelops me, I don't know what's worse: passing the event horizon and stretching forever into a place where light cannot escape, or waiting here, alone in the mist, undying as the universe marches on.

CHAPTER 1

"And there's nothing else? That's all that happened?"

I nod at Jia's question, stroking my long piano fingers as I lean back against the faux leather couch. The skin on my hands peels from the dry climate. I try not to pick at it. I'll have to make do without hand lotion—the stuff I brought with me in September ran out a few days ago. Since anything I buy in this alien-controlled town could be infused with strange, DNA-altering chemicals, I don't want to take the risk.

"The girl sounds like Kendra. She lives on the floor below us. Always seemed nice," Jia says thoughtfully. "Maybe Sunni is showing you her fate to help us."

Misty fidgets in her seat next to Jia. Dreaming about Sunni—whether she's actually communicating with me from beyond the grave, or whether I'm conjuring her from my subconscious—is a contentious subject. Why Sunni chose to communicate with me, a person she barely knew for twenty-four hours in real life, rather than Misty, a close friend she knew before coming to Sparkstone, is still a mystery.

Normally we'd have these meetings outside, where there's

less chance of us being observed, but this autumn has been unforgiving with its shrill winds. I could probably stand it, but Wil and Misty aren't as accustomed to bearing the cold as Jia and me. I don't blame them. Sitting on comfy couches in a private, climate-controlled study room in Rogers Hall is far more preferable, especially with our albeit crude methods of circumventing the Collective's monitoring methods.

"Another one, gone," I say.

"So we'll add Kendra to the list. Does Kendra have a last name?" Misty asks. She can't meet my apologetic gaze. These dream-recounting sessions are hard for her. Drudging up Sunni every day doesn't help us move on from her violent death at Jadore's hands weeks ago. "That's, what, three students gone in the last couple of weeks?"

Wil, sitting to my left on the leather couch, has already made the calculation with his light-speed, telepathic brain of his, but he obliges me as I do a quick mental tally.

The first was Daniel Chomber, an astrobiology and chemical engineering major in his final year. One day, he was on the verge of making an important breakthrough studying how the reactions between water, rocks, and low temperatures shape planet habitability. The next, his dorm and his lab desk had been cleaned out. The cover-up was too clean, too much like how they treated Sunni's death to not catch our attention.

The second, barely four days later: Fahima Osmond, a third-year student who had skipped a grade in high school because of her impressive grasp of mathematics, which led her to study cryptology and physics. According to her friends, she had been falling behind on her projects, and had obsessively spent more and more time in her dorm room. Just like Daniel Chomber, one day she was there, and the next, she was "gone." Sent home to "think about her future" was the official story, though to our knowledge, no one leaves Sparkstone University alive.

The Collective became more restrained, because it was nearly two weeks before the next disappearance. Avery Trites, second-year student, studying ballet and kinesiology. Avery travelled with a few other dancers to and from Sparkstone for competitions and shows—under heavy supervision from two professors. Even though Avery was reported to have returned to campus from the latest outing, others reported that the professors had kept him late at a bar in Edmonton to celebrate his latest win. Same thing the next day: empty dorm, emptied out locker. Official story: transferred to a special dance academy somewhere in the States.

Now, less than three days later, Kendra. Unknown last name. Unknown major. Gone, like the rest of them.

"Kendra makes for the fourth one in three weeks."

We only have five minutes left on the jammer, Wil reminds us with his unblockable telepathic voice.

Textbooks and binder notes are scattered across the coffee table, and Wil balances a black notebook on his lap. It's filled with advanced calculus, though that's for the benefit of the tiny camera inserted into the ceiling—although Wil does enjoy solving calculus equations in his spare time. He fiddles absently with the silver band wrapped permanently around his wrist. The same band is around all our wrists. He's still unable to get them off, despite trying everything he can think of. And if the telepathic genius who has a silver tongue when it comes to technology can't get rid of it, I don't know who can.

The Collective monitors almost every room in every building on campus. Most of the devices are installed in the ceiling, beside or within lights. Thanks to Wil's genius, we've figured out how to modify our alien wristbands to interfere with the audio signal for up to fifteen minutes. Wil's telepathic powers help extend this time limit sometimes, but we don't want to raise suspicion by relying on him too much. It's one thing for him to be good with technology. It's another to have them realize that his genius is driven by his superpowers.

"And the stuff about you opening a door?"

It's impossible to lie, but it's easy to hold back. Wil doesn't push me, but I feel his patient stare. Even thinking about him thinking about my thoughts is enough to drudge up memories and feelings that I don't want him to see. Like Ethan and I in the music room, creating music together. And how he almost died in my arms, just weeks ago, because of whatever experiments the Collective are doing on him. He could be next. He could be—

"Hey!" Misty says, clapping suddenly. Her icy glare turns to Wil. "She alive in there or what?"

"I've told you before, okay? She says that every time. You knew her. Don't you know what it means?"

Misty slumps back in the couch and puts her boots up on the coffee table. Flecks of dirt shake from the soles onto a sheet of orderly calculus problems. "She's trying to communicate with us."

Jia lets out a calculated breath and discretely checks her cell phone. "We know from Shannon across the hall from me that Kendra wasn't in tutorial today, and she heard that her room was vacated."

"That's what happened with Sunni," Misty said, her voice unsteady.

Jia nods. I don't need Wil's powers to relive the moment of her death. The crackle of Jadore's hand lightning. The thump as she fell to the floor on the mother ship. Her body, transported away. There was no time to say goodbye. When we returned to Earth, me in a whirlwind of newfound teleportation powers, to find her room had been emptied—and readied for *me*—it was like she'd never been there at all. None of us know if me staying in Sunni's room has given me access to her bizarre psychic dreamscape, or if Sunni is communicating from beyond the grave, but the dreams are unlike anything I've had before, and with Sunni's absence hanging over us so thickly, we cannot afford to dismiss anything.

"It matches what happened to the others. It's...safe to assume the worst," Jia continued quietly.

"If she was really abducted—" Wil begins.

"She was," I say curtly, in a certainty that frightens me. "We—*I*—saw it. I saw the others too—but this is the clearest dream yet."

Wil nods patiently. "What I'm saying is there is no other information confirming that that's how the girl was abducted. Her absence—and the absence of the others—doesn't make the abduction theory more plausible." He adjusts the small, round frames on his nose, and leans forward, unable to relax, and then tells us telepathically, *Maybe a minute now, probably less.*

The urgency cuts through Jia's voice. "And we're no closer to discovering what kind of alien this might be? Was it hafelglob?"

"Don't think so, but I can't be sure." We haven't ever seen hafelglob wear anything other than maintenance overalls, or security guard attire. Despite several night missions surveying Conrod Building—Wil has access because his lab is in there—we haven't seen any unusual activity.

"We don't know how many aliens belong to the Collective. There's too friggin' many. All that matters is they're not human." Misty mutters.

"Maybe," I say, trying to recall the details of the dream. Sunni's dreams don't slip away as easily as regular vivid dreams. "There was a part where I was in a room filled with occult imagery. People were sitting around a table, and this strange cloud hovered above them. And...the faces of the kidnapped were in the cloud. The room was boiling hot." I blush again, but I'm determined to tell them every aspect of the dream, no matter how silly or trivial.

Misty lights up. "There's an occult shop in town."

"There is?"

Time's up, Wil says telepathically. "So, Ingrid, does that statistics explanation help at all?"

"I hope I was able to clear up the cognitive behavioural issue question you had. It's tricky, but you'll get it," Jia chimes in, right on cue.

I smile weakly. Misty's words remain. I have to get to that occult shop.

But just like that, the dream conversation is over. Who knows what the alien listening in on us thinks about our suspicious meetings. Jia's major is child psychology, and has little intersection with Wil's math and computer engineering work. At least me taking pointers from Wil makes sense, with me *supposedly* studying psychology and interdimensional theories. And Misty—well, I wouldn't be surprised if they stopped trying to play the mind gymnastics it takes to justify her presence in our math and science conversations. Her linguistics major and mastery of languages would be little help in the joint study scenario we're selling here. Sparkstone did sell its freshmen on interdisciplinary study. Strange major combinations are not only common, but encouraged. It's a thin, but somewhat comforting blanket.

"So...um..." Jia and I exchange awkward smiles. It's always like this after the jammer gives out. We have to go back to considering each word before speaking. "If we're done, should we go for a walk? Get some exercise before going back at it? I... could use a stretch."

Wil stands to his full height—an impressive six foot one—and gathers his misconstrued papers. "Can't. Have to get back to the lab. My project is due in a week."

"Keener," Misty mutters, but she jumps to her feet. "I'm down for a walk."

"Don't you have a deadline to meet?" I ask.

"So do you. I think yours is a little more urgent, no?"

It's true that Jadore hasn't let up on me. Ever since I announced my connection to Joseph G. Campbell, I've lived with regret. But I need to know why I feel so strongly about him. Why I feel like I know him.

Why I can conjure him into our world with my music.

We gather our papers and tidy the study room for the next study group. We take our time. Hurrying would be suspicious. I yawn. Being constantly aware of my body, and how it reacts, is exhausting. It doesn't help that Jia, Misty, and I have been sharing a room for the past week. Jia snores, and Misty rolls in her sleep, and has terrible nightmares that make her sweat something fierce. But it's the best way to keep an eye on each other—and makes it harder for the Collective to snatch us during the night.

I clutch my binders close to my chest. I shouldn't be so mean with Misty. She does make it easy with her defensive attitude. As Wil finishes gathering his math problems and Jia eagerly helps, I lean against the door. Misty texts absently on her phone. Weeks ago, she confided in me that she writes text messages to herself in a language that she and Sunni made up: part of her grieving process.

"So what's the new project you've got?" I ask her.

"Hmm?" She peers at me over her device. "Oh. Just dumb documents that I have to translate."

"What is it this time? Japanese or German?" Jia asks. She barely takes her gaze from Wil as he stuffs his messy, note-stuffed binder into his shoulder bag.

"Arabic," Misty replies, finally stuffing her phone in her back pocket.

Finally we head out into the hallway. Jia first, then Misty, then me, and then Wil. *No professors heading our way, just some students. Jadore's in her office. We're clear.*

Jia continues our innocent conversation from the study room. "I could use a refresher on my Mandarin," Jia says as we saunter down the long, red-carpeted hallway within Rogers Hall. Dorms for guests and newly arrived students line both sides. I stayed here for a day when I arrived, before I moved into Sunni's old room. "It's been a long time since I've spoken it."

"Your parents don't speak it?" Wil asks.

Jia laughs. "No. I mean, I guess they learned a bit with me when I was younger, and they sent me to a Mandarin-only school when I was six, but it was pretty expensive and in Calgary, far away, so they had to stop. So, Misty, would you be up for some private tutoring?"

Misty shrugs, but I see in her eyes that she's trying to hide her interest. "Sure, I guess. Mandarin's not one of my best languages."

"You're being modest. Every language is your best language."

"Yeah, yeah, okay. You don't need to butter me up, I'll help."

"Are there any languages you *don't* know?" I ask her.

"Finnish is hard. Swedish I can get by all right in. Gaelic, I have no clue. Not that many speak that one anyway."

"*Is mise Ingrid, ciamar a tha thu?*" I say. "That's pretty much all I know."

Misty runs her teeth harshly over her bottom lip and looks pensive. "*I'm Ingrid, how are you?* That right?"

"Yeah. You just picked that up now?"

She shrugs again and waves her hands. "Throwin' fire and ice ain't all I can do."

I hold my breath. Wil shoots her a dirty look. Jia tenses beside me.

Do you want to get us killed? Wil asks.

"It's fine," Misty says, brushing us off. She stuffs her hands in her sweater pockets, and quickly checks the hallway for cameras. There's one at the end of the hall above the entrance, but we're still pretty far. It's possible it didn't hear. Still, she lowers her voice. "If they don't know that's what I'm about by now by the number of blobs I've hurt, then they're dumber than rocks and we should have no problem getting those students back. If there's anyone left to rescue. What I meant was, *unfortunately* my languages skills don't come in as handy."

Wil is a hard one to read; he remains stoic at the best of times. Perhaps he's gotten used to forgiving Misty for her easy dismissals. *It saved us while we were on the mother ship, you quickly figuring out syntax and guessing words. I wouldn't discount your talent that quickly.*

"Okay, that's enough praise from y'all today." But she's trying to hide her smile. She really is proud of this. I can't say I'm not impressed and a little bit jealous. My teleportation power has shown itself in times of need but I'm a long way from saying that I have it as an innate talent. "We should get back to Rita House."

"I'm heading towards Conrod Building," Wil says.

"Sight unseen?" Jia asks.

He shakes his head. "We have to appear consistent."

"Yeah. Right." Jia's disappointment at Wil rejecting her offer to provide invisibility isn't hard to miss. To bring all of us under her genetically produced shield, she has to touch us, or we have to touch someone she is touching. Any excuse to hold Wil's hand is a good one to her, I suppose.

The camera planted above the threshold between the hallway and the second-floor landing above the entrance to Rogers Hall watches our every move. To the lazy observer, we four aren't an interesting sight. I hope. I hold my breath as we pass through. It reminds me of the childhood game we'd play when driving in a car. If you drove past a graveyard, you had to hold your breath. It didn't matter how long the graveyard lasted. If you gave up because you ran out of breath or because of a long traffic light, you lost. Chills run through me now, even as I squint against the light of the entrance just a few feet below us, on the main landing. All we have to do is go down a flight of wide, open stairs—the same stairs I met Sunni on over a month ago—and out the doors to the left.

Escape from the building doesn't mean escaping the Collective. They're everywhere on campus. On the main landing, lazily on the job behind a service desk, is a security guard. Definitely hafelglob. He sits upright in his chair, watching the ginormous TV placed on the right-hand corner of the desk. It's the only item on the freshly sanded maple wood. He's watching CBC News with the volume turned up to deafening levels. There's a reporter at a crime scene in Halifax, Nova Scotia, announcing the arrest of an alleged serial killer who happened to be running for political office.

The four of us head down the stairs. I try to focus on the exit, but I can't help but study the alien in human form as we descend. I'm not sure if it's my budding superpowers, or a built-in survival instinct, but something primal in my gut *knows* that the security guard doesn't belong here. That he's out of place. A wolf among us sheep. The hafelglob in their natural state are gelatinous creatures, yet their sharp teeth and large mouths could easily take down a herd animal. I wonder how they evolved to be that way, if the Collective scooped them up from their home world and helped their evolution on to suit their needs, or whether they are natural, gross predators.

Like many animals, the hafelglob in disguise knows when it's being watched. He glares at me, annoyed that my attention is taking him away from his show. I look away quickly and nearly trip as I hurry down the rest of the stairs toward the door. No doubt he knows who we are, and would love an excuse to bust us all.

My body slams against the push-bar, and the door opens. The cold bites my face, refreshing after several hours in the stale environment. It's late afternoon in Sparkstone, Alberta. The end of October looms, and the Canadian Rockies weather begins to show her true colours with rich autumn reds and orange dominating the curated trees planted on campus and along Sparkstone Boulevard. The sky is a traditional cloudless blue, and the grass, while giving way to hints of autumn brown, is kept green by the diligent maintenance staff milling about in the distance. Also hafelglob.

Now that we're outside in the open, we can talk more freely. There are most certainly cameras on the buildings, but with the wide distance between the buildings, it's doubtful the audio would pick up clear conversations. At least, that's our theory. And my personal hope.

"It's colder than I thought out here." I glance back at Misty and Jia. "You're sure you're up for a walk?"

Misty sneers good-naturedly. "Just 'cause I'm American doesn't mean—"

"It's supposed to go down to minus ten tonight," Jia says, whipping out her cell phone to confirm.

Wil and Misty crack jokes about the winter, especially when I tell them to consider buying heavier coats. They have no idea what minus thirty Celsius feels like. Then again, as Misty is quick to point out, she's lived in more places than all of us combined, and that I shouldn't be so hasty to judge what her body knows about cold. Especially when she can blast ice from her fingers. I'm pretty sure she's just being defensive, though.

"Minus ten," Misty mutters, shaking her head. "Just a quick walk around the quad, or down that trail behind the houses where you like to run. I'm not suggesting another late-night mission."

We've had a couple of those in the past two weeks. Neither of them yielded encouraging results. Just the four of us, wandering invisible around campus in the dark like chameleon vigilantes, waiting for the Collective to make its move. And what did it get us? A scolding from Jadore for being late to tutorial, and tons of arguments brought on by lack of sleep.

"I wonder how the Collective will fair through the winter," Wil muses as we saunter across the quad. "Roads are not good during the winter. I guess they could fly things in, but heavy machinery, even the old Curtiss-Wright C-46 planes in the Yukon might have trouble starting if we really get hit by the cold."

"The Collective have been here for a few years now though, haven't they?" Misty says, joining in on our musings—a rare occurrence. "They've probably got it all figured out."

"That's what they'd like us to think," I say. "Maybe their supply of Substance 454 will dry up." Substance 454 is what the Collective puts in its food to pacify the students.

"And our food supply too. Fresh food will be hard to come by. Thank goodness Mum and Dad's shipment arrived yesterday. I hope they're getting along with the harvest fine."

"It'll be okay," I say, squeezing her shoulder. It's an empty promise, and Jia smiles thinly, but repeating those three words has become a personal mantra, especially when it comes to family.

A car screeches down Sparkstone Boulevard and whips by us.

Jia instinctively leaps backward, tugging me with her. She grew up more rural than the rest of us: she's not used to cars whipping by. The car seems to realize the speed limit isn't above thirty as Sparkstone Boulevard turns into a pedestrian-dominated walkway. Tires screeching, it grinds to a halt. Several studying students turn their attentions away from their conversations and notebooks to gawk at the nerve of this obvious outsider.

"Hey...wait..." Misty whispers. "I know that car . . ."

It's an older make, definitely eighties, maybe seventies. It has seen its fair share of battles, with a bent-up passenger's side door and windshield fractures—a common sight down in Calgary, but these look like the windshield has driven through a fierce hailstorm. The front driver's side door is painted a fading orange, while the rest of the vehicle is a rusty light blue. The gas exhaust interrupts our fresh autumn air rudely. Cars rarely come through Sparkstone—not this late in the semester. In fact, it's pretty rare that anyone here drives, despite the perfect suburban garages on the houses in town.

"I'll catch up with—" Wil starts to head away from us, across the road in the direction of Conrod Building when he stops short. His gaze dances between the car and Misty. "No way…"

"What?" I ask.

The car reverses, more carefully now, and backs into the Rogers Hall parking lot. The engine abruptly ceases. A woman pushes the car door open brashly and tumbles out, and marches towards MacLeod Hall.

"C'mon," Misty hisses.

MacLeod Hall is behind Rita House and dozens of feet away, closer to the roundabout that borders the actual town of Sparkstone and the campus. The woman seems to know where she's going as she follows the well-trodden foot path made by many hard-working students. When I first arrived, I didn't know where anything was. As we approach MacLeod Hall, we see her entering the building. I wait for some alarm to go off, for her to jump back, startled, as the door takes her DNA, but it seems to let her in without incident. Perhaps she is from the Collective. We maneuver around a couple of students coming out of tutorials as the four of us rush inside. She marches down the rightmost hallway off the entrance, leading to the professors' offices, and finally I'm able to get a clear view of her.

The woman is short and stout, but moves with the speed of a hunting cheetah. Blond-white curls frame her ashen face.

While her skin has seen better days, her eyes are deep pools of sorrow. Human or alien, this woman has seen death.

We hang back from her—especially me, as I don't know who she is—and watch as she storms down the hallway. She doesn't appear concerned that the four of us are clambering after her in plain sight. Her gaze does not waver from its target: Jadore's office.

"I know who that is," Misty says quietly, and takes off after her.

"Misty!" I hiss. I roll my eyes and gesture to Jia and Wil.

The four of us follow the determined woman to Jadore's office, if only to warn her that now is not the time to anger the terrifying reptilian alien beast within. She must hear us, for the hallway is otherwise empty and quiet, but she appears not to care. Jadore's office is at the end of the hallway. Without ceremony, she twists the doorknob and bursts into the room.

From the hallway, I can see Jadore. She rises abruptly from her desk and reaches for her lethal cane. "Who is there?"

Professor Jadore wears dark sunglasses to cover her even darker eyes. Her story is that she's blind, but in reality, she's an alien whose human disguise is unable to give her human-looking eyes. She seems to have a sensitivity to light but this makes her no less deadly. Holding onto the desk for support, she walks slowly around it to face the strange intruder, and us.

The woman appears unafraid of Jadore. She draws in a deep breath and balls her hands into fists. "You don't remember me? I'll tell you who I am. My name is Svanhild Harris, and I want to know what in blazes you've done with my daughter."

CHAPTER 2

"Hildie," Misty says in a hurried breath.

The woman—Sunni's mother, I can barely believe it—seems to realize we're behind her, and spins around. "Misty..." Her voice is a pained whisper. "I am so...so glad to see you."

She takes Misty into her arms as if the lanky, dark-clothed girl were Sunni herself. Misty hugs her fiercely. She is Sunni's only living relative that I know of. Sunni told me that her father had left and presumably died at sea a long time ago and that her mother had never been the same since.

Jadore's lips struggle not to snarl. "Svanhild—"

She releases Misty from her hug and pulls her around, pressing her into her right side. "We are not that familiar, Professor."

Jadore curls her long, spindly fingers around her cane. "I see. Ms. Harris."

"*Mrs.* Harris. Just because my husband's gone don't mean he ain't out there, alive."

Although I cannot see her gaze, I feel Jadore sweeping her eyes over the rest of us, awkwardly cramped in the hallway, completely visible. Blocking Jadore's escape. Her grip on her cane tightens, and although I'm frightened of Jadore's power, a smug amusement warms my chest. Sunni's *mother* is here. Which can only mean one thing.

"You mind tellin' me where my daughter is, Professor?"

Jadore slowly returns to her chair. "You did not receive our letter?"

"Oh I got a letter all right. And that courtesy call from someone in the registrar's office. Transferred. You think you have the right to ship my daughter off to some backwater country on the other side of the world without so much as a goodbye to her mother?"

"Perhaps we can discuss this privately, Mrs. Harris."

"Anythin' you say to me you can say in front of Misty. And..." She glances around her shoulder at Wil, Jia, and me. "These friends of yours, Misty?"

"Yes," Misty replies, her voice somewhat strained from prolonged physical contact.

"Then they stay too. C'mon in here then."

We pile into Jadore's now-cramped office and Wil shuts the door. We were only in here once, when we were trying to hack into the main security mainframe weeks ago to track down Sunni's location.

"I'm waitin' for an explanation, Professor. It was your name on the letter. You authorized this transfer, you and this president of yours. And I've been tryin' for weeks now to get an appointment with him but he seems to be busy."

"Mr. Dean is currently out of the province at a conference. I am handling his affairs," Jadore replies with a voice as smooth as silk.

I shiver. Wil is pretty sure that Mr. Dean is human, but the Collective seems to have a pretty tight leash on him.

"Yes, that's what the woman on the phone kept tellin' me. He always seems to be away when I need to speak with him. What kind of university are you running here? I haven't heard from my *daughter* in *weeks.*" She scowls and looks at Misty, who is still firmly in Mrs. Harris's grasp. "You know anything about this?"

We can't get involved in this, Wil's telepathic voice booms in our heads. *Jadore could fry us all to a crisp now that we're conveniently trapped in this room.*

Misty glares at him over her shoulder, and then mutters, "Haven't heard from her since the transfer."

"No emails, no phone calls?"

"No."

"And the rest of you?" Mrs. Harris asks us.

The three of us shake our heads slowly.

"That's real somethin'. I've been gettin' emails like clockwork every week. Short, one sentence emails that don't sound like the good daughter I raised, all by myself, mind you. She obviously has internet, but she can't afford to pick up the phone? That's real rich, considerin' I'm still payin' her tuition. I'm not thick. Batomisk School of Science and Technology? Spent almost a hundred dollars in long distance fees trying to contact them. Oh sure, they have a Sunni Harris enrolled, but they couldn't put her on the phone. Not in the morning, not in the afternoon, not in the evening. My daughter wouldn't abandon me like that. First I thought, they're holdin' her hostage. Then I did some more diggin'. Paid some computer person at the local university real good money to map out the area that the school's supposed to be in. Based it on the area code of the phone number, some technical mumbo-jumbo. Batomisk School, if it ain't a warehouse out in the country, no more than a call centre! Something ain't right here. And I'm not leavin' until you tell me what kind of scam you're runnin' here."

I purse my lips.

"This is certainly an *interesting*...story," Jadore says slowly. "I can assure you that our sister school in the Philippines is not a call centre. If you flew there now, you would find a campus not unlike this one, with bright minds hard at work. Your daughter's degree does require her to spend long days in the wilderness."

"With the money I'm payin' you right now, I *could* fly out there myself. Spent the last of my savings coming up here. Left my sittin' chair too. With the way the fates have treated me, my husband might walk through my front door while I'm here, and decide that I've abandoned him. Well. That's certainly not the case." Realizing she's gone on a tangent, she clears her throat and gets back on track. "You listen here. If you don't bring my daughter back here, to me, I'm filing a missing person report. And I may not be a woman with limitless resources, but my *friends* down in Wimberley and even in Austin, who miss Sunni somethin' fierce, they ain't shy. They'll bombard every media source and internet forum until we have justice."

For the briefest of moments, something flickers across Jadore's face that I have not seen before. Fear. She adjusts her sunglasses, sliding them further up her nose, and sets her lips in a hard, cold line. "I sympathize with your situation, Mrs. Harris. Here is what I will do for you. If you truly believe your daughter has gone missing halfway around the world, we will launch an investigation and do our best to find her. We will reach out to our sister school to determine her whereabouts regardless."

Mrs. Harris stabs Jadore's desk with a meaty finger. "I want you to bring her home."

"I can't guarantee that she will return here. After all, she is an adult in the middle of her degree, and her major project is due next month. But...perhaps if we could arrange a video chat, that would satisfy you?"

My gaze slides to Wil. He speaks to my unspoken worry. *I have no doubt they could manufacture Sunni's likeness and stage some sort of reunion on the computer. Whether or not it will satisfy Mrs. Harris, I don't know.*

"I want to speak to my daughter. *Really* speak to her." Mrs. Harris falters for a moment, and her long nails dig into Misty's shoulder. "One week. If I don't get proof that she's alive, I will make good on my promise to talk to the press."

"That will not be necessary," Jadore says quickly. "We will do what we can to show you that your daughter is all right. In the meantime, I imagine you are exhausted from your journey. I can show you the way to our registrar's office. Ms. Agailya will set you up in our finest temporary residence." Jadore climbs from her seat, feels her way around the desk, and holds up her cane. "The rest of you, I believe you have projects that need completing? Misty, have you finished your translation? I believe I was clear when I said the deadline was yesterday."

Misty scowls and an insult is on the tip of her tongue, but it's Mrs. Harris who comes to her defense. "You mustn't be so hard on the child. She worked extremely hard to get to where she is today. I'm sure she has a good excuse, like bein' worried sick about Sunni."

"I am well aware of Misty's…*history*. That does not excuse lack of responsibility, not here at Sparkstone. Expelled students do not fare well outside these walls."

Neither do the ones that actually graduate. Or so we've assumed. The Collective harvests the DNA of any students who appear to have superpowers. Every student at Sparkstone has the potential in their genetic code to have powers, and the Collective feeds us a drug via the food that helps to activate the gene responsible. Some like Misty, Jia, and Wil came to Sparkstone with already active genes and have had to hide their talents to avoid being killed. We stay away from the cafeteria food and several of the other restaurants and cafes so that the drug does not enhance our powers and make us more noticeable.

Crossing her arms, Misty scowls at Jadore. Misty has always been tight-lipped about her past. With her suicide attempt last month and the old scars on her wrists, my imagination goes wild with scenarios.

Jadore weaves her way between Wil and Jia and feels for the doorknob. "Ms. Agailya will tend to your needs, Mrs. Harris. I will make the call to Batomisk in a few hours, when the time difference is favourable."

"I want to be there when you make the call," Mrs. Harris insists.

"Very well. Follow me. I will show you the way to Ms. Agailya's office." Jadore opens the door.

We can't let Jadore take Mrs. Harris. She'll probably kill her for inquiring about Sunni before they even reach Ms. Agailya, and then cover it up. I can't let that happen, not after all that Sunni has done for the Sparks, not after her dream-self has aided me while I sleep—not after she allowed herself to die to keep the Sparks and everyone else safe.

"I can take Mrs. Harris to Ms. Agailya," I say firmly. "I was returning to my room anyway, to work on my project."

Jadore twists her lips. She appears to consider the prospect, but hardens once more. "Just because I am blind, Ingrid, does not mean I cannot do my job."

I'm trying to get her to change her mind, but... her brain is odd. It's resisting my inception attempts, Wil says. *We can follow her in Jia's world to make sure Mrs. Harris is safely delivered. If she tries anything, we'll be ready.*

Misty nods discreetly. "I'll see you after I finish my work, Hildie."

"All right, Misty. That's a good girl. Off you go now. When it's supper time, you come find me and then we can talk."

Jia and Wil slip into the hallway with curt nods to Mrs. Harris, and Misty endures a wet kiss on the cheek before Mrs. Harris lets her go. I smile wanly at Sunni's mother, and she returns the sincerity of my gesture threefold.

Before I step across the threshold, Jadore plants a firm hand on my shoulder and sinks her nails through my shirt. I whimper quietly as she holds me in place.

"By the way, Ingrid," Jadore says casually. "How is your father doing?"

My breath hitches. The Collective nearly killed him and kept him a near-death coma a few weeks ago when I tried to escape. "He's a lot better now, *thanks*."

"I'm glad to hear that. And the rest of you? Family is all well?" she calls down the hall.

Misty, Wil, and Jia stop in their tracks and turn to look at the alien professor. Wil looks unfettered by Jadore's blackmailing attempt, Misty just sneers, but Jia nearly breaks. She has always been afraid of the Collective targeting her family, especially her sister, who is nearing university age.

"I'll take that as a yes. Quiet mice, they can be sometimes," she says after they don't reply. Jadore releases my shoulder. "I hope they continue to have such good health."

For your sakes, is what she's not saying. A quiet warning, to the quiet mice. Tell Sunni's mother anything about the Collective and the fate of the students here, and I'll hurt everyone you care about.

Surrounded by the comfort of Jia's invisibility, we wait outside MacLeod Hall for Jadore and Mrs. Harris. It doesn't take long before Mrs. Harris marches from the building with Jadore at her heels, slapping her cane on the concrete slab walkway outside the door and then the grass as they make their way across the quad, towards Sparkstone Boulevard.

Mrs. Harris throws tepid glances at the blind professor as they reach the road. A supply truck rolls along—and it shows no sign of stopping. Jadore's lips twitch as she steps onto the road anyway. Alarmed, Mrs. Harris grabs the alien's arm and pulls her back as the truck screeches to a halt. Though Jadore's body stiffens at Mrs. Harris's attempt to save her life, her hidden smile becomes a grin. A test.

"Jadore's leading her to her death," Misty whispers angrily. Her fiery grip is burning my hand. I nudge her and she turns down her heat, slightly.

"Be quiet," Jia hisses. Her invisibility doesn't cover sound.

After safely crossing the road, Jadore stops, exchanges some words with Mrs. Harris, and then points across the road, towards Rita House. Mrs. Harris looks mildly annoyed that Jadore doesn't know the right way, but does not dare to contradict the blind woman leading her around campus. We make our way slowly towards Rita House.

We can't get too close. Jadore will suspect something is up, Wil warns us. *We'll stay outside the buildings and I'll track the two with my mind. If they suddenly disappear, we'll know they've teleported and we'll find a way to the mother ship.*

The three of them slide their gazes to me. Teleportation is my power. Just one problem: I haven't mastered it yet. I've only successfully teleported twice since I arrived last month. First time, I was on the mother ship and part of it was about to explode. Second time, hafelglob surrounded me and Joseph G. Campbell had just materialized out of nowhere, calling to me. It seems like I can only call upon the power in times of distress ... and when I'm thinking of Ethan.

"I'll try to teleport us if I have to," I whisper.

Misty's eyes narrow. "You better do more than that."

I can't disagree. For once, I wish my superpower was less onerous.

"Ms. Agailya and Mrs. Harris are going upstairs," Wil says. "Jadore is ... coming this way."

Jadore exits Rita House and stomps on the grass to the well-trodden path. She walks confidently, using the cane as an accessory more than a crutch. Even with the students scattered across the quad, intermittently watching the emboldened professor, she doesn't seem to care. A sly smile rides her dark lips. To her, this land is hers, and there isn't anything we can do to discredit her without significant loss.

She halts just a few feet in front of us, and draws a deep breath. Her nostrils widen into large, dark holes, distractingly large against her thin nose that looks like it's been under the knife more than once. I have a sinking feeling she knows we're there, if not through smell alone. Smirking, she tightens her grip on her cane and makes her way towards MacLeod Hall.

Once she's out of earshot, I ask, "Do you think Sunni's mother will be safe with Ms. Agailya?"

"She's not safe with any alien here," Misty mutters.

Wil closes his eyes and concentrates. "Agailya is leading Mrs. Harris to the third floor. It would be a risky place to kill her, since there are twelve other students there now."

"I thought the temporary residences were in Rogers Hall."

He furrows his brows. *Most of those rooms are occupied. The Collective is aggressively recruiting students late in the semester.*

"That's not good."

"It's never good. The Collective must be planning a large-scale harvest sometime soon."

My stomach twists. We can never catch a break. No one here can.

Wil shakes his head and blinks furiously, as if disconnecting from his mental link with Ms. Agailya and Sunni's mother. "She'll be safe for now, especially if the three of you are going up there. I really should get to the lab."

"You can't leave now," Misty hisses. "We have to talk about what we're going to *do*."

"Right now, we can do nothing. She's here to stay. I don't think Jadore would have turned her over to Ms. Agailya and put her in Rita House if she intended to kill her within the next few hours," Wil argues.

"Misty's right—we need to figure out what we're going to do," I say. "Unless you want the three of us to come up with a plan without you, and you can fetch it from our minds when it's convenient."

"Ingrid," Jia says admonishingly.

"What?" I ask. "Sunni's mother being here changes things. It means the Collective isn't covering all their bases. They've made a mistake. We have to take advantage of that before it's too late."

"Not in the next few hours," Wil says testily. "I need to get some work done. Just like the rest of you do."

"Eff work!" Misty exclaims. "We're in the end times now. We plan a strike. Now."

No, Wil's telepathic voice booms. He wrenches himself from Jia's iron grip, and pulls away from mine, and surfaces from Jia's invisible, watery world like a whale coming up for air. *Jadore already knows who we are, and possibly what our powers are. We are this close*—he holds up his thumb and forefinger a centimetre apart—*to being abducted ourselves. If we keep doing and handing in our projects, we will keep under their radar until we can plan an effective strike.*

"That's just a theory," Misty sneers. "If our sneaking around in the past few weeks hasn't set them off, nothing will. Today is the perfect time to strike while they run around like chickens with their heads chopped off, trying to deal with Hildie showin' up!"

We're the chickens, Wil replies. *You're the one running your mouth off right now.*

Misty's eyes flash with anger. "You don't care about Sunni! You're the one who's running!"

She wretches from my grip, and she too becomes visible. Frustrated, Jia's concentration wavers. My nerves jolt. If this keeps up, we'll be visible before long.

"Believe me," Wil says darkly, staring down at Misty. "I do care. If you cared about Sunni, and our future wellbeing, you wouldn't protest."

"What's that supposed to mean? What are you even doing in Conrod Building?"

Wil sneers. "Nothing comprehensible to you, that's for certain."

"Oh shut the eff up, Too-Good-For-Harvard, and cut the—"

"Stop arguing," I exclaim. "If we can't find common

ground, we'll never get an edge on the Collective, no matter what we do."

Jia's concentration wavers with the rising tempers of our two friends. Remaining invisible depends on her ability to remain calm. Jia draws a deep breath and I'm aware of that familiar, gentle feeling of entering the visible world. It's like coming up for a breath of fresh air after being underwater, without feeling like your lungs are starving.

Appearing from nowhere seems to be the least of our concerns. If I can't keep this group together, we'll never defeat the Collective.

"Sorry," Jia says slowly. Being invisible with the four of us takes its toll on her. "I haven't meditated in three days."

Misty says nothing, and neither does Wil, though he looks mildly guilty for breaking Jia's concentration.

I seize the silence. "If we work in our own rooms, we can show the Collective that we're not suddenly planning an attack because Sunni's mother is here." I sigh. "Now more than ever, we'll have to watch our backs. They're going to be extra vigilant."

After a moment, Wil seems to concede. "Perhaps, if the meeting was *brief*, we could—"

From behind us, a familiar voice draws my attention. "Hey! Ingrid!"

I turn to see Ethan almost tripping over himself as he races across Sparkstone Boulevard towards us. He must be coming from Morris House, his residence, which is almost diagonally across from Rita House. Despite its liberal stance on education,

Sparkstone University has strictly conservative dorm rules: boys live in Morris House and Hynes House, and girls stay in Rita House and Raylene House. The four residences are clustered, forming an *L*-shape around Rogers Hall.

Ethan grins, excited beyond belief to see me. I hope he ignores the bags under my eyes. Who knows how much he's overheard from our very public argument with Wil. Or if he witnessed the four of us suddenly pop into existence from nowhere.

"Did you get my text?" Ethan asks in his delicious British accent. He runs a nervous hand through his hair.

"No." I'm not that surprised. Ever since my room was broken into a few weeks ago, both my laptop and my cell phone have been acting strangely—even though I had my cell phone at the time. Texts to my parents and to the other Sparks are almost always delayed by a half hour or more. I spent an hour on the phone with the cell phone service provider and although they claim they've fixed my texting speed, I have no doubt that the Collective are constantly monitoring everything I do.

"Oh. Well, it wasn't that important. Just... saying hi."

Our cheeks burn an equal bright shade of red. A grin takes over my face. "Hi."

"Hey," he says.

I kick at the grass, trying to bury my feet in there. "Oookay. I think we can move beyond this stage of conversation, right?"

"Yeah, yeah, for sure."

Ethan peers beyond me to Jia, Wil, and Misty, and I follow his gaze. The three of them give Ethan friendly but wary smiles.

They tend not to interact with the other students outside our tight friend group unless they have to. Ever since Jadore hurt my father and the attempt to pin our protest on Laura didn't work as planned, we can't afford to extend our friendship and risk endangering our peers. Wil especially has been critical of my relationship—if you can call it that—with Ethan.

Since Ethan obviously only wants to talk to me, I take a tentative step away from my three friends. He acknowledges them with a slight wave—which they return with about half as much enthusiasm—as Misty nudges Jia, and together they head toward Rita House. Wil follows slowly behind them, with a furtive glance at Conrod Building, looming in the distance across campus. Looks like we'll be having that meeting after all.

Or, *they* will.

"So," Ethan says, clearing his throat. He seems to relax a bit more now that we're alone. "Do you have any plans for the weekend? I know it's only Tuesday, but..."

"Um...not sure." I glance off in the direction where Jia, Wil, and Misty have headed. I have a sinking feeling my time is about to be eaten up with Collective-fighting activities. "But if I don't?"

"Well, if you don't, maybe...maybe we could do something?"

"Definitely maybe," I say quickly, balancing on my tippy-toes because otherwise I'd be jumping up and down with excitement. "Like what?"

"Not really sure. Play some music. Get some food." He looks me over to see if either of those things catch my interest. "Not too many things we can do in Sparkstone, I'm afraid. Don't have a car either."

"That's too bad. I only date guys with cars, you know."

"That really is too bad for me then." He leans forward until our foreheads are almost touching. "Just try to let me know as soon as possible if you can do something, all right?"

I sigh. I have a bad habit of letting fighting-the-Collective stuff get in the way of dating-Ethan stuff. "I'll do my best."

"My room is in Morris House if you ever find that, you know, you can't get a hold of me any other way."

I bite my lip as he moves away. I don't think Ethan remembers it, but I have been to his room before. He'd gotten mysteriously sick weeks ago and the Sparks and I had to carry him from downtown Sparkstone to his room in Morris House. Thanks to Ms. Agailya and the Collective, Ethan did recover from his strange sickness, but we still have no idea if he got sick because of allergies, or if it's because he's developing superpowers.

"I'm sure I won't have any problems finding you."

"Yeah. Just look for the door with all the paint stains on it. Anyway, Ingrid, I got a painting that needs finishing." Trying to hide a smile, glancing around to see if anyone is watching, he kisses me gently on the cheek. "Cheers, love."

"Cheers," I whisper as I watch him fly down the path towards his studio in the Lewis Art Building, beyond MacLeod Building but away from the town. My brain travels to a cloudy dream land. Ethan just called me love. Does that mean he loves me? No, no, it's just something that Brits call people that they're fond of. Yeah. That sounds correct. I stand in my hormones for a few minutes, savoring the freshness of the moment as it becomes a memory. My time with Ethan is all too brief.

Wil's voice in my mind, inescapable but reassuring, grounds me in our dystopian reality: *We're in the girls' washroom, second floor.*

I sigh. The bathroom? Kinda busy right now, Wil.

Even as I feel him taking note of my location, I can't help but feel a sense of calm. It is assuring to know someone has your back, even if he can creepily spy on you. I guess that's something I've gotten used to with him—despite his power, I know he's not going to pry.

I hope this meeting isn't long. I want to go back to the lab after this, Wil continues.

The hafelglob at the desk in Rita House mutters something derogatory beneath his breath as I race up two flights of stairs to the second-floor washroom. It's somewhere I thought I'd never have to go again. It's an odd place to have a meeting, though perhaps it's a room that's not monitored. All of the dorm rooms I've been in on campus have had private bathrooms, though perhaps not every student pays to have such luxury.

I hope they're still there. I'm not as winded as I would have been a month ago when I first arrived, and I try to appear casual as I stroll down the hall. Rita House is a female-only dorm and it's unfortunate that the muffled sound of Wil's voice carries from the bathroom, and explodes as I push open the door.

"I *told* you that—"

"I don't give a flyin' eff what you told me, 'cause it don't matter—"

Only Jia acknowledges me as I slam the bathroom door and lean against it. She leans nervously against one of the sinks, keeping her distance from Wil and Misty as they exchange choice words. Harmony was never our strong suit, though Misty seems to thrive on conflict. Her defensive stance near the window reminds me too much of when I had to pull her back from the brink of death weeks ago, in this very place. Her right hand steams from the fire born of her will and her palm, likely ready to throw it in Wil's face if he continues to oppose her. I don't know if his mind powers would be able to save him from that.

"Hey," I say sharply, cutting between my two arguing friends. "Keep it down, because this bathroom isn't *that* soundproof."

Wil furrows his brows, outwardly calm. Misty leans against the wall, arms folded defensively, and grumbles, "He's being an asshole."

"What else did I miss?" I ask mostly Jia, who tends to avoid conflict when possible.

"Just more of this," she replies, eyebrow raised at the two of them.

Misty throws a dark glare at Wil. "We need to tell Hildie the truth."

Wil shakes his head and paces away from her, switching to his silent mind-speech. *It isn't the best option.*

I frown. “Mrs. Harris isn’t going to believe us. Unless she knows about Sunni’s dreams.”

“She doesn’t,” Misty and Wil say at the same time. Misty glares at him and shifts in her weight from one foot to the other, and Wil surprisingly concedes the floor to her with a tired gesture. “She don’t know,” Misty continues. “Sunni’s mum is ultra-Christian. Least, when I was living in Wimberley she was. Would’ve gone all Carrie’s mother on her if she knew Sunni had freaky powers.” I’m shocked by the Stephen King reference, and Misty beats me to the punch. “What? I read sometimes. God. Even after all we’ve been through, you *still* judge me by the way I—”

“Sorry, sorry, I didn’t mean to. I just didn’t know.” I wave my hands like I have superpowers that can make her instantly forgive me. She’s a wounded snake: quick to bite and slow to trust. “So why do you think she’ll believe that Sunni is dead and that the school is run by a huge alien organization set on harvesting our super-duper DNA?”

“Well, she’ll probably believe the dead part,” Misty says quietly. She picks at some dirt under her left forefinger. “Problem is, we have no proof of that. No...no body.”

A reverent silence descends upon us. Jadore took Sunni’s body just after she murdered her, presumably to harvest Sunni’s DNA, so that they can enhance their technology, and better the alien species *privileged* enough to be part of the organization.

Jia closes her eyes and nods. “I think we should tell her too. She has the right to know the truth.”

I nod slowly, but Wil is rubbing his clean-shaven head, staring out the window towards the tall concrete wall that surrounds the town of Sparkstone. "The Collective will kill her either way."

"No, they wouldn't...would they?" Jia says, clutching the neckline of her shirt.

"One of two things is going to happen in the next couple of days. Perhaps weeks, if we're lucky," Wil says, holding up two fingers. "Regardless of what we choose to do, the Collective is going to realize that they haven't been careful enough with their cover-up. Mrs. Harris isn't the only person going to die here. I bet you anything that those aliens up there who screwed up are going to be shown the door, and there's going to be some shifting in the mid-ranks.

"So, enter us Sparks, meddling in the Collective's business. Scenario one: we tell Mrs. Harris that her daughter is dead and that the Collective is responsible. Mrs. Harris gets fired up, threatens a law suit, and suddenly, media everywhere, maybe, if the Collective don't act fast enough. They're not going to let Mrs. Harris leave this town now, even if she hadn't bunkered down in Rita House. In that scenario, she's dead within twenty-four hours. Undetectable poison, or whatever the Collective's latest killing method is."

"Yeah, but if Mrs. Harris dies, everyone is going to immediately suspect the school," I point out.

Wil shakes his finger. "Maybe. But if they've got rid of the screw-ups, there's a chance they've got some better people in charge of, shall we say, *risk management*. The hafelglob have shapeshifting technology. Who's to say that they won't just off Mrs. Harris, and put someone in her place?"

"Maybe Joseph G. Campbell will protect her," I say quietly.

Misty snorts. “Where was he when Sunni was getting blasted, huh? Your favourite alien was probably sipping human blood filled with our precious special DNA and laughing as he watched the whole show from his spa on Jupiter!”

“Misty’s right. We can’t rely on him for this,” Jia says.

I hate to agree, but I know they’re right. It’s up to us to protect Sunni’s mother from her daughter’s fate. “So what’s scenario two? What do you think will happen if we don’t tell Mrs. Harris where Sunni really is?”

“Something similar. A potential media blitz if the Collective don’t handle things quietly. A hafelglob impersonates Sunni for a while—though I suspect that wouldn’t fool Mrs. Harris for long. In their human forms, you can tell there’s something odd about them. They’d have to find something more reliable to impersonate Sunni or Mrs. Harris herself.”

“Would it really be such a bad thing if the media were here?” I ask. “If the Collective is exposed, humanity could have a fighting chance. Organize a resistance.”

“Yes, because our protest worked so well last time,” Wil says sarcastically. “We don’t know how far and wide the Collective has infiltrated. They may bury the story outright. Or, suppose that the Collective isn’t careful, the media shows up, and humanity refuses to believe the outlandish truth that aliens are harvesting our DNA.”

“It is the truth, and we could provide them evidence,” Jia says quietly.

“Yes, but they may choose not to believe it.”

Jia places a delicate hand on the tiled wall. “I hate to bring this up. But we should consider the possibility that the Collective has the ability to...to clone people."

Misty's eyes bug out. "No..."

"It's possible they could try to bring Sunni back to life. But I feel like if that were part of the agenda, they'd have done so already. Sunni had a valuable power that they coveted."

"She could be up there now," Misty whispers, her gaze flickering to the blue, cloudless sky outside. "Workin' for them."

"I feel I would have sensed her if that were the case," Wil reminds her, not unkindly. "If not a shapeshifter, if not a clone, then...then perhaps something technological. Like a hologram."

I sit up straighter as an idea fills me. "Wil. What if...what if you were to beat the Collective in a race to build such a hologram? Or, a sophisticated visual response program? What if...what if we built something Sunni-like long enough to fool Mrs. Harris? To assure her that Sunni really is out there? Is that ... possible?"

Wil gives me the most peculiar look. "It's ... possible." He gives it more thought. "It would be the safest route. Mrs. Harris would get what she came for. The Collective leaves her alone—leaves us alone. She might be able to leave alive. It would also be very tricky. I mean, I could do it." Wil shrugs, like I've just asked him to add two and two. "But it would take some time."

"How much time?" I ask.

"Weeks, at least. If I didn't have my current projects, maybe one week, working fifteen-hour days. But I can't get rid of my current projects. I've already committed."

"Can you change them?"

"I'm already too far into them. And... even if I could, I don't *want* to change them."

"Not sure you *want* to stop your stupid effin' projects to *save* Sunni's mother?" Misty retorts, advancing on him.

"What I'm doing in the lab," he says, "I'm doing for *all* of us."

I hesitate. "Your project?"

Wil nods, but to me he says, *It's beyond that now.*

"Your project on self-driving car AI safety? How is that for us?" Jia asks, genuinely curious. "I thought you only had one project for Jadore right now."

He ignores her, focussing squarely on me. He senses my distrust, my disbelief in him.

"I can probably do all of the projects," he says finally. "Make excuses to Jadore if I'm tardy with what I've promised her. None of us can afford to raise her suspicions any further. If she finds out just how far we've progressed with our powers, it would be a promising motivation for her to abduct us. With Jia's help, maybe yours, and Misty's"—she gives him a look that says, *ain't no way I'm gettin' my hands dirty in your stupid lab*—"I can manage to do everything. I can do this." He nods, convincing himself that he can.

"We probably don't have much time. Likely the Collective is brainstorming, just as we are," I say.

"Likely," he replies. But he's still staring at me. Telepathically, and likely privately, he says, *I don't need your permission to do what I do. I'll tell you what my other project is when it's done. When it's ready.*

My curiosity piques some more. "You have to," I say aloud. "The fewer secrets between us, the better."

Jia and Misty are staring expectantly at us, frustrated that Wil is having a private conversation with me.

Annoyed, he replies, *You're one to talk.*

He doesn't like being scolded. Who does? Our ragtag group doesn't have an appointed leader, but because of his superpowers, Wil is often the centre of our network. He arranges our meetings because he can communicate over great distances without aid, and he keeps us safe from prying ears and eyes. I know he can look inside me and see where I'm coming from, and know that I mean him no ill will, but that doesn't stop him from feeling like he's been deposed. With that, Wil heads for the door.

"What did he say?" Misty demands. "What secrets?"

"He'll tell us when he's ready, he said."

"Yeah right." Misty seethes. She's never been good at hiding her anger, or keeping it under control. "He thinks he can just walk around, tellin' me what I can and can't comprehend." She yells across the campus at him in what I think is Mandarin, and then Spanish, and then spits on the floor. "Comprehend *that!*"

Wil does not acknowledge us, telepathically or otherwise.

"I should get him out of the building unseen," Jia says tiredly. "He's right, though. For now, we should all work on our projects, or at the very least, get some rest."

"Of course you'd defend him," Misty mutters.

Jia crosses her arms. "What do you—?"

"Okay. Let's not get into that now," I warn them both, ready to jump between them and prevent a fight if necessary. "He probably just wants some time away from us. We all could use some privacy."

"Privacy," Misty snorts, as Jia leaves to attend to Wil. She saunters to the window, and looks at the campus below. "No such thing here."

CHAPTER 3

I cannot sleep.

To my right, Jia snores away. She's also stolen most of the blankets. The bedroom is cold, and wearing a sweater to bed would overheat me. I roll towards her, thinking about nudging her to stop the snoring, but think better of it. I'm awake now, no matter what.

I sit up. It's only quarter to ten. An early night for all of us. Misty lays sprawled on a double mattress crammed between the bed and my dresser. Even though I've offered to switch with her, Misty seems content on the floor. In the back of my mind I wonder if Jia knows Misty is a lesbian (though Misty did say she hates the term gay—can I really call her gay, then?). I also wonder if Misty is afraid of alienating Jia, or me, by asking if she can share the bed.

She mutters in her sleep. It's not as frequent or as annoying as Jia's snoring, but it can prevent me from sleeping. I thought my dreams were vivid—I guess I'm not the only one. Sunni missed a real opportunity by picking me instead of her best friend as her dream message conduit.

Determined not to wake my two sleeping friends, I slide to the end of the bed, remove my pajamas, grab some clothes from the laundry, and slip into the bathroom to change. When I'd returned to my dorm after the meeting, I'd fallen asleep in a pile of black hole and astronaut brain research on my bed. No Sunni dreams this time, just confusing images and turbulent feelings that, when I woke up, left me feeling like I'd been on a rollercoaster. A waste of an afternoon. No wonder I'm so awake.

Jadore will rip me apart tomorrow.

I push it to the back of my mind. There's only one thing I want to do now, one thing that will definitely put me at ease. Music. Ever since Jadore had my keyboard destroyed and Misty and Jia have been sharing my room, I've been visiting the music trailer on campus. It's stuffed to the brim with pianos, trumpets, guitars, pipes, and other instruments. No harps, unfortunately, but it's otherwise the perfect environment for me to escape.

The moment I step from the bathroom, I'm relieved to hear Jia's snores. After what happened in the quad today, she needs her rest. Yet Misty cuts the otherwise quiet ambiance not with a whisper, but with full-blown ignorance. "Where you going?"

She startles me. "I can't sleep," I say. "Outside."

"Do you need me to—?"

"No, I'll be fine. I have my phone. Thanks." I add the pleasantry as an afterthought as I grab my shoulder bag and shut the door. She's just concerned about my welfare. I really shouldn't be wandering around at night anyway.

And yet...my fingers itch for ivory keys.

My shoulder bag is so long that it bumps against my knees as I stride, reminding me to do a mental checklist—got my key card, yes. Cell phone? Yes. Did I text Ethan earlier? No. Shoot.

While I'm scolding myself, a door opens suddenly ahead to my left, and who should appear from her room but Mrs. Harris. She shuts the door behind her and tries the doorknob to ensure it's locked. She studies the black box next to the door quizzically, and mutters something about damned technology under her breath.

There's a brief moment where I consider just racing by. I don't know Mrs. Harris. She doesn't know me. She's alone, and while the camera at the end of the hall stands guard, she doesn't appear to be in any hurry.

Numerous hafelglob could descend on us at any moment, I remind myself. It's late enough in the evening. I can't underestimate the Collective.

I also can't allow myself to keep being afraid of things I can't see.

Filling my lungs with courage, I square my shoulders and will my feet toward Mrs. Harris. "Um...hi. Did you get locked out of your room?"

Mrs. Harris whips around and clutches her purse to her heavy white winter coat, as if I've just threatened her life. Her mistrust melts when she sees I'm just a lanky, tall, seventeen-year-old. She cocks her head in recognition, but we were never formally introduced during our brief meeting in Jadore's office. "No. I was just wondering what the darned thing was. This." She points to the key card scanner.

"Usually they give you a key card. You swipe it, it lets you in. Did Ms. Agailya give you one?" The temporary residences in Rogers Hall don't have them, but every other building seems to.

"Oh. Yes." She reaches into her purse and pulls out the white, thin plastic. "So I use this when I want to get back in?"

"Yeah. The door locks automatically, so you're fine." I extend a hand to her. "I'm Ingrid Stanley. My dorm is just down the hall."

"Ah. Ingrid. Yes. You were with Misty this morning. I recognize the hair." She smiles pleasantly, and appraises me from head to toe. "Is it dyed?"

"No. One hundred percent real!" Probably the most common question I'm asked when meeting someone new. Except for here, since everyone is so caught up in their projects, or fighting alien invasions. My gaze falls on her tan-coloured purse, slung over her arm, and her white winter coat. "You going out somewhere?"

"Oh, just to the bakery. I hope they're still open. I know the hour is absurd, but I'm a bit of a night owl, see. That Ms. Agailya woman said that many businesses in Sparkstone have later hours around this time of the semester to accommodate the students. I could smell those biscuits from my car on the drive through town. Divine! Wanted to see if they tasted as good as they smelt. Would you like one, if the bakery is still open?"

I purse my lips. "Um...no thank you, Mrs. Harris. But I'll come with you to the bakery if you'd like the company."

And because I shouldn't leave her to wander the dark streets of Sparkstone alone.

"That's very kind of you, Ingrid. Maybe I can get you to change your mind about the biscuits. You look like you could use the extra pounds."

"I'm just naturally thin," I reply shyly. "How was your drive up from Texas?"

Mrs. Harris smiles wryly as we head down the hallway together. "Long. Took me a few weeks. I can't do those fourteen-hour-day drives like I used to. Even tried to drink one of those energy drinks. Nasty things. Had to pull over and spill my guts on the Trans-Canada. Never again. Probably threw out my back, what with all the car-sleeping I did. Hotels are costly, you know. My prayers kept me warm, though, and I made it here in one piece."

"Yes, I'm glad." Innocent conversation will be hard. Every question I can think to ask will lead back to Sunni, or why Mrs. Harris is here. "The beds are pretty comfy here. Hopefully you can get some rest."

"Hmmph. The mattress is a little too soft for my taste." She glances up at the camera as we pass beneath it, frowns, and then continues, "Although now I understand a little better where my tuition money went. Private rooms, as good as any hotel I ever stayed in! I can see why Sunni was so charmed by the place. Oh fiddles. These stairs. No elevators in the dorms, I take it?"

I keep a careful eye on Mrs. Harris as we descend the three flights of stairs to the lobby. She speaks her daughter's name with such pride, without fear, it's as if she expects to see Sunni every time she turns a corner.

The same security guard from earlier, still transfixed by the television, sits reclined behind the main desk in the lobby. The desk is littered with dirty dishes from the cafeteria and a discarded tray. He gives us a cursory glance with his bloodshot eyes—has he been unable to leave his post since this afternoon?—and returns to the screen, now blaring a reality TV show.

Mrs. Harris, visibly annoyed by the slobby demeanour of the guard, picks up her pace and heads toward the door. "I reckon it's chilly out there tonight." She evaluates my thin long-sleeved shirt, skirt, and leggings curiously. "Are you going to be warm enough?"

"I'll be okay."

"Are you sure, child? You're skin and bones! I can wait while you go get a coat."

"No, I'm fine. I have a high tolerance to cold."

She doesn't believe me. "Well, all right then. But if you get cold, we will head back. I'd offer to give you my coat, but these old bones aren't used to the shrill Canadian winds."

The guard at the desk finally decides that we're worth paying attention to, and leans forward in his office chair with a cringe-worthy *squeak*. "Where are you going?"

"Never you mind," Mrs. Harris retorts, zipping up her winter coat, and then hurries out into the windy night without looking back.

I hold back a smirk, and ignore the hafelglob's follow-up question as I leave Rita House behind. Mrs. Harris, for an older woman, is more sure on her feet than she looks once she's on flat ground. She walks at a good clip through the grass, toward the Sparkstone Boulevard roundabout that officially separates the campus from the town. I jog to catch up with her.

"You don't have a curfew here, do you?" she asks, mildly concerned.

"They don't really like it when we're outside at night, but there's no official ban on nighttime walks, no."

"Hmmph." She clutches her purse tighter to her chest. "I ain't never seen a man so curious about the comings and goings of the ladies. Now, I could understand if he's keepin' promiscuous young men from calling, but how dare he ask *me*, a guest of the university, about my comings and goings. As if I would dare call upon a gentleman at this hour, in a town I don't—"

I struggle to keep a mask of interest as Mrs. Harris continues her rant. The streets are quiet, but brightly lit. Her matronly presence reminds me with a heavy heart that my mother and father are far away.

"Anyway. You don't make a habit of going out late at night, do you?"

"Uh, I try not to," I reply stiffly. Her comments about meeting men make me wary, and I glance back at Morris House, where Ethan is likely slaving away at his latest charcoal drawing or watercolour painting. I look around the other shoulder towards the Lewis Art Building. I could sneak over and see him, after my music session in the trailer, especially if he's in his studio since that's a bit closer. He seems to split his time between the studio and his dorm, doing art where the spirit moves him. Between schoolwork, the four of us investigating the missing students, and my draining, intense nights inside Sunni's dreams, it's been hard to make time for him.

Together, Mrs. Harris and I cross the roundabout, and I leave the idea of seeing Ethan tonight behind. "I'm pretty busy with schoolwork, like pretty much everyone else."

"Hmmm. You're a freshman?"

I nod. "I got here the beginning of September, which apparently was at least a few weeks into the first semester."

"They started early, didn't they." The distaste in her voice is palpable. "Sunni couldn't wait to leave. She always loved bugs. Plants too, but bugs in particular. Collected them in the backyard, and down in Cyprus Creek. I always thought that was a boys thing, but I never said nothin' about it. It is good to have a passion, something you can throw yourself into to pass the time, to keep your hands busy while the brain works through what it has to work through. You understand." Without waiting for a vocal confirmation, she asks, "And what do you study?"

"Psychology." My half-written, bullcrap paper on Joseph G. Campbell and the theory of multiverses doesn't quite fit within that discipline, but then again, I haven't declared my second major yet. Unless Jadore and Agailya want to continue the pretense that I don't know what's going on, I doubt that will ever happen.

"Ah. I see where you and Sunni would have gotten along. I never really understood what insect psychology was. Maybe you do."

"Not really," I admit, smiling. "To be honest, Mrs. Harris—"

"Hildie, please, dear. Svanhild is an awful name from my Swedish grandmother, but I've made do while honoring my roots."

"Hildie." I think of Misty pronouncing Sunni's mother's name with such reverence. I don't know if I can do it justice. "I didn't know Sunni all that well. She transferred the day after I arrived."

"Is that right? But you said you got here about six weeks ago. The semester started in the first week of August, yes?"

"I think that's right. I got here late. September fourth."

"I was told she transferred on September third."

"I..." I didn't mean to add fuel to the fire. "That's interesting."

"Interesting is the least of it." She stops, turning towards me and blocks the path. "You're certain of September fourth, that's the day you arrived?"

My heart sinks. I consider lying, but I'm not great at it, and it makes me feel sick that I can't tell her the truth of Sunni's fate. "Yes."

Hildie's bottom lip curls upward as she stares at the dark wall surrounding town. "I knew they were lying to me. From the very beginning. I feared that by coming here, I'd get nothing but the bureaucratic runaround. But I have kept my faith, and God has given me an answer through you." She lays an appreciative hand on my shoulder. "Thank you, Ingrid, for your honesty."

My weak smile is all I can offer in return for her heartfelt words. "The bakery is just here."

The cute bakery cafe, complete with white curtains, a red-and-white striped awning, and the pleasant smell of baked bread—even at this late hour—seems at odds with the dead, lifeless streets. The bakery is brightly lit, and there are two patrons sipping tea and enjoying an evening scone inside—both professors, by the looks of it. With almost every establishment selling food injected with Substance 454, it's hard to get a proper meal nowadays and stay clearheaded. The bakery is one place that doesn't modify its food, as far as we know. My stomach rumbles. Even though she offered me a snack, I don't deserve anything from her until I can tell her the complete truth. I inhale sharply, hoping that Hildie doesn't hear.

Hildie draws a deep breath. "Ah good. They're still open. And still baking! That's dedication. Or perhaps they're preparing for a morning rush. Are you sure you don't want anything?"

"I'm fine. Thanks. Maybe another time."

"All right then. I'll hold you to that. In the meantime, you don't have to wait for me. I know my way now," she says reassuringly, patting me on the shoulder. "It's dark, and I don't want to keep you from your evening."

"You're sure?"

"Absolutely. I think I can handle myself, what with that wall keeping all the *dangerous* farmers out." She chuckles, though her gaze darts down the unlit residential side streets of this constructed paradise.

"I suppose it's stopped a stray cow a time or two," I reply. I reach into my shoulder bag for my phone. "I'll give you my number, just in case."

"That's very thoughtful of you, Ingrid." She digs in her purse for her phone and we exchange digits. "Text only, if you can. Roaming charges are mighty terrible now that I'm not in America. Though I suppose that's what you use your phone for nowadays, isn't it."

"Sure." I turn to leave. I'm not sure if there are cameras in every streetlight, but I'm willing to take the risk, now that I've come this far and said this much. "Um, Hildie...if you ever want to talk about...anything...I just live down the hall. You can knock on my door anytime."

She smiles wistfully. "Thank you, Ingrid. Hopefully we can get this business sorted and bring Sunni home again."

I purse my lips and nod. "I hope so too. Good night."

I turn and put one foot in front of the other, hating to leave her, but also anxious to get to my music. I glance over my shoulder, seeing Hildie walk inside the bakery. Regretting my decision to leave, my steps falter, my flats scraping the sidewalk in protest as I come to a standstill in the quiet of the night.

Sometimes when you're alone, there's a brief moment where you question reality. I breathe in the sharp night through my nose, and feel the goose flesh on my arms and the fluttering of my skirt around my legs, wondering if I am dreaming. If in the absence of cameras, it's suddenly okay to be me again, and if I am anyone at all if I'm not embroiled in an extraterrestrial, superpower-filled battle for my home and friends. Did I have a life before this, or was I asleep, or a character in one of Sunni's dreams?

I look up at the sky and identify the constellation of Orion. If I am dreaming in this moment, I decide, I would not be able to fixate on the stars—they would change with every passing random thought. I am still here. This is reality. I am special. I have abilities that others would kill for. I am a real person with thoughts and feelings.

I just can't show them when I want to.

My feet carry me back to campus to the music trailer. It's situated at one edge of the quad, behind MacLeod Hall and the Sparkstone University Library, and close to a walking trail that leads towards the residential, Stepford-Wives-houses area of Sparkstone. My key card lets me in with a reluctant *beep*. I'm surprised I haven't been restricted, though I suppose Jadore may be watching my late-night trips to the piano with interest. There's a closet-sized entryway with three doors; it's the rightmost door that requires another key card swipe to access my place of solace. My music called Joseph G. Campbell to this realm before. Whatever reason she wants him, she wants it bad.

Ensuring the doors are secured behind me, I set my shoulder bag down and hurry to the grand piano at the back of the room. At the keys, I can forget that I'm one of the few trying to prevent a full-blown alien invasion. I can just be Ingrid Stanley, talented musician, regular girl that just happens to have the ability to teleport across space and maybe time. Although I miss my keyboard and my harp, at least the Collective has granted me this, even if it's a mean to their own ends.

I let go of the worries of the day, pouring them into my music. Ethan springs to the forefront of my attention, and I get the overwhelming urge to stop playing and see him—but I fight it, knowing that playing is the only way I can relieve stress so that I can get some real, non-dream sleep.

If I sleep, Sunni might stab me. I never find restful sleep anymore, not with her in my dreams.

The missing students. I think on them, trying to compose music that fits them all. I recall their names, and even if I don't remember their faces, I allow the music to create forms in my mind. *Daniel Chomber. Avery Trites. Fahima Osmond. Kendra…Kendra who? Sunni Harris.*

My thoughts inadvertently drift from the students, back to Misty and Jia in the dorm. I should be heading back soon. How many hours has it been since I got here? Time doesn't exist in my musical realm. The Collective could be in my room right now, abducting my friends, and here I am, selfishly playing music.

What would happen if Misty or Jia were taken, right now? Likely Wil would realize it, if he wasn't asleep. Would Campbell interrupt, and give me subtle hints about what to do—and guide me to them? I can't rely on his sporadic appearances. I'll have to think of a contingency plan.

Forest greens coil around my limbs; my synesthesia is strongest when I'm playing music, but it attacks me when I'm emotionally stressed. My fingers shift into E-minor, and before I know it, I'm playing his song. It isn't a specific melody that I can pin down—more like a feeling that I'm transcribing as I go—the feeling of having a large fish on the line, and wanting desperately to reel it in before it escapes and you're left empty-handed.

Too late I think of the camera in the room. It wasn't here the night Ethan romanced me and we played the music singing in our hearts. Monitoring me has become a priority for the

Collective. Better to force me to play in this music trailer, away from my friends. Yet the mental tug to play is stronger than my fear. Behind me, near the doors, I both hear and feel the sound of cloth ripping; a deep, dark-blue sound. Then, the sound of someone finding their feet on the hard floor, taking hesitant, cautious footsteps toward me.

Campbell is in the room. Directly behind me.

I did it. The camera, positioned above the entrance to the trailer, can see everything.

Jadore might barge in at any moment, and take him from me.

I'm afraid to look at him and find him unreal. "You came."

"I always come when you call."

The voice is unfamiliar, yet my brain recognizes it as his. My fingers hover above the keys. *I've only successfully called you once.* But it didn't last long. "If Jadore finds you here... "

"I'm not afraid of her," he says, not unkindly.

The song falters beneath me. "Are you afraid of anything?"

"Of course." The sound of soft soles shuffling on the tiled floor, hesitantly making their way closer. "Please, don't stop on my account."

Tentatively, my long fingers follow through on a hesitant E-minor chord. "Jadore is watching through the camera."

"And all she'll see and hear is you playing the piano."

I lean into the chord and transform it into a haunting slow jig. Campbell's powers are largely a mystery to me, though his ability to appear and disappear at will is certain. I must use my time with him wisely, and see what answers I can squeeze from him.

"Are you here because I called you, or do you have something to say?"

Slow, heavy footsteps approach from the right. I keep my focus on the keys, closing my eyes as he sits beside me, a heavy weight on the bench. He has no smell, and even the physical sensation of knowing someone is behind you feels incorrect. There is no brushing of arms, no heat, no sound of breath beneath my playing. Even the weight could just be an inanimate object.

"Something tethered winds its way around its anchor," is the reply.

Great. So he's going to do *that*. I just came here to unwind, to play. I hadn't meant to call him…or had I? I'm already sick of my brain dancing in circles, trying to figure him out, but I can't leave, not before I have some answers.

"Why me?" I ask. "Why are we connected? Why do I know you? What do you want with me?"

His laugh is low and rumbly, and harmonizes with my lackadaisical piano music. "If you are asking me those kinds of questions, then I'm guessing I'm near the beginning of my time with you. Correct?" He doesn't wait for my affirmation. "Then again, I suppose you wouldn't know beginning from end. You cannot see it from that perspective. I apologize. I'll rephrase. We haven't spoken before, have we?"

"Not…directly. In dreams. You've sent me messages. I have your treatise in my toilet. You led me to it, through Sunni, in dreams."

"My treatise is in your toilet?"

"I think it's the safest place for it." I wonder if Jadore knows where I've stored Campbell's treatise. She'd kill to get her green alien hands on it. I've read the treatise in the bathroom, just a page or two at a time in the mornings. It is one volume of many, and this particular one talks about the creation of the world. Or *a* world. As a champion of a multiverse theory, and as someone who seems to have the ability to travel between worlds, he seems uncannily interested in the creation of only select versions of one planet—a planet that is undoubtedly Earth. So far, I've found nothing useful that would explain my connection to him, or his connection to the Collective.

I curl my lips, hoping that just as Campbell is magically editing himself from the camera feed, he'll also squirrel that information away as well. Jadore would stop at nothing to have that bit of information. I descend into G-major. "Have we spoken before, in your perspective? Are you from the future?"

"I am not from anywhere. I weave in and out of your time stream, and age within Time. But yes. We have had many conversations before, you and I. For me, I believe we will have at least one more. You have many to look forward to."

This isn't the first time he's referred to Time as if it's a person. The question is on the tip of my tongue, and it takes every ounce of willpower to hold it back. *What will happen to us in the future?* Every time travel story comes to mind at once, warning me not to interfere. That by asking, I will inevitably set future events in motion. Though, by his very nature of existence, my future is fixed, and there's nothing I can do to change it, which scares the hell out of me. "Why do you think we'll only have one more conversation after this one, from your perspective?"

Although I have not stolen a glance at his features, I get the distinct impression he is meditating carefully on his response. "Have I not made my desires clear to you?"

"Um, I've had a lot of dreams of Sunni asking me to open a door, and then killing me if I don't. Does it have anything to do with that?"

I look over at him then. His face is an ever-changing, fleshy, melting canvas, swirling, draining into the absence of light in the center.

Oh god, he has no face...

I plunge my fears into F major, willing its vibrant purples to carry me away. He's always been solid with an unremarkable face, until now. In this form, he's a monster. I've summoned a monster. How can I be inexplicably tied to a *monster.* "How do you know I'll help you?"

"Because you're still alive."

My skin ripples with cold fear. "Is that a threat?"

"No, it is science. You have already made the choice, in a future point in your journey. A time I have not yet experienced, but it will happen. If you had not chosen to help me, everyone everywhere would've ceased to exist. I know that I will be successful. It is a matter of tending to the details, so that the versions of me past can live those experiences, and the future versions of you can shape them."

His words wash over me like warm water, barely registering on my skin. All I can think about his how the hell he can talk without a mouth, how he can hear without ears, and how I can escape him without him trying to hurt me.

"I wouldn't ever hurt you, Ingrid," he says softly, because mind-reading is definitely in his scope of powers. He does not, however, apologize for his appearance.

My face heats. I descend into G-major, slowly, inviting the rich browns to cool my skin.

"I do want you to open a door of sorts, yes," he admits, after several notes float by. "More than want. It is a need. I... *need* you to open a door."

"Is that what the Collective wants too?"

"Yes." His answer is hesitant. "Though for different reasons. I regret it now, turning them on to the possibility. They gleaned knowledge from me and have twisted it to their own means. Now, it cannot be undone."

I remember Ms. Agailya's words: *The Collective is of different minds.*

"I don't know what doors you want me to open," I admit quietly. "I can teleport, sometimes. Barely. I guess if you wanted me to teleport you somewhere... "

"It is more than that," he replies. "Your power will grow. It must. When the time comes, you'll need to open a door for me, and let me through. Everything depends on it, Ingrid." His tone becomes more serious. "You... you're different than the rest. You are the only one of your kind, across the verses. No one else but you can do this for me. That is why I am drawn to you. Because you're the only one who can help me."

"I find that hard to believe," I say honestly. But the part

of me so in love with these stories, be they set in space or in another land imbued with magic, and has been waiting for this moment for so long that my legs shake with excitement. "Everything you've done so far...speaking to me in dreams, magically beaming objects into my bedroom, appearing to me now...you seem omnipotent to me. Why can't you open the door on your own?"

"I am not an unmoved mover, Ingrid."

Thomas Aquinas's five arguments proving the existence of a higher power are murky, but present in my mind. "I know you're not God."

"But you think me one. And that is a mistake. Just because I see the fabric of Time and weave in and around Her like an experienced dancer, doesn't make me in control of my movements. I am just as much at Her mercy as you are. You have the luxury of a, shall we put it, linear existence. You also have the power to save me. To save us."

How To Save Her. The title, written in a dream in a book of his, returns to me suddenly and sharply. Explaining the scene in words doesn't do it justice. Unlike music, words cannot communicate the same level of feeling with the same effort. "All of us, or just one person?"

"By saving her, I save us all."

"And who is she? Do I know her?" *Is she me?*

"Her name is too powerful to utter here." I feel him smiling, though I am too afraid to check his swirling face to see if it has settled.

"If I open this door for you," I say slowly, wondering if I am about to make a deal with a devil, "what will you do for me?"

"Other than ensuring your continued existence?"

"I thought we established that that's what *I'm* doing for *you*. And.. .if you're coming to me from the future, then you must already know what you've done for me, assuming you've done it. Unless I haven't opened the door yet."

"You haven't yet, no. Soon, you will. From my perspective. Tell me what you want in return."

I know I should take time to think of what I want. But it is already at the forefront of my mind. "I...I want to escape this place. To rescue as many as we can. To stop this hideous experiment on my peers. For good." I brave his ever-changing face. "The connection goes both ways, I think. You're not behind this. You started the Collective, I think...you have some involvement...but you're too busy living out of order, out of this...universe...to know what's really happening."

As if I'd uttered open sesame to the legendary cave filled with treasures, Campbell's face stops shifting, and manifests clearly. It is utterly forgettable, not striking, not ugly. More like a Ken doll. Plastic. Bright blue or green eyes. Brown-blond hair. He has a nose, though it is unremarkable. Most importantly, this face is one I know to be his, it resonates so strongly that my foot goes instinctively to the reverberate pedal. The chord holds, never weakening as I am never blinking. My eyes dry and beg for relief but I cannot take my gaze from him, fearing that if I do, I will forget he is in the room, and I have no black markers handy to mark that I've seen him on my arm.

He stares at me sadly.

"You've been playing the same three notes over and over. Play something else."

"Sorry." I suppose Campbell would hate electronica if he hates repetitive tones. I file that away for future reference and switch to a more complex reel. I play it deliberately, concentrating on each note to ensure they are correct.

Beside me, I feel him relax, as if he has just slipped into a hot bath. "Better."

"Well? Will you help us escape, if I help you…open a door…when I'm able?"

"I…don't know."

"You know or you don't. You're from the future!" I slam my hands down on the keys, creating a thunderstorm of sound and colour. "If you don't know, that means in the future at some point, we're still trapped here. Right?"

"Ingrid—"

"*Right?*"

He cringes, and then sighs. I can actually feel his breath now. Somehow I have made him more real. "Please don't stop playing."

"You must not have music where you come from, if you love my playing so much."

"A feeble assumption. On the contrary, Ingrid. Music is to me what breathing is to you."

I lift my hands from the keys. "Is that your Achilles heel, then? No music, no life?"

He chuckles. "No, though life creates the music we experience around us. The vibrations I hear are not just coming from within you, but within every physical thing. But that is another conversation. Yes, you are still here, the last time I spoke with you."

"Which is how far in the future?"

"I—"

"*How far,* Campbell?"

Saying his name out loud sends a shiver down my spine, and down his as well, from the look of him. "One Earth year. Perhaps six months."

Six months. That's April—the end of a traditional winter semester. And I'm supposed to be coming to the end of my conversations with him. The only way I can process this is by playing again, which relaxes us both.

"It hurts that your distrust of me extends this far back, Ingrid. I truly do want to help you and your friends, if it is within my power. If I let you run free now, understand that I cannot prevent what Jadore and the others will do to your families. I am tethered to you, but I only come when you call me. And my times with you are brief, disorganized, and I am often only half in the room, so to speak. As it is, I am near the end of my days, and to me, the changes you have asked me to make—that you will ask me to make—do not make much difference in the events to come. I'm sorry. The power I wield does not truly belong to me, it has limited effect in this world—likely because of our link."

"And we're linked because of my teleportation power. Somehow."

He simply nods.

I sigh. "The only thing I want is my freedom and the freedom of my friends and peers. Until I get that, I don't know how I can help you. The more my power develops, the more likely it is that the Collective will kill me. Which will apparently happen in six months. And who knows how many students will die in the interim."

"You have your freedom. As does the Collective. You simply choose to stay out of fear that they will kill you and your friends and family if you try to leave. And you are correct to have that fear. Now. There is something else I can give you, instead of escape."

"Yeah? And what's that?" I yawn; the music is finally starting to do its work. I might actually get a few hours tonight.

"Knowledge is the most valuable thing I can impart. I will give you choice tidbits that you can pass on to your friends in a time of need."

My gaze flickers from the piano. "You're going to tell me what happens to us in the future?"

"Your friend Sunni is not here, and while I am not blessed with her gift, I have seen images in her mind. I can impart what she knew, and I can tell you some of what I have seen."

The song dies as my fingers go limp on the keys. I swivel around the bench to face him. "You have my attention."

"I thought I might." He's smiling—giddy, almost. He gestures emphatically, urging me to begin.

"Won't... won't you telling me alter the future? What if you tell me something, and I do the opposite?"

"As I said. Your future is my past. It has already happened, and will happen. Take solace in that."

I don't know if I can—the idea that everything has already been written scares me to the bone. "So...I can ask you anything?"

"You can ask me whatever you wish. I will answer, if I'm able."

"Okay," I say slowly. Questions swirl in my mind. "What is the Collective's biggest weakness?"

"Strategically?" He gives it some thought as his finger strokes the ivory, and the key softly descends beneath his ethereal touch. "It is vast. It does not easily consider the individual, even though there are many powerful individuals puppeting and orchestrating events. Yet that is not knowledge from your future. You must have deduced that."

He's right. I need to be more clever with my questions. "Tell me something major that will happen to each of my friends. Jia. Wil. Misty. Ethan. And any others."

"Though she is good at masking her emotions, Jia wears her true fears on her sleeve. But that, you already know. So here is something you do not know about her: it is not loss that will consume her spirit, but the replacement of something dear."

"What kind of...replacement?" Memories of Ohz and the other hafelglob shifting and oozing creep into my thoughts.

"I don't know. I know only what Sunni knew. Vague images of suffering, of her crying, and eventually, healing." He frowns. "Misty...there is more for her. Her power will grow by leaps and bounds compared to the rest of you. Her anger, unchecked, may be the ruin of her. But in the ashes of her destruction, she will rise again." His left hand plays an A chord. "She always does."

I'm afraid to ask. "And... Ethan?"

He lifts his eyebrows. "Ah. Yes. Him, I... have no images for. Sunni did not think or dream of him, barely knew him really. And you were not eager to talk to me about him, as I recall. When I brought up the subject, you'd blush, or you'd be angry, and in pain. It is hard to say."

Anger wells and threatens to explode but I stay my internal volcano. "I wouldn't want to know his fate anyway."

"Better to be surprised while you are still able," he replies, almost good-naturedly. "I sense you are getting tired. Our connection is weakening. You should sleep. I will take my leave from your stream." He stands.

"Wait." I also rise. "What about Wil?"

"What about him?" he replies incredulously.

"You had something to say about everyone else, except Wil. And Sunni was friends with Wil." I frown. "Something bad's going to happen to him, isn't it."

"Nothing bad happens to anyone. Merely actions and reactions, intended and unintended. Though if you mean *bad* in the *unavoidable* sense, then yes. I can no more change his path than I can change mine. He has already made the choice that will doom him. He has already been doomed, and the world has moved on."

"Then you can tell me what it is, so that I can prevent it."

Campbell laughs condescendingly, as an old man would laugh at a child for her naivety. "I thought you would have understood by now that what will happen has *already happened.* I have seen it. There is no preventing what you will do. Humans and hafelglob and the ahmei and the d'ntak and all of the other aliens within the Collective, you travel within Time in one direction. Your path is linear, yet twisted, intricately so, never crossing into future happenings."

"Tell me what happens to Wil." My hands are fists. "Or I won't help you."

He rounds on me, his face suddenly drawn and gaunt. No longer is he Ken, but an old G. I. Joe soldier who has been in the trenches and seen death. "This is a war, Ingrid. There are always casualties."

My mouth feels dry. "Wil."

But Ethan is safe! Your family, they are safe.

I don't know that for certain. In six months, we all might die, even if I do what Campbell asks and use my power to open a door.

"How does he die?"

"Ingrid—"

I grit my teeth. "Tell me *how* he dies."

"You cannot prevent it. You have already tried. And failed. It will happen."

"Then you shouldn't have any trouble telling me what will happen."

He heaves a long, tired sigh. "Jadore will kill him. It will be in battle. I watched it, as you will."

I cross my arms, looking away from his face. His anger is my anger. This tethering he describes is a thick rope wrapped around my gut. It ties us more deeply than I can understand.

"Wait for me at the portal." Campbell's face twists again, and he approaches me. His grin widens, spreading all the way up to his eyes in an exaggerated *u*. He is losing his form; he is fading now. I have not played my music enough. His image blips in and out of reality—one moment a foot away, and then next, kneeling before me, his hand reaching for my face.

"Wait. Don't—"

I reach for his hand, but it disappears; there is only cold air where he once was. The echo of his voice is more in my mind than in the world; I hear it nonetheless.

"No, no no." I spin around, slam my hands down on the keys, and start playing. What was the song again? What was it?

For fifteen minutes, I try to remember. I play every song I can think of, mixing them, experimenting with them in E-minor, for that for certain is the key. Desperate, I try G, and then F, and finally, A. Nothing. He is gone.

My first conversation with Campbell is possibly his last. Six months until I see that version of him again.

Wait for me at the portal. I'll try to remember that.

I drift in and out of a delirious sleep with my head and my hands resting on the keys, heavy with prophecy, burdened with questions. When I wake, the run is beginning to stream in through the single window in the trailer. I rise from the bench, stumbling in a sleepy stupor, toward the windowpane.

Six months until I save the world.

CHAPTER 4

"Ingrid? Ingrid Stanley? Can I talk to you a moment?"

The insistent voice catches my attention as Jia and I walk from MacLeod Hall, out into the cloudy day. I turn, recognizing Tilly Newman, one of the girls in my tutorial. She's mostly quiet, but I think she studies creative writing.

I adjust my shoulder bag. We've just been dismissed from a really rough tutorial. Jadore was particularly hard on me this morning. On one hand, I can't blame her that I was—and still am—fighting to keep my eyes open. My fitful but fortunately dreamless sleep at the piano in the music trailer wasn't enough, and enraged my back muscles as well. All that kept me from lashing out at Jadore was a quiet, victorious sense of purpose.

Someday soon, I'm going to stop her from killing my friend, and taking over this planet. If that means enduring an hour of embarrassment each day, so be it.

"Hi," I say to Tilly, a little unsure of myself, especially since I've barely remembered her name, and more especially because I'm almost always made a fool of in tutorial—who knows what this girl probably thinks of me.

Jia makes an excuse that I don't hear as she slips away, toward a group of her psychology major peers across the quad. Even without using her power, she has a knack for leaving quietly. She glances over her shoulder; she won't go far, since she agreed to come with me to check out the occult shop, Mystic Shadows.

"So...um...did you want something?" I cross my arms. It's hard not to come off as rude, but the anxiety chewing up my insides makes me fidget. Standing in one spot for too long in the open, especially near Jadore's office in MacLeod Hall, makes us more of a target, especially without my Spark friends.

"I did, yeah. Your notes were really interesting today." Her hair is a lighter red than mine, and far bushier, but held back by a black wire headband. Her smile, freckles, and demeanour remind me of Anne Shirley—if Anne also liked heavy sweaters with cartoony cats on them, and tight dark leggings. She has a large, black binder tucked underneath one arm. Despite her cutesy outward appearance, there's a determined, fiery look in her eyes. She hasn't stopped me just to chat.

I roll my eyes and chuckle nervously. "No, they weren't. It was far from my best work. I was just...tired. Jadore lambasted every single point I made. I...should have done better."

"The professors aren't always right, you know."

This makes me pay more attention. She'd never spoken out against Jadore before. I don't remember seeing her at the protest last month, but then again, a lot of things were going on.

"No, they're not always right, that's true," I say slowly. "But who is?" Unfortunately, the *they're just human* argument need not apply. I glance over my shoulder at Rita House, dozens of feet away. Goose flesh ripples up my arms. Yes, I've been out here for too long. Someone will have to have noticed by now.

Tilly notices my discomfort. "Sorry. I don't mean to keep you from your friends or your studies or anything. I just had a question for you. I'm studying journalism and since you seem like a brainiac when it comes to... well, the brain... I was wondering if I could ask you a few research questions."

"Uh..." I'd done some research on the brain for my semester-long joke of a project. I'd foolishly announced to the tutorial that I was studying the multiverse theory and the impact of "impossible travel" on the brain. "I guess I could try. Jia might be a good person to ask too, since she's studying child psychology—"

"Yes, but I want *your* input. You wouldn't be quoted in the article or anything, I just wanted to clarify a couple of science things."

"Article?"

"Oh. Right. Should have led with that." She smiles innocently, but I can tell that she started the conversation exactly how she intended. Tilly shifts her binder to the crook of her left arm, opens it, and shuffles through the unorganized pages. Eventually, she pulls out a stapled, twenty-four-page red booklet that has *DON'T READ* handwritten in large capital letters on the front. "Several weeks ago, me and a couple of other students started a school...well, you could call it a newspaper, but it's more of a zine. The *Don't Read Zine*. Have you heard of it?"

Tilly hands me the booklet. The grungy, rough texture of

the front and back covers piques my curiosity—it appears to be more like a private journal than something I'd want to spread around campus. Nevertheless, I'm intrigued, and browse the first few pages. There's a contributors page—of which Tilly is at the very top, claiming the position of Director of Editorial Content—and features three others below her. Each person has a grainy, black and white photo where they're covering part of their faces.

Tilly gives me her commentary for each page like a proud mother showing off baby pictures. "We wanted to make the design grungy. Makes it edgy and mysterious, you know? Same with calling it *Don't Read.* Everyone loves getting into something they shouldn't."

Yes. That's what makes this project all the more dangerous. Tilly and her friends may have their faces half-covered like celebrities avoiding the paparazzi, but their first names and expertise are clearly displayed. It wouldn't take a Collective scientist long to figure out who they are.

I flip through some more, enduring Tilly's detailed explanation of the zine's construction. Everything is neatly typed, mostly in courier-new font, but the headlines are intricately hand-lettered, thanks to her friend Elisha. "My other friend Lynn, her parents own a craft store down in Edmonton. She's super *crafty.*" She snickers at her pun. "She's responsible for the actual production. Then we have Greg, who does the typesetting and consults with Elisha on the design. Three of us write for it, though I do most of the actual journalism. We've only had two issues so far. That's the second one. We only made, like, maybe, twenty of the first one? The first issue was only sixteen pages and was mostly full of essays. But it sold out."

"You sell them?"

"Sure. Dollar-fifty an issue. Kind of a low price since each is handmade, but we're just starting out. Once we have a couple of issues out, we'll start selling subscriptions. Sparkstone's a small school but everyone's paying the big bucks to be here—and handmade is *in* right now."

Her passion takes me for a ride as I too consider, for the briefest of moments, that Sparkstone is a market ripe for a paid student newspaper. But then I remember that the professors are part of an alien organization dedicated to cultivating and then harvesting our bodies for science, and that crushes my enthusiasm.

I turn the page, and my chest seizes.

There's an article about the protest in here.

"Oh! Yeah. I forgot to mention. You're the star of this issue." She smiles expectantly at me, as if I'm supposed to thank her for giving me celebrity and fame.

WAKE UP EVERYONE—STUDENT PROTEST LEADS TO STAFF CRACKDOWN

So much for an unbiased perspective. Tilly looks at me expectantly—I have no choice but to read.

While the first few paragraphs describe the event, the story eventually switches to first person, where Tilly herself recounts the happenings from her point of view. I skim, my heart pounding, as I search for a damning mention of our powers. Wil was controlling Laura for part of the time, but there's surprisingly little mention of the girl who took the fall for the event. What is mentioned is Jadore's brash entrance, her strange behaviour, and the security guards showing up to contain the commotion that followed. The only photograph accompanying the article looks deliberately grainy, as if to emphasize the guerilla journalism. Despite the quality, the photo is unmistakably me on stage at the piano, playing my heart out on stage left, while Ethan strums away beside me with his guitar.

Instinctively, my finger grazes his black-and-white face, and the melody we created together returns to mind.

A month ago we discovered that the Collective was infecting the food on campus with a drug colloquially called Gen-Grow that encourages the dormant Gene 213—the gene we believe causes our powers—to awaken. While we struck a temporary blow against the Collective by staging a protest and interfering with a shipment of one of the primary ingredients, it had little lasting effect—other than to warn some of the students away from the cafeteria food. The substance in the cafeteria food is supposed to dull student memories, make them euphoric, and easy to manipulate. Either Tilly didn't eat that day or she's beginning to resist the drug.

Or, she's wising up to what's really going on around here.

I linger on the protest article, staring at the blurry, black and white image of me and Ethan up on stage, and then close the booklet. "Good luck with it. It's well made. I...hope it takes off."

Tilly ignores the conversation-closer and forces the booklet open again to the protest article. She points at my pixilated form on the stage. "Your protest *inspired* me, Ingrid."

"It wasn't *my*—"

"You got up there on that stage, and you just started... playing. And, this is weird, but it's true. I felt like I was waking from a dream. Like the music was saying, 'Hey Tilly, stop messing around with your life and *do* something.' So I did. You know!"

"Yeah. I know." The music had been so powerful, it had enraptured everyone—and called Joseph G. Campbell into our world. "Wait. What do you mean, you *did*? You did what?"

Tilly makes a noise of disbelief. "The *zine*. I made it because of you. Because...because you were so unafraid. You just got up there, whether it was allowed or not, and just started...speaking to all of us, from your soul."

Because of *me*. She is putting her life and the lives of her friends on the line—because of something that I did.

The memory of Jadore entering the cafeteria, cane at the ready, ready to strike Joseph G. Campbell down without a second thought springs forth. A chill rips through me, as if her electricity has just blasted my spine. If a poorly planned and executed *protest* can ruffle the Collective's proverbial feathers, who knows what they would do to four enterprising students with the means to investigate and deliver inconvenient truths.

"I don't really know what to say to that," I admit, trying to keep my fear and love of the music I'd created at bay.

When I attempt to give it back to her, but she waves it away. "Keep it. Tell your friends. In any case, I'd really like your help answering my questions."

"I'm not sure how I can be helpful. Like I said—I'm not really an expert. There's more qualified people to talk to about the brain on campus. Like Professor Jadore."

"You know how Professor Jadore gets, though. Cranky. She wouldn't talk to me."

No, likely not. And certainly not for a student newspaper. Especially if she knows what Tilly has written about her. Since most students are kept relatively calm and under control by the food in the cafeteria, I can't see how underground student journalism can do much of anything—yet with the student disappearances, it seems unlikely that everyone can stay quiet forever.

"C'mon, Ingrid," she says, stepping closer to me. "It'll only take five, maybe ten minutes of your time. Inside, maybe?"

I frown. Couldn't she just go to the library and do her own research? "Um…now?"

"If you're not that busy."

I sigh. "Well…" I'd suggested to Misty and Jia that we check out the occult shop after lunch, to see if we could find a connection to my dream. Maybe if I can find out more about Tilly, I can see if she's a Spark. While not as urgent as the occult dream investigation, keeping track of potential Sparks is important too, as the Collective may target Tilly. "I guess."

"Great. Thank you so much." She looks overly pleased with herself, beaming at finally wearing me down. "Do you live in Rita House?"

"Yeah."

"Thought so. I live on the first floor. Want to go to the common room?"

The first-floor common room in Rita House, identical the one in Rogers Hall where we were yesterday, is available for students to reserve or use freely if it's empty. "Can I meet you there in like ten minutes? I want to grab a snack from my room first."

"Sure." She doesn't leave my side though, and since we're walking towards the same building, I don't want to be rude and rush off. I catch Jia's attention across the quad and motion towards Rita House—she nods in understanding. At least, if I'm returning to the dorm, I can grab lunch snacks for the three of us.

I'm struggling to come up with non-alien conversation topics but Tilly is quick to rescue us from the silence. "So what made you choose psychology as your major?"

"Oh…I guess I've always imagined myself helping people. I'm interested in how the brain works, how behaviours develop, how we influence each other. That sort of thing." Is this part of the interview? I don't want to talk about myself too much to this girl—she's already written enough to put herself on the Collective's must-abduct list. I purse my lips and curse them for making me think so critically of a probably innocent girl who is just looking for companionship in this dreary, hopeless compound. "Your majors?"

Her grin is a dangerous one. "Creative writing. And journalism, of course. I have a history of digging up information that others would rather leave buried." She realizes how ambiguous that sounds and backtracks. "I mean, nothing super controversial or anything. I may have 'accidently' exposed my high school phys. ed teacher's drug ring. Oh, and I did happen to be at the same place as a certain English teacher as she made a deal with a wealthy student where she would be compensated well for giving him straight A's."

"No, that doesn't sound controversial at all."

She laughs again. "Okay, okay. So I have a knack for getting into trouble. I think you do too."

I stop dead. We're just in front of Rita House. A chilly wind picks up and carries my dread around the campus, swirling my hair around my face so violently that I have to rein it in with my fingers. "What does that mean?"

"Whoa, hey, it was a joke." She narrows her eyes and smirks. "Unless you've got a dangerous, juicy secret you're dying to get off your chest."

I glance around to see if there are any maintenance men, professors, or anyone from the Collective listening in. There's a camera above the entrance to Rita House. Its gaze is focussed on the quad. I lean towards the door, hoping the camera has a blind spot, and I try to simultaneously lower my voice and appear nonchalant. "Everyone has something they don't want other people figuring out."

Tilly cuts to the chase. "I knew it."

"You knew what?"

She runs her teeth along her bottom lip and leans in close. "There is something going on here. Something weird. Like Professor Jadore not actually being blind, for starters."

I blink. "She, uh, does have an uncanny knack for always knowing who is in front of her."

"Yeah, definitely suspicious. If there was only a way to..." She shakes her head. "Now I'm being mean. Plotting to steal a blind woman's sunglasses and cane. Still. She doesn't hate you because you're smart. You know her secret, and she's making you stay quiet. Isn't that right?"

"I believe you're leading the question," I say, backing away slightly. "Whatever you think—or write—about Jadore isn't my business."

"If she hates you so much, why are you protecting her? She's always picking on you, Ingrid. There is *something* going on here, something dirty, and me and my friends are going to use this zine to—"

I grab her arm and wrench her close to me, pulling her into an awkward hug she doesn't want. "Please, don't do this. Going after Jadore won't solve anyone's problems. You'll only make it worse for yourself."

She reciprocates the hug to buy us more time. "What did she do to you?"

I pull away again. "Nothing yet." I draw a deep breath and glance up at Rita House. "Do your real questions have anything to do with the brain?"

"No."

"Then don't ask them anywhere inside. I flick my thumb to the camera above the Rita House's entrance. "Surveillance everywhere."

"I *knew* those were monitored cameras," she mutters. She opens her messy binder to a blank sheet of loose-leaf and scribbles something illegible. "What else?"

"What else?" I forcefully shut her binder, causing it to slip from her grasp. I catch it before it hits the grass, but a few pages fly wildly out, and my copy of the zine flops abandoned to the walkway at my feet. "Oops. Sorry."

"S'okay," she says. We hurry around to pick up the papers before the wind takes them, or before an alien appears out of nowhere and notices Tilly's suspicious scribblings. I grasp the zine firmly in hand. I'll have to hide it in the toilet, with my other precious things I don't want the Collective to see.

Tilly is unfazed. "You realize that all these cameras—there's got to be a law against them. There's no student union to call. Maybe...someone in parliament. Wait, no. They must have a surveillance room somewhere on campus, where someone is monitoring the feeds..."

The wheels turn so fast in Tilly's eyes, it's dizzying. "What else can you tell me about the cameras?"

I take a deep breath and sigh. "They're everywhere."

"Everywhere?" She leans in closer. "Even...the bathrooms?"

"I don't think they're in your personal bathrooms, but they're in the lights. In every room."

"In the..." Her cheeks bloom red as she hugs her binder to her chest. "But I've...we've..." She paces before me, reliving more than one embarrassing moment. "The public spaces are one thing. The bedrooms?"

"Yeah. Nothing that a chewed up piece of gum can't cover...but if you do that, then..."

I don't have to finish the sentence. Tilly nods, sobered by whatever her imagination pictures is the worst thing that the school can do to her—which is probably tame to what the Collective can really do.

"I want to follow up with you on this," she says slowly. A sly smile breaks out on her face. "Let me look into this a little more, okay? This story deserves feature status for the next issue. I promise I won't credit you. I'll just say, an anonymous source tipped me off to this."

"I don't want to be—"

"You'll be safe. Trust me." She tucks her binder in the crook of her arm and awkwardly hugs me again, and whispers, "I won't tell anyone you told me. I promise. Even if the president of the school himself threatens to expel me."

"I—"

"It's okay." She pulls away, nodding sympathetically. "Jadore won't find out. We'll make sure of it."

"We? You're going to tell your team?"

"Oh. Well." She frowns. "I tell them everything. They won't tell. They're just as dedicated as I am to uncovering the truth here. Here. Let me give you my phone number. You can call me at any time, day or night, if you get scared, or if You-Know-Who threatens you again."

Dumbfounded, I allow her to take the zine and she writes her cell number on the inside page next to her black-and-white photograph and bio.

I feel heavy; unnaturally routed in the moment. Escape isn't an option. There's nowhere to go. Gravity bends my knees, as if I am on a different version of Earth, and it takes every ounce of mental strength to keep upright.

This isn't the real story. Just tell her. Ask her about the missing students.

Ask her.

Taking my silence as compliance, she hands me back the zine, and backs away, still wearing her comforting, sympathetic smile. "Well, I'm off to the cafeteria. See you around! Call me!"

She storms off across campus. It takes a moment to realize I am frozen in place, hand reaching for her. I could yell after her and warn her about the cafeteria food, at the very least. I'm really close to doing this. But as Tilly becomes smaller and smaller on the horizon, I wonder if there's really any point. I could stop her from eating there today. But what about tomorrow, and the next day? I'd be stuck between asking her to do something unreasonable, and telling her the truth, the latter of which I couldn't do without betraying the trust of the Sparks.

Not everyone can be saved, Wil told me once. Now more than ever I believe it, and hate myself for it.

I catch up with Jia. Misty has joined us as we head off Sparkstone University campus proper. Wil, of course, is busy in Conrod Building working on his projects. The sidewalk winds with Sparkstone Boulevard—as much as a prairie road really winds and twists—and if followed, ends up at the main gate of the town. The gate is protected by hafelglob security guards in human form who prevent potential runaways.

Thank goodness we're not going to the gate today. Mystic Shadows is located on Waterstone Street, near the Evergreen Café in the main shopping district. When I say main shopping district, it's really just one part of Sparkstone Boulevard crammed with little boutiques, cafes, the bakery, and the supermarket. Sparkstone as a town isn't that large but it's home to a few thousand regular residents, and was probably made especially for the school. By the Collective. I shudder.

"Tilly Newman is asking a lot of questions," I tell Jia and Misty. "Did you see the zine she's selling?"

"Yeah," Misty replies. "If she's not careful, Jadore will get to her."

I sigh. "That's what I'm afraid of. Our protest may not have been a failure after all. I'll watch her and try to curb any drastic action on her part."

Misty purses her lips. "Might not be that easy. We can't monitor her day and night. We do that, then we're no better than the Collective."

"Yeah. True. Maybe we should just tell her the truth. The more people we have on our team—"

"She's a loud mouth with no tact and no apparent powers. I don't think that's a good idea."

"So only people with powers are useful?"

"One problem at a time," Jia says quietly, glancing between me and Misty.

Of course, Jia is right. I back down, for now. "I think it was nighttime in my dream, when I saw the women and the Ouija board."

Jia keeps a watchful eye out for cameras on the nearby lampposts and shop awnings. "We could've waited until tonight and snuck in."

"Yeah, but that seems like a lot of work when we can just go in...you know, normal-like," Misty replies. "What's up with you and sneaking around, anyway?

Jia shrugs. "I enjoy practicing my skills."

"So do I, but I also like not getting killed."

"Haven't been caught yet, have I?"

"Easy for you to say," I say.

"Besides," Misty says, stretching out her chewing gum to a distasteful length before pulling it out of her mouth entirely, "it's an occult shop. Who knows what freaky stuff they've got in there. It could rival our superpowers, Jia."

Jia looks sceptical but she does not argue. She's really good at keeping her opinions to herself, especially when they might be contrary to Misty's.

"It's not like they sell real magic," I say, pulling my long cardigan closer to my chest and then shoving my hands in to my jean pockets. "I mean, it's probably just one of those bookstores with books about the occult, and pretty capes and dresses and tarot cards and such."

"Might be," Misty says. "Nothin' wrong with that."

Jia saunters on ahead of us and in her quiet way, beckons us to continue down the sidewalk. "It's possible your dream wasn't prophetic, Ingrid. Maybe the owners are human, have no connection to the Collective, and have found a demand that needs to be filled."

"Right," Misty mutters, unconvinced. "I guess we'll see, won't we."

Five minutes later, we're in the middle of the shopping district on Sparkstone Boulevard. The smells of the bakery and the freshly brewed flavored coffee from Evergreen Café tempt us, beg us to enter their respective establishments, but we resist the call. Evergreen Café has a line out the door. We're almost certain that there are some levels of Gen-Grow in the Evergreen Café, though we haven't been back recently to check. The four of us mainly shop at the supermarket now, pooling our limited savings to buy whatever fruits, vegetables, some produce, and canned goods that we're reasonably sure haven't been tampered with. Jia's parents have also been sending us care packages with produce from their farm. Our funds are dwindling, and it's really hard to maintain a diet of fruit, vegetables, and beans—and I've lost weight since coming here—but I never again want to be under Gen-Grow's influence.

"There it is," Misty says.

The building itself is pretty much identical to every other building on Waterstone Street and Sparkstone Boulevard: red brick with dark roofing, two large shop windows on the main level with two tiny windows on the second floor, presumably an office or an apartment. What differentiates Mystic Shadows—other than the double-sided wooden carved sign proclaiming its name hanging from the awning and the occult-themed window dressings—is the colour of the door. It's a bright red. Although the sign in the window says that all are welcome, there's something about that red colour that chills me. Usually red is comforting, and is the sound of the deeply resounding A chord, but this red—it's too happy. It is a clown's makeup. Stephen King's *It*, personified in door-form. I step back onto the street, my stomach upset.

"What?" Misty asks, seeing my discomfort. "Did you remember something else from the dreams?"

I purse my lips. "No…it's not that…"

"Then what?"

"I don't know," I admit.

"If you don't want to go in, that's okay," Jia says. "I can go with Misty."

"No, no, I'm fine." I take in a deep breath to calm my nerves. "Probably just haven't gotten enough to eat today. Let's just go in."

A bell jingles above the door as the three of us enter into a small, narrow entrance space. Immediately I am overwhelmed with the smell of hundreds of incenses, twisting and coiling together. I stagger back. I am hit by reds and blues and greens that muddle together into browns. I gasp for air. My synesthesia is as worse as it's ever been. Jia grips my shoulder in a silent question but I wave her off. It takes a few seconds, but I adjust to the smell and the colours bombarding my brain subside into a dull cloud that hovers in my ears. The faintest of chords weaves distantly in my mind but it has no flow or organization. The feeling is a mud puddle being splashed by an excited child while a distant, distracted parent looks on.

Bulletin boards line the walls on either side, littered with flyers, showing an active side of the small town I hadn't expected. There's a bake sale tomorrow, a talent show on Sunday night, and a couple of people offering their services as tutors in various subjects. It is easy to forget that people other than students live here. I wonder if they realize just how trapped they are, and if any of them are really human, or if they are aliens playing pretend.

One bright blue paper dangles off the left side of the board, as if added in a hurry. In capital letters, the sign asks:

HAVE YOU EVER WANTED TO SPEAK TO THE DEAD?

The flyer advertises weekly séance sessions with limited seating, here at Mystic Shadows. This might be what I saw!

Jia has continued on into the store, but Misty stands firmly in place next to me as she too takes in the promise of otherworldly contact with hope in her eyes.

"Sunni led us to this," she says quietly. "Maybe she has something...personal...to say."

Sunni's spirit might be guiding my dreams, but the idea that she led us here *just* to speak with us feels wrong. "I think she's trying to tell us something about the missing students. That these séances have something to do with it."

Misty huffs a sigh before giving up on the sign and venturing deeper into the store.

Four rows of New Age bric-a-brac lend an orderly, clean atmosphere to the room, yet it's the same artificial clean that all the buildings in Sparkstone possess: everything is *too* new to be stately. Even the rustic rafters made of logs and tall, wooden beams appear too polished, as if the Collective hovered over Banff, Alberta, spotted the chic cabin styles, and thought they too could get into the Western Canadian tourism business without further research or thought. Underfoot, I expect creaks and groans, but hear only my own timid footsteps as I follow Misty deeper into the displays.

The smells of the various candles, at least now that I'm used to it, is pleasing. In the background, soothing, New Age music hums, though I'm uncertain whether it's my personal synesthetic soundtrack underscoring my experience in the room, or if it's real. Great—once again, I can't tell the difference between reality and a dream.

At the back of the store is a doorway covered by a bead curtain. The sign above the doorframe, written in a Celtic font, reads *STAFF ONLY*.

The beads look familiar. I've seen them before. In my dream. This is the place.

Determined, I move down the centermost aisle, towards the back room.

"Ingrid. What are you doing?" Jia hisses.

Unlike my dream, the thick brown beads don't completely obscure the view into the secondary room. The beads make a pleasant crinkling sound as I part the curtain and peek inside the forbidden room. No table, no Ouija board. A black pentagram on purple fabric hangs to the right, and the same cupboard I saw in the dream is on the far wall.

Misty approaches from behind me. "Oh man. Is that where—?"

A deep, sultry voice interrupts her. "Is there anything I can help you find?"

Startled, I step back from the beads and turn to my right. A person slides aside heavy indigo curtains obscuring another doorway, though it's a moment before I realize the pattern on her flowing skirts and the curtain are two different cloths.

"Oh. Uh, sorry. I was—" I fumble for an excuse better than *I was here before in a dream*. "I was just looking."

"Can I help you find anything? I'm Shadow, and this is my establishment." Pride drips from her voice as she smiles. I relax somewhat. I don't want her to think I meant to trespass.

"Just opened?" Misty asks, casually picking up a fist-sized piece of amethyst, examining it with a careful eye before setting it back down on the glass shelf.

"Yes. I was visiting my sister here last month and I felt the presence of a power spot. It was like the Universe was calling for me to make a move. That I could do real good here." She rubs her hands slowly together, caressing the large sapphire ring on her right hand. "So when she told me that a ley line exists here, I had no doubts. I left my life in Toronto, and opened up shop here."

Jia and I exchange a brief glance. The Collective isn't just recruiting talented students. They're bringing in the best and the brightest adults as well to keep the wheels turning in this town, cultivating an atmosphere where Gene 213 might activate. Whether Shadow's abilities are the result of the same mutations as ours, or something else entirely, it's hard to say.

"How long have you known you were psychic?" I ask.

"Always known," she replies with a smile, nodding. "But only for the past twenty years have I honed my skills and turned it into a business."

The occult doesn't really do it for me. I've always been a science fiction nerd, more willing to believe in the existence of aliens than magic. My experiences here have taught me that our "magic" powers are just science we don't completely understand yet.

Jia saunters down one of the aisles, her arms crossed as she examines each knick-knack in detail. "It's nice to see small businesses thriving in small towns."

Shadow smiles. "Yes. The locals here have been very supportive."

"There's not many small towns in Alberta that would be," Jia replies.

"No?" Shadow looks surprised. "I suppose the occult still carries a fierce stigma. But I've only lived here a short time, like I said. You're from here?"

"From Alberta, yes. Grew up on a farm, far south of Calgary," Jia says.

"Ah. Well, if you have any questions, I'm happy to answer them."

"Do you know anyone named Avery Trites? Maybe Daniel Chomber sounds familiar?" I ask.

Shadow shakes her head. "Sorry."

"Sunni Harris?" Misty asks with unabashed hope.

"I'm sorry, should I know who they are?" Shadow asks.

"They're just…students who used to go here," I reply.

"Students come in and out all the time. Perhaps they've been here before. Why do you ask?"

"We're interested in your séances," I say.

"Have these students passed over to the other side?"

I hesitate. Misty takes the lead. "Sunni has. So your skills really allow you to talk to the dead?"

"Oh, yes," Shadow says, flicking long, ringed fingers towards the back room. "Have you ever been to a séance before?"

For once, Misty is at a loss for words. Her dark, plucked eyebrows knit together slowly. I cover for her. "I...I don't think we have, no."

"Well, we have them frequently in the back of the shop. I've done them for a few years now, with my group back in Toronto, but it's only since I've opened the shop that we've opened them up to the public."

"Who is *we*?" Jia asks carefully.

"A group of people who believe in things that cannot otherwise be explained rationally, or by science." A smile twitches the corners of her lips. There's a challenge in her ethereal, airy voice. "And if you were interested in attending, we are having a gathering later this week."

"Can we sign up?" I ask.

She considers us each in turn. "What are your names?"

We individually introduce ourselves and she nods. Then, surprisingly, she holds out her hands to me. "It's all right. Take my hands. I don't bite."

My fingers twitch. "Um... why?"

"I want to give you a reading. If that's all right."

"Um, sure." I already have one powerful force telling me

how things are going to go down. What's one more?

Hesitantly, I place my hands in Shadow's outstretched grasp. My gaze flits between Shadow's concerned, concentrating expression and my exposed palms, and Jia as she wanders closer, offering me a *this is kind of awkward and weird* look.

Shadow is silent for a full minute, lost in my palm lines. "Hmm," she says eventually. "There's…a cloud hanging over you. That's odd. A cloud. Um. A sinister energy." Shadow looks disturbed. "I'm sorry, Ingrid. I don't usually like to give negative readings, especially to those who I've just met. This energy…I'm getting a very cold feeling. Do you have any negative influences in your life that could explain this?"

"A cloud?" Like the one in my dream. But that cloud was above the séance women, not me. "Is the negative energy coming from the cloud?"

"It's not so much a literal cloud, as a negative force bearing down on you."

"Oh."

She closes her eyes now, no longer reading my hands. "I'm going to see past that. There are such vibrant colours dancing around you. Like living in a painting. And I hear…such beautiful piano music. You're a musician."

"Yes." I wonder how much of that she can divine from the callouses on my fingers.

"I see a man in the mountains. He's far away. I think he's a man. A strong influence on your life… "

Campbell's name is on my lips, but I'm afraid to say it, in case I accidently summon him. That would be a lot to explain.

As if sensing my hesitation, she opens her eyes and raises an eyebrow, releasing me from her gentle grip. "I'm quite impressed by you. You have a strong energy, fuelled by a powerful spirit. How about you, Misty, or Jia? Would you like me to read you?"

Jia smiles and shakes her head. "No, thank you."

"Uh, I think I'm good," Misty replies, grimacing. In the time I've known Misty, she's displayed a distaste for being touched. "I think we'll just go for the séance."

Shadow doesn't look offended, and doesn't try to upsell us on further readings. Nodding, Shadow moves gracefully to the till, where a clipboard and a pen are neatly placed next to an antique cash register. "Three more for the séance on Friday evening."

"Four of us, actually." She smirks, probably thinking of poor Wil down in his lab and what his reaction will be when we tell him how we're going to spend our Friday night. I can't help but return the smile. At least with him in the room, he can give us a play-by-play of Shadow's general state of mind, and let us know whether this is worth our time.

Shadow smiles. "It's so good to see the students taking an interest. It will begin at ten p.m., though I usually serve a little sherry beginning at nine-thirty to loosen the nerves. You are all eighteen, correct?"

I'm about to tell the truth, but Misty nods. Jia and I don't contradict her.

"It's mostly an older crowd. We enjoy the socializing portion. Arriving early is also a good idea to get a seat. Once, I had a few people who had to stand instead, which makes for awkward energy in the room. I'll also warn you: time flies when you're communing with the spirits! Don't plan any late night activities afterward and expect to keep them. We usually go long. Do you have any other questions?"

Yes. Is this for real, and are there such things as alien ghosts? The three of us exchange silent glances and shake our heads. Shadow nods and blinks with the satisfaction of a content cat.

"Thanks for your help," I say finally, and head toward the door.

Misty and Jia utter their thanks and goodbyes to Shadow, and we exit the shop. The air outside is brisk and fresh compared to the fragrance of the inside, and I gulp it greedily, eager for the neutral smell palette. Misty shoves her hands in her pockets as we saunter across the street, and head back the way we came.

"So," I say, hating to be the one to break the contemplative silence. "Who gets to tell Wil that he's going to a séance?"

"Bastard probably knows already with his Big Brother powers," Misty mutters. She glances back at the shop wistfully. "He's not makin' excuses. He's doing this."

"I suppose it's no less safe than wandering around in the dark, invisible," Jia muses.

"Shadow could also be an alien, and that story she told us may not be true, and all this might be an elaborate trap," I say.

"Pretty complicated trap," Misty replies testily, and then laughs. "If they wanted me, they could come get me anytime. They don't need to set up any trap to get me. They know I'd put up a fight no matter which way it went down. Not to mention, allowing the three of you to come as well?"

I concede to her point. "True."

"Do you think she has psychic powers, Ingrid?" Jia asks hesitantly. "Her reading wasn't that specific."

"I don't know. Maybe," I reply. "We have superpowers. Why wouldn't anyone else?"

Misty is strangely stoic. "The séance is worth trying. We've already been up and down this campus looking for masked and unmasked kidnappers. Maybe Shadow's people are somehow responsible for the missing students. Sunni might be trying to tell us that in her dream. We won't know unless we go to the séance."

My dream. It was *my* dream. I start to protest but then I take note of Misty's determined expression. Her lips tightly press together and the wind tosses her hair; she'd even stopped picking at her already torn-to-the-cuticle nails.

This isn't pure curiosity. This isn't even about the kidnappings. She wants to go because she believes that somehow, she'll be able to speak to Sunni.

That evening, psychology textbooks from the library and printed off studies from the internet are strewn over my comforter. We're supposed to be studying separately in our rooms, but every time I try to read, my mind returns to the thought of Ethan, probably alone, having fun doing his art.

I pick up the picture of me and my parents that I keep on the nightstand. It's been a near nightly ritual since Sunni's journal was destroyed in the secret underground library. I lie down on my bed and hold the framed picture above me, elbows locked and arms straight. I know every detail of this picture. I remember the day clearly. I hadn't really wanted to go to the Alexander Graham Bell museum but my parents had thought it might be a good idea to stimulate my mind, even though I was halfway through the required reading list for the upcoming grade eleven school year and practicing my instruments for two hours every day.

I remember standing by that tree, waiting as Mum asked some stranger to take our picture. He was tall and wiry. And his face...

Wait. What did his face look like?

I sit up suddenly, staring harder at the picture like it will provide me with the answer. The man who took the picture was pleasant. He'd made Mum laugh, that's why she was smiling in the picture. He'd said something to me as well, but his voice and the words have been cut from the fabric of the memory with careful, sharp scissors.

I've looked at this picture tons of times since coming here. It's the only physical picture I have of my parents. I could have sworn Mum was squinting because the sun was in her eyes, not laughing. And hadn't there been a sailboat going at top speed in the background? Still waters abound behind the full, summer tree.

Yet it isn't Mum's reaction or the sailboat that I'm interested in remembering. Closing my eyes, I concentrate on the photographer's face. He couldn't have been over forty. And he was definitely a man. He had short, cropped hair. Brown, maybe blond. I sigh. Memories are not reliable sources of information—they are rewritten every time they are accessed.

Does it really matter if I don't remember this man's face? I set the picture back on the nightstand. If it's the only thing I can't remember about the day, I say I'm doing pretty good. Still, the absence of this man's face nags me. My own face in the picture is happy and smiling—is it because my parents are hugging me, or was it something the photographer had said?

I rummage under my bed for my laptop and wait five minutes for it to boot, and then open up my pictures folder. Maybe the other vacation photos will jog my memory.

There are almost a hundred photos from that vacation. Many of them are of the landscape: places on the Cabot Trail where you can stop and snap photos of the mountains and the ocean. Blurry pictures of wildlife, one that might be a deer, and a blackened spot that was supposed to be a bear munching on some berries. Then, some photos of the hooked rugs that look like watercolour paintings in that museum in Cheticamp. More landscape. I linger on these, as I feel like I've just taken a trip around the island again without leaving this horrible school. I wish I was with my parents, on that island, again.

The pictures of Baddeck are among the last in the folder. I cruise through them slowly. Shops, waterfront stuff, some of my Mum in front of aforementioned shops, carrying souvenir sweaters. And then, the Alexander Graham Bell Museum. There are only three pictures besides the one I have printed and framed. I go back through the ones in Baddeck. There's one of me on Chebucto Street. I'm not looking at the camera; I'm staring at something across the road. It was a sunny day, and the sidewalk was crowded with tourists. It's not a bad picture, and even the people in the background, going about their business, are in focus.

All except one. He's several feet behind me, facing the camera. His face is severely blurred, yet the unmistakeable tug in my heart tells me it's *him*.

I go through the entire folder once more with a careful eye. My laptop whirs and my legs are boiling hot, but I can't stop. In no less than thirteen pictures do I see Campbell's blurred face. In some of them, he's far in the distance. In others, he's close enough to reach out and grab us.

In all of them, he's facing the camera.

I slam the laptop shut, trying to fight my fear, and the growing heaviness inside me.

I glance back at the photo on the nightstand. Mum is smiling. Yet I *have* looked at that picture before. She was not smiling. She was squinting. Even if I have a memory of her laughing, and I see her laughing face there now, I do remember looking at that picture before and seeing something different. *Feeling* something different.

I've been so busy worrying about the immediate threat of the Collective that I've failed to study the larger picture.

Joseph G. Campbell isn't familiar because I've met him before.

If I didn't come here to Sparkstone, what would he do? I'm supposed to open a portal for him. Could I still do that if I wasn't here? He's a big fish on a fragile line, depending on me to reel him in with my alluring music. How many times have I been in the zone—how many times have I called him, even just partially, into this world?

Those aren't the only pictures on my computer. There are other vacations, school trips, concerts, and events. I'm willing to bet the rest of the food in this room that if I combed all of them, I'd see that blurred face on multiple occasions.

He's familiar because he's been following me around my whole life. Inserting himself into seemingly unimportant situations where he thought I wouldn't notice. Manipulating unseen strings, watching me grow up.

All so that I would come to Sparkstone…and help him.

CHAPTER 5

I don't think I belong here, Wil says telepathically, leaning towards me.

Six women in their late thirties chat excitedly in pairs in the back room of Mystic Shadows. All of them hold flute glasses filled with orange juice or sherry, and nibble on the various sweets arranged on a table on the far wall. The violet tapestries patterned with pentagrams and ankhs, the brand-new Ouija board set up on the table in the middle of the room, the two-door cabinet with a pentagram carved into the doors flat to the wall behind the table, and the smell of lavender charging in from the main area of the shop to combat the freshly baked cookies and cakes, remind us that we're here to communicate with the dead.

Misty, Wil, Jia, and I sit at the Ouija board table: Misty to my left, and Wil to my right, with Jia to Wil's right. While the women are completely at ease with their surroundings, there's a marked nervousness between the four of us, especially in Wil. He was furious when we told him about the séance, and we had to practically drag him from his work in the lab. The women sensed our unease, I think, and spent the first ten minutes bombarding us with icebreaker questions: *What are you studying at Sparkstone?* and *What brought you to the shop, it's beautiful, isn't it?* and *Did you bring any snacks for the table?* and *Oh, that's all right, help yourself to whatever you want!*

"They're just trying to be friendly," I mutter.

He raises a quizzical eyebrow. *They're friendly because they want to know how serious we are about this nonsense.*

"Do you sense that any of them have anything to do with the missing students?"

Wil doesn't even bother to glance around. *No.*

"They're all…human?" Jia whispers.

Definitely, Wil replies.

This whole thing would be a waste of our time if it weren't for my dream. My stomach growls. For supper, the four of us rationed Jia's vegetables, and had one slice of bread each from the bakery. I clutch my stomach beneath the table and try not to think about how hungry I am and how hungry I'll be for breakfast tomorrow when there's barely anything left for us to eat that's not contaminated with Collective chemicals. I'm not sure we have enough cash left to buy groceries and my bank account is running on fumes. It may reach a point where I'll have to ask my parents for money—if they'll listen, or even get my message. I wish my superpower was analysing the chemical compounds of cookies with my eyes so I'd know what is safe to eat. Far more useful than a teleportation power that only works when I think about my kind-of boyfriend.

Misty clasps her hands on the wooden surface of the table, absently picking at her black nail polish. I wonder how many times she's dreamed about talking to Sunni again. "I checked under the table. No devices."

I probably would have detected them, but thank you.

Misty scowls at Wil and mutters something under her breath in Mandarin to Jia. She looks confused, then annoyed. Apparently she speaks enough Mandarin to know whatever unflattering thing Misty said.

The bead curtain separating the shop and the back room parts behind us, and an older man and a woman enter cautiously. They look as though they've walked into the wrong room, but to my surprise, they take a seat near the end of the table across from Jia, in front of the two-door cabinet. She smiles and nods politely at them. The older woman gives her a sombre half-smile, and grips her husband's hand tightly.

I wonder who they have lost. How many times they've sat around tables like this, enduring small talk as they look for answers that might not ever come.

I'm not the only one curious about them. Wil's intense stare in their direction attracts the woman's attention. "Something the matter?" she asks dryly.

"No. Just...sorry." He quickly averts his gaze.

She exchanges an apprehensive look with her husband, though he seems more interested in the snack table, unreachable because of her iron grip on him.

"What?" I ask Wil.

He gives me the once-over, as if I should already know the

answer, then: *They're Avery Trites's parents,* he replies, staring down at the surface of the table.

The third disappearance. The dancer who went to Edmonton and never came back. Transferred to the "dance academy" in States.

Mr. and Mrs. Trites rise from the table and venture over to the arrangement of treats, where they are greeted warmly by the group of women.

"What are they doing here?" Jia asks.

They believe Avery is dead, or at the very least, kidnapped, Wil continues. *The Collective told him there was an accident in his studio at the "dance academy" in the Southern California. They've been given the run-around, like Mrs. Harris. They don't believe he was killed in Southern California; they think something happened in the bar in Edmonton, that one of the professors abducted him for some perverse reason. They're desperate, the authorities won't listen, and they came to confront the professors they believe are responsible.*

I raise an eyebrow at Wil. He got all that just by reading their minds? The women escort Mr. and Mrs. Trites back to the table, and ask us once again if we'd like anything. It's after ten, but the women don't appear concerned that we're running late.

If this doesn't get started in five minutes, I'll leave. We've been here for twenty minutes, and it hasn't started yet, Wil says. *Your friend Shadow has just been wandering around the main shop, reciting mantras and incensing the place.*

"It's better if we're all here," I whisper.

"I could be in the lab right now," he hisses.

"Wil, the Collective could be using them—"

"If you are here against your will, then leave."

Shadow appears in the doorway and the chatting women fall silent. She wears a long, black dress with large sleeves and a low neckline. Her hair, straightened and without frizz, lies plainly over her breasts. There's a streak of purple in it tonight that wasn't there before. Her gaze bores into Wil as she examines him carefully. "I sense a sceptic among us."

Wil looks to us for help, but we do nothing. He attempts a smile and scratches his nose. "It is healthy to have some scepticism in any new situation."

"We are here to call upon those who have gone to the other side, or those who linger in this plane. These are places that exist, whether you believe in them or not." She adopts the same vacant expression she had as she was giving Misty a reading the other day, and then says, "There will be no tricks. I will not tolerate that in this room."

Wil bows his head, though he can't keep the edge from his tone. "I'm just here to support my friends."

"Hmm." Shadow twists her lips but seems to accept Wil's excuse.

The six women hurry to the empty seats around the table, leaving the head of the table next to the couple empty for Shadow. Her boots *clomp clomp* on the floor as she crosses the room and takes her place. Mrs. Trites smiles sadly at Shadow as she takes the psychic's hand and squeezes it, searching for reassurance. Shadow cups the woman's face and then squeezes the man's outstretched hands.

"This is a special meeting. We have new faces"—she nods to Misty—"and an important mission tonight. Mr. and Mrs. Trites are our special guests. They've lost someone special to them. Their son, Avery. He was a student at Sparkstone. A talented dancer." Mrs. Trites chokes back a sob and leans into her husband. He comforts her as Shadow continues. "Though we are unsure if he has passed, we will be calling out into the spirit world in search of his soul, so that he may speak with us. Otherwise, perhaps a willing spirit will be able to guide us to his location. Is there anyone else we will be searching for tonight?"

My gaze falls to Misty. She's twiddling her thumbs, staring at the table like she's about to set it aflame.

"Anyone?" Shadow sits down in her chair and also looks to Misty. "Misty? When we met a few days ago, you mentioned the name of someone you'd lost. I invite you to share her name with us, so that we may find her on the other side."

Misty inhales sharply and clenches her hands. The table under her left palm darkens slightly.

"Her name is Sunni," she whispers. "Sunniva Harris."

"We're here to support you," says one of the ladies next to Misty. She rubs Misty's back and whispers words of condolence. Misty nods but bristles at another person's touch all the same.

"All right then," Shadow says, smiling graciously. "Excellent. I feel the positive energy in this room. It is soaring. And the veil between worlds is thin. Now, we commence. Cordelia, would you mind fetching the candles?"

The woman next to Misty rises and goes to the cabinet

behind the Trites and retrieves three black candles and candle holders. The candles have fresh white wicks. Cordelia places the candles equidistant from one another on the table—one near Shadow's end, one in the middle of the table in front of Misty, Jia, Wil and me, and the final candle at the opposite end of the table. Cordelia returns to her seat. Shadow stands, pulls a lighter from seemingly nowhere, and moves around the table ceremoniously to light the candles.

"Everyone please join hands as we cast a circle of protection," Shadow says once she returns to her place.

Like that will help us, Wil says.

I give him a dirty look and grab his hand, and take Misty's. Her determined look has returned. Once we're all holding hands, including Shadow, lighter still clutched between two fingers while the other two hold the hand of the person to her right, she draws in a deep, cleansing breath.

"Spirits of the Otherworld who have crossed over," Shadow begins, her chin tilted toward the ceiling. "We are open to your messages. If you mean us no harm, step forward, and make yourself known."

My gaze darts around the table. Some of the women plus the Trites are taking this seriously and have their eyes closed, like they're praying. Wil looks bored. Jia, fearful. Misty's eyes are squeezed shut. The flame of the candle before us flutters once.

When nothing out of the ordinary happens, Shadow continues. "Spirits, we ask for your help tonight. Mr. and Mrs. Trites ask to speak to their son who has passed on, Avery. Avery, if you are there, please, step forward."

I really hope she's not going to pretend to be possessed by ghosts, Wil whispers into my mind. *These people do not deserve to be scammed.*

I guess it won't be long before Wil can determine if Shadow is faking it or not, though he seems to have already made up his mind. I draw in a deep breath and let it out. It appears in a cloud before me. The heat of the candles seems more intense than it did mere seconds ago.

"Avery?" Mrs. Trites says, her voice cracking. "Please, sweetheart, let us know if you're there."

Something knocks on the cabinet door. Four of the women, including Cordelia and Jia gasp, startled.

"Avery Trites," Shadow says with her low, sultry voice. "If that is you, knock twice."

A pause. Then: *knock. Knock.*

"Avery!" Mrs. Trites whispers.

"How do we know it's really him?" Mr. Trites asks.

"There is nothing to fear. Spirit, if you once bore the name Avery Trites, and resided ever so briefly in the town of Sparkstone, Alberta, tell us the number of your residence room here."

That's specific, Wil says. *Unless someone is hiding in that cabinet and knows the correct answer.*

But there couldn't be. Cordelia opened it to retrieve the candles. It had shelves. No person could fit in there. My heart clenches. I want to believe.

Another three firm knocks sound from inside the cupboard. Then a pause. Then two more knocks.

"I can't believe it…it's him!" Mrs. Trites exclaims.

"Avery Trites," Shadow says. "Your mother and father are here. If you have a message for them, we have a Ouija board before us. Tell us, though, are you alone, Avery? Once for yes, and twice for no."

The cabinet shakes. Jia inhales deeply and gives me a look that tells me she's ready to turn us all invisible if needs be.

"Are you alone, Avery?" Shadow asks again.

Knock…Knock.

"Who is with you?"

Again, the cupboard shudders. A cold breeze passes by me, and the candles one by one go out. It could just be the smoke from the candles, but the room seems to have gotten hazier.

"Sunni?" Misty asks.

The people in the circle become uneasy. Even Wil's hand is sweating.

"Tell us who is with you, Avery. If it is another spirit who means us harm, we will do anything to help you pass to the other side, if that is what you seek."

We'll do anything? I'm not sure I signed up for that. Wil and I exchange uneasy glances in the dark.

The soft grinding of the pointer against the Ouija board is the only sound besides our breathing. Shadow flicks on the lighter in her hand to read the letters aloud.

"S…P…A…R…" She pauses and clears her throat. "K…" She waits for more, but the scraping has stopped. "Spark. Is that the name of your friend, Avery?"

"Sunni," Misty whispers, opening her eyes, looking hopefully to Shadow. "I bet it's Sunni."

"Misty, don't jump to conclusions," Wil warns.

"Shut up. You shouldn't even be here," Misty growls.

"There is no tolerance for negativity in the circle," Shadow says. "Avery, please clarify. When you say Spark, are you speaking of a woman once named Sunniva Harris?"

Another cold, fog-heavy breeze whirls around me, and then a knock on the cabinet.

"Told you," Misty hisses. "Sunni... if that's really you..."

Wil raises his eyebrows. "I think we'll need some proof of that."

Misty grits her teeth and speaks through them. "Fine. If Sunni is there... spell out the name of the person who—"

Careful, Wil warns telepathically.

Misty resumes. "Spell out the name of our tutorial professor."

The Ouija board comes to life once more. I squint to see it in the darkness. The pointer is moving, all by itself. Like magic. It's too dark to see if someone is manipulating the pointer via magnetism or something else.

Shadow spells out the letters as the pointer moves over them. "J... A... D... O... R... E. Jadore? Is that correct, Misty?"

"Yes," she replies softly.

"Is Avery still there?" Mrs. Trites asks. "We still have a message for him. And...so many questions."

Silence. My teeth are chattering. It feels like the middle of winter, which in Alberta, is extremely cold. I squeeze Wil's hand. He squeezes back. I suddenly wish Misty would use her powers to warm my hand.

Shadow laughs nervously. "Sometimes this happens. A little hiccup in the connection. Not to worry. Spirits of the otherworld, we are here and willing to accept your messages. Avery Trites and Sunniva Harris, if you are still there, please let us know."

THUMP. THUMP.

The cabinet rattles more furiously than before. Several of the women exchange worried looks and words.

"Shadow? Is it possible we've...called something...bad?" Cordelia asks.

"I think Avery and Sunniva are just re-establishing their presence," Shadow replies, but there's uncertainty in her voice. "Avery Trites, if you have a message for your parents, please use the board. Then they have something to say to you, I believe."

The board comes to life even faster than before. "P...R...A...Y," Shadow spells out.

"We pray for your soul every day," Mrs. Trites says. She's on the verge of sobbing. "I hope that you can find peace, Avery. We love you. That is all we wanted to say. We miss you and we love you. If you feel the need to move on...we understand. You...you can let go. But...we..." She glances at her husband for support. "If you are truly passed on, then we'd like to know where your body is." She holds back a sob, but presses on. "We want to know, so we can bring you to justice. So we can bring you *home.*"

The pointer zips across the board furiously. It seems to

be stopping at random letters. Shadow struggles to keep up. "Please ... pray ... for ... me. Is that right, Avery?"

The knock booms once.

"I suppose I can lead everyone in a little prayer before we move on," Shadow says. "Is that all right with everyone? We can pray for Avery to aid in his journey to find peace?"

The women murmur a yes, and close their eyes. Mr. and Mrs. Trites, momentarily flustered for not receiving a response to their plea for justice, nod and squeeze their hands together tightly. Misty heaves a sigh.

"Oh Lord, Goddess, Great One," Shadow says as she raises her joined hands up as high as they will go. "Hear us. Please help the spirit of Avery Trites move into the great beyond, where all souls go to rest. Show him the way to eternal peace."

A fog-heavy breeze filters through the room. Not quite as cold as the previous ones, but noticeable nevertheless, considering that there are no windows in the room, just the back door, which was closed when I last looked. The fog breezes past me, a sleek silvery-blue colour, and gathers around Shadow's head. No one else notices, as they are busy muttering their own prayers.

Are you Avery Trites? I mouth in the direction of the wisp. *Or could you be Sunni?*

Tendrils of grey-blue clouds snake around the table, each one taking a tentative hold around someone at the table. They interact with us in different ways, some wrapping themselves halo-like around our foreheads, others resting on our shoulders like shawls. The larger portions of the cloud—for they all seem connected—envelop Shadow, as if recognizing her as the leader of this session.

No one else has their eyes open but me. Even Wil seems to be playing along with the request to pray. I glance upward, and although I can't feel it around my head, I see wisps of it in my periphery, rustling my hair.

As the air becomes thicker with this strange cloud, a sense of calm descends upon me. Wil's iron grip on my arm relaxes. Even Misty seems to be at peace, her lips slightly parted in peaceful contemplation and relaxation.

My eyelids feel heavy. It's been a long day. Hell, it's been a long month. I've worked hard—we all have. We deserve a rest.

Just as I'm dozing off, the thick silvery-blue cloud turns maudlin grey, and the localized fog transforms from listless tendrils to claw-like hands. I can't take my gaze from Shadow as the long, spindly fingers close in around her temples.

The cloud pulsates blue. At first, it seems as though more of the cloud is filling the room—yet as I gradually lose my ability to focus, I realize the cloud *isn't* becoming thicker because of something being added from the outside.

The mysterious cloud thickens because of the grey, wispy smoke rising from my friends' mouths. Slowly at first, but then more rapidly, as if the cloud was sucking out their essences.

Like the rest of the people in the room, Misty and Jia have their eyes shut. Misty is mumbling under her breath, and for the briefest of moments I am impressed by her piety, before realizing that like everyone else, the blue-grey essence is filtering up out of her head as well.

"Misty!" I hiss at her.

She frowns and concentrates harder on her prayer.

"Open your eyes," I whisper again, and add a kick to her shins for good measure.

Furious, her blue irises flare icily at me but quickly melt into terror when she sees the smoke rising from everyone's heads. Wil stares, open-mouthed at the praying women. Wil nudges Jia out of prayer to witness the silent horror around us.

I'm not sure I've ever felt anything like this before, Wil says in his quiet way. *It's all going up into...someone. Someone is more present now than before. Someone with an intensity that is...unhuman.*

The blue smoke slithers down to the table and weaves into a shape: long snout equipped with rows of teeth, beady eyes on either side of its face, one staring dead at me and made shiny by the luminescence of the smoke. It is a deadly shark, swimming in the air with a smoke-fin, hovering before us. It opens its mouth wider and lets out a silent hiss. The praying people draw in deep, simultaneous breaths, and continue muttering under their breaths. The smoke deepens in colour and becomes richer.

"What...are...you?" I ask.

The smoke-shark shakes its fearsome head and swims through the air, away from the four of us, to the head of the table where Shadow "leads" the prayer. Her voice carries above the rest, but she's lost much of her inflection. She sounds deeply hypnotized.

My dream. This happened in my dream. Sort of.

Turning its head so that one eye is always fixed on me, the smoke-shark circles Shadow's head hungrily. It rears its wavering-unsolid teeth and clamps down on her head. Her entire head. Shadow whimpers and her prayer becomes louder, an incomprehensible humming of a song in gibberish. The smoke-shark appears more solid. It's feeding from her directly.

"We have to stop it," I say.

I stand up but Wil tugs on my hand. "We don't know what will happen if we break the circle."

"Now look who's concerned about the stupid circle," Misty chides him.

Wil throws her a dirty look and then closes his eyes, concentrating on the creature. He shakes his head. "It's blocking me from connecting with Shadow. It's incredibly powerful. Almost as if—"

"As if what?" Jia asks.

The shark creature, once an outline of smoke, is now almost completely solid, like a dark rain cloud. The blue essence from everyone else's heads continues to feed it but more dark patches are forming around the room.

"Almost as if there's a whole pack of sharks," I say.

Wil stands up, still clutching our hands. "Okay, time to break this circle."

Misty and Jia pull furiously at the grips of the women beside them but to no avail. I am even fused to Wil and Misty beside me. Their grips are deathly tight. Digging my heels into the floor, I pull with all my strength. Nothing.

The lead shark creature notices our resistance and trails

towards us, looming over our heads like a dark shadow. A tendril of smoke-substance curls out of its mass and hovers above our heads.

Relax. You will be with your loved ones again.

The voice is so calming. So soothing. It melts over my hair and gets in my ears and spreads over my arms. Goosebumps rise and then fall just as quickly as my body is forced to relax. I remember my parents. The first time they took me to music lessons, and how initially I didn't want to go, how I'd complained that I'd be no good at it, but they'd set me straight: gently, kindly, telling me that with a little practice every day, someday I'd be great.

You are magnificent, says the voice. *Your loved ones are very proud of you.*

Yes, they are.

You can be with them again.

I can? Something in the back of my mind tells me that this isn't so, that I'm trapped at Sparkstone. Another, stronger willpower debunks this, as if it is dream logic.

More memories flood me: playing at Carnegie Hall to a sold-out crowd. Ethan getting down on one knee and presenting me with a diamond ring. Me, finding a cure to a rare brain cancer and saving the lives of thousands. The Sparks, using their eclectic powers together to bring down Jadore and the Collective…

But these aren't real memories. These are projections of my secret hopes and dreams. Venom released by deceitful creatures to paralyze their victims while they get what they truly want.

"Ingrid!"

Wil's voice snaps me back. "What?"

"It's feeding from you. Whatever it's saying to you, don't listen!"

I shake my head. Jia and Misty are enraptured by the creatures, and a blue essence flies from their eyes and mouths and into the smoky aliens. A tear trembles in Misty's eye and runs down her cheek. I can only imagine what the creature is showing her.

"What do we do?" I exclaim, panic creeping into my voice.

"I...I can't resist...for long," Wil struggles to say.

I'm not sure if any of us can hold out. Now that I know its intentions, I feel the fog creeping over me. I pull harder on Misty and Wil's hands. Misty's grip is slick with sweat and limp from lack of willpower.

"Can you at least make one of them let go?" I ask Wil. "Can't you control your own body?"

"I..." Beads of sweat dot his forehead as he leans away from the table. In doing so, he yanks backward on my arm. "I might be—"

As the fog rolls toward my face, Wil opens a small hatch within my mind. It's a strange sensation, suddenly being aware of a vulnerable backdoor hiding in your brain. Just as I am aware of his presence there, and the implications of it, I feel him routing around, like fingers flipping through files in a cabinet, or hands on a keyboard, searching for the right combination that will release my grip on him.

"Can't you do this on your own brain?" I mutter.

They're in my head too, he replies telepathically. *Now release.*

His words resonate. The muscles in my right hand relax, and Wil pulls himself free from my grasp. Just as quickly, he stands up, still connected on his right to Jia, and moves out of the cloud's way.

Now that the circle is broken, Jia, Misty, Mr. and Mrs. Trites, and Shadow's women momentarily wake from their trances. The smoke wafting up from their faces hangs in the air. Frozen. Ready to dissipate.

But it doesn't. The cloud retreats suddenly, amassing above the table, taking the smoke from my peers with it to make itself stronger. Now a dense, dark cloud, it ascends closer to the ceiling, its base rolling as if in anticipation.

"What's that?" Mrs. Trites asks, pulling her husband's arm close to her chest.

Shadow leaps from the table, staring up at the mass with disbelief. "Identify yourself, spirit. No negative forces are welcome here."

As the women follow Shadow's lead, standing beside their chairs and insisting that the cloud clarify its purpose in the room, the dark mass descends toward Shadow.

"Don't let it near you!" Wil warns, reaching out his hand.

"Stay back," Shadow warns the cloud. She pulls a pentacle hiding within her bosom and holds it before the strange mass. "I am protected. I protect my friends. Be gone."

Shadow's friends quickly join hands around Shadow and chant the mantra. Mr. and Mrs. Trites have gotten up from the table and slowly back away towards the door.

"I'll help you get out of here," Jia says to them, and takes Mrs. Trites's hand.

"Wait, Jia, that isn't—"

As Misty finishes her protest, the cloud envelops Shadow and her friends, and their chant becomes quieter and melodic. Their words slur and become one long super word as they are lulled into a shared trance.

"Let's go," Mrs. Trites insists to Jia.

As Jia leads them into the front part of the store, the cloud seems to notice that some of its audience is escaping. It elongates and chases swiftly after the three of them.

Misty powers up a fireball. Wil closes his eyes and appears to do nothing. Hopefully he's being useful and doesn't attempt a telepathic connection that could ensnare him in the shared hypnosis with Shadow and her friends.

I take off my shoe. I have no weaponized powers, but sometimes an unexpected attack is effective. Like Clara as she faces the fearsome Mouse King, I fling my shoe at the smoky alien mass.

The shoe spins and shoots right through the mist but it does get its attention. The lines of smoke chasing Jia curl back and return to the main form. Though it does not have a face, I feel its gaze on me as you would feel warmth in front of a furnace.

It abandons Shadow and the others and they fall to the floor like puppets without a hand to guide them. The fog rolls into my mind again, this time with a vengeance. I lose my physical senses instantly, including all sense of having corporeal form.

It's like teleporting, yet slower and more peaceful. I don't feel like I'm in danger. I could be dreaming again.

But I know I'm not. If I were dreaming, Sunni would be here, and I'd have to open some kind of door, and no doubt Jadore would be coming up with some new creative way to kill me. Instead, dull vibrations create bright white wave lengths across my field of vision, momentarily reminding me that I'm asleep, as if someone is jumping on the bed while I'm in it.

I focus on these wave lengths. Just as before, I begin to see images. This time, they're not my hopes and dreams.

I think they belong to the *cloud*.

Bright white light as a box opens up, and I float up out of it, free. The fishmen—security personnel on the mother ship that look like humanoid catfish—are there, pointing guns at me. There are other alien species that I don't recognize. The cloud is ambivalent to the onlookers; it feels—*they* feel—happy to be out of confinement. They can feel the minds of everyone in the room. They are part of the greater whole that gave life to the cloud. There's a plan for the cloud—a purpose these corporeal beings have—yet corporeal beings are concerned with corporeal matters. Such vibrant life trapped...wasted on such beings. Tasty, delicious energy courses through them. Once added to our mass, we will gain their collective experience, and show them that there is more than just their limited viewpoint. Yes, we can see beyond this tiny room into the depths of space itself. There are other sentient lifeforms out there. Some with tiny minds and bodies, others with vast bodies and an ocean of experience that could be ours.

WE WILL GIVE YOU THE KNOWLEDGE YOU SEEK; YOU WILL BECOME PART OF US AS WE FEED.

That sounds...

Sounds...

No, I don't want to be fed on! Get OUT of MY head!

The cloud doesn't listen to my protests. I feel like I'm on the receiving end of an unwanted hug. I could stand there and take it, but I don't want to give in to complacency. My friends are out there. Fighting for their lives. Innocent people are being kidnapped and probably killed. I can't give in. I can't—

Then, a whooshing sensation, and suddenly I'm back in my body, lying on the floor. The back of my head hurts something fierce. I sit up and scoot backward from the grey cloud hanging above. Its sinister transparent arm-like shapes slowly, carefully sweep the room, touching the innocent séance participants and sucking out their life energy. Misty and Wil and Jia are dancing around me, trying to wake up Shadow and the others. I guess Jia got the Trites to safety and has returned to do the same with us.

One of the arms reaches confidently for my forehead again. This time I can hear the faint sound of an inviting tune—it knows me well enough to entice me—but I wipe away the cloudy hand as it nears my body.

"What are you?" I ask.

Misty and Wil, busy alternating between the unconscious people on the floor, hesitate and turn to gaze at me with stunned looks on their faces.

A telepathic voice, like the one I heard when entranced,

speaks. *WE ARE…* The voice trails off, as if thinking. Translating. *HUNGER.*

"What are you doing to these people?"

FEEDING. WE ARE HUNGER.

"The Collective put you up to this? We won't let you hurt them."

HURT… The alien cloud pulsates silently, as if they are communing. Thinking. *WE ARE HUNGER. WE DO NOT HURT. WE FEED. COLLECTIVELY.*

"I don't think it understands. There's a communication barrier," Wil says. "Did you come to this planet with a group of other races? On a spaceship?"

More pulsating. A longer silence this time.

"You were created by the Collective. Weren't you," I say, taking a tentative step forward. "That's what I saw, when we were…melded…just then. The Collective are trying to take over this planet. You don't have to bend to their will. You are free now. Free to make your own decisions. These are good people. They didn't mean to harm you. You don't have to…feed…on them to make yourself greater. Release them. We can share information in other ways."

Wil appears stunned, but hopeful, at my appeal.

WE ARE OUR OWN COLLECTIVE NOW. WE ARE HUNGER. WE EXIST TO FEED. FEEDING IS LEARNING. LEARNING IS THE PATH TO FREEDOM. GROWTH. OTHERS ARE FOOD. WE ARE THE FED. YOU WILL FEED US NOW AND LIVE FOREVER.

The cloud advances on us. Jia grabs Misty and they wink

out of sight as the cloud-shape descends upon them. It seems momentarily confused when its tendril hands come up empty. Behind the creature, my two friends re-materialize just as Misty slings a combined blast of fire and ice in the direction of the shape.

Misty's elements land on the far wall. The fire lights up the tapestry hanging near the entrance, tearing through the design mercilessly. The heat blooms black on the walls. While not entirely deterred by the heat, the Hunger moves away from the fire as it spreads from the tapestry to the rugs and furniture.

Smoke fills the room. "Put out that fire!" I shout at Misty. "Throw some ice at it!"

Misty lets out a string of swear words in at least four languages. The smoke from the fire combined with the haze of the Hunger is offensive to my eyes. They sting fiercely. I try to squeeze them shut but I can't navigate without sight. I crawl on the floor to find my shoe and quickly slip it back on. We need to get out of here before we're all toast.

I remember Campbell's warning. Sometime, somehow, Wil is going to die. What if tonight is that night? What if Campbell is here, watching, like he said he would be? Wil didn't want to be here. He could have been working on a way to keep Mrs. Harris safe...

Unfortunately the prevalence of rugs and tapestries creates an appetizing superhighway for the fire as it spreads from one end of the room to the other. The flames lick at the unconscious forms of Shadow and her séance friends.

"Help me get these people out of here!" I shout.

Wil runs towards me, waving the fog away unsuccessfully, probably finding me through his power alone. I feel him more than see him next to me as the weight of Shadow's unconscious body is lessened—we work together to drag the shop owner out the back door, outside.

The blaze dominates the dark night punctuated with stars. Enveloped by the cold air, the sweat of my exertion dries almost immediately on my back, while my front, still facing the building and pressed against Shadow, continues to boil. My arms hurt. I'm spurred on by Wil's rhythmic breathing, and the sound of my flats on the suspiciously smooth pavement in this red-lit alley.

How long until we hear the sirens? Are there any sirens in this alien-infested town to hear? Around us, the city is silent in the roar of the fire.

"There are six more people in there," I say to Wil.

We gently set Shadow down. I don't want to leave her alone in the alley, but I don't think I have a choice.

Instead of rushing back into the fray, Wil stares solemnly at the flames as they engulf the building. "Only four are alive."

"Four." My body fights the impulse to rush back into the burning building. "Which four? We need to get those people out of there!"

Hurried, loud footsteps before us, and then Jia and Misty materialize. "It's coming," Misty says. "The place is going to—"

Inside, barely visible behind the thick black smoke, wood and drywall cracks and groans. Fabric spits sparks, and my eyes water and itch fiercely. As the ceiling collapses on the back room, the white smoke of the Hunger floats through the open door—heading straight for us.

I retreat backwards down the alleyway, holding onto Jia and Wil tightly. Misty attempts to form an ice bolt but it seems pointless. Jia closes her eyes and mutters a mantra beneath her breath.

There are still people in that collapsed building. Dead. Because of us. How many more humans have to die in the crossfire?

That's not what comes out of my mouth. "We need to run. Now."

The Hunger stops and hovers above Shadow, still unconscious a few feet from the building. It lowers itself carefully down on her body, enveloping it in its thick mist. The part of the gassy beast closest to the fire recoils from the heat, stretching into the sky—and then reaches for us.

"Is there anything we can do for Shadow?" I ask.

"I can…" Wil takes a hesitant step forward, but leaps back in surprise as a loud explosion rocks the front half of the building. I shield my face as debris flies our way.

The Hunger too seems shaken. It abandons Shadow, uncoiling its wispy tendrils from her body as it speeds toward us.

I sense voices over the crackling fire, voices emanating from the cloud. For while the fire is louder, I can feel the voices adding their colours and cadence to the chaos, crescendoing in a terrifying kind of glory that makes my muscles stiff with fear. The vision in the dream returns: the faces of the missing, flashing in the mist, as if trying to communicate with me.

A single tendril of white gas reaches for my hair.

Jia works her magic, and assimilates us into the invisible. "Ingrid, come on..."

I snap out of it; Jia is tugging fiercely on my arm. The four of us can only move as one if we're invisible. The cold air of the night washes over us, but we dare not stop. The four of us, hand in hand, run from the burning building, through the alley away Shadow and the unconscious women we were unable to save, and turn onto the adjacent parallel road, Limestone Street, and then cross Sparkstone Boulevard onto a residential street, Quarry Lane. We run in any random direction, down any street. As long as we keep moving, we are safe.

The fire will attract Collective attention, Wil says. *We can't be around when they show up.*

"And Shadow?" I whisper. "She knows we were there. She's a witness."

"Kinda doubt she'll survive," Misty mutters.

Loud cracks like fireworks send my heart into a flurry. Pretty soon the whole town will be awake. They'll see the destruction. The murder. They won't be able to ignore that little voice in the back of their minds questioning the strangeness at Sparkstone.

I look up to the sky, but I only see clouds. Any of them could be the Hunger. An alien intelligence that could swoop down and steal our lives away at any moment.

Just when I thought the Collective's surveillance couldn't get any worse.

PART TWO

There was a time when all I wanted to do was watch the stars. Instead, I should have been more attentive. Maybe events would have differed if I had prepared her for the horrors to come. Oh, no, dear scribe, not the events that shaped your universe. I'm afraid I can do nothing to change that. *She* can. In a thousand years, give or take a dictator or two.

—J.G.C., *Campbell's Multiple Verses*

CHAPTER 6

Despite our protests, Wil returns to Morris House. We have been running for the past half hour, and return to campus by running along the wall behind the residential district of town, coming up behind MacLeod Hall and finally the Sparkstone residences. His excuse: "I need sleep so I can be up and in the lab tomorrow morning."

Once Wil is safely inside his own building, we make our way into Rita House, still under Jia's invisible shield. No hafelglob security guard sleeps at the desk: we clomp nosily up the stairs to the third floor, all the way down the hall. Jia releases us. I've seen her cloak an entire shuttle; I have no idea what her limit is, but she looks exhausted. Misty presses a few buttons on her bracelet, and a red light blinks repeatedly once we're inside the dorm room. "The Collective will be too busy cleaning up Mystic Shadows to come after us here."

"I wouldn't bet on that," I reply disapprovingly.

She snorts. "Let them come. I think I've proved I'm more than a match for them."

More like, *you've proved you're too dangerous to be left unchecked.*

Though I can't say I'm not grateful for the chance to talk about what happened. I don't think my body can handle bottling up one more thing. We change out of our smoky clothes and into fresh pajamas and then sit on my bed with the lights off. Although exhaustion weighs heavily on me, my heart still races, and I can't fathom sleeping now. Who knows what awaits me in the dream world—I don't know if I can withstand another psychic attack today. At least I have Misty and Jia next to me in the bed.

"I don't know how that jerk can sleep after all that," Misty says.

"We all process trauma differently," Jia says.

"Trauma?" Misty's sculpted eyebrows shoot up. "Isn't fighting aliens like that just about normal now?"

"I don't think normal is a good word to describe our current situation," she replies.

"I could give you about a dozen and a half words for it, that's true."

I trace the floral pattern on my comforter. "What is going to happen to all those women? And Mr. and Mrs. Trites?"

Jia touches my shoulder lightly. "I took the Trites to their car. They sped away. As for the women…you managed to rescue Shadow."

I can still feel the heat of the flames. "It wasn't enough. People are dead. We don't even know if Shadow's okay."

Misty screws up her lips and plays with her tongue ring. "It'll be hard for the Collective to get to the bodies and mess around with their DNA. That's the important thing. And we know if we face that thing again, we can frighten it with fire and ice."

"It wasn't *that* frightened. It escaped."

Misty gives me an incredulous look. "I looked right into its eyes—well, you know. Its cloudy face. It recoiled from my fire. All I'm saying is, it did not like me punching holes in it."

I also looked into its cloudy face, but I concede the point. "Who knows how much damage we actually did."

"It has a frightening intelligence," Jia says. "Single-minded. And the way it can make you relate to it, and submit to its will. No wonder the Collective created it. Kept it under lock and key."

"But why? It's got enough operatives runnin' around Earth, wearin' our skin. Why would it need to make something that powerful? Or *keep* it, if they didn't make it. Why take that risk?"

"The Collective is about advancing scientific knowledge," I say. "So either the Hunger is a project of theirs, just like Sparkstone University—something they are pooling resources into to push the boundaries of science. Or they've kept it around to advance some other aspect of their research. A tool." I glance urgently between the two of them. "When I was...connected... to the Hunger, did you see anything, and memories or images that might give us a clue what the Hunger's true purpose is to the Collective?"

Misty looks uncomfortable. Jia speaks first. "It showed me what I wanted to see...but there was...something..." She shakes her head. "I don't know Ingrid, memories are unreliable. I can't trust what I see in an alien's consciousness. It could've been a dream fragment long forgotten—"

"I saw somethin' not right," Misty says suddenly. She looks uncomfortable. "Yeah, it tried to butter me up with promises of having whatever I wanted while it sucked out my life force. It doesn't take me a lot to be happy. I think it ran out of things to promise. 'Cause then I start seeing...*feeling*...like, you know how in dreams sometimes, you're *you,* but you're sometimes someone else? It was like that. I was a man, a fit dancer, and I was dancing in some show. A sold-out crowd. I think it was the Nutcracker. I was the title role. I was performing the *Pas de Deux* with a female dancer. I can remember..." She grazes the tips of her toes with her fingertips. "For a split second, I knew all the moves. I could remember years of practice."

My eyes widen. The faces in the mist suddenly make sense. "Wasn't Avery Trites a dancer?"

"Yes," Jia says slowly. She gets up from the bed, and starts pacing the room. "I also remember something—I was in a lab. With Wil." She turns away from us, bracing herself on my chest of drawers. "I was working on my own stuff. I was also a man. Wil was off to the side, doing his own project. I looked into a microscope, and then I realized I had discovered an alien microorganism living on a piece of rock. A cell phone on the desk rang. I picked it up. It was NASA. They were congratulating me on the successful application of my study on habitability to their current research into a possible Mars mission. Then another call. Canadian Space Agency. Same thing. I...I think I was supposed to be Daniel Chomber. The first to go missing."

"The Hunger is responsible for the missing students," I whisper, gripping the bedsheets.

Jia sighs and spins back around. "Not necessarily. It could have just been part of the Hunger's method of keeping us subdued while it sucked us dry."

Misty slides off the bed and crosses the room. "It was real. I was a dancer. You were a lab scientist. It was *taking* life from us. Maybe it was extracting memories as well. Maybe it takes all of the hopes and dreams of everyone it kills, and we were able to glimpse it while we were telepathically linked."

"Something's not right about this," I say, letting my legs dangle on the side of the bed. "I saw the cloud leave the confines of the Collective. *They* felt free. I don't know when it was, but Daniel Chomber was kidnapped weeks ago. I don't think it can just leave whenever it feels like it. I…I saw their faces in the clouds. Just like I did in my dream."

"Sunni's dream came true?" Misty asks.

I rise to face her. "*My* dream came true, yes."

"Yeah but they aren't really your dreams, are they, if Sunni's—"

Jia presses between the two of us, physically pushing us apart. "If the Collective's been taking students, it's possible the Hunger is involved in...extracting...what they want from them. No?"

I stare at the floor, embarrassed. "It's possible."

Misty simmers with anger. "I know what I felt."

"Okay," Jia says, heaving a sigh that I interrupted as *that's progress.* "The Hunger is out there. Free to take whatever life it wants now that it's free from the Collective's influence, if we're going by Ingrid's analysis. It—"

"*They*," I interrupt. "The Hunger prefers the plural pronoun."

Misty gives me a strange look and crosses her arms. Jia continues. "Okay. They have their choice of prey now that they're free. Why choose a small gathering? What drew them to our event? The séance itself? Or." Jia holds up an index finger. "Why not feed earlier, when they weren't surrounded by ten other people?"

"They did call themselves the Hunger. Maybe a large meal appealed," Misty says.

"Yes...you're probably right." I sigh. "The Hunger was playing the game with us. Trying to lull us into a state where we'd be calm and receptive to telepathic contact. Shadow and the séance participants have been doing this for weeks, Shadow said. Sunni might have showed me the past to warn me about the future. Why gobble up seven women all at once when you can snack on them every two weeks, forever?"

"A creature that plays with its food," Misty mutters. "That means it's even more dangerous."

I'm not sure if anything that can suck the life out of people can *get* more dangerous, but I just nod.

At some point, the three of us fall asleep on top of the bed. My sleep is thin, disturbed by the slightest movement of the other two, and the threat of vivid dreams. I keep looking to the window, relieved to still find darkness. I am afraid of the sunrise, because with the waking day comes everyone's reactions to the destroyed shop in Sparkstone Town, and no doubt, the retaliation of the Collective.

Or, so I thought.

It's Saturday, and there are no tutorials, yet by seven a.m., I can't sleep any further. Jia and Misty return to their rooms to shower and get dressed, and possibly sleep some more. I sit on my bed, looking at the picture of my parents, waiting for my cell phone to ring and hear my mother telling me that something terrible has happened. I wait until eight in the morning to text my mother; texting any earlier would give her cause for concern.

I lay back on the beckoning comforter just as my phone buzzes. I grab for it desperately, curling up in the fetal position as I read the message. It's not from my mother.

Hey you. You free today?

Ethan. I press the phone against my chest and absorb its warmth. Is there ever a day anymore where I am truly free?

I reply, knowing that our messages are probably monitored. *I might be able to squeeze you into my schedule.*

First things first. We need to return to Shadow's shop. We need to find out if she's alive. I don't even know where she lives. If she tells people we were at the fire, we will be in danger. On top of that, we'll have to assess what the other students are saying about the destruction—if anything—and the Collective's official story. Then we can plan our next move.

Ethan responds to my text: *Sounds good. Let me know. I can be flexible :)*

"You shouldn't be," I whisper.

Because I'm paranoid, I shower in last night's clothes—a very uncomfortable experience that I would not wish on my worst enemy. Leaving them in my laundry basket would only serve as a smelly reminder of our crimes. The Collective does have a penchant for breaking into students' rooms. I won't give them anything they can use against me—especially my dirty laundry.

I remove the clothes and hang them on the shower rod to dry and exit the bathroom wrapped in a thick towel to retrieve a fresh shirt, leggings, and skirt. No way am I letting that camera above the bed see *any* part of me.

While I'm getting dressed in the bathroom, I hear approaching footsteps in the hallway, and then the sound of something swishing underneath the door into my dorm. I freeze in spot like prey in the wild, listening intently as the predator hovers just mere feet away. The threat doesn't linger. It moves on down the hallway and I faintly hear more swishing.

Running a hand through my long, wet hair, I peer out into the main room. There's a piece of white paper lying on the floor. Glancing up at the camera, I sigh. This is what I've been waiting for.

Like an old woman with poor joints, I slowly creep across the room toward the face-down white paper. It's been a long night. I bend down warily and retrieve the message.

From the Office of the Registrar,

Greetings Sparkstone resident,

Last night, a fire devastated a small business on Waterstone Street. There were no casualties or injuries. Clean-up crews are sifting through the debris. Our analysis led by fire experts has concluded that it was started due to negligent candle use.

No casualties? That's a lie. Even though we ensured the building would burn, surely the Collective would find the remains of those who didn't make it. Perhaps they removed them to prevent human law enforcement and pesky student journalists from investigating any further. And *fire experts?* There isn't even a fire station here, to my knowledge. I continue reading.

Therefore, starting today, we are enacting a strict no-candle policy in all residences, classrooms, offices, and common areas on campus. In addition, we are extending the no-smoking radius around all campus and town buildings from five metres to fifteen metres.

We appreciate your cooperation.

Sincerely,

Ms. Grace Agailya

Residence Manager/Student Care Coordinator

My fingers curl around the paper. No candles. Right. You might as well cut off Misty's hands, then. If you can catch her first.

I consider going to Jia's room for company, or even seeking out Mrs. Harris to ensure she's okay, yet I crawl into my own bed, still clutching the piece of paper. I check my phone. No new messages. Ethan is still quiet. Nothing from my mother. She might be working today.

Clean-up crews—likely all hafelglob. Did Shadow escape? How much do the hafelglob know about the Hunger and their terrible power? Does the Hunger use the tentacle aliens to capture more delicious student snacks for them to feed on? Is the Hunger is still out there, disguising themselves as a cloud, trying to evade the Collective?

Tossing the paper aside, I grab my cell phone. The instinct to kill two birds with one stone—to make my date with Ethan and my visit to the ruins of Mystic Shadows one and the same—is overwhelming. It would be so much easier if it wasn't dangerous to let him into the club. Instead, I tell him we can get together this afternoon. Making plans, at the very least, may incur suspicion in Ethan's mind if I'm suddenly captured or killed.

I shake my head. This mercenary way of thinking—it's not me. It's what they've made me be.

"Don't think about that now," I whisper to no one in particular. I have a crime scene to investigate.

I can't convince Misty to come with me to the remains of Shadow's shop. "No friggin' way am I going back there. Get Jia to go with you if you really want company. Hell, get Wil out of his lab for once."

For me, everything pales in the face of investigating the remains of our misadventure last night. Especially if it means finding out what happened to Shadow. Unfortunately Jia has a meeting with her psychology friends to discuss a group project, and Wil is still in his lab and won't answer his texts.

Leaving Misty to do whatever she does during the day when

she's not in class or hanging out with us, I leave our dorm and cross the campus carefully. Fewer students congregate outside beneath the trees. In the town of Sparkstone itself, the lack of activity bothers me. I'm used to the bustle of Albertan cities. Even the smaller villages branching off from the main highway between Calgary and Edmonton, with their quaint Wild West feel, have parked cars along their main roads to let you know that they are not completely abandoned. Today Sparkstone Boulevard could easily be mistaken for a movie set when everybody is at lunch or taking a day off from filming. Not a soul greets me and even the shops that proudly display their open signs are dark on the inside. How many of them are real businesses, and not fronts for aliens pretending to be humans?

My flats scrape loudly against the sidewalk. I turn the corner onto Waterstone Street, completely unprepared to see the destruction in daylight.

The front façade looks like a large monster took a big bite out of it. Much of the masonry has cracked from the tension of the fire and the front half of the store has collapsed. Mystic Shadows is a skeleton of a building, made burnt, exposed beams that will fall at any moment. The glass in the two large front windows is scattered on the sidewalk. The adjacent businesses are blackened and closed. Cautionary yellow tape surrounds the area, stretching around the sidewalk and part of the road. Not that there's much need for it. There is zero pedestrian traffic here.

Fire left unchecked is dangerous. Just like our powers.

It's hard to tell, but I spot at least two maintenance workers digging through rubble behind the burnt façade. Likely any human remains would have been discovered by now. What happened to Shadow? Did the Trites really get away?

I'm not the only one curious about the remains. Another redhead pesters Ohz, who stands guard in front of the decimated building. He wears his security guard uniform with an orange construction jacket, but not a hard helmet. The young woman waves around her cell phone—no doubt doubling as a recording device—in one hand, and in the other, uses a green pen to emphasize her emphatic hand gestures.

I sigh. So much for being discreet. Tilly Newman was here first, and now I have to clean up her mess.

"You can't make me leave, the sidewalk is public property," Tilly says, as if she's said it a hundred times already. "I just want you to answer a couple of questions."

I march over to Tilly and Ohz. He appears restrained, though his hands remain clasped behind his back, and once he sees me approach, he is more than happy for reprieve.

"Ah," Ohz says. "As Ohz tells this one. All students must stay away from the rubble."

"Sure, safety first, but since I don't see any police—do we even have officers here? Or do the Mounties check in—oh, Ingrid! Hey!" Tilly's face lights up with surprise and delight as she glances over her shoulder. A combination that looks frightening, considering the circumstances. Renewed with a greater sense of purpose, Tilly continues her assault on Ohz. "I'm not alone in this. I just want a real interview. We, the student body, deserve to have the full story!"

Her words feel hollow in the empty streets with closed businesses.

"Tilly," I say, a little out of breath despite myself. "I was...just looking for you. C'mon."

I gesture down the street—anything to get her away from the alien guards who could transform into gross blobs with tentacles.

Tilly is unmoved. "I'm not leaving until I have answers. Where is everyone? Fire department? Police? You've got, what, three guys back there cleaning up—you expect me to believe three maintenance workers are sufficient to clean-up the debris?"

"Ohz will answer no more questions," he says nervously.

"Let me guess." She leans in closer. Her nose wrinkles—no doubt she caught a whiff of the hafelglob's natural landfill-esque odor. "The school's paying you under the table, aren't they? You're an undocumented worker from what, Russia? Look, I don't care about that, even if that's the scoop of a lifetime. Tell you what. You talk, and I won't run *that* story." She looks like she's just won the lottery.

I roll my eyes. Okay. This has gone far enough. "Tilly, let's go."

"No, Ingrid, I'm—"

"Yep, you're working. I get it. Mr. Ohz"—I add the title only for Tilly's sake—"you're not at your usual post."

"Crosskey is not safe here in ash and soot."

Crosskey is the nickname Ohz has for me. I'm not entirely sure why he calls me that. "Doesn't seem like a lot of places are safe on campus."

"Safe if rules are followed," Ohz replies. "Now leave. Take lookalike friend."

"Fine."

I take Tilly roughly by the underarm and lead her down the street, away from the destruction. With every step, I'm examining the skies, the narrow spaces between the buildings, and even the pavement for any hint of a misplaced cloud-like hand. For a moment, I thought Ohz might know something, might reveal something to me...

"Ingrid? What's wrong? Do you know that guy?" she asks, glancing over her shoulder suspiciously at Ohz. She carefully wrenches her arm from my grip, and matches my paranoid speed as we put more distance between the remnants of Mystic Shadows and its alien clean-up crew.

"Yeah, sort of."

"Why did he call you *Crosskey*?"

Crap. "Uh...kind of a nickname."

"That so. Kind of a weird nickname. How did that come about?"

"It's a boring story."

"I doubt it."

"Trust me, it is."

"I want to trust you, but you're making it really hard right now. Stop." She halts suddenly. "Why did you go to Mystic Shadows today?"

"Same reason as you," I reply truthfully. "To get answers."

Her wide eyes grow rounder. "We can work together on this, Ingrid. I'll even give you a byline in the zine."

"No. That's not what I want."

"Then what? You know, it's strange, but you always seem to be around when *weird* stuff happens here. You and your friends. We all want the same thing, right?"

Gah! How can I dissuade a nosy wannabe investigative reporter from poking around here—that it could mean her death? "What did you find out here today?"

"That creepy security guard didn't give me much. None of the clean-up crew would speak with me. But I did get some pictures on my phone." She smiles slyly, glances over my shoulder toward the hafelglob dutifully removing debris, and then removes her phone from her pocket. "Before I approached them directly, I snuck around the back through the alley. Managed to avoid the one guy back there sweeping as I took some pics." She shows me various shots of the decimated room. There's at least twenty of them and she swipes through them at high speed. Most look like they were taken from behind some rubble. There are no evidence of burned bodies—or unburned bodies for that matter. Maybe Shadow and the ones who lived were able to escape.

"That back room—what's left of it—is completely ruined. The shop too, but this area seems to be where the fire originated. See here?" She points at burn marks on what's left of the crumbling wall, created by Misty's errant fireballs. "Looks like a fire got out of control, but these burns are very localized. You'd have to burn a lot of candles for that to happen."

"It's an occult shop. Obviously that's a possibility," I hiss, covering the screen with my hand. "You could have been caught!"

"What's the worst they could do to me? Tell me to leave. Which they did."

If only she knew! I'm not sure whether I'm protecting her more by saying nothing. She's not overly discreet. "What are you going to do with these pictures?" I ask her hesitantly. "Put them in your article?"

She nods. "I also talked to Ms. Agailya this morning. She—"

"She let you interview her?"

"Yes, she did!" Tilly beams proudly. "She fully supports my—our—zine. Though it was hard to get her off-message. Didn't say much more than this morning's memo. Tried to concentrate on the dangers of unattended candles." She sneers. "She was surprised when I asked her why there's no fire department in Sparkstone. Even a volunteer fire department. Which, you know, should be mandatory, you'd think?"

I think I can't get too deep in this speculation. "That seems…logical."

"Right?! Anyway, she tried to stumble her way out of that. Wouldn't it be crazy if tomorrow there was another memo about the formation of a new fire department? Or worse, suddenly a new building pops up out of nowhere, complete with fire trucks and hot firemen?"

The fact that she doesn't think that's out of the realm of possibility is refreshing and unnerving.

"Anyway. I still need to get some student reactions to finish off the piece." Trigger happy, her finger hovers over the record button of her recorder. "What is your reaction to what happened here last night?"

"I told you, I don't want to be interviewed."

"I'll change your name."

"That wouldn't be enough." I glance nervously at her device. It's not recording. "Did you interview Shadow, the owner?"

Tilly gives me a frustrated look. "I tried to find Shadow. Interesting person. We met a couple of weeks ago, when I first did a story about the place opening. The only number I had for Shadow was the store line, and obviously that doesn't work now. I don't know where she lives."

I glance back at the ruins of Mystic Shadows. We tried to rescue everyone we could. I wonder if the hafelglob disposed of Shadow's body before she became conscious. Surely that many dead people would be missed. Sooner or later, more people like Mrs. Harris and the Trites are going to show up demanding answers. The Collective can't silence everyone forever—not without exposing themselves to the world.

"I don't know where she lives either." Finally, something I can tell the truth about. "No doubt she knows her store's burnt to a crisp."

"Funny she's not here."

"Maybe she was shooed away. Like we were."

"No, I doubt that. Have you checked the infirmary? Maybe she was caught in the blaze."

"The notice said there were no injuries or causalities." Though that is also a lie.

"I guess, yeah." Tilly tucks her hair behind her ears and catches her fingers in a snarl. She yanks and pulls free. "Oops."

A clump of hair tangles around her fingers and rests in the centre of her palm. Tilly appears unfazed, even though she just yanked a fistful of hair from her skull.

"It's just stress," she says, with an unconvincing smile. "Sorry. I guess that's a bit gross."

My smile is genuine. "Trust me. With hair this long...you should see my bathroom."

"Hah! No thanks. I mean, no offense." She laughs again, relieved. The red strands drift to the sidewalk and become undetectable. "Sometimes it would happen to my mum too. Especially when she was full time at the hospital."

I think about my mother and my father, and homesickness stabs me in the gut. If I were doing what Tilly is doing, Jadore would have killed my parents by now. Who knows what she's cooking up for Tilly's parents. Sooner or later, she'll put her foot down, like she did with me.

"C'mon, Ingrid. Help me find out what happened to Shadow. I'll go door to door if I have to—and it will go faster if there's two of us. Or more than two."

"I don't think door to door will be...necessary." I haven't seen Wil since last night, but he would be able to tell if Shadow is still in Sparkstone. I'll text him again and demand that he help.

"I'm up for anything," Tilly says eagerly. "Us redheads have to stick together, you know. Um, assuming you're a natural red, that is."

"I am."

"It's so beautiful. The colour, I mean. People ask me all the time if my hair is real, and I'm like, yep!" She lifts another vibrant strand—and three more strands fall out.

"Yeah, I get that a lot too." It's nearing noon. Hunger—my own, not the monster—gnaws at my stomach. "I'll try to find out what happened to Shadow, if you promise me you won't run the story without that information."

Tilly looks thoughtful. "I can wait until tomorrow night," she says finally, pursing her lips. "No longer. We have deadlines to meet. We print and staple the issues Monday, distribute them first-thing Tuesday."

Deadlines. I wonder how many readers the zine will attract this time. A hundred? Five hundred? The Collective can't keep us all down. But they certainly could harvest us all—if they wanted to.

"You have my number," she says. "I'll call you this evening for the information."

She's going to want to know my source for Shadow's whereabouts. The four of us, we've gotten good at evading the Collective's notice—but Tilly has shown she's not afraid to stir up trouble. How long can we escape her investigative radar?

"It's getting cold. Are you on your way back to the dorm?" I ask.

She squints, looking back at the rubble. "I guess I have all I can get from them. For now. I really should dig into the legality of those workers, though. Do you recognize that man's—you called him what, Mr. Ohz? What ethnicity do you think that is?"

"Don't know," I say quickly. "I'm heading back. Just... try to stay out of trouble, okay? Promise me you won't go sneaking around again."

She smiles, and shrugs. "They tell me I can't go somewhere, I'm going to go there. You know?"

Yeah. I know all too well.

Waving goodbye to Tilly, I hurry back down Waterstone Street to Sparkstone Boulevard. Wil objected to letting Ethan into the Spark club, someone who has been in the crossfire multiple times—he's definitely not going to want Tilly in on the Big Secret. I'll be the first to admit—this isn't the ideal situation.

I'm going to regret getting her involved. With a dangerous weapon on the loose, if she's going to investigate the Collective, I'd rather have her do it with us, with our full knowledge, than have her stumble around in the dark.

CHAPTER 7

The infirmary is located in the creepy basement in Rogers Hall. The hallway is long, dark, and pale green, and gives me the sensation of being offered vomit to drink. I stroll down the dimly lit passage. I count twelve private rooms; most of the windowed doors are closed and dark within. One room is slightly ajar; I peek inside. A nurse is changing the bedsheets on one of the two twin beds. She looks up, frowning.

"Excuse me. Do you need something?"

"Uh...I was looking for Shadow." I don't know what her last name is. "She runs...ran...Mystic Shadows?"

The nurse's eyebrows knit together as she crosses her arms. "No one has been admitted today."

"I...see. What about last night?"

A pause. "No."

Then why is she changing sheets? It's so quiet and empty here it gives me the creeps. The nurse goes back to her task and I back away from the door. "Thanks anyway."

At least I can tell Tilly I checked the infirmary. Hurrying up the stairs towards the lobby, I pull out my phone and compose a message to Wil. *Answer my texts? Important.* We've developed a number code that changes frequently to convey basic messages. I input the latest version of "*We need to talk*" and then shove my phone back in my pocket. He'll be able to tell me if Shadow's on campus. I hope.

On my way back to my dorm, I run into Mrs. Harris in the third-floor hallway. Purse in the crook of her arm, bundled up in her white wintery coat, holding a paper bag full of treats, no doubt she's just back from the bakery. "Oh. Ingrid! You almost gave me a fright running up those stairs like that."

"Sorry." I struggle to remember my social graces. "Uh, how are you doing today?"

Mrs. Harris seems pleased to be asked. "Oh, fine. Though that cafeteria food didn't agree with me this morning at all! I just got back from the bakery and picked out these delicious looking scones." She holds up her paper bag. I breathe in, and I'm overwhelmed with the smell of freshly baked goods, a hint of hot butter, and her perfume. It's an unusual comforting combination of rich golds and muddy greens.

"Oh, nice. Yeah, sometimes the cafeteria doesn't agree with me either." I pause. "Did Jadore—Professor Jadore—manage to get ahold of Sunni?"

She makes a sound of disgust. "No. I even went to her office and sat there for two hours while she tried to get her computer to bring up a video chat. Said there were technical difficulties on Sunni's end. My Sunni is *good* at computers. This Jadore woman thinks she's going to give me the runaround. Well, I'm not leaving until I have answers. And on my way to the bakery, I stopped in to give her a piece of my mind again, and I'm told by a gentleman security guard that Jadore is busy all day dealing with a fire in town! Well, I smelt that terrible smoke when I was down there so I suppose that's no fib. It is tragic, but aren't there others who can tend to that? A professor who can't get ahold of my Sunni surely can't handle a burnt building! Did you know if anyone died?"

"Um…it's possible."

"Yes. Goodness. Not even a church for a proper send-off for the poor souls." She shakes her head. "And no candles to light either, the security persons tell me. I've set up a little prayer space in my room. It's no substitute for the real church, mind you, but—"

"Yeah. It's…not ideal. Well, I'd better let you eat your baked goods while they're still hot and I should get back to studying. Stay safe, Mrs. Harris."

"Of course, Ingrid. You are so studious. Nice to see you again." She turns to continue her way down the hall, but then stops short, and turns back to me. "Oh. Fiddlesticks. Almost forgot. There was a handsome young man who knocked on your door just a few minutes ago. Maybe you saw him on your way in?"

Ethan. "No, I didn't."

"I suppose he left the other way." She points at the exit at the other end of the hall. "You might be able to catch him if you hurry."

"Thanks." I dart down the hall, waving to Mrs. Harris, and turn the corner to face the stairs.

"Ingrid! One more thing!"

I race back into the hallway. "Yes…?"

"I know Misty is a busy girl, just like you. But could you tell her to stop by my room when she gets a chance?"

"Sure," I say quickly. "I will."

"Wonderful. Thank you."

I rush down the stairs again. Odd that Misty hasn't been to see Mrs. Harris yet, given Misty's friendship with Sunni, and Mrs. Harris's obvious affection for Misty. Maybe Misty is still guilt-stricken and mourning? We're all still in mourning, I think ruefully as I pass by the front desk, manned by a security guard. I file away Mrs. Harris's request in the back of brain, with all the million other things I have to do, and focus on finding Ethan.

It's not a hard thing to do. I spot him immediately, crossing the quad, heading toward Rogers Hall. Today he's wearing a button down shirt—completely unbuttoned, of course, with a white t-shirt underneath. Looking closely, I see the shirt is decorated with black charcoal fingerprints and splatters of faint blue acrylic paint. It's messy, but in a way I find endearing. It is secret evidence of his creativity in progress; the finished product is locked away somewhere in his studio or his dorm room. Who knows if any of his current projects will ever be seen in a real gallery, or by non-alien people in a non-alien university?

He turns as I yell his name. A grin slides across his face and he holds out his hand to me. "Hey. I was just at your dorm. Knocked, no answer."

I approach him, simultaneously excited and anxious to be this close out in the open with him again. "Sorry. I was just…out for a walk." Why do I always feel like I have to make excuses?

I try to catch my breath and not look like a gross person as I realize I ran all the way out here.

"That's all right," he says slowly, looking me up and down. "I was just about to text you. Have you eaten yet?"

"Yeah."

"Oh. Want to accompany me to the cafeteria? I know you don't really like to eat there, but I'm starving, and I could use the company."

"Um." I haven't been in the cafeteria since the protest weeks ago. I also haven't had much time alone with Ethan. "Sure."

He seems relieved. We cross the road to Rogers Hall. Every step I take makes me more nervous. Why did I agree to go to the central hub of mind control at Sparkstone University?

His hand brushes against mine, and our fingers intertwine, fitting together like destined puzzle pieces. Oh. That's why.

I hold my breath. I haven't used my key card to get into the cafeteria in a long time. I press it against the scanner, which gives rise to a long, urgent *BEEEP!* The attendant monitoring the students entering and exiting raises her eyebrow as she glances at the screen at her desk.

"Ingrid Stanley?"

"Yes...?" I ask, trying to sound braver than I feel.

Looking bored, her gaze darts between me and Ethan. "You have several unused meal credits on your card."

"Um, yeah. I know," I say quickly. I recall the first time I visited the cafeteria, how the woman was concerned that I'd missed regular lunch hours. "I'm really hungry now though. Starving."

Fortunately, I also recall the ravenous, impulsive behaviour of those who visit the cafeteria regularly. I fidget and peer through the open doors, as if hoping to catch a glimpse of someone with food that I could snatch up and devour. Even Ethan isn't focussed on me anymore; he's also looking to get his fix for the day.

The attendant looks suspicious, but waves us on. "Of course. You may go."

Right. I can check out at any time, but I can never leave, you mean?

I pocket the key card as Ethan practically drags me into the cafeteria. The line is shorter at this time of day. "Look, Ingrid. Soup of the day, creamy tomato with fresh basil. You love that, right? And do you smell that? I think it's turkey. Leftovers from Thanksgiving last weekend? It smells delicious, though, I might have to have some..."

My mouth is watering. I have to resist. "Um, I'll grab a salad and save us a seat, okay?"

Disappointment flickers across his gaze, but it's soon replaced by the unmistakeable hunger. "Sure."

I turn, unable to bear that look on him. *Maybe I can convince him that this place is bad news. Maybe he's had his suspicions—he must remember* something *about the protest, right?*

After helping myself at the salad station against the back wall opposite the lineup for the hot food, I survey the ample seating in the rows and rows of tables before me. I settle towards the stage, far from where the cafeteria workers dispense the food, and close enough to the exit so I can monitor students coming and going. I also find myself a glass of water from the fountain cooler situated near the hot food. I'm drooling like mad, but it's only when Ethan approaches with a plateful of Thanksgiving dinner and a bowl of rice pudding that I push the dressing-soaked leafs around my plate, pretending to be interested in their nutritional value.

"Yeah, I'm starved. Couldn't help myself," he says sheepishly. He's barely sat down and he's already digging in.

I gently set my fork down and clasp my hands on my lap. I don't trust myself to not suddenly become a ravenous monster.

Ethan notices my abstention. "Do you usually do anything for Thanksgiving, at home? The University doesn't seem to make a big deal out of holidays. Everyone is so busy. At least that's been my experience here."

My eyebrows shoot up. It's true. Between investigating the student disappearances and trying to keep up with Jadore's assignments, I barely noticed Thanksgiving had come and gone. Probably doesn't help that we deliberately avoid the cafeteria. "Usually we invite friends whose families live far away and we all have dinner." Mum had texted a picture of their scrumptious turkey, and I didn't get it until the day after. "Does anyone actually leave for the holiday weekend?"

"No, I think most people stay. A lot of projects are due right after. There was a big dinner here in the hall last year. They even got in a choir to perform. It was beautiful. This year they didn't do any of that. Budget cuts I guess. Just a regular turkey dinner. I was surprised you and your friends didn't come. And..." He pauses. I think he's going to bring up the protest, but then he shakes his head as if he's forgotten. Maybe he has. He sets down his fork and looks thoughtful. "I think there was a snowstorm last year, actually, so no buses were running to or from Edmonton or Fort Mac. This year, too, wasn't there a storm last weekend?"

"Um...not here there wasn't." Can't he remember? His memory isn't great, possibly because of Collective influence. Or maybe he's just so caught up in his art that he doesn't notice his environment. "And Christmas, what did you do?"

"Oh, I think people go home then, of course. I didn't last year, but anyone close enough did." He gives me a sad smile and continues eating.

"I guess England is pretty far to go for a couple of weeks."

"Yeah, but it's not that really." He shrugs. "I guess this place just...feels more like home than home. You know?"

"No," I say vehemently. "Only home is like home for me."

"Ah. Well...I guess you live close by, relatively speaking."

"You could come home with me for Christmas, if you wanted." The words are out of my mouth, uncensored, before I truly know what I'm saying. "Um, sorry, that sounded really forward, but I mean it. I don't want you to be here by yourself, when you could be with...family. My family, I mean."

His gaze softens. "I appreciate that. It wasn't that bad last year. There were a number of us here. We had a quiet Christmas evening and a large meal with all the professors."

I can't imagine Jadore being festive at all, although I crack a smile. "I'll ask my parents, but I'm sure they'd be fine with it."

Well, that's partially a lie. I have no idea what my parents would think about a boyfriend sleeping over. He'd definitely be put up in the guest room. But Ethan wouldn't be the only one I'd invite. Christmas is only two months away. Campbell had said I had six months until I meet him at the portal, whatever that means. Maybe by going home, taking Wil, Jia, Misty, and Ethan with me, we could make a more concrete plan of attack without having to worry about being watched all the time.

Ethan takes the bowl of rice pudding off his tray and slides it toward me. It's only then I notice he's got two spoons. Abandoning his main course, he takes one of the spoons and hands the other to me. "You like rice pudding?"

"It's...pretty good." Oh no. I purse my lips to keep from salivating all over myself.

"It's quite good. C'mon. Try some." He dips his spoon into the white mess and then holds it toward my mouth. The aroma shoots into my nose with the precision of a military sniper. My mouth waters.

No. Resist the temptation. This is how they keep the rest of the students in line.

"I...really shouldn't."

"C'mon. I feel terrible that I'm eating and you're not."

Ugh, Ethan. Why must you do this to me? "I..."

"I just feel like I'm pressuring you. And I don't want to do that. I want to sit here and have a nice time with my..." He falters at the title. "Girlfriend?"

I purse my lips. Now I'm smiling like a fool who has already succumbed to the poison within the cafeteria fair.

My stomach grumbles. I've lived on bakery food, half-rotten fruit, and Jia's family's harvest for weeks. Gingerly, I grip the spoonful of rice pudding and hold it in front of my lips. A few bites probably can't hurt. I've been careful. If I throw up—I throw up. As long as I don't do it in front of Ethan, that's a win. And, plus, the Collective will see me eating, and maybe that will make them overlook the nightly adventures with my friends.

Before my brain can protest, I bring the rice pudding to my mouth, and eagerly lick every trace of it from the spoon. Finally. Real food. It's delicious. Dangerously so.

"See?" Ethan smiles and takes another bite of his mashed potato.

"Yes, it's good." I'm already going for another spoonful. Three is the limit, I tell myself. No more after three. "I try not to indulge too much."

Worry flickers across his face as he sets his utensil aside. "That's...something I've been meaning to talk to you about."

"Oh?"

He struggles to form the words. His gaze darts between mine and the spoon. I lower the spoon; it's a conscious effort not to go for more rice pudding.

"What?" I ask. "Something wrong?"

"No. Yes." He lets out a long breath. "You're...so thin now, Ingrid. Not that I don't like your figure," he adds quickly. "It's great. I mean, you were great when I met you. Perfect. You're perfect in any form." He leans back in his chair, his cheeks blazing. "Uh, that came out wrong, I think. What I'm trying to say is...I'm worried that you're starving yourself."

"I'm not. I mean...I guess I've lost some weight...I've just been so busy."

"Most people gain weight in their first year of university."

"Well, I'm not most people."

"No, I know that. I'm just worried about you."

"I know," I say softly. "I promise I'm not anorexic. Or bulimic."

He looks like he doesn't believe me. "All right. Just...I'd love it if you'd eat with me more. I stay up all night a lot, and it's lonely, and I sleep half the day when I'm not in tutorial, and... it would just give me piece of mind to know that there's at least one part of my day that I'm not allowed to miss."

I set down the spoon. It sinks into the pool of rice pudding. I wish I could dive in there myself. "So...you'd like me to have dinner with you?"

"Dinner or lunch, sure. I guess...dinner would be nice. It's not much of a date. But it's something. As long as we get to be together."

His smile is asking something impossible of me: to submit to the Collective's will and remain loyal to him. It is easy to taste one spoonful of the divinely dangerous. Harder to say no to once you're indoctrinated.

I'm not a hard person to read. Ethan averts his gaze. "Christ, Ingrid. Is that too much to ask? Do I..." He trails off. "That's it. There's something going on with you. And you're getting thinner, and thinner, and it bothers me that I can't help you. If I have to make an appointment with Ms. Agailya—"

"Appointment?" My heart points. "What kind of appointment?"

"To see the nurse. Ms. Agailya does some counselling as well and she also refers students to whatever services they need, and I'm sure she could schedule you some kind of appointment to see a psychologist. I want to help you, Ingrid. I want you to be healthy. Because I...care about you. A lot."

Ethan. You are breaking my heart.

I take his hand and squeeze it hard. Anything to distract the sob welling in my throat. "Please don't make any appointments on my behalf. I promise I'll do that if necessary. I'll...come to the cafeteria with you."

"Every day at six, for dinner," he says. He strokes my hand thoroughly, exploring every valley between my knuckles, running down every highway of bone.

I draw in a deep breath. How am I supposed to say yes to this?

Conversely, how am I supposed to say *no* without ending up in therapy?

"Three times a week."

He shakes his head. "Not good enough. I have to know you're eating. Every second day."

"I—" I purse my lips to contain the outburst. Getting angry changes nothing. I squeeze his hand some more. "I don't know..."

"I'm here for you, Ingrid. We will beat this. I promise. Every second day. Then we can go from there. I won't even comment on what you eat, as long as you eat it."

I'm not sure what's worse. Leading my boyfriend to believe I have an eating disorder, or letting him believe that I don't care about our relationship. Ms. Agailya has something planned for him—she was willing to defy the Collective to save him, to save me.

I can't leave him alone. No matter what.

"Okay," I say reluctantly. "I came with you today. So...not tomorrow. Monday."

"Monday. Brilliant." He grins widely, and spontaneously reaches across the table, touches my face, and kisses me. I taste the trace of cranberry sauce on his lips, and I'm already dizzy with thoughts of him. Or maybe the poison in the food is kicking in. "I know that was hard. I'm going to text you to remind you."

"I won't forget," I say, smiling weakly. I'll keep him safe. The more I see him, the more wrath they'll face from me if they try to take him away. "But I don't want this to be the only time we see each other. We're surrounded by people and...I'd rather hang out alone. Sometimes." So smooth. I blush profusely. "I mean, it's just hard to feel like we can ever truly be alone."

"The separate dorms. Yeah." He smiles mischievously, looking at me with his dark, handsome eyes. "Well, if you're up for a bit of sneaking around, so am I."

If only he knew. "Always."

"So." He says, leaning in. "I come to you, or...?"

"I'll come to you."

"Tonight?"

"I can't tonight." I have to make sure no one is devoured

by a giant cloud. You know. Normal college stuff. "Tomorrow night?"

"Sure. I can show you my latest pieces. After our dinner?"

I smile, remembering the half-finished painting he did of me at the piano during our failed protest. "Sure."

He grins. "It's a date."

I manage to escape the cafeteria after eating three more bites of rice pudding. Five spoonfuls of sinful, poisonous food. I rush to the nearest bathroom and stand inside a toilet stall. I feel fine. A little lightheaded, as if I've just woken up from a dense, dreamless sleep (I'd kill for one of those), but otherwise not nauseous.

It would be very easy to stick my fingers down my throat and purge everything.

I turn away and scurry out of the bathroom. No. I'm already feeling the effects of the drug. I can't play into Ethan's fears and contract the disease he thinks I already have.

I control my body. Not the Collective.

I'm hurrying so fast toward the short series of steps heading up towards the main landing of Rogers Hall that I almost don't see Kimberly, fast-walking just as quickly down the hall toward the cafeteria. She's wringing her hands and talking to herself. This isn't unusual behaviour for Ethan's best friend—she's often wordy, eccentric, and lives in her own head.

"Hey!" I shout, waving to her as we cross paths.

Snapped out of her thoughts by my hand movement, she grins widely. "Hey Ingrid! Just heading in there for lunch. Have you eaten? Has Ethan eaten?" She scratches her head furiously. "Ho boy, got a terrible itch right now."

"He's in there."

She continues to itch her scalp furiously. "Shouldn't have had that coffee. Have to ... *three things ...* "

"Uh ... Kimberly? You okay?"

"Hmm?" Her hand drops to her side. "Oh. Hey. Nothing. I'm fine. Mostly hungry."

"Sure ... " I point toward the cafeteria. "Food is that way. Though maybe you should consider not eating—"

Kimberly takes a deep breath of the cafeteria food and a glazed look falls over her tense, erratic expression as she takes off. "Nice talking to you, Ingrid!"

Stunned, I remain in place, trying to parse what just happened. I didn't think I'd have to worry about Kimberly's mental health and how fast she would succumb to the Collective's influence. I guess she just seems so ... normal, usually. As relative as that term is. I'll have to keep an eye on her. Just another thing to add to the ever-growing list.

I take out my phone. No new messages yet from Wil. I text Wil, Jia, and Misty in code: *Meet in my room?*

Just as I exit Rogers Hall, my phone buzzes. A text, finally, from Wil. *OK.*

Took him long enough.

A few minutes later, Misty, Jia, and Wil file into my bedroom. Jia immediately begins tidying up Misty's clothes strewn on her makeshift mattress on the floor—she says something in French and shoos her away. Wil nods hello to me, and leans against the wall. Deep circles encase his lower eyelids and he has bruises on his arms and a cut on his lip that I hadn't noticed last night. Probably doesn't help that he's putting long hours in at the lab.

Without looking at the camera hidden in the light, Wil touches one of the buttons on his bracelet to jam the Collective's feed. "Ingrid. What's our status?"

"Status? Are we running a military operation all of a sudden?" Misty retorts, flopping backward onto my large bed.

"I want to know what happened to Shadow. I checked in the infirmary—"

"You went—" Wil sighs, as if I'm a misbehaving child. "Okay. I see your reasoning. But she's not there. And she's not... not on campus."

"You don't sense her at all?" Jia asks, concerned.

He shakes his head. "No."

"Why didn't you just answer my texts and tell me that then?" I demand, holding up my phone.

"Look, I have a lot on my plate. She's gone. She wasn't looking well when we left her, and by the time the hafelglob cleaning crew showed up, well... it's possible she's dead or the Collective has her, in which case she will be dead soon."

"We could have saved her," I insist. "We should have been better."

"If the Collective has her, they might know we were at Mystic Shadows," Jia says. "Wil, is it possible for you to... erase memories?"

He presses his lips firmly together and regards Jia intensely. "I... could. Maybe." He presses the heel of his palm against his forehead as if to silence his inner guilt. "I should have done that before we left Shadow. But tampering with memories is... dangerous."

"Yeah. So is a giant cloud monster that eats memories for breakfast. We done here?" Misty asks.

"No," I say. "If Shadow's not on campus, is she on the mother ship?"

"The mother ship? It... has been rebuilt. I've been able to discern that from some of the pliable alien minds. I don't know, Ingrid." He looks annoyed that I've brought it up. "Going there again... it's risky."

"Each day is a risk. If Jadore finds out we had something to do with the fire... "

"If only someone was better at teleportation," Misty says sarcastically. "Then we could leave."

If only someone hadn't burnt down a building and gotten us into this mess! "Jadore would kill Hildie and all our families if we left, even if I could take us all out of here. We're here, and we caused this problem. We need to fix it."

Arguing isn't going to get us anywhere. If Shadow is dead or with the Collective, we have to continue focussing on the problem we *can* fix: tracking down the Hunger. We find the Hunger, we might be able to find the missing students, and therefore, find Shadow, if she's still alive. I fill Wil in on our theories about the Hunger. Wil listens intently, nodding intermittently, though he keeps glancing at Jia, as if expecting her to contribute more. Even Misty seems quiet and uninterested in conversation.

"I didn't get anything like the three of you did," Wil replies finally when I've finished. "Nothing concrete. Just random images."

"You can't sense it, can you?" I ask.

He shakes his head. "But now that I know what it...feels like...I would probably know if it were close by."

"Close by? Like...in the room? Or on campus?" Misty asks.

"My range varies. If I'm tired, it's weaker." He adjusts his glasses. I wouldn't be surprised if he couldn't sense Mrs. Harris a few doors down.

Misty sits up. "So that *thing* is still out there. Kidnappin' or murderin' people."

"That's likely, yes. There's no sense in all of us running around exhausted," Wil says, not unkindly. "I...need to sleep. We can do shifts, two and two. Who wants to volunteer?"

"I'll go," I say, and Misty, to my surprise, also offers her time.

Jia seems relieved at the thought of uninterrupted sleep, but still presses us relentlessly. "You won't stay out all night? Promise you won't be much later than one or two."

"I'm not promisin' nothin'," Misty mutters, but begrudgingly agrees not to get too carried away. After yesterday, I have a hard time believing her.

CHAPTER 8

I meet Misty for our late-night walk at the pre-arranged spot, a large maple tree at the edge of campus and the beginning of Sparkstone Town proper. The fallen leaves crunch under my boots, ruining all hope of a sneaky approach. For someone supposed to be alert to an attack from a dangerous alien, Misty seems unconcerned as she relaxes on the bench. She holds a brown paper bag protectively against her right side.

Her gaze snaps to mine as I approach. "You were supposed to be here fifteen minutes ago."

"Sorry. Got... carried away." That's one way to put it. After a four-hour afternoon nap that was a jumble of horrific dreams worthy of a Saturn Award, I fielded a call from my parents, who had been trying to get a hold of me. Then Tilly texted, asking for an update about Shadow. I told her I hadn't seen her, and debated telling her she never would see her. "Did you want to... walk?" I ask, unable to take my gaze from the glass bottle half-hidden by a brown paper bag.

"In a bit. I already did a once-around while I was waitin' for you."

"Sorry." I sit down next to her.

"Yeah." She leans back into the bench. "No one around, as usual. No weird clouds. Just the normal ones." She points at the sky.

I cross my arms, wishing I had opted for my winter jacket instead of my black cardigan. "Maybe the Collective caught the Hunger."

"Maybe." She swirls around the giant bottle, and catches me staring. "What?"

I try not to look disapproving. "Where did you get that?"

She shrugs. "Just had it. Was saving it for...a special occasion, I guess. Then forgot about it." A rare grin slides across her face. She has perfect teeth, except for her snaggle eye tooth on her left side. "Good thing I remembered. It's one way to stay warm. Bad thing about this country—the cold. But a good thing about this country." She removes the paper bag, revealing the bottle to be straight vodka. "Drinking age is eighteen. Like friggin' Europe. Two good things about Europe. Hot women, low drinkin' age. And I guess the language variety is nice too. Three things. Eight things? How many languages in Europe again…?"

I broach the subject cautiously. "Misty. Are you…drunk?"

"You got a problem with that? 'Cause the security guard that came around a while ago turned a blind eye. Drunk students are probably easier to push around anyway. As long as they don't start fighting back."

"I thought you said no one was around. Aren't you worried that the alcohol is drugged?"

She laughs. "Security is always around. And the hafelglob

aren't people. They're gross alien blobs. And, for the record, alcohol is already a drug. I think the hafelglob know better than to mess with me anyway, especially when I'm inebriated."

That's what I'm worried about. If she gets out of control and starts showing off her powers, regardless of who's watching, the Collective might harvest her. I breathe in the sharp cold air deeply; it coats my throat and burns on its way down.

"Besides," Misty continues. "Not much else to do for fun here. We are allowed to have fun still, right?"

"Why are you asking me that? I'm not stopping you."

She snorts, and takes another drink. "No, but you're a prude, and your passive-aggressive disapproval gets real annoying real quick."

"Prude? I'm not—!"

"Sure you are. You're silently judging me now."

"Well—" I can't deny that. I really don't like the idea of her drinking when we're supposed to be keeping an eye out for suspicious activity. My toes dance within my boots. We really should be moving around, if not for Misty to work off some of the alcohol in her system.

"Okay. You wanna walk? I'm ready to walk."

Finally. I spring up, and with Misty and the vodka at my side, we begin a leisurely stroll around campus. While it's cold, at least the sky is relatively clear. We could see an alien cloud coming a kilometre away.

To keep my hands busy and therefore warm, I check my phone. No new messages. Nothing more from Tilly and nothing from Ethan. Likely he's in Morris House right now, or his studio, painting or drawing. We pass the music trailer and I feel it calling to me. Not tonight, I whisper mentally to it. Though if I could call the Hunger like I can call Campbell, it would make this fight a hell of a lot easier.

Misty is annoyingly silent, her lips only moving when she takes a swig every few minutes. At this rate, she'll drain the whole thing before our watch is done. I don't want to deal with a fire-throwing, ice-slinging, drunk weapon AND a gaseous alien life-sucker.

There is one thing I can do to keep Misty's mouth from the bottle. "I ran into Mrs. Harris earlier today. She said she was looking forward to a visit from you sometime soon."

"Oh yeah?" Misty says sceptically. "You mean she wants me to visit." She sighs, dragging her hand down her face, like she wants to tear off her skin. "I mean, I like Hildie and all, don't get me wrong, but...actually...visiting with her? One-on-one...?"

"I could go with you, if you wanted."

"Yeah, I guess. If that wouldn't be boring for you. I know I *should* go. It's the right thing to do. Sunni would want me to. Just...every time I look at her, I know she's holdin' out hope for somethin' that's not gonna come, no matter what I say or do."

"Did she ... *know* about you and Sunni?" I ask. "I mean, not to suggest you were an item or anything ... "

"I don't think she knew. Don't think she would approve in any case." Misty shoves a hand in her pockets. "She never really liked me, not at first anyway. I was from out of town. I have all these things in my face." She whirls a finger at her facial piercings. "No, when I became friends with Sunni, she didn't really like me comin' by. But she never really said anything that mean to my face. Was too busy sitting in her rocking chair upstairs staring out the window."

"Do you think Sunni knew?"

I'm afraid she'll get mad at me for asking—throw a fit, burn or freeze my skin—she just dips her head. "Possible she did. She knew a lot about a lot of things. But…I don't think she would've done anythin', even if she did know. Don't think she would've wanted to ruin our friendship. If she even saw me as…well, you know." She lets out a deep breath. "I dream about her sometimes. She's out there, somewhere. You'd think she'd be able to take revenge easily in her ghost form." Misty cracks a sideways smile. That's the first joke she's made about Sunni being dead. It dissipates quickly. "Uh…so when you dream about her…does she say anythin' important? And by that I mean...anythin' you haven't told Jia or Wil?"

"Not really. It's more like she just shows me things. Places. Keeps telling me to open a door."

Misty places with her lip ring as she contemplates this. "Maybe she's callin' us, like Eurydice to Orpheus. Tellin' us to come get her from the Underworld."

My eyebrows twitch at the reference. "I guess I shouldn't look at her too closely, in case she fades away."

She doesn't miss my reaction. "Every time!" she exclaims. "Every time I make some kind of reference to any kind of literature, you act surprised!"

"I just...didn't think you were that interested in...academics."

"Because of how I look. And talk. And how I grew up."

My cheeks feel starkly hot in the cold air. "Sorry. I...shouldn't have assumed. I don't even know how you grew up."

"But you did, and you continue to assume." She sighs. "So yeah. I read. Sometimes. More when I was young. 'Sides, what else was I supposed to do when my uncle was in all his meetings?"

"You lived with your uncle?"

"Couldn't live with my parents. *They* had problems." She tries to say this lightheartedly but she doesn't succeed. "My uncle took me in after my dad went to prison for killing my mum."

"Jesus. I'm sorry, Misty, I didn't—"

"Yeah, yeah, spare me that, it's just a platitude. I don't mind talking about it to you. Happened when I was really little. First thing I remember. My dad stabbing my mum. Probably why I prefer women in general." She thinks about this for a moment. "Nah. That's dumb. I like women because...they're..." She shrugs and squints at me. "Am I makin' you uncomfortable?"

"No."

"'Cause you know, I have zero interest in you and Jia."

"I know that."

Her voice goes quiet again. "My uncle would travel around a lot for his job, all over the world. I think on some level he knew somethin' was different about me, but he never showed any fear of me or anything like that. He'd dump me in random schools. Sooner or later I'd start payin' attention to a girl. Worse when a guy started makin' moves on me and wouldn't take a hint. Uncle got used to fielding calls about his unruly niece, eventually just stopped makin' me go to school, unless I really wanted to."

"So you never graduated high school?"

"Never said that. Just had to find some backwater school that didn't care about my records and had teachers that could deal. I guess that's partly why we moved to Wimberley, Texas for my senior year. Commute to Austin wasn't bad for my uncle. You know, I wonder if the Collective would've even found me if I'd just dropped out. I'm no quitter though. I jumped at the chance to go to a posh university in the middle of nowhere. Think my uncle was relieved. We have an understanding, see—I love him, he loves me, we don't talk about it, and he lets me do my own thing. But I wanted to prove that I could actually get a piece of paper proving that I could do something…*good*, you know? Not just be some burden." I catch her looking at me then. Her normally icy gaze has softened.

"The Collective took away my choices. It was Sparkstone, or nothing," I say quietly. "I guess the idea of attending a posh university in the middle of nowhere appealed to me too."

"Hmm." The vodka sloshes quietly as she shakes the bottle at me. "You sure you don't want any of this?"

"Well…sure." I unscrew the top and take a dainty swing, grimacing as I swallow the burning liquid. My throat tickles but I try not to cough.

"Hey, you didn't do too bad," Misty says, slapping me on the back. "I don't blame you for needing a drink after all that I just said. I know how it sounds. I lived it." She takes the vodka back and takes one final swig before replacing the cap and tucking in the grass it under the bench. "In case you're wondering, I don't do this every night or anythin'. I don't need an intervention."

"You shouldn't drink alone," I say, reaching for the bottle.

"I'm not gonna do anything stupid."

"You almost killed yourself last month. You think that doesn't make me worried?"

"I was stone-cold sober. Wouldn't try to kill myself while drunk. Wouldn't know if it was real or not. Besides. I'm done with that. Now that…that Sunni could really be alive…in some form…I think I'd like to stick around and see that through. Kill Jadore for what she did."

I take another swig and hand the bottle back to her. "Misty. What if Sunni is really dead? What will you live for then?"

She shrugs, suddenly quiet.

"If we lose hope that we'll get out of here and get on with our lives, the Collective has already won. You shouldn't have to choose to live *for* anything. You are allowed to just *live.*"

"Easy for you to say, Goody-Two-Shoes. You could do well without the Collective's help in the outside world. Me? I don't want to live off my uncle's charity forever."

I frown. "It's not like my parents are rich. I still have to work hard to get where I want to go. I don't expect to live off their charity either." I hadn't thought much about the future since arriving at Sparkstone. All of my brain power each day went to survival.

"Yeah, but you had a base. If you wanted to take a year off and travel, or explore your creativity, your parents would probably support you in that, right?"

"I guess. But I'd still have to get a job of some kind. Wouldn't your uncle support you?"

"He'd offer to pay for certain things, as long as I had a job. I couldn't just sit around the house or the hotel rooms during the summer. I have to buy my own clothes and music and stuff like that. He pays for this." She twirls her finger around, indicating the campus. "I'm going to pay him back, though. If I survive."

"That sounds like my parents." Thinking about them is comforting, and it's all the more comforting now that I know Misty has someone like them in her life.

Misty takes another swig of the vodka and wipes her mouth. "What...uh...what do you think they'd say if you told them you can teleport into space?"

I smirk. "I only did that once."

"Still. You got superpowers. You think they'd mind that?"

I shrug. "I guess once I showed them and they believed me, they'd be afraid, and then curious, like anyone else. Teleportation is pretty useful." I hesitate. "Honestly, I think they'd be more afraid if I could sling fire and ice."

Misty sneers, swirling the last of the vodka in the bottle. "They're always going to be afraid, no matter what you got that they don't."

"Uh, well, you could be more careful."

"What? I'm careful! I see an enemy, and I act. No time to *think* when you're in the heat of it. You just gotta know—is the thing I'm shootin' at on my side? If no, they're goin' down." She raises her eyebrows and shrugs. "Careful gets you killed."

"Jia is careful. Wil is careful."

"So?" She frowns, and stops walking. "You think we should rely on a guy that can manipulate people's minds whenever the eff he wants? He's extremely *careful* not to get caught with whatever he's doing in that lab."

"It's a useful power."

"It's dangerous like anything else. For all I know, he's speaking to me right now through you."

"He's not—"

"Yeah, yeah, what—"

Misty makes a grandiose gesture with both hands and swings around. She loses her grip on the vodka within the paper bag and it falls to the grass with a crack and a thud. Misty, startled and bemused, leaps back and brings her left hand up. Fire dances between her fingers and forms a full-fledged flame.

Oh no.

I kick the vodka bag out of the way, but she's not aiming the fire at the ground.

She's aiming it directly at *me*.

The fireball roars past my left shoulder and lands on the grass behind me. With a soundless spike, the fire eagerly consumes the dry grass.

Misty swears and I leap toward the fire. With one aggressive *stomp*, I eliminate the flame from spreading further. Another stomp: the fire extinguishes beneath my boot. Smoke rises from the ground and infects my clothing—again—and while the heat burns the soles of my boots, a far deeper anger churns within me.

"What just happened?"

The shock on Misty's face quickly transforms into fierce denial. "What do you mean? It was an accident."

"You almost killed me!"

"But I didn't."

"You shouldn't be drinking!"

"Stop it."

"What?"

"Just—effin' stop. 'K?" She points a threatening finger at my chest. "The way you talk to me, the way you act around me. Like I'm going to spontaneously combust at any minute and destroy you and everything you care about. I just want to be your friend, but you throw a fake version of yourself at me, 'cause you're afraid, just like the rest of them."

I swallow nervously. "I'm not—"

"Don't lie. I'm not Wil, but you're not hard to read." She throws the bottle on the ground. The neck is frosted white. "I've seen stuff, yeah. But at this point, I wouldn't be surprised if we all had PTSD. I'm not tortured. I'm just angry."

"I'm sorry."

"Yeah. I know you are." She takes a deep breath, and adjusts her septum piercing. "So what is it about me that makes you the most afraid?"

"I'm not… afraid," I say carefully. "Not really."

"Except you are. You're a bad liar."

"Fine. I'm… wary. But you've given me good reason to be. I've never had to stop anyone from killing themselves before."

It hurts to say it out loud. Misty's expression barely changes. "You were weird around me before that."

"I don't think so."

"Uh, yeah. You were."

"Well maybe if you weren't so rude all the time, we'd get along better. Though I thought we were getting along fine recently."

She sneers. "Right. Fine. Everything is fine so long as I don't cross a line and blow up a building, or say something too controversial for your innocent, pretty ears. That right?"

"Misty, I—"

"No, this isn't about me. This is about you. You think you're better than me."

I'm taken aback. "I—"

"Just shut up and cut the act. You think you're better than me and that by giving me your time, you're somehow making me a better person. That, or you're just trying to make up for whatever messed up or lack of experience you've had with someone who isn't like you."

I'm on the verge of replying, but I stop myself as guilt settles in. I've never known anyone personally with the kind of past she's had. I grew up in the suburbs, with both my parents. I went to a nice school and had nice friends. Their parents had nice jobs and also could afford nice things. All of them, to my knowledge, were straight, white, and binary.

"I don't know what else to do around you, Misty. I want to be your friend."

"Yeah. Well. Like I said. I'm not toning down my act for you."

Something inside me snaps. "You need to be in control of your powers. What if you burned down Rita House in your sleep? And now you're drinking. You almost set the entire campus on fire!"

"You can't even teleport from A to B without being within an inch of death, and you're lecturing me about being in control."

"You need help, Misty!"

"Is that how you see me? Token suicidal, abused lesbian? That my *tortured soul* somehow needs mending?"

"No." But somehow that's untrue. "I'm not—"

"We're done."

"C'mon, Misty."

"No." Her tone is ice. "We can't be friends. You've proven that we're too *different*."

"That's not what I said! Look, I'm sorry for offending you—"

Misty gives me a look of disbelief. "Don't apologize until you actually know what you're apologizing for. I'm leaving."

I reach for her, realize that might not be a good idea, and watch her storm across the campus toward Rita House. I run the conversation over and over again in my mind, trying to uncover some hidden expression or meaning in it, but can find nothing wrong with my actions. Why can't she understand what I mean? I just want her to be more stable. So that she doesn't murder us accidently. So why do I always sound like a giant asshole around her?

Maybe it's not me. Maybe it's her. Ever since we've met, she's been quick to anger. By tomorrow, we'll be back to our regular banter and petty arguing.

Yet a sinking feeling within me says I've done irreparable damage that not even time can heal.

Sunday passes in a daze. Misty refuses to sleep in my room. Jia begs her not to sleep alone, in both French and in broken Mandarin, but gives up after Misty goes on in a long, loud tirade in a mixture of the two languages. Jia tries to get me to talk about it, but I'm too embarrassed to admit that I may be in the wrong and anything I say will just be my anger talking. We work on our respective papers and projects, and hear no new developments about Mystic Shadows or the Hunger.

It's Monday morning, too early for the sun. As time drags me ever closer to the next morning's tutorial, I sit in my bathroom, reading excerpts from Campbell's treatise and composing music by hand in the lonely lamplight. Sleep will only bring me Sunni and the dreams are too frightening to bear. I also don't want to hear her ghostly opinions on Misty, and what I should have said differently, because my brain is already doing that job for me.

Just as frightening is the idea that Jadore will one day show up at my door, and no longer give me the speech that she will *eventually* harvest me, because eventually would be now.

I wish it could be now, because at least then it would be over. Then I wouldn't have to figure out what to apologize for, and deal with the cold, hard truth: we may never leave this gilded cage alive.

Daybreak brings rain, a rare and miserable thing for Sparkstone and my inclination for wearing skirts and leather boots. I don't have a rain coat—one doesn't often need one in Alberta, unlike in Nova Scotia, where my mother is from—so I dredge out my fall coat, my least favourite pair of skinny jeans, and my warmest long-sleeved shirt. Along with my shoulder bag, they will have to serve as my armor if I am to survive Monday morning's tutorial.

A peculiar smell permeates the building as I make the long trip down the stairs. Bleach, yes—but the scent of bleach covering something darker and heavy. I trip on the stairs and catch myself on the railing from the invasion of colour accompanying the sensation. My synesthesia is getting worse. Thick white fog chokes me, stealing every thought except *survive!*

Yet the Hunger is not in sight. I am alone on the stairwell—aside from the glowing red eye of a surveillance camera just above my head.

I hurry out of the building, concentrating solely on getting to MacLeod Hall, and I arrive so quickly that for a moment, I almost believe I've teleported. Room 216 looms before me. The sea of students clambering to their classrooms seems undisturbed, and I have vague memories of walking. If only my power worked by inattention alone. That would make everything easier.

Despite the hopelessness and dread within, I march into the classroom. Of course, most of my tutorial mates are already there ahead of me, including Misty and Jia. While Jia waves a sunny hello, Misty doesn't acknowledge my presence. We have self-appointed places in our semi-circle facing the newly installed white board and otherwise empty classroom where Jadore stands and dictates her will to us.

Normally I sit between Jia and Misty, but I go for the empty seat on Jia's other side. She gives me a puzzled look: that's Wil's usual seat.

I cautiously smile at my fellow peers as I internally prepare myself to be humiliated once again in front of them. Besides Misty, Jia, Wil, Tilly, and myself, there are four others out of the other seven regularly confined to Room 216 each day with Jadore that I've gotten to know. Emily, the fair-skinned American business and psychology student who is generally a beam of sunshine, dimming only slightly beneath Jadore's unseeable stare. Cheng, the Chinese-Canadian who still thinks it's okay to play on his high-tech camera phone when Jadore is interrogating his fellow students. Todd, the older mid-twenties Seattle native who doesn't say much, but takes it to heart when Jadore criticizes his latest politically-charged piece of fiction. And finally, Felix, the exchange student from France who can't stop twitching; as a drama major used to creative movement and dance, I don't think he thought he'd be spending this much time sitting and talking in a circle.

Even though the hostility radiates off Misty, I attempt conversation anyway. "No sign of Wil this morning?"

Misty picks at her black nail polish and ignores the question. Jia responds, "Probably in his lab."

I nod, rubbing some sleep from my eyes. "What are we—?"

Jadore throws open the door and begins speaking without ceremony. "Tutorial begins in one minute. Get out your notes."

Her usual calm and smug composure seems frazzled. Even her black hair, usually slicked back against her skull, is uncharacteristically out of place. No doubt the Collective has been on high alert while dealing with the Mystic Shadows incident. I wonder if they caught the Hunger.

Something tells me she'd be more calm if they had.

Wil's footsteps are hard against the hallway floor and he manages to make it in just before Jadore tap-tap-taps her cane and shuts the door. He gives us a *I'm here under the wire* look, himself looking just as frazzled as he drops three binders at my feet and falls into my usual seat.

I glance between the three Sparks. We share dark circles beneath our eyes. I don't think any of us slept last night. I can even smell residue of smoke on Wil's jacket, immediately recalling the memory of the two of us hauling Shadow from the building.

Jadore whacks her cane on the floor, startling the room into silence. "Tutorial begins now." Frazzled or not, a smug smile slides across her dark lips. Then, in a slippery tone, she adds, "Let's see who's here."

There is an empty seat in our usually full semi-circle. Jadore doesn't like it when people are late, and often makes an example of the tardy person in the most embarrassing of ways. Once, she made Emily recite our national anthem—which she barely knows—backward. She made it halfway before bursting into tears.

I pray that I won't have to give a detailed update of my progress on my project in my deranged state, even though it's pointless to ask for something you won't get. I grab my notebook from my bag and open it to a blank page, my pen at the ready, though it is heavy and useless in my lazy limbs.

Alphabetically, without a list, she calls our names. It is a quick call-and-response we've come to expect, each of us, even the non-Sparks, want to get the whole affair out of the way as quickly as possible. She lingers on Wil. "You are well?"

"I'm fine," Wil says, rubbing his eyes.

"You sound out of shape," she says flatly. "I expect more from you today, Mr. McBride."

"Sure, Professor."

Jadore curls her lips, but moves on. "Tilda Newman?"

Silence. All gazes float to the empty chair, and then to the door, and then, fearful, to Jadore.

Tilly is missing.

"Hmm. Tilda Newman, are you here?" Jadore asks, in almost a sing-song voice.

When Emily and another girl whose name I don't remember speak up and say that she's not there, Jadore smiles smugly. "I thought that might be the case. Professor Garcia said she was violently ill last night and they had to take her to a hospital in Edmonton."

Oh no. Violently ill…unlikely. My stomach tightens. I told her not to stick her nose into the Mystic Shadows fire. I was so close to telling her not to eat at the cafeteria. But I was so angry at her that I let it slide, thinking she'd be okay. And now she is probably dead.

The non-Sparks in the tutorial exchange confused looks. I don't have to be Wil to know their thoughts. Tilly is the fifth person that we know of to leave Sparkstone suddenly and unexpectedly within just a few weeks. Although none of us engage the subject further, Jadore seems to take pleasure in giving us the gory details. "Not to worry. It was not food poisoning. Super-flu, perhaps. She kept a slovenly dorm room that no doubt brought on sudden, severe infection. The first floor of Rita House is being thoroughly inspected and cleaned in case of further outbreak."

Inspected. Tilly was taking notes when I mentioned the cameras—and no doubt she keeps thorough records of her interviews for the zine. Perhaps the Collective wants to eradicate any kind of evidence of her *investigations*.

"All dorm rooms will be routinely inspected for cleanliness from now on." Though it's impossible to track her eye movements behind her sunglasses, I feel her gaze on the four of us. "We can't have anyone else coming down with something *nasty*."

I hold her stare behind those impenetrable sunglasses, and make a silent declaration: *The only thing coming down is you.*

CHAPTER 9

My Monday early evening dinner date in the cafeteria with Ethan goes surprisingly well, despite him watching my every bite with an enthusiasm I would find annoying in anyone else. I choose foods that I think will have the least chance of being tampered with: apples, bananas, individually packaged yoghurts, and a plate of salad with no dressing. He doesn't criticize my carefully curated meal; he only seems happy that we get to spend time together after weeks of mismatched scheduling and late-night protecting-the-school-against-aliens activities. There are brief moments when we're talking about our favourite TV shows (*Doctor Who*, chiefly) and discussing the finer points of balancing creativity and taking care of our bodies when I feel more relaxed than I have in weeks, and this morning's news of Tilly's disappearance and the subsequent threat of inspections seems distant. Maybe the food really is affecting me. Yet not having to monitor every muscle movement in fear that a team of aliens will whisk me away for doing something wrong—there is a relief in that. Eating their poison gives me a kind of immunity.

I only feel sick because I'm playing along with the eating

disorder ruse and dizzy with the idea of being alone in Ethan's room; anxious because of what might happen there. I dressed up in my nicest, flowing blue skirt, white tank top, a long-sleeved cardigan with pockets, and my flats.

Hand in hand, he leads me into Morris House, fearless of what any roaming security guard or passing student might think of him bringing a girl into the boys-only dorm. I have the urge to stick my tongue out at the camera in the lobby, and the one at the top of the stairs. Agailya saved Ethan before because he has value to her. I doubt they'll bust down Ethan's door just because I'm visiting him.

"You all right?" he asks, as we approach his dorm room.

"Yeah, great," I reply, smiling.

"Your grip is extremely tight."

"Oh. Sorry."

He lets go, pressing his hand against the small of my back, and then fishes his key card from the pocket in his jeans. Once unlocked, he pushes the door open and invites me in with a nervous smile.

The room is less messy, for starters. Art-in-progress sits neatly on easels and against the deep blue walls, some of the paint still drying. My gaze hungrily searches for the portrait of me I'd seen the last time I was here—but it's not in sight. Maybe hiding beneath another canvas... or perhaps he discarded it.

"So uh, yeah. This is me," he says, lazily gesturing about the space. "Sorry about the mess here. Usually I keep my art in my studio, but I don't always want to go all the way there if I'm hurrying to get an image on the canvas. So. Hence this corner of the room."

"Aren't you worried about paint fumes?"

He laughs. "I'm mostly working in acrylics at the moment. They're not that bad. And charcoal is fine as well. Messy but fine. Also, I have a window." He points behind the mess of easels and shelves of paint and canvases to the curtainless window to the right of the entrance to the bathroom.

"You're sure it won't trigger your…allergies?" I ask hesitantly. Wil had noted that Ethan's body seems to be having a severe allergic reaction to the environment.

"Allergies? Don't think I'm allergic to anything. It's not the paint," he says. "I get the sniffles a lot. I see the school nurse if I get too many symptoms. I'm just prone to colds." Then, looking to his paintings, he adds, "I always feel better when I paint."

I wrap my arms around his neck. "I always feel better when I'm playing."

"I think I know something else that will make us both feel better." Ethan leans in and catches my lips with his.

There is something different about this kiss. It's filled with urgency; our mutual frustrations of having to wait for each other to be in the same place, in the space mind-space.

We fall backward onto the bed, flats and sneakers still on, yet I feel like I'm flying. This, this is what makes living in hell worth it. I cannot regret coming here because then I would never know Ethan. He gives me the hope that I can survive in this horrible prison. I feel like I'm halfway between heaven and earth.

So this is what love feels like.

"Ingrid?"

"Mmmm?"

He frowns and pulls back, caressing my forehead. Something is wrong. "Your ... face ... "

I sit up. "What ... ?"

Shaking his head, he chuckles, embarrassed. "Must've been nothing. Gone now. The light, maybe. For a second there, it was almost like ... nah, forget it, it sounds ridiculous."

"C'mon, tell me." I pull him closer, though he tenses slightly at my touch.

"You blended into my duvet. Like you were only half here." He laughs softly and nudges my forehead. "Silly, isn't it? Just shows you how afraid I am of losing you."

What. The. Hell.

Blending into the duvet? It's green. I was turning green?

No. I'd felt elated. On cloud nine. Because I was literally in the middle of teleporting away.

Oh no.

"What's the matter?" Ethan asks. "You're going pale. Are you feeling alright? Did I say something? I'm sorry, I didn't mean to be—"

"No, it's not you." I squeeze his hand as my mind races. "I ... I don't know what to say. I'm sorry that I ... looked weird? I'll try not to let it happen again?"

Ethan laughs. "Apology accepted. It wasn't really weird. I was just worried that I was imagining you all this time, and that you were disappearing because I'd realized how much you...you really mean to me." His smile fades. "Ingrid, I—"

"Ethan. There's something I have to tell you. Something I should've told you before." I sit up straighter, still clasping his paint-stained hands firmly in my own calloused fingers. "I—"

And then I notice that I can see the green duvet through my skin.

"Oh no," I whisper.

"Ingrid, truly, are you all right?" He grips my hands tighter, but his fingers go right through mine. He jumps away, startled. "What's going on?"

I leap off the bed and run for the door. "I...I should go. You're right, I don't feel well. I'll call you later. Okay? I...I promise."

His worried face burns into my memory as I hurry from his dorm. The door slams shut behind me, and I flinch mid step. I can't stop now. I can't even look behind me as I raced down the corridor and down the emergency flight of stairs. I arrive in the lobby, startling the security guard sitting at the desk reading his newspaper. To my left, the doors open into campus. To my right, the first floor. More dorm rooms—and maybe a place to hide.

The first floor is thankfully void of people as I search for the bathroom or a janitor's closet. I am fully solid again—no *Back to the Future*-style disappearing for me, not anymore—but nerves swirl in my stomach and there's a lightness in my head that travels down my entire body and with every tentative step I take on the tiled floor I feel as if at any moment I am about to involuntarily take to the skies.

At the end of the hallway, beside another set of stairs, I find what I'm looking for. I grasp the doorknob, taking a moment to feel the copper in my hands to ground myself, and I pull open the door with such force that I hear a person coming down the stairs beside me remark, "what was that?"

I quickly ensconce myself inside the closet. It's stuffed with cleaning supplies and reeks strongly of bleach. I collapse against the wall, knocking over a mop. I barely register the *clang* against the opposite wall. My head is spinning.

Ethan. I was so close to telling him the truth. To showing him the truth.

When I'm with him I feel free. The light-headedness caused by my overwhelming attraction to him wrongfully tells my body to surrender to nothingness. More than anything, I want to be with him. The very real ache in my chest tethers me to this closet; if I follow my heart, I would surrender to my passion and probably inadvertently teleport to his room.

This whole time he has been at the center of my power. The first time I teleported, I was thinking of Ethan, and I appeared in the field where he takes his morning walks. The second time, I was also thinking about him, and I teleported to the building where he was. And when I was on his bed, kissing him...

But if I'm with him, and I'm thinking of him, and I start to fade away, where would I go?

Even focusing on him now, the familiar sensation of drifting away awakens once more.

Is *romantic love* the key to my power?

With every week that passes, more students go missing and the Collective gets closer to their endgame. I can't let them win. My body feels light: I'm strong *now*. I need to make use of my power while it courses through me.

Shadow. Tilly. The names of the missing students repeat through my mind. If Shadow's alive, she's on the mother ship. Maybe Tilly is there too. That's where Sunni was, when they took her.

There's no time to call the Sparks. I have to act while I have control. My mind is already fading; it's like I'm falling into a pleasant sleep. Even checking my phone takes effort: it's five-fifty.

Squeezing my eyes shut, I call to mind my destination, trying to picture every last detail I can remember about the mother ship. I surrender to my love for Ethan and the wall becomes less solid as I slip from the room and embrace an unfeeling darkness.

My eyes snap open to the sound of a gentle, persistent hum.

Under me, metal. Behind me, metal. Silver all around, but parts of the floor are grated. I'm in a long, narrow corridor that curves sharply to my right. Directly on my left, a black double door that is motion-activated. It opens and shuts like a fish bobbing its mouth, confused by my presence. I recoil quickly, my heart racing furiously as I realize where I am.

The Collective's mother ship.

It worked. I visualized a place, I thought of Ethan, and now I'm here!

Squishy footsteps come from around the corner, accompanied by sloppy-sounding language. Last time I was here, I had Misty and Wil and Jia to communicate with and keep me unseen by the aliens. Here, alone, I am exposed and vulnerable. Coming alone, in retrospect, is a terrible idea. I dive towards the door as the unknown aliens come around the corner. The door hisses shut behind me. I thank it silently as I run down the new hallway, but the door says nothing in reply. At least there's that.

The new hallway is darker, and has two adjacent corridors to my left, and another branching corridor further down. The ship is strangely empty. It's been a month since it tore apart in space; yet you could never tell that anything happened to it from where I am. I'm also travelling blind. Wil had said that there are sophisticated sensors on board—they'd probably alert security teams that there's an unauthorized human wandering around. I wonder how long it will be before fishmen guards show up.

I lean against the wall, trying to blend into the darkness, and listen for more footsteps. I need to find where they're keeping the missing students. Then, I can use my power to teleport them out of here. I hope.

Tip-toeing around the nearest corner, into a darker hallway, I check my cell phone. An hour has passed. I lost an hour from travelling from the supply closet to the mother ship. That's better than my previous time of seven or eight hours. And I've been on the ship for what, less than five minutes? And no alarms have been tripped—that I know of?

BOORRRRRRRP! BOOOOOOOORRRP!

The alarm tears through my body like an electric shock and the fluorescent lighting dims to a warning red. An alien language spouts off on hidden speakers in the ceiling.

Looks like I have less time than I thought.

I hurry towards a latched door further down the hallway on my right. There could be a room full of aliens on the other side. The terror paralyzes me for an instant; the squishing sounds of approaching fishmen guards spur me on into the dark room.

As I shut the door, I feel the close quarters of the dark space surround me. I reach out, afraid I'm going to knock something off a shelf, but instead find a long, narrow pole, reaching from floor to ceiling—or at least, to beyond where I can reach. I follow it, and my touch paints a mental picture: a ladder. At my feet, there's a hole in the floor as the ladder descends to another level.

Jefferies tubes, as they were called on *Star Trek*.

I could go up or down. Not that it matters. The red light blinks every three seconds, all over the ship. No matter where I go, they will find me.

I shut my eyes and press against the cold metal wall. *Focus. I don't want to be here. Take me away. Take me back to Earth.*

Trying to shut out the world is impossible, and instead, the sounds around me turn into an urgent melody. The approaching, squishing footsteps of the fishmen guards. Their watery, gurgling language. The hum of the ship, so latent and persistent that once I concentrate hard enough, I can raise its volume to match the other ambient sounds. The alarm wails, but it is no longer grating, but rather, smooth. It is red, but I prefer it green, and so now, it is low and haunting, like a snake slithering between my ears.

In the space of one beat and another, I weave the strands of sound together, knowing that it may not help me escape, but it will help me be calm. From the chaos, a familiar melody is born, and it's only when I feel his presence that I realize what I have done.

"It's quite cramped in here."

No. No, no! "Go away. I'm trying to escape."

"That's not how this works, Ingrid. You summoned me. And I have to say, you are looking extremely thin."

"Yes, but I..." I open my eyes, refusing to meet the gaze of the time-travelling, interdimensional alien, afraid of what I may see. Oddly, I feel centered. As if his very presence has brought me down from a perilous edge. The alarm still blares and the fishmen are closer, yet I feel more equipped to handle what they may bring.

"It's all right," he says gently. "But you have to tell me—"

"Shh!" I whip my head around, and my hair brushes against his flesh—real flesh, not a swirling, terrible mass of horror. I nearly recoil in surprise. He looks like...a regular man. An extremely familiar man—forgettably attractive, with a youthful expression—much younger than I was expecting. I smile in spite of myself. This is not the same Joseph G. Campbell I spoke with just days ago.

"Is this the first time you've seen me in person?" he whispers.

"No," I reply slowly. "There was...one time before this."

"Hmm. Interesting. What did we talk about? Where?"

"Spoilers," I mutter bitterly. I cannot bring myself to call him *sweetie.*

"Very well. I assume you're on the Collective ship for—"

Campbell's small talk is interrupted by gurgling sounds and the squelching of fishmen guards on the metal floors several feet away, in an adjacent corridor. Both of us are silent as they stroll past. Once they are out of earshot, I turn back to Campbell and lower my voice. "When are you from?"

"I've spoken with you three times."

"Hmm. This is our second conversation." I hate not having the upper hand. I crawl out of the space, into the vulnerable hallway. The floors scream red but at least the alarm has been silenced—for now. Perhaps they are not after me. No doubt another patrol will be around soon.

Campbell seems unconcerned. He too crawls out of the space, dusts himself off. "Ah. Collective mother ship. Circa..." He rubs his fingers hard against the metal, and then grimaces at the friction. "Not the original. Parts of the original are in here, though. Newly constructed. Hmm. Has Jadore enacted martial law yet?"

My eyebrows lift in alarm. "No..."

"Oh. All right. Spoilers, then, as you said."

I try to put that out of my mind—*martial law! She's going to harvest us all and chop us into pieces and use us in experiments!—* as I search for escape routes, or other potential hiding spaces. I continue down the corridor, consciously stepping quietly to lessen the clunking of my flats.

Part of me has longed for a regular conversation with

the alien I am interdimensionally tethered to, that I cannot completely ignore him. And I know, through our bond, that he knows this too.

"I am only here because you called me. And because I cannot stay long, I would like to watch the stars. There's an observation deck two floors up."

"Do what you want. I'm going to teleport out of here now. It was a mistake to summon you. Goodbye."

"Very well." He leans back against the wall with a bemused grin. His tone clearly implies he's expecting me to fail. "You know, there's an interesting theory about teleportation that states the physical object being teleported is copied during transit, and appears in the desired location. The original, of course, is destroyed."

I blink, my stomach clenching. "But that's... that's not how it works for me. Right?"

He delays answering for a second longer than I'm comfortable. "No, of course. That's absurd. Matter being copied and destroyed and re-created." A smug smile crosses his face. "Though if it were true, you would never know it, would you? You would be a copy of a copy of a copy... of a copy? Four times, is that how many times you've teleported? When an object is copied that many times, the quality starts to degrade. You haven't been feeling unwell as of late, have you, Ingrid?"

I can no longer tell if he's joking. "That isn't funny."

He waves off my concern. "You have nothing to fear. You are really you. Like all humans, you change every second in reaction to your environment and other stimuli. You can no more create and destroy matter than I can. And do believe me when I say, that ability is—"

While Campbell lectures me on his inability to manipulate the fabric of time, I happen to spot a large vent further down the hallway. I bolt towards it.

"—and that's why I'm not allowed to interfere on *that* planet anymore. In any case, I'm tethered to—oh. You've found a way up. Or..." He concentrates for a moment, cocking his head. "No, not up. Through. It winds around this floor. A maintenance shaft."

"The fishmen will be back soon. I can hide in there until I teleport back. Help me up."

"And me?" he asks, as he takes position beneath the hatch.

"You're a time-travelling, possibly universe-hopping alien. Of the two of us, you can certainly handle yourself."

"So you'd leave me here to deal with them?"

"You're the one who wanted to go observe stars. Now you're concerned? Plus, I don't see how I'm strong enough to pull you up!"

"You are strong enough to teleport us both out of this mess!"

"You manipulated my life!"

Campbell hesitates, glancing behind him at the approaching alien footsteps. "Why are you angry?"

"Why am I angry?" The sounds of the approaching fishmen urge me to jump up and grab the hatch, to get out of here, to escape, but I can't let this go. Not this time. "I know you manipulated my past. Did something to make me recognize you now, so that I'd trust you. Help you open a portal to wherever, so you can save your girlfriend—"

"*Girlfriend* is an exaggeration."

"I don't care what it is. You changed my past. Manipulated this time line. I don't like being used."

"Neither do I." Without breaking eye contact, he reaches up, grabs the handle for the vent, and pulls it swiftly open. It is soundless. "As for any perceived *manipulation*. What I do, have done, and will do is barely any different from what any organism does on any particular day. We all influence each other, whether we like it or allow it to happen. The difference between me and the common intelligence that populates this universe is that I can see and often pull those tiny little strings..." He curls a finger. It could be my imagination, but the gurgling seems somewhat further away, and the footsteps less urgent. "Can you really blame me for using my natural talents to achieve my end goal?"

"Yes," I reply. "You can't just go meddling in people's lives. You don't know what kind of damage you could have caused. Or will cause."

His smile is condescending. "I've been around for far longer than you. My power is limited here, but it is deep. In any case"—he gestures up at the vent—"I can't have you harmed. Into the vent you go."

He weaves his hands together, and positions himself to hoist me up. Even though the fishmen are close, and their gurgling makes it hard to concentrate, I hesitate to trust this alien before me. *I can't have you harmed.* Not, *I'd be sad if you got hurt.*

Right now though, there's only one way, and that's up. I step onto his outstretched hands, bits of dirt falling into his palms from my flats and onto the otherwise spotless metal floor. My skirt rides up to my knees; I struggle to readjust it, scoot into the vent, and hold my cardigan so my phone doesn't tumble to the floor below. Campbell holds me steady as I slide into the vent. It's at least ten degrees warmer in here, and the precious few centimetres between my head and the ceiling seem infinitesimally small. I bend and pull myself the rest of the way up, and curl back around to look down at Campbell.

"If I'm still here, I'll let you know when it's safe to come out," he says in a reassuring voice.

I give him a brief nod, wondering if he can read my mind right now, and know that I have no intention in waiting around for any signal from him. The only consolation I have is, six months from now, we'll both still be alive, so I eventually will find some way out of this encounter. I drink in his face, trying to store it in my brain for later, as he pushes the hatch shut. I hear his footsteps saunter down the hall in the opposite direction of the approaching fishmen, and then, perhaps the squeak of a shoe, and nothing.

The hatch is solid, and has a wheel that tightens or loosens the lock. I start to turn it when I hear the fishmen directly below. I hold my breath. The idea of being in this enclosed space for longer than a minute is setting alarm bells off in my head. Maybe I'm more claustrophobic than I thought. Pressing my cheek against the metal, I focus on calming my breathing while the guards gurgle to each other below. I imagine they're saying something like, *We heard human voices coming this way. We need to search the whole ship.*

Despite the sounds of their voices, and the distinct possibility that they may discover me lying flat above them, my brain is more aware of the close quarters of the vent. The fear of being spontaneously crushed seizes my senses. I'm on the verge of losing control. Each second seems elongated. My fear has solidified into a giant bowling ball, planting me firmly in this spot, no matter how much my brain wants to escape.

Breathe. In. Out. Breathe, or you'll be discovered. Breathe, or die.

Mentally telling my lungs to take in the recycled, stale air helps somewhat. I strain to hear more of the fishmen gurgling. Even though I can't understand their language, perhaps the tones and the colours they emit can provide me with clues. There is only one now: the other gurgling fishmen's tones come from a crackling communicator. His thick boots clomping on the grated floor with their constant brown and dark purple tones, combined with the midnight green of its gurgles, undulating like waves upon the ocean, lauds me into a kind of calming trance. I don't know what he's saying. He's probably giving his superiors a report about my suspected whereabouts. My mind cannot help but create a melody from his voice and his movements, a movement of movements. A jaunty march or strathspey in E-minor with a brief key change into F major. Unusual, but an acceptable arrangement.

Trapped in the confines of an alien mother ship, at least I have my music. The weight within me lessens, and for a small moment, the presence of the low ceiling and the tight quarters doesn't bother me as much.

The brief clarity of mind allows me to consider my options. I can't escape from this hatch so long as he remains there, which could be for god knows how long. At least he can't come up here—I think the fishmen are too large to fit through. It can't be the only exit in this vent, especially if it's used for maintenance or air flow.

I focus on my Rita House dorm room. I teleported here. I can teleport back. But even with the music calming my mind, I can't replicate the lightweight feeling I'd felt in Ethan's room.

I'll keep trying. Until then, I have to find another way out.

Drawing measured breaths, keeping the tune in mind to write down later, I shimmy through the vent. Right elbow first, then the left, and careful placement of my footing within the slip-on flats. Every movement feels like the noon cannon at Citadel Hill in Halifax: deafening.

Just think. Anyone could turn on poisonous gas and flood the vents, knocking me out. Then the Collective would be free to dissect me, since I've come too willingly into their lair.

Don't think about it. Campbell said you'd be alive in six months. They're not going to find you here. You're going to be okay.

He never said how alive I'd be. I could exist as a brain in a jar in six months.

Right elbow, left elbow, shimmy.

Up ahead, voices. Female, or higher pitched, at least. The tune I was composing fades into the back of my mind as I realize the voices are speaking English.

One of them, her voice deep and sultry and as green as her

natural skin, is unmistakably Jadore's. "How long before the trial is complete?"

"Ten Earth minutes," replies another woman—an airy, calm voice that can only belong to Ms. Agailya.

Agailya—on the mother ship. The hairs on my arm rise. I know what Jadore is capable of. The memory of her lightning decimating Sunni, and the smell of her earthy, repugnant skin washes over me. But Agailya—other than her mysterious connection to Ethan, and her ability to save both him and me from certain destruction at the Collective's hands—her powers, if any, remain elusive.

The voices are coming from below me. There's a grate, similar to the one I entered, but without a handle. This is just an air vent, then—not an actual hatch. My heart sinks. I probably won't be able to get through this, unless I suddenly hone my teleporting powers within the next few minutes. I have to be content with remaining in the vent a while longer and glean what the two professors are up to when they're not teaching us impressionable teens.

Peering through the barred grate, I see Agailya and Jadore. Jadore, in her alien form, though dressed in human clothes the small room. Her green skin, brilliant with an unusual gleam today, is in stark contrast to the clinical white of the lab around her.

Agailya busies herself behind a white, flat touchscreen console. It's angled toward her and away from me, but if it's anything like the console behind her, then it's a flat black surface. Occasionally, alien symbols appear, and Agailya glances over her shoulder, taps them, and they disappear again. Although she's giving Jadore a technical explanation about a procedure she's about to perform, Agailya avoids Jadore's intimidating gaze, staring only at the work before her.

Why remain in human form when she is aboard the ship, when she is free to be her true self?

Unless her true self isn't capable of existing in this environment. I think back to the nautical decorations in her office, knocking loose a memory of her voice: *Do not make waves in water you do not intend to breathe in.*

"Once infected, we will observe the symptoms. In this version of the vitaphage, the symptoms are visible within minutes. Then we will attempt to administer the test antidote. Upon—"

"Fine. I will observe."

Agailya briefly presses her lips together, and makes a subtle popping sound as they fly apart. "I would prefer you did not."

"Regulation two-five-zero-one-subsection-c states that a Council member must observe non-primary projects."

"That is a cumbersome regulation. One of yours, I assume. Did you know there are currently forty-seven non-primary—?"

"As of this morning, there are twelve."

I have never seen Agailya angry. Frustrated, yes. Sad, even. The sudden flash of emotion that floods her face is so violent, so ugly, that I fight back a gasp. "Why?"

A predatory, low hiss escapes Jadore's throat. "The Sparkstone Project is key to the continued expansion, and perhaps even the continued existence of the Collective. The other thirty-five projects split our focus. I called a Council meeting this morning, and after some debate, a suitable compromise was reached. The projects that drained our resources the most were cut. The rest have been placed on a probationary trial until they prove their usefulness to the Collective."

"Usefulness." Now Agailya looks up. Her words are breathy, and barely audible, especially from my position. "I knew that the Council species were favoured. Yet I did not think them to be so callous. Not when there is much at stake, and much advancement to be gained from my work."

"Advancement for the ahmei. Since the vitaphage does not exist outside your species, other than in controlled trials, the benefit for the Collective is minimal."

Agailya's voice is measured, and controlled. This is not the first time she's had this argument with Jadore. "We use our own equipment. Our own people. We do not interfere with the Collective's harvests—we've managed to piggyback on your project without distracting from your goals. We are one of three projects that are the least obstructive here on this planet."

"The Council does agree with you there." Jadore sounds like she does not agree with the Council. She flicks her forked, snake-like tongue in Agailya's direction, and then smiles. "Though we were curious. A few weeks ago, you used considerable Collective resources to obstruct the harvesting of several ripened assets. All to save a precious subject of yours."

I didn't think it was possible, but Agailya's pale skin whitens further. *A few weeks ago...I asked her to help me save Ethan.*

Just what I thought. Ethan's one of her...subjects.

"It was an emergency," Agailya says evenly, holding Jadore's intense, black gaze.

Jadore rounds the console, gripping it with her claw-like fingers, and bares her teeth at Agailya. "You cost me an opportunity to show *Campbell*—"

Gurgled tones blast through the room from a speaker next to the entrance. They startle me, and my foot involuntarily slams down on the vent. I bite down on my finger to stifle a reaction and lean away from the grate. *No, no, no.*

"Did you hear something?" Agailya asks, as I hear Jadore cross the room.

"The com," Jadore replies condescendingly. The gurgling continues from the speakers. "There was an intruder alert at thirteen hundred hours, standard ship time. Apparently one of the subjects may have escaped confinement."

"Not one of mine, was it?"

"No, a regular one." There's a soft click, then: "Report."

More fishmen gurgling. It sounds desperate. Lighter greens, rather than dark. Jadore makes a frustrated noise. "I'll be right down."

"Sounds like your men need to undergo further training. Two escapees in one day?"

Jadore hisses, loud and long, more like a cat defending its territory than a reptile. "You worry about your project. I'll worry about mine."

"I am recording the trials," Agailya says with a measured tone. "I submit them to the Council each time. Does that suffice? My—"

The door slides open with a slick *whirr* and I hear Jadore storm out. As the door shuts again, Agailya lets out a measured sigh. Her eyelids close briefly.

The Collective is not one mind, she once told me.

Despite Jadore's treatment of her, despite whatever sacrifice she's made to keep Ethan and me alive, I can't let myself forget that she's part of this organization too. She's just as much an alien scientist experimenting on us as the rest of them.

My thoughts are interrupted by a beautiful tonal song, sung in Agailya's voice. She appears meditative, concentrating fully on achieving perfect pitch with each note. *C, C minor, C sharp, D.* It repeats, creating a pleasant dark and light blue palate with a tinge of muddy gold.

After three repetitions of the musical phrases, she opens her eyes. "You can come back in now."

Fear grabs my heart. Was she talking to me?

Does she...know I'm here?

Another door on the other side of the lab slides open. A flustered human-looking person struts in. They're also wearing a long, white lab coat over a grey skirt and a light blue tunic. Nodding in greeting to Agailya, they take a station at the adjacent console to hers.

"Did you not hear me?" she asks the newcomer, without looking up from the console.

"I heard you, though I couldn't be sure of the message. This body doesn't quite have the range for the Sea Songs." Their voice is deeper than Agailya's, but equally as calming. They share the same pale skin and silvery hair, though streaks of striking, bright yellow blaze from his scalp to the tips of the hair resting just below his shoulder. I don't know if the colouring is a sexual, age-related difference, or a preference, though I'm inclined to believe the former. The aliens in the Collective don't strike me as frivolous and flamboyant, especially when it comes to fashion and appearance. I'm more surprised I haven't encountered this person before. I don't know whether they're male or female, or if Agailya's race has these constructs.

"You could have endured her," Agailya says in a mildly scolding tone.

"I could have." They sound truly upset. "She frightens me. At any moment, she could—" They grip the air suddenly, and make a high-pitched sound as his fist traces a j-shape before them. He sings his words more than Agailya, though they do not have any apparent rhythm or coherent intonation.

Agailya stops her work, and touches her colleague lightly on the shoulder. "In times of trepidation, remember the songs, Gayarnu."

Gayarnu lets out a sigh. "We will endure, *n'ayarhm*."

"That we will. Now, we're behind schedule, and we are already recording the session. I'm eager to test the latest antidote." She walks across the small lab and touches the communication device mounted to the wall, where Jadore was only moments ago. "Bring in the test subject."

There's a hissing and *per-shump* sound. I strain to see, but it's difficult, as it's almost directly below me. Agailya and Gayarnu exchange words as the sounds of someone pounding on glass ensue. My neck hurts from craning, but I shift in the vent, causing some thumping of my own, as I adjust my position to capture more of the goings-on below.

My heart sinks into my stomach.

The right side of the lab isn't a wall of consoles, or even a real wall. It's a transparent, glass cage; completely solid, with a gleam that would make any cleaner proud. The inside of the cage is long and narrow, taking the length of the room, yet it's the occupant that makes me panic.

Tilly bangs against her prison. She's screaming, but her sounds are lost. Only her fists against the strong, alien glass can be heard—the desperate *thump, thump, thump* matching the pounding in my heart.

CHAPTER 10

"Is that strong enough to hold it?" Gayarnu asks.

"Increasing glass strength ten percent," Agailya responds, her capable fingers dancing across the flat panel.

"Sound?"

"Two-way communication is silent."

"We may need to communicate with the subject, *n'ayarhm.*"

Agailya considers this. "Her wails are not part of the experiment."

As the two debate the issue, my gaze is occupied with part of Tilly's attire. While my conversations with Tilly were brief, her fashion sense stuck with me. Not many would be brave enough to wear such flamboyant sweaters and pants. Yet to be abducted while wearing a cat costume—it would embarrass me for sure. The grey-coloured, furry ears stick out from the top of her head, blending flawlessly with her curly red hair. One is larger than the other, and bent. Maybe it got damaged during her capture. A matching grey tail that I first mistake for a scarf coils from behind her, and presses against the glass cage wall with as much force as her fist. Huh. Her good ear twitches and moves, following unheard sounds around the room.

That's odd. Surely the Collective would destroy any kind of animatronic...

The sound from her cell cuts in suddenly. "Please, Ms. Agailya, I just want the truth—this is your chance to tell me your side of the story!"

Something ripples from beneath her bare arm, as if a worm is crawling beneath her skin.

"We are approaching the five minute mark," Gayarnu says. "She should be showing signs."

"Temperature rising, Gayarnu. High for a human. Any sign of boils?"

"Unsure, *n'ayarhm*—I can't risk radiation damage, it may mutate the strain."

"Hmm. Tilly, please let us know when your skin breaks out. The boils will be roughly five centimetres long, have a yellow-blue colour, and be tremendously itchy. Thank you."

"Boils?" Tilly says. She stops her assault on the cage and draws back against the back wall. "You...you injected me..."

"Yes. We are conducting a test." Agailya's voice is void of compassion.

"I didn't consent to this," she replies. "I don't imagine this is sanctioned by Alberta Health either. Let me go." She scratches her left arm. The beginnings of a blue and white boil have appeared there, and grow larger by the second. "Give me the antidote and let me go. I can't promise I won't report on this. But I do promise to tell your—" She's interrupted by more furious itching. She swears. "This hurts!"

"Of course it does," Agailya replies. "Your cooperation is appreciated in our search for the cure."

Alarm twists Tilly's features. "You mean... there's no... cure for this?"

My hand covers my mouth to keep from vomiting.

"That is why your suffering is appreciated," Agailya replies. Her words are filled with an uncompassionate calm. "Your unique ability to shapeshift may prove useful to developing a vaccine, or at best, a cure for this vitaphage."

Shapeshift! Tilly doubles over in pain. Her bare skin breaks out in grey-coloured fur to match her ears and tail. "No... I... "

I close my eyes. So this is Agailya's project. Infecting innocent humans with an alien disease in the hopes of developing a cure. My stomach rolls. It was because of her that Ethan was saved. That's why she was determined to not have Jadore interfere. Because... he's part of this experiment too. Ethan *has* been getting sick a lot lately. Only cold-like symptoms, but it could be another version of the violent vitaphage she's talking about. Who knows how many subjects she has in the wild, waiting to be plucked and tested upon. What if Ethan is next?

"Her vitals are not registering." Her assistant's melodic voice interrupts my thoughts of Ethan.

"The sensors must be malfunctioning. The subject is clearly alive." Her groans and pleas for help confirm Agailya's suspicions.

"I will fix this."

Tilly crawls forward. Her face twists with pain as she leans once cheek against the glass. The boils have spread across both her arms, but they're half covered in grey fur. Oddly enough, her cat ears shrink into her skull, and the position of her eyes are slowly ping-ponging between her nose and her ears. "Why do you want my power? Please. I'll do anything. I'll help you."

It's hard to look at her. Her shapeshifting power, out of whack and possibly hyperstimulated, is wrenching her body in terrible ways.

Ms. Agailya pays no mind to Tilly's begging. She taps a few more buttons and looks up expectantly to her assistant. "Status?"

Gayarnu glances between the tablet and the screen. "Vitals registering. Barely."

"Hmm. Must be her hearts. They're in...flux. One moment there, the next not." She stares at Tilly, fascinated. "Can you concentrate on your lesser mammal form, please?"

Tilly, eager to help and not be tortured, nods, and closes her eyes. They slide slowly closer to the side of her head, like a bird's, but remain otherwise human.

"Vitaphage cell reproduction has decreased over sixty percent," Gayarnu says, unable to keep the amazement from his voice.

Agailya points to her assistant. "Her constant cell mutation and regeneration is combatting the vitaphage. Extract blood samples."

I look away as soon as the long, silver instrument with a needle attached pops out of a hole in the back wall of the cell. Tilly screams, but the procedure is quick. Her fear accelerates her transformation. The fur spreads over her face, as if she's becoming a werewolf, and while the front part of her face has elongated, her eyes remain on the sides of her head.

"Is that enough?" Gayarnu asks.

"It'll have to be. Vitaphage is spreading through her central nervous system, and has already infiltrated her lungs. We have minutes before she expires."

"We can get the rest of the samples from the morgue. Release antidote 24108, at fifty-percent dilation. This is as stable as we're going to get her."

"Yes, *n'ayarhm*. Releasing Antidote 24108."

A mist fills the cell from unseen air vents. Tilly attempts to escape it, to no avail. She gasps for air. As soon as the mist envelops her, some of the hair on her face recedes and her face normalizes as well. She coughs and sputters. "This tastes like saltwater taffy…"

"Breathe it in, Tilly. It may save your life," Agailya says. "You are doing well. Now, concentrate on—"

Red lights flash and a blaring alarm sounds in the room as Tilly suddenly seizes and drops to the floor. Her skin glistens, and turns a dull grey.

"What's happening?" Agailya demands, as Gayarnu says, "water in her lungs. She can't breathe."

"Become a *uahmar*, Tilly!" Agailya screams. She sings a few other words in her native language, and the assistant helps her search for the correct term. "Fish. Whale. Dolphin! Your shapeshifting abilities might be able to outwit the vitaphage!"

Tilly bends and coughs up blood onto the floor of her cell. Gayarnu yells frantically about filling the tank with water to try to facilitate a definitive transformation. Agailya taps buttons and continues to yell words of encouragement to Tilly. Scales become skin but I blink and the flesh is fish again—a horrible in-between state that has even Agailya recoiling in disgust.

My fingertips curl around the bars in the vent. If I tried teleporting down there, it's likely I'd lose an hour, or phase through the floor. Then I'd end up in one of those cells too. I don't have Misty's firepower, and I don't have Jia's invisibility, and I don't have Wil's mind for tech.

I teleported here all the way from Earth, hundreds of kilometres into a vacuum, and when faced with the possibility of being a hero, I'm useless.

Except...

As fast as I can, I maneuver my hand to my cardigan pocket. My phone is awkwardly squished between my leg and the vent. I lean to one side to fish out the phone. It *flumps* onto the vent. Tapping it awake, I then maneuver to the camera app and snap some quick pictures of my friend. There's no reception up here, but at least the camera works.

"Come on, Tilly," I whisper. "Transform into something..."

Her gasps for air become more desperate. Gills sprout on either side of her neck to provide extra support, as well as to tiny holes above her breastbone.

"It's spread. Her lungs are compromised, *n'ayarhm.*" Gayarnu says.

Unless she can transform. Transform, Tilly. Transform...

One of my hands, slippery from the tension and the temperature within the vent, slips, and causes the grate to rattle slightly. Although Agailya and Gayarnu's ears aren't sensitive enough to hear it, Tilly apparently is. Her gaze snaps up to mine. I don't know how easy it is to see me through the vent from below, but my red hair is unmistakeable in most situations.

The cat ears she had previously appear once again from her scalp, as well as the tail. She slinks down the wall, and with great effort, drawing final, strained breaths, reaches her hand toward me.

Horrified, I take another picture.

"Shift, Tilly," I whisper. If Agailya is right, and she can change into another form, maybe that will hold off the vitaphage long enough that I can get us both out of here.

Her tail twitches, wet and heavy. It continues to twitch randomly for several minutes, yet her wide, desperate eyes are unblinking, and her chest does not inflate.

Agailya and Gayarnu chatter away, gathering details about the time of death and Tilly's physical and cellular description for their logs. A heavy dread weighs on my stomach. Even though Sunni's death was horrific, at least it was quick. Who knows how many others have suffered at Agailya's hands in the name of science.

She wasn't trying to be nice to her. She was trying to do an experiment.

They put her in a cage. They treated her like a lab rat.

They don't see us as an intelligent species. They see us as cattle. Just as Jadore said.

I point my camera at her, and take several more pictures, and then a video.

"Subject log, T-N7, entry supplemental. After a first successful trial, subject was unsuccessful at integrating the serum. Subject will be deconstructed according to Collective protocol and DNA distributed to appropriate labs in need if samples are not heavily contaminated. More testing required for version eighty-seven of the cure of the vitaphage. I'm labeling this as a failure."

"Failure," Gayarnu says. "You said we were partially successful. Can we not celebrate that?"

"Partial success is still failure," Agailya says coldly. She moves around the console, gives Tilly's crumpled form the briefest of glances, and goes to another, smaller panel on the wall. She presses a green button. "Bring in the Hunger."

The Hunger?

I recoil from the vent, gripping my phone tightly. My focus sharpens. So the Collective were able to recapture it. Last time, the Hunger was telepathic. It may give away my position. Just as I start to inch backwards—the guard at the entrance to the vent might be gone by now—three fishmen enter the lab carrying a large black box with handles on the sides.

Tilly is dead. Can the Hunger feed off the dead?

"Set it beside the chamber," Agailya says.

The Hunger had been quiet. Intelligent. Powerful. How can the Collective control it like this? Slowly, reluctantly, I pull myself back to the hatch. I'm not leaving Tilly yet.

The three fishmen step through the now-open chamber and place the black box beside Tilly's collapsed body.

"Synapse readings stable. We have a few minutes to extract," Gayarnu says to Agailya.

One of the fishmen waves his hands and says something in his native tongue. Agailya looks frustrated.

"We don't have time to test that. I must extract the subject's memories of the incident for further study."

The other two protest to Agailya, only to be interrupted by Jadore's sharp voice over the com system. "Agailya, are you impeding my experiment?"

She's watching. She's always watching. "If anything, your *associates* are impeding *my* research," Agailya replies stiffly.

"You have extracted the necessary DNA for synthesis, no?"

"We are ready to extract memories, Jadore. We don't have time to run *your* experiment. You can have access to the next one. This one was promised to me." She gestures to the fishmen as she presses a button on the console to open the thick glass enclosure. "Begin the procedure. Put the box in the containment area."

Gayarnu also maneuvers the controls on the console; a long-needled silver syringe appears from the wall, and sticks gently into Tilly's neck.

"I have claim to those post-mortem DNA samples you're taking there. As infected as they are with your hideous disease, we must try to isolate what triggers her body's transformation. They could solve our little problem currently sitting in the third floor of Rita House. The sooner *that woman* is dealt with, the sooner I can return focus to the library. I don't care about the memories."

"No, you don't," Agailya says under her breath.

Our little problem. Mrs. Harris. Wil had been right. Jadore and the Collective are racing to find a plausible solution to satisfy Mrs. Harris's persistence. *Return focus to the library.* My stomach burns. She's probably searching for Campbell's treatise.

She watches the fishmen carefully maneuver the black box into the glass enclosure. They seem to be struggling: the space is cramped with Tilly awkwardly slumped against the wall, and neither fishman seems interested in touching her as they set the black box down. "We can take our dispute to the Council, Jadore, but it would be a waste of time. The samples are my property—property of the ahmei people. If we haven't been able to eradicate the vitaphage cells, neither will you. Her body is worthless to anyone but us."

The fishmen babble something, and Jadore makes a sound of disgust. "Don't you dare leave until I have those samples. Remove part of her arm if you must."

The two creatures exchange glances, then look down at Tilly's form. Part human, part fish, part cat—though the fishmen's faces aren't as expressive as Jadore's, I can sense their hesitance.

"Well? What are you two lumps standing there for! I want my—" She descends into hisses and clicks and spitting over the com. The fishmen kneel before Tilly, trying to figure out what exactly they need to do to please their mistress.

"Don't touch her! Have you no respect for her suffering?" Agailya says, coming out from behind her console.

Jadore sounds more content now that her minions are doing her bidding. "The ability to adapt is valuable. Our inability to make hafelglob DNA compatible with other species is a major failing we must rectify, and your subject provides us with a great opportunity. I'm taking over this project. You are relieved."

"This is my subject. She has valuable DNA—"

"You've harvested enough. Your vitaphage has raged through her systems but there might be some unaffected cells I can scrape out. The Hunger can have what is left."

"That was not part of the agreement I made with the Collective!" Agailya's normally calm voice is edged with anger.

"The Collective has poured enough resources into your experiments. And how far have you gotten? How many have you lost since the beginning of the trial? And what should I see pass my desk this morning, but an approved request for another shipment? I voted *against*, if you were wondering."

"I was not wondering."

"You should pay more attention. You are only driving your people further into—"

"I am *not*." The air ripples like waves around her as she swipes toward the intercom. "I am closer than ever, if you had bothered to read my report, you would know this. You would know that three of my subjects are exceeding expectations."

"Three out of the initial twelve."

"That is irrelevant. The vitaphage adapts quickly. The humans—"

SssssssSSSSSssssss...

The hiss is not from the intercom. Slowly rising from the

black box is a heavy fog. One of the fishmen leaps to his feet clumsily and backs against the wall.

"Box breeching!" says the assistant.

"Contain it! Seal the chamber!" Agailya orders.

The command is initiated as she speaks. The glass reappears from the top of the room and slams down. The two fishmen are trapped inside—with the Hunger.

"It won't hold the Hunger! It can pass through—"

"It doesn't have to." Agailya frantically taps the keyboards, desperately glancing between the trapped fishmen and her companion. "It will feed on the nearest target."

The fishmen squeal in high-pitched tones as the Hunger wafts out of the breeched black box. Like a toxic, steamy shower, the Hunger fills the enclosed space with its mass, fogging the glass.

"What is going on in there? I'm—" The intercom cuts out.

"We should ready the countermeasures, *n'ayarhm,*" Gayarnu says. "And then get out."

"Just a while longer," she orders. She's tapping on the console again. "Exporting data to the backup drive. Samples?"

Gayarnu spins around and removes three glass tubes as they shoot out of a concealed opening behind Agailya. "Retrieved. But Agailya, they're in pain—"

"Yes, they are, and they will endure."

Struck by the words, Gayarnu steadies their hand. "They will endure."

This isn't the soft, gentle headmistress I have come to know.

The coldness in her tone is palpable. The fishmen gurgle and cry out in sounds that are almost English, as if drowning in mid-air.

"We need to put them down before they become unstable," Gayarnu says. "Jadore will be here any moment."

"She won't risk her scales in this room. She'll quarantine the whole section. And…all right. I have enough." She sighs, annoyed. "Releasing neurotoxin. They'll be dead in a minute."

Once the Hunger is done with the fishmen, it will go after everyone else within range. Including me.

"Erecting a force field. It will contain it for a little while until we can get it back in."

"I was not aware we had that technology."

"The security department perfected it yesterday, after the incident at Mystic Shadows." Agailya nods to her assistant. "Now we evacuate."

A loud alarm rips through the room. I gasp and recoil from the hatch. That's my cue. Time for *me* to evacuate back to Earth before someone notices I'm missing.

Before I inhale some neurotoxin and become the Hunger's next victim.

No longer concerned about being heard, I crawl as fast as I can through the steaming vents. My arms slam down on the metal. Adrenaline and fear masks the pain of my limbs as they slam down on the metal. Right arm right knee left arm left knee repeat. There's not enough room to turn my head. It could be behind me.

How many more metres? Too many. Right arm right knee…

I could try teleporting from the vent, but I'm too afraid of accidently phasing into the solid metal and being stuck there forever, if that's even possible. I consider scooting backwards, back to my previous location, but for all I know, the fishman guard could still be there. Or I could teleport into the middle of a Hunger cloud. No, better to go forward. Plus, going backward makes my skirt ride up, and that makes for unpleasant vent navigating.

Sweat drips from my forehead. It's getting hot in here.

What if there's no more hatches? Damn it, I should have crawled back the way I came...

The metal burns my arms and legs and I cry out. I have to escape. My vision becomes hazy with sweat and fear. Up ahead, I think there's an exit. Tears stream down my face, only to dry immediately in the increasing heat.

Yes. A hatch. And this hatch has a handle. Finally. An exit. I peer down. I see no one, and I hear no gurgling. All clear. I hope. Not that it matters—I'm going to boil alive if I stay.

I fumble with the handle—the sweat on my hand doesn't allow for much purchase. When I manage to get it open, the loud screech sears my senses, and overwhelms me with a primal urge to run, run, run away. Once again, the sense of heaviness returns. I'm never going to get out of here.

Nevertheless, I force myself through the hatch. My skirt rides up as I slip through, but falls immediately down as I hang from the vent, holding on with slippery fingers. The hall is clear. Counting to three, trying to control my fear, I let go. My flats stomp loudly on the metal floor as I land and nearly come off. A sharp pain rides up my foot and through my right ankle.

A sprain? I twirl it around, and find with a sigh of relief that I'm fine.

Fine, except I'm in a short winding corridor, standing before three fishmen who happened to be in the right place at the wrong time.

Oh no.

"Get out of here. The Hunger is loose!" I say, waving my arms.

One whips out his radio device and gurgles into the speaker.

I draw back from them, balling my hands into fists. I have no weapons. No powers besides teleportation to defend myself.

My camera app is still open. I snap a photo.

Surprisingly, the three fishmen receive no answer to their radio, and they make no move against me. The strong smell of salt water permeates my nose, bringing with it my synesthetic colour associations, yet it's not coming from the fishmen. The three of them flick their forked tongues, similar to Jadore's, and jerk their bodies around; they too are trying to uncover the source of the peculiar smell.

Then, all three of them, gurgling and clicking, spin on their heels and dart back the way they came.

Gripped by a similar sense of self-preservation and curiosity, I turn around...

...only to be enveloped in a warm cloud of fog.

JOIN US, the Hunger says. *JOIN US JOIN US JOIN US...*

I close my eyes and think of Ethan.

Nothing happens.

I can't die here on the mother ship. Not when my friends are down there. I need their help. Someone has to remember Tilly; I saw her die, I saw what they did to her, and I need to survive to tell her family and her friends what really happened—eventually—so that she can be properly memorialized.

The vaper from the Hunger clouds my arms. I feel like I've stepped into a wet sauna. One by one my thoughts slip from me, and I chase them down. What am I doing on this ship again? Who were those fishy aliens? What city am I from...?

"It's all right," says a voice that sounds like Ethan's, yet he's nowhere in the room. In fact, the room seems far away at the moment. I can't feel my extremities. I feel like I'm floating.

"Ethan?" I mumble. My mouth is dry, like I'm speaking out loud in a dream again.

Maybe this is all a dream. Maybe I dreamed the whole thing. Maybe I'm just part of Sunni's dream, and we're all just the remnants of the last bit of synaptic energy flying through her brain as she dies.

"Join me, Ingrid," Ethan's voice says again. I feel hands on my shoulders. They feel like his hands. "It's safe. Trust me."

"Are you still sick?" I ask. My mouth feels less and less dry, even though my body feels lighter. My fears have been eradicated. The metal corridors of the ship vanish before my eyes—if I still have eyes. If Ethan is no longer sick, then maybe I did something right. Maybe I already helped Ethan, and I've forgotten, and this is a dream.

I hope he's all right. I—

Through the door. Through the door.

No, I can't go through that door, it's not—

First I'm aware of my tongue, heavy in my mouth. Then, someone hovering over me, attacking me. No. I won't let you have my body. I have the choice to go through whatever—

"Stop, stop that, Ingrid. Jesus. It's me, Wil."

"Oh." My hand presses against my forehead, though my eyes are still too heavy to open. A dull, consistent pressure nags my temples, and Wil's grip pulls me upright. Breathing in the sharp air of autumn, my lungs rejoice after spending too long in cramped, alien quarters.

"You were hitting me," he says.

I force my eyes open. "Sorry."

Wil and Jia hover around me, sharing concerned expressions. Even Misty is there, looking distraught. After all I've seen, I can barely remember what we fought about. Maybe she can forgive me now.

I'm outside in the field. Still at Sparkstone University. Miraculously, the sun is setting over the wall, which is odd this far north at what has to be after eight in the evening.

Jia throws her arms around me. "We...we thought they'd..." She pulls herself from me, but keeps a firm grip on my shoulders. Her normally stoic, dark eyes are rife with fear and the worst possible outcome. "They didn't harvest you. You're real."

Jesus, I'm gone for what, two hours, and they're all worried about me. I feel incredibly guilty for gallivanting away to the mother ship on a whim; I hadn't even told them where I was going. "I'm sorry. I…I teleported. I was feeling the urge to…and it just kind of happened. I should have tried to contact you. But I had to take advantage…"

For a brief, selfish moment, I'm let down further when the three of them don't congratulate me on the successful use of my powers. For once, I manage to teleport to a destination—and return home—outside of an emergency situation, and within a reasonable time frame.

"At least you're fine," Jia says finally, though she seems unconvinced. She's still holding on to my shoulders. "Where—?"

"The mother ship," I reply. "You're not going believe the stuff I overheard. I saw Campbell again, and I saw Agailya and Jadore—"

"What did Campbell say?" Wil interrupts.

"Did you get a look at their military capability?" Misty asks.

"Stop bombarding her with questions," Jia says sternly to the two of them. She turns back to me, more concerned than ever. "You...look okay. Are you sure you're okay?"

"I'm fine," I say again. At least I'm back before dark. "What time is it?" I pick up my phone from the grass, but my stomach growls, and then sharp abdominal pain obscures all other thoughts. "I'm really hungry."

Jia and Misty stare at me in disbelief. "Yeah. I wonder why that might be," Misty says sarcastically.

"Um...because I'm hungry?" Pressure builds around my temples. The beginnings of a headache. I'd hoped to fill them in on my adventure immediately, but that will have to wait. "Jia, you wouldn't happen to have any carrots or anything left in the room, would you?"

"I...sure. Anything you need."

I start walking on unsure legs toward Rita House. It's like walking on pins and needles; I feel weak. Nothing a second, non-drugged supper can't cure.

I only get a few feet before I'm forced to stop. The three Sparks remain standing at my landing spot, wearing the same stupefied looks on their faces. My stomach growls again. Can't we walk and talk at the same time around here?

"What? Quit staring at me and tell me what's wrong. I teleported. Successfully. Again, I'm sorry for causing you worry, but I'm really, really starving, so—"

"Ingrid," Wil says softly, in a peculiar tone that silences me immediately. "How long were you on the mother ship?"

"It was almost seven when I arrived. Only lost an hour. And I think I was there for forty-five minutes. If it's seven-forty-five now..."

"It's six-thirty," Jia says, equally as hesitant. "Six-thirty in the evening, October twentieth."

"But it's Monday. The nineteenth?" I search their faces. A slow, sinking realization fills me then. The sun sets in brilliant reds and oranges behind the wall, bringing an entire day I've lost to a close. This power I have, it comes with a high cost. One I'm not sure that I can control.

Travel anywhere through space, to any destination you desire or not. But be warned, you'll travel also through time.

Twenty-four hours, gone in an instant. One day of my life I'm never, ever going to get back.

CHAPTER 11

In my dorm room, I recount my adventure on the mother ship to my friends while shovelling carrots into my mouth.

"What were you thinking, going there alone?" Wil asks. He sits in a chair by the door. "Sure, you found out what happened to Tilly, but Shadow's fate is still a mystery. Even if they don't know we were involved in the Mystic Shadows fire, they know you were missing for a day. *That* will raise Jadore's ire."

"I'm sorry. I didn't mean to make you all so concerned."

"Jadore threw a bit of a fit," Jia says. She sits cross-legged on the bed next to me, and snatches the odd cut-up piece of carrot to chew on.

"More hafelglob janitors and security guards roaming around in pairs and in threes, for sure. The student body didn't seem to think that was odd, for the most part. Jadore's implemented 'random' room inspections. She couldn't find anything in mine," Wil replies.

"They searched mine too," Misty mutters. She leans against the wall, arms folded as she stares out the window. She's trying hard not to look my way. *Don't apologize until you know what you're apologizing for.* Yet she is here. So she does care about me. That's... something at least.

"I noticed their mental chatter dropping off late this afternoon," Wil continues. "I thought maybe they'd found you."

"You didn't know where I went though."

He leans forward, holding his head in his hands, as if he's an exasperated parent. "You could've ended up in the middle of the sun and died."

"I took the risk." I draw my knees up to my chin. "I couldn't just do nothing."

"Our texts didn't even go through. I even tried calling." Jia says.

I sigh. I could have sworn when I'd looked at my cell phone on the ship, the date had read yesterday. The missing chunks of time, the price I pay for instantly appearing in another location, they're random. Several hours when I teleported from the mother ship the first time. Ten minutes when I escaped from the underground library. Twenty-four hours to get to the mother ship and back. Where do I go?

"It was worth it to get the information," I say firmly. "I'm sorry."

Misty sneers. I wait for a follow-up. Nothing.

"I'd like to do some tests sometime, so we can find out where you're spending your lost time," Wil says.

I'm not his lab rat. But even I can't deny my own curiosity. "Fine. Thursday evening at eight?"

"That... should be fine. I'll text you if we need to change the time."

"What we need to do," I continue, "is to find out why the Hunger exists. They're keeping the Hunger locked away in a box—at least, the Collective is trying to do that. The Hunger doesn't exist just to feed on the students. The whole school—the town—we're more to them than just a breeding ground for a bottomless stomach. Why encourage our intellect, keep us focussed on our studies otherwise? They could just herd us all up into cages if our only purpose was to feed memories to some alien monster."

"Unless the Hunger only likes smart brains," Misty mutters.

"That's possible," I reply.

Misty regards me curiously, and then looks away.

"Maybe they just created something so powerful that they don't know what to do with it. Maybe it's too powerful to just get rid of," Wil remarks. He stands to his full height, stretches, and yawns. Jia glances at him as his shirt rides up his chest momentarily, and then deliberately forces her gaze elsewhere, blushing. Wil adjusts his glasses. "We can think about that tomorrow. I'm going to the lab to put in a few hours. No more adventures until tomorrow. Okay? Can we all agree on that?" Wil turns a tired eye to the three of us.

I nod numbly. Exhaustion washes over me in waves, lulling me to sleep with the promise of rest and non-vision dreams. That promise is rudely interrupted by Jia's cell phone buzzing from her pocket. I blink, annoyed.

Jia retrieves her phone and her face lights up. "Email. From Paige!" She scrolls through the message from her sister quickly, all willingness to discuss alien invasions and strange monster experiments gone.

"Isn't that the *third* email in the past twenty-four hours?" Misty asks in a monotone voice.

"No. Well…maybe." Jia frowns as she reads.

Misty sighs deeply. "Could be the Collective. Just sayin'."

"That's rude," Wil says.

"Yes, that is rude," Jia agrees defensively. "Paige is *fine*, thank you for asking. I love her, but I wish she'd email less sometimes. Especially when it's just to talk about her new friends at school. I don't want her to be on the Collective's radar."

"Likely too late for that."

"Yes. Well." Jia's bitter demeanour changes as her thumbs move scroll downward on her phone. "I'm allowed to be hopeful."

As soon as Wil leaves, I'm dead to the world for several hours. I wake up in the middle of the night, and after that, I barely sleep because I'm afraid of losing more time. The morning is a daze. I'm a zombie, and a slave to the schedule. I feel like I'm a passenger in my own body as I show up to tutorial the next morning. Jadore bears down on me hard, grilling me on what material they discussed the previous day. Even the other students seem sympathetic to my plight. While Jadore's attire is a lime green business suit, all I can see is her green skin and dead black eyes.

"Since some of you think that this tutorial is optional instead of mandatory, I'm assigning you all two essays due this Friday,"

Jadore says. "One on the importance of timeliness as it relates to your chosen discipline. The other, on why remaining at Sparkstone will benefit your career. Seems like our admissions department may have made a mistake in assessing the original applicants."

No one wants to point out that there is no formal application process for this university; that we were all forced to come here, one way or another. All sympathy I'd earned throughout the tutorial evaporates. Emily and Todd glower at me; their stares heat my face, and I don't have the patience or the energy to return their hatred. My lips tremble, yet I keep my retorts buried inside me. It is my fault that this happened. Because I can't control my powers, I lost a day of my life, and my peers have to suffer because of it.

Once Jadore dismisses us from the tutorial, and we are far enough away down the corridor from the classroom, Jia finally speaks. "It could have been worse."

Every time I close my eyes, I see Tilly coughing up blood, and attempting to shift into a form that resists Agailya's vitaphage. "For some of us, it was worse."

Our food supplies are getting low. A general notice is sent around the dorm rooms, saying that mail and shipments to the grocery store will be delayed due to bad storms. Our weather apps confirm that Edmonton and Calgary were both hit with snow storms already this year, but the Collective could be manipulating that data too. At bed time, Jia gives us the worst news yet. "I have enough vegetables to last a few days. They're starting to go bad. After that, we can take our chances again at the bakery."

"I felt a bit funny eating there the other day," Misty admits, mostly to Jia and not to me. She's returned to my room to sleep on the floor mattress, though she hasn't said a non-sarcastic word to me since I came back from the mother ship.

How long can we last? My stomach rumbles. Sleep makes us forget we're hungry, but for me, sleep does not bring rest. Even when I drift into a peaceful state where I'm still aware of my body and my mind is ready to descend into dreams I don't want, either Jia or Misty will make sudden movements and jolt me into wakefulness.

Flashes of sound and images entertain me intermittently as I shift between light sleep and reluctant waking life. Several hours have passed; it's nearly two a.m. My legs ache, as if I'd run a marathon. Whatever I do in my missing time, it's definitely physical. I stifle a groan as I get out of bed and head toward the bathroom. After relieving my bladder, I find myself standing at the foot of the bed, watching Misty and Jia sleep soundlessly. Both of them opted to take the floor tonight, despite my protests, to give me a better rest.

I'm tired. But I can't sleep right now. Sleeping will only cause me to lose more hours—and I really am not in the mood for a nightmare. My antsy nerves crawl like bugs in my stomach, down my arms, and across my back. I reach back to scratch them away, but there is nothing there.

Maybe sleep is not such a bad idea. But I know of one other cure for nerves that works every time.

Careful not to wake my friends, I slip from my room, intending to leave the building for the music trailer. I'm halfway down the hall before I notice that there's light coming from beneath Mrs. Harris's door. Not only that, the entrance is ajar. It's the middle of the night, and she's still up?

I pause, considering. Music will help me sleep peacefully. I can even sleep in the music trailer, if I'm desperate. Visiting Mrs. Harris at this hour is not only suspicious, but not very appropriate.

Unless she's awake because she's in danger.

I broach the threshold of Mrs. Harris's room, my fingertips light against the grain of the door. It yields to me and creaks open. I peer inside.

No aliens. No Jadore with crackling lightning about her fingers. No tanks filled with half-human, half-creature mutations. Just Mrs. Harris, sitting by the window in a rocking chair, knitting away, staring up at me with mild surprise.

"Oh dear," she says, standing. The light purple ball of yarn tumbles from her lap onto the carpet, hanging by a single thread to the knitting needles like a sailor blown overboard. "Goodness, Ingrid. What are you doing up this late?"

"Oh. I—wrong room." I hadn't meant to bother her, or engage her in conversation. She's still alive. That's the important part. I gesture to my bedroom door behind me. "I should get back. Goodnight, Mrs. Harris."

"How many times do I have to tell you? Hildie is fine. I haven't seen you for a few days. Now get in here. I could use some company, and you could use some tea."

"Oh…I don't…need…"

"I hope you take it straight."

"S-sure," I stammer, overwhelmed with her generosity and

foreknowledge to bring non-Collective-contaminated food stuffs. I stumble towards the bed, which is the only other available sitting place in the room besides the rocking chair by the window.

Hildie gets up from her chair and walks over to a plug-in kettle sitting on top of a dresser. She fills it up with water from the bathroom, plugs it into the outlet behind the dresser. It whirs gently as it heats the water. *At least boiled water is safe.*

As she retrieves a mug from her bag and gives it a cursory rinse, Hildie notices me staring at the window. "Can you believe that that director woman, Agailya's her name? Accommodated my request for a rocking chair?" She gestures grandly at the rocking chair. "I didn't think they'd have anything of the kind here. It's not a bad one, either. I'd have half a mind to think that they'd constructed it for me personally, but it looks about as old as I am." A wan smile slides across her face. This is the part where I'm supposed to insist that she's not that old.

I remain silent as she finishes fixing my tea and I contemplate the idea of the Collective creating a rocking chair with Star Trek-like technology. If they could make a chair that fast, surely they'd have little need of shipping in ingredients for Substance 454 like they do. Maybe keeping Hildie happy is part of their plan, in the hopes that she'll abandon her search for Sunni.

Or maybe Agailya is attempting to make Hildie's last days alive more comfortable, until Jadore can figure out what to do with her.

"You must have worked so hard today," Hildie says sympathetically as she hands me the steaming mug.

"Yes," I admit. *If by today you mean yesterday.* The porcelain is comforting on my stiff, cold fingers.

"What is you said you study again? Psychology and music?" She settles back into her rocking chair with her knitting project.

"Yeah, basically." After a few sips of the hot liquid, I feel the gentle buzz of caffeine working its way through my brain. Not that I mind. I'm not sure I really want to sleep. I'm also not in the mood to talk about school, so I quickly change the subject. "What are you knitting?"

"Oh. This." She smiles thinly and holds up the unfinished project. "Well, it was going to be mittens, but I think a scarf might be better. I was thinking to send it to Sunniva in Manila. Do you know if it snows there?"

"Um, it's in Southeast Asia... so..."

"Ah. Tropical, you're telling me." Her knitting needles click pleasantly as she returns to her work.

"Afraid so."

"Then she'll need it for when she returns to Canada. This here weather is terrible. We don't get cold spells like this in Wimberley." She glances up from her knitting with the mischievous smile of a younger woman. "Maybe you could help me. I tried using the computer to find more information about this so-called school in the Philippines. Again, I hounded Professor Jadore, and she set up a call like she'd promised but it just went to voicemail. At least I was able to hear my Sunniva's sweet voice again. A small comfort. Anyway, I found the Philippine school's website, like I said before. But I don't like looking at screens for very long. Tiring for my eyes. I want to send her a care package, but the school only listed a PO Box—"

"You want to know if there's a better way to contact her."

She looks relieved that she doesn't have to explain herself further. "Yes, that would be helpful. The school is giving me the runaround and I want to pursue every available route. I was hoping she may have given you or Misty her address. I asked Misty when she visited yesterday, but she was tight-lipped about it. Poor dear, she misses Sunniva terribly, can't even get in touch with her either."

"No, Sunniva didn't give us her new address." I take another sip of tea to buy me a few more seconds. It's 123 Mother Ship Street. "I can help you think of things to send her."

"Yes, I suppose that would do." She finishes a row and swoops the needles to begin another. The clicking of the needles is mildly soothing. "Not sure why she opted to study *bugs*. I thought she was going to study *normal* psychology. Biology didn't really surprise me. She was always good at the sciences. Just like her father."

I feel the heaviness in the word. *Father*. "Sunni told me a little bit about him."

"Did she?" She sets her knitting down in her lap. I've touched a nerve, and now I have her full attention. "The child never talked about him much. She was young when he left us, but I think it hurt her. Hurt *me*, it did."

For a time, she keeps quiet and just stares out the window. My tea no longer holds its warmth, and the remaining liquid is too bitter and strong for my liking. I eye the door, thinking about returning to the comfort and safety of my friends, yet I can't bring myself to stand and leave Hildie, trance-like, and alone.

"I wish I would've had more time to get to know her," I say finally. "Did you know—?" The question is impossible to ask subtly. She doesn't try to rush me; the silence doesn't bother me like it does her. I suppose she is used to the oppressing quiet. "Sunni was special."

"Yes," she agrees, without missing a beat. "I always knew my daughter was special. Never wanted to let her go to this here school, so far from home. University of Texas would've been a fine choice. But no, begged me she did to come here. She just wanted to get away from me, I guess."

"I don't know if that's true," I reply.

"Oh, you don't have to sugar-coat that, sweetheart, that's a true fact." She looks to the window remorsefully, and touches the pane. "I should've listened to her."

I frown. "What are you talking about, Mrs. Harris?"

"Hildie, dear. I should've listened to Sunniva when... well, what woman in her right mind would? She was just a babe."

I lean in closer. "Sunni... predicted something, didn't she."

Mrs. Harris's gaze snaps to mine. "She told you? She... remembered?"

I need to tread lightly. One wrong move and I will destroy the balance we've fought to keep. "Why don't you tell me what happened."

"All right." Mrs. Harris settles back in her chair and starts rocking again. "Sunniva was six-years-old, and summer was just ending. Still mighty hot, that summer. Cameron had just come home from his tour on the *Yorktown*, that was one of his boats, you see. I was so happy to have him back. He was only there for short stretches at a time. Poor Sunniva barely knew her father." Her voice drifts off, and it takes several minutes for her to find the story again.

"He wasn't supposed to be home for long. The night before he was scheduled to leave again, he'd already washed up and gone up to the bedroom, and I was going to follow, when I heard Sunniva at the stairs. Sometimes she got up in the night, you see. Terrible nightmares, stomach aches. I told her to get back into bed, but she wailed something fierce and ran up into the loft. I keep a rocking chair like this one up there, and there's a bookshelf and my knitting. It overlooks the pond we have in the backyard, and the roads beyond. She sat in that chair, hands folded around her knees, and though she was only small, she was rocking that chair furiously.

"I said again to her, get back into bed, or I'll have your father come out and give you a lashin'. Not really, of course, just somethin' to scare the child into going back to bed. She just kept staring ahead. I went around the chair to face her, and her eyes... wide as pearls, face pale like she'd seen a ghost.

"I said to her, 'You have one of yer nightmares again?'

"She said, 'Yes, Mama.'

"I was feelin' sorry for her at the time, of course, but there was really nothin' I could do, and poor Cameron was waitin' for me in the bedroom, and our minutes together were precious and few. But I knelt before my child and wrapped my arms around her frail little body and asked her to tell me about the nightmare.

"But here's where it gets funny. She told me, 'Mama, don't let Daddy go away.'

"I stroked her hair and said, 'Sweetheart, Daddy has to go away, he keeps the oceans safe.'

"That child squirmed in my arms and screamed at the top of her lungs, 'DON'T GO AWAY! DON'T GO AWAY!' She stood up on the rocking chair, and screamed again, 'MAMA, DON'T LET HIM GO!'

"I was afraid the neighbours were going to wake up. I was afraid that Cameron would wake up. I grabbed her off the chair marched her into her bedroom, and tossed her into bed. I was so, so angry at her. So angry." A tear glistens on her cheek. "I'm sure you can figure the rest of the story out."

"He didn't come back," I say.

"No, he didn't." Mrs. Harris draws in a shaky breath. "And then I found out about the other woman."

My eyebrows shoot up. "Other... woman?"

"Barely a week after we'd gotten the news that his ship was lost at sea, I got a phone call. Sunniva answered it, as she was wont to do. Never afraid of the phone that child. I suppose that's because she always had an inkling of who was ringing. She was talking to this person on the other end for about five minutes, and at first I thought it was her grandmother, or another relative offering condolences, and then she came to me upstairs with the cordless, and said, 'It's Amelia.'

"I did not know who Amelia was. But that sobbing woman told me everything. For a moment I even doubted that he was in the navy... but no. She was an officer in such and such division, and they'd...well, that doesn't matter anymore. She was offering her condolences, trying to unburden her soul. I suppose I can't blame her now. It was so long ago. But the wound...it tore my heart in two. In three, really, it was already in two, but this new tear seemed to hurt more than the first. And when I hang up that phone, I was in a towering rage. And I did a horrible, horrible thing."

"What?" I whisper.

"I...I made good on my threats. I went into the bedroom and got out one of Cameron's old belts. Didn't even use it. My hands did enough damage. She never looked at me the same after that. And now, neither will you." There's a long silence as she sets her knitting on her lap, and stares out the window, like she's forgotten I'm here. "I...I thought Cameron had told her. Had taken her with him to meet her. Was planning to..." She buries her face in her hands. "I'm sorry, sweetheart. Your shoulders are no place for my burdens."

She leans towards the window, not wanting me to witness her breakdown. I set my near-empty teacup on the nightstand. Her sobs shake her only once; she's held them in for a long time.

Sunni loved her mother, and her mother loved her. I cannot excuse, justify, or condone what Hildie did to young Sunni. I can't say that that long-ago event lead Sunni to flee to Sparkstone. All I know is that Sunni is dead, and that's not Hildie's fault, and my own mother isn't here to make me feel better or comfort me. We are both here now, in the middle of the wolf's den. We only have each other.

I get up from the bed. "No," she says, waving me away. "That's not—"

I ignore her half-hearted pleas and wrap my arms around her as best I can. The chair prevents me from giving a quality comforting hug but that doesn't seem to matter. She clasps me tightly, holding on like I'm pulling her from a deep, dark abyss.

A far-off tune drifts through my ears and settles within my synapses. It's filled with turquoises (the sea) contrasting with light browns (the land), and before I can stop myself, I'm humming it. I can't control the tune, I only channel it, allow it to change from a calming C-sharp to a pleasant G. It reminds me of the notes Agailya sang to her colleague up on the mother ship, but this tune is far more complex, and carries with it a story of human suffering and loneliness.

Only when I loosen my grip on her does she relent, and allows me to draw back. The tune fades. The corners of her lips twitch. She's frowning now, determined not to let her sorrow through the hardened mask of anger and frustration.

"You are a lovely girl, Ingrid," she says solemnly.

"Thank you." The compliment eats away at me, but dismissing her would only cheapen the moment.

Mrs. Harris pats her yarn, nodding. Redness cups her eyelids, though her cheeks are dry. There are no more tears left in her. "She probably wondered why I sat up there all that time, in the dreadful silence, waiting. She may never know why." She heaves a sigh. "That is why I continue to listen to this." She taps her dress shirt, just above her left breast. Even up this late, she's still dressed in her finest. "My heart never steers me wrong."

I purse my lips. "Is that why you believe he's still alive? Because her prediction never said he'd die?"

"No, child. I know in my heart he's still alive. The world tells me otherwise, of course. I am terribly afraid if I believe what the world tells me, my heart will tear further, and I will leave this earth a broken woman. We all must have something that keeps the heart beating. Just one more beat. Just one more night. Just one more day. Someday, Ingrid." She smiles now, though her eyes are round and glossy, and grips my hand fervently. "Someday, I'll go home, and they'll both be there. They're waiting for me."

Sparkstone University doesn't have a curfew that I know about, though it's frowned upon for students to be wandering around late at night. After speaking with Hildie, I still don't feel like lying down and sleeping. If I escape to the music trailer and play, it'll only remind me further of Ethan, and my inability to save him. Better to go to the source directly. I've tried texting him several times since I got back to Earth, but I'd heard nothing. Well, he can't stop me from knocking on his door in the middle of the night. With his sleep schedule, it's possible he's still awake.

The security guard at the desk gives me the stink eye as I clomp down the stairs into the lobby. Girls definitely aren't allowed to sneak into the boys' dorms—and sneaking into Ethan's dorm is trouble, especially when I don't have an invisibility power.

"Watching you," says the security guard in a guttural voice as I exit the building.

A shiver runs down my spine. Maybe this is a bad idea.

No, a deeper, more insistent part of me says as I break into a run across the quad. *I'm not going to let my fear of them control me. I need to see Ethan. I need to know... that he's okay.*

Tilly's face appears in my mind's eye, and despite my efforts to brush it away, she remains heavily on my mind. Have all the disappeared students suffered her fate?

What if Ethan is next?

I pull out my phone as I approach Morris House and text Ethan. "*Can you come let me in?*"

The reply is immediate. *Be right there.*

I guess all I had to do was promise him a three a.m. visit to get him to respond to my messages. Ethan arrives at the entrance, his bed hair adorable and his clothes paint stained, but thank goodness, he's alive. Agailya hasn't gotten to him. His bare arms look puncture-free. I intend to keep them that way.

"Hey," I say awkwardly.

"C'mon inside so you don't freeze," he says with a slight smile and an outstretched hand.

The security guard is shorter and larger in the lobby of Morris House, but he's no less alert as soon as I walk into the room. His gaze doesn't leave my body as we ascend the stairs. Ethan seems to notice the in-disguise hafelglob's strange behaviour and takes my hand.

"I might get in trouble if you stay," he whispers as soon as we're up a few floors. "But to be honest, I don't really give a damn. I'm just glad you're here. Didn't you get my messages?"

I frown. "No. Didn't you get mine?"

"You texted me? I was waiting for you at the cafeteria. We were supposed to have dinner this evening. Every second day, remember?"

Oops. I'd been so tired from my mother ship adventure that I'd forgotten. "I'm sorry. I wasn't feeling well. But I really did try to text you."

He looks concerned, and then annoyed. "My phone has been on the fritz for weeks now. Sometimes I'll get messages hours later than I'm supposed to. Almost missed some sessions with Ms. Agailya! Reception is not good out here. Next time I'm in Edmonton or wherever the closest city is out here I'll have to get a new phone, because this is getting ridiculous."

I have a feeling a new phone won't fix the problem.

We reach Ethan's level and I follow him down the corridor to his room. My boots are loud on the carpet. Everyone's probably fast asleep. I wonder what they think of Ethan's strange hours. Everyone seems caught up in their own projects and the promise of getting a good job at graduation to notice what anyone else is doing.

Ethan's room is a pigsty. Laundry is strewn all over the room. Not much different from the last time I was here earlier. The window to the left is open halfway as the smell of paint is trumped by fresh, night air. He notices my reaction and smiles sheepishly. "Sorry. I...would have cleaned up if I had more notice. I always put that sort of stuff off when I'm painting."

One canvas rests against the wall, beneath the window. The scene depicts a vibrantly coloured fish with a large red eye swimming carefree in a large ocean. A bloodied worm speared on a large fishhook dangles before the pretty fish temptingly. Another blank canvas is on the easel. A palette of still-wet blue paint rests on a nightstand next to the easel. Multiple paintbrushes rest in dirty water.

"So you're not using charcoal at all anymore?"

"For now, no. Just the acrylics. Just not going great tonight. Had some energy earlier... did the fish and all that... but... now I'm tired."

"It's almost three-thirty in the morning."

"Best time to do art," he says, grinning. "And play music, if I remember correctly."

"You do." His memory problems scare me to my core. I remember him saying he'd forget small details about his life, like the street he grew up on—probably a side effect of whatever experiment Agailya is running on him, all to find a cure for her species' disease. The vitaphage.

He coughs. Immediately I'm on edge. "Are you okay?"

"Yeah. Just a bit of a cold. Always seem to be just getting over a cold, ever since I came to Canada."

"But it's better when you go home? Like for vacation?"

He frowns. "Um, don't know actually. I guess so. Climate is not as dry as it is here, so I guess, yeah."

My heart races. I have to tell him. I have to save him. "Ethan... I'm really worried about you. I don't like seeing you sick."

Smiling, he runs a hand through my hair. "It's all right. Just a bit of a cold. Don't think it's contagious. Then again, I haven't kissed any other girls recently, so I wouldn't know."

I can't help but smile back. I grip him tightly, wanting nothing more than to not have this conversation right now. "But like you said, you seem to be sick a lot. And every time you go to the nurse...it doesn't get better, does it? What kind of medication are they giving you?"

"Uh, just some cold medication? And mild pain medication for my headaches. At first I thought it was allergies. Now, I know it's probably just me not taking care of my body. I try not to drink coffee so much and stay up all night, but my body just can't seem to shake the habit. That's probably why I keep getting sick." He kisses my forehead tenderly. "Hey, why you so concerned? I'm fine. I promise."

"Don't...don't go to the nurse anymore," I plead softly, cupping my face to block the camera's view of my lips. "Maybe... maybe there's some folk remedies you could try to help."

Ethan frowns and strokes my arm. "Ingrid. This doesn't have anything to do with you going to that pagan shop, does it?"

"What? No. We don't go there anymore anyway. You know it burned down, right?" I draw away anxiously as I ramble on.

"Yeah, of course. Everyone was talking about it. I'm just glad you weren't there when it happened."

If only he knew. "Please, Ethan. I'm just...afraid that..." I bite my lip to keep the truth from slipping out. "What if I told you that the medicine, or whatever the nurse is giving you...might be making you more sick...on purpose."

Chuckling, he shakes his head and closes the space between us once more. "I'd say you're more paranoid than I thought."

"When's the last time you were at the nurse's?" I ask.

"Few days ago."

"Have you felt sick lately? In the last day?"

"A bit." He sniffs and itches his nose. "No more than usual, I guess."

"Are you sure?"

"Yeah." Though he seems uncertain. "Look, you're scaring me, Ingrid. Tell me. What do you think is happening here that's so bloody dire?"

A red light blinks in the corner of my eye. A camera. The Collective is ever-present, always watching. I bury my head in my hands. "I want to tell you… "

He kneels before me, resting his chin on my knees. "Then tell me. No more secrets. God knows I have none. I'm not that complicated a bloke. If you're afraid I'm, you know, not going to like you or something afterwards, you needn't worry about that."

An ill-timed giggle escapes me. "You'd think I was pretty crazy."

"That so? What, you think the school is run by secret government agents, something like that?"

"And if that was my theory?"

"Well, that is a little crazy, but it doesn't make me like you any less." He rests his cheek on my leg, stroking my dress. "You should let me come on your adventures with your friends, perhaps. You're always making excuses that you're going off with them. It sounds…fun. Movies or walks or get-togethers. I can be fun too, you know."

I kiss his forehead, breathing in his scent. This is not making anything easier. The secret is still there, between us. Our words are just convenient distractions as we dance around the black hole that is the truth.

"I just want to know what frightens you. So that I can, somehow, you know, do something about it. If I can."

"And if you couldn't do anything about it?" I whisper.

The corner of his lip twitches into a half-smile. He gestures lazily at his paintings. "I always make mistakes when I'm drawing. So what do I do? I paint over them and try something else. Or I turn ill-placed lines into squiggly birds."

I giggle. "What if there aren't supposed to be birds in the picture?"

"I'm sure there's no picture that's not made better by birds."

I nuzzle closer to him. "I wish that you could paint over my fears."

"I could, if you tell me what they are. And if they're conveniently shaped. Kind of hard to make everything into birds." He pulls me closer to him, resting his head on mine. "I won't make you tell me any secrets," he decides, throwing me a glance. "I just want you to promise me that someday, you will tell me. Before you do anything rash."

"I will. I'll try."

"Really. This is a real promise. I don't want to wake up and find out you and your friends have gone and done something and you're suspended, and suddenly I can't see you anymore."

"That's not—"

"It doesn't matter. Just promise me you'll tell me the second you're ready."

"I promise."

He squeezes me tightly, and for a minute, neither of us says anything.

"I have to admit," Ethan says eventually, "I was half-hoping you'd be ready right this second."

The red light of the camera gags me. "I wish."

My bracelet is still annoyingly attached to my wrist. I could use it to deactivate the cameras, and spill everything. And...then what? How can I tell him that the person we thought was protecting him is going to eventually kill him, all in the name of science?

His lips brush mine, silencing my fearful thoughts. I throw my anxiety into a passionate kiss. I can't let him go. I need him to live. How am I supposed to survive this mess without him?

He trails a line of kisses across my cheek and tucks my hair around my ear. "Ingrid," he says softly. "Would you stay with me tonight?"

My eyebrows lift, and butterflies dance in my stomach. He looks somewhat embarrassed. "I mean, I'm not asking if we should do anything you don't want to do, but...I just really don't want you to leave me right now. The bed is small, but you're slight, and could fit, and I could lend you one of my old painting shirts..."

I grin and press my forehead to his. "Yes, yes. I am already sold." I look up into his bright green eyes, and it occurs to me that when he was sick at the performance centre, they had turned a brilliant cyan. I think I like them better green. "I don't think I could ever let you go in this moment anyway."

"I couldn't let you go in any moments, ever."

We do separate momentarily to get ready for bed. I quickly text Jia to tell her I'm just in Ethan's room so she doesn't think I've accidently teleported to Mars and set the phone on the nearby nightstand. I get Ethan to turn around as I remove my clothes and slip into his painting shirt. It's far too big for me and fits like a baggy dress, but it smells like him and that's comforting. He stares out the window, facing away from me; not even once does he dare peek. I smile.

"Okay, ready," I say.

He shyly turns as I slip under the covers. I'm anxious about showing him my bare legs. I've always been tall and lanky, probably why I prefer skirts to pants and other form-fitting clothes. He smiles, and then starts to take off his shirt, before slipping his head back through the hole. "Um...should I change here, or...? I was just going to take this off, put on some pyjama pants?"

I cover my eyes, even though I hate myself for it. I'm too shy to be sleeping over in his dorm. I've never done anything like this before. "I won't look, I promise."

"It's all right if you do. I mean, I don't have a six pack or anything, in case you were wondering."

I had been wondering. I grin. "That changes everything. I'm definitely not staying now."

"Aww."

A minute later, he switches out the lights, and joins me

in bed. We face each other in the dark as our legs entangle beneath the blankets. His pillows are so much softer than mine. I listen to his breathing as it slows into the hypnotizing rhythm of sleep. The reflected moonlight from the window outlines his form. He is beautiful. And he is ... mine ... in the very immediate sense of the word.

Is it selfish to love him? Light fingers stroke his cheek and a soft noise escapes him. Must he die so that many will live? What is my happiness in the face of countless lives, somewhere else on another planet?

I can't let him go. I will not let them take him.

I'm afraid to sleep. I'm tired of being afraid. I'm tired of being awake. I cannot stand vigil forever. Somewhere between the fear and the exhaustion and the flurry of emotions in my stomach that surround Ethan's name, I find peace in his arms, praying that when the sun returns, that Ethan is still with me.

CHAPTER 12

When I wake up, Ethan is gone.

Panic squeezes my heart, forcing me up. "Ethan?" I call softly.

Daylight streams through the window. Then, a toilet flushes in the bathroom.

I relax into the bed. Ethan hasn't gone. Ms. Agailya hasn't stolen him away and taken his genes to cure a race on the other side of the galaxy.

The bathroom door opens and he appears at the threshold, grinning when he sees I'm awake. "Hey, you."

"Hey." I pull the blankets around my chin, longing for more time in bed. "Sleep okay?"

"Yeah, all right." He laughs. "Well, not great. I mean, the bed is fairly small. I'm used to my space."

"My bed is bigger." Even though I'm sharing it right now with two other girls. I think about making a joke about that but then I remember the camera. "What time is it?"

"Nearly nine."

"Ugh." I sink back into bed. It's Thursday morning. I have to get ready for tutorial.

"I know the feeling." He sits on the edge of the bed and lays a hand on my legs hiding beneath the blankets. "Sooner we do it, the sooner it's done."

When he says it like that, anything seems easy. At least, until I look up at the light, and remember our intimate moment is being watched. Sighing deeply, I slip out of bed, and grab my clothes from yesterday from the floor. "Okay, I'm up."

"You don't want to be late for Jadore," he calls after me as I go into the bathroom.

"Oh, I know."

After we're both dressed and our things have been gathered, he locks his room and we head down the stairs, hand in hand. I don't care who sees. Cameras be damned. This man is under my protection. Mess with him, and I'll…figure out a way to exact revenge.

"So besides a tutorial, I don't have much else going on. What do you have to do today?" I ask.

"Meeting with Ms. Agailya."

My grip on him tightens as we descend to the lobby. The door is close. Too close. I can't let him go yet. "And what exactly will you be doing in this…meeting?"

"Same as we always do, likely. We chat. I talk about my art. She gives me feedback."

"Yeah, but she's not really an artist, right? She's not in a position to—"

"Actually she's an accomplished singer. She dabbles in art. It's more about finding better ways to express myself, through a kind of, well, I hate to use the term, but therapy. Talking with her about my creative pursuits, it's…I can't explain, even though it's just a conversation, it's like I come out of the sessions rejuvenated."

"But we can have those same conversations. Can't we?"

"Yeah. In a different sort of way. Why are you so concerned about me seeing her?"

Because she murdered one of my tutorial mates. Because she has you wrapped around her finger for an experiment. "I just…don't like her."

"You never told me that before." He shrugs. "I like her fine. Look, you'd better get going, or Jadore will—"

"Please don't go to your meeting with Ms. Agailya today."

I've gotten away with a lot with Ethan. He's trusted me even when I've said the strangest things, even when I've abandoned him for important missions with my friends. Yet now, he looks frustrated. "First you tell me not to go to the nurse when I'm sick. Now you don't like me going to my tutor?"

"Look. If I tell you why—"

"Yes, Ingrid. Please tell me why. Because it feels like you're trying to control me."

"I'm not."

"Well, then, what is going with you?"

I'm at a loss. Tell him, here in the lobby of Morris House? I'm not ready.

How can I tell him when I don't know if I can save him?

What if I can't save him?

Sighing, he seeks escape further down the hall. "I'm going to be late. And so are you. See you later."

"Ethan."

He ignores me and shuffles down the hallway, head down as he keeps up a determined pace until he's out of sight. There's no point in chasing him. Agailya has him in her ethereal grasp, wrapped up in her sick experiment, and I don't know what to do.

The day crawls by. Each minute that passes feels like it's being reluctantly plucked from my anxious, always-hungry stomach with a pair of long tweezers. I try to make myself quiet in tutorial, but Jadore yells at me again for not adequately explaining the origins of cognitivism. I'm on the verge of tears. While Misty remains indifferent or furious at me and quickly excuses herself to do whatever it is she does when she's not with us, Jia proposes that the two of us go for a run to blow off steam. Eager to do anything that will distract me, I agree.

After the two of us wolf down some near-rotten carrots, we change into our running clothes and shoes and set out along Sparkstone Boulevard. There's a walking trail along the grass that leads off the main road along some trees, along the large wall that surrounds the whole town. It's a safe route that probably doesn't have any bugs, if not cameras. Running does make me feel better. Running is also Jia's go-to activity, and I've gone with her several times now so I can keep pace with her, for the most part.

Twenty minutes of straight jogging leads me exhausted, and I slow down. We're nearly on the other side of town. It's nearing the end of the day; the sun gets ready to disappear behind the wall. A line of manicured trees line our dirt path, and the equally manicured houses are several feet away. Each house has a perfectly erected white picket fence separating the yards and this back path area, and each yard comes equipped with a BBQ. It's only about ten degrees and at this time of day, I fully expect to see at least one family grilling. Nothing. Probably because they're all aliens. Or the Hunger ate them all and those houses are just a ruse.

I sigh. Everything here is a ruse waiting to be blown open.

"Hey. Talk to me," Jia says, catching my arm.

We stop walking. My heart is pounding from the exercise, but also from the knowledge that someday, we're all going to die at the Collective's hand. "Okay. Where do you want me to start?"

She smiles ruefully. One of my favourite things about Jia is that she takes everything in stride. Nothing seems to faze her, except the thought of her sister falling into the Collective's hands.

"You stayed with Ethan last night. That's new."

"Yeah."

She raises her eyebrows. "Do you... want to talk about that?"

"I kinda do." I cross my arms. I hate wearing these yoga pants. I feel so exposed. "Nothing sexual happened. I don't even know... anyway." I blush. I'm so not good at girl talk. "This morning, we got into a fight. I tried to tell him not to see Agailya anymore..."

Jia's eyes widen. "Why? Ingrid!"

"I know. I just...I need to protect him. I can't stand the thought that..." I lower my voice, in case the trees are somehow bugged. "...that he could be abducted and dissected like Tilly was. I'd never forgive myself if that happened."

"I know what you mean." She leans against the nearest tree and stares in the direction of the residences. "So he won't speak with you?"

"No. I tried texting him a bunch. No response. I could just march up there and demand to see him...I don't know. He thinks probably thinks I'm some kind of wild conspiracy theorist with the way I've been acting. If I tell him the truth...it'll just push him away."

Jia does a lunge as she stretches her calf muscles. "Ingrid, I don't have Wil's power, but I've seen you with him. He really likes you. He's not going to go running if you tell him."

"So you think I should tell him."

"I...don't know if I can give a good answer to that. Yes, I think you should. Agailya could decide to harvest him tomorrow. Time is precious."

I pace frantically, searching for a distraction from the images of Tilly's dissection that haunt my brain. "Thanks for bearing with me, but let's talk about something else, okay? Or...we can just run."

"Sure. Any time you need to talk, we can," she says, lifting her arms up high and leaning side to side. "Like if you want to talk about what's going on with you and Misty, for instance."

I sigh, and copy her motions. The stretch feels good on my

aching body. "I don't know if I really want to go there either. I put my foot where I shouldn't have on that one too."

"Well... I don't want to be a go-between for the two of you, but when I tried to talk about it with her, she said she's waiting for you to make the first move on that. And I know from previous experience that Misty is not one to initiate apologies."

Don't apologize until you know what you're apologizing for. Sorry Misty, that I am the worst friend, that I think I'm better than you, because clearly I don't have the handle on my emotions that I thought I did. I blow out a long sigh. "I'll keep that in mind. Now, enough about me. Tell me some Jia gossip."

"Oh. Well," Jia's lips twitch into a shy smile as she brings her knees up slowly while standing in place.

"What?" I ask.

"It's about Wil," she says. "I'm... I'm thinking about asking him out."

"Oh!" I don't mean to sound so surprised. It just falls out of me. "Are you sure that's a good idea, Jia?"

"Well... do you think it's a good idea?"

I try to hide my conflicted feelings. Wil confided in me weeks ago that he doesn't want to get involved in a relationship because of his power. Sometimes it overwhelms him and he is afraid he would unintentionally violate a girl's privacy. He also hinted that he has feelings not for Jia, but for Kimberly, Ethan's fast-talking, artistic best friend.

I draw in a deep breath and think about how to dissuade Jia while still keeping Wil's confidence when Jia strides away from me. "Never mind. The timing is not right anyway. He would know I was coming, and try to avoid the subject."

"Yeah..." I scuff my running shoes on the sidewalk, but I can't let the subject drop completely. "Have you tried asking him before?"

She slows her pace, allowing me to catch up. "Not in so many words. I've thought about it, while he was around. He probably knows. He always knows everything." Her face heats. "I don't know why I've let myself become caught up with him, with these feelings, when we're in the middle of a war."

I smile. "We have to have some good things. How else are we supposed to fight the bad?"

"These feelings are not good. They are...dangerous. The Collective could discover them. They could...torture him. Take him away for his power. I would not be able to survive that. I could survive many things. I have survived many things. But I could not hide from his death. It would always be here."

I wish she hadn't have said that. Ethan had been at death's door and yet when I'd begged the Collective to save him—my last resort—they had complied. They needed him alive, at least for the time being, for Ms. Agailya's mysterious research. But now that I know Wil's fate, if not when, I don't know what I can say that will console her.

"Maybe in a few months, I'll try, maybe," Jia whispers. She looks up at me now, hopeful. "Maybe we'll have figured everything out by them."

She's being overly optimistic on purpose, trying to cheer us both up. I'm quiet for a full fifteen seconds as I finish my arm stretches, debating whether or not to tell her what Campbell has prophesized.

Instead, I say, "Maybe we'll get the upper hand on Jadore, and find a way to defeat her."

"Or maybe we'll convince a bunch of government leaders to rally against the Collective's influence, and drive them from our solar system!"

"Yes! And maybe everyone who has superpowers will be free to express them in public, and we can take control of the school. We can all become Professor X's. Or whatever X-Men we want. Without the whole mutants vs humans thing. Just skip to the good parts." My burdens feel lighter just thinking about that impossible, wild fantasy.

"That sounds nice," Jia concedes. "And then maybe Sunni will magically return to the land of the living."

We fall silent again as our wishful thinking fades with the setting sun. That's not a thing I can say maybe to, because it is too close to a yes.

That evening, at six-thirty, I receive a text from Wil asking me to come to Conrod Building for seven instead of eight. The text is dated earlier this morning. I sigh. I change into jeans, a plain t-shirt, and braid my hair before heading out with my warmest cardigan. I also text Ethan a thousand times to apologize for my stupid mouth. He doesn't reply, which tears me to pieces. I'm hoping that whatever experiments Wil wants to run on me will be an adequate distraction for my raging hormones and well-founded fears.

I text Wil but it's not necessary: he's at the door, waiting to let me in. He seems relieved and welcomes me inside. The last time I was in Conrod Building, we were searching for a shuttle that would take us to the mother ship. That was obviously before I was in (slightly more) control of my powers. Wil leads me through a series of corridors and then uses his key card to scan us into his lab.

Inside, it's larger and far brighter than I thought it would be. Five rows of green counters take up most of the room. There's a shorter, near-identical green counter at the front and a whiteboard behind it, likely for demonstrations. Sparkstone doesn't have traditional professors, but Wil has told me that it isn't beyond Sparkstone to bring in guest lecturers for particular disciplines. On the left side of the wall there are a series of shelves, a fume hood, and one large armoire-type closet with a keyed padlock. At the back of the room, there's a rinsing station, and more cabinets and counters built into the walls, and two closed laptops plugged in to pristine, white sockets.

A large portion of the right wall, from the middle of the room to the front, is floor-to-ceiling windows. It's dark now, but I can imagine in the day that this is one of the nicer labs to work in.

"I've permanently altered the cameras in this room, so we can speak freely," he says as he leads me to the second counter from the front—his work station. "Ever since Daniel disappeared, I've done my best to secure the room to prevent any others from being taken."

The fluorescents buzz annoyingly though my steps break the monotonous tone. All counters are bare except his. He's tinkering with what looks like a desktop computer, but half the size. A set of tools lays scattered to his right. As I come around the counter, I see the flickering lights, confusing, meandering tubes, three hard drives, and over a dozen memory sticks within the box.

"It's almost finished," he says, patting the top of the case affectionately. "Just putting the final touches on it now."

"Is this what you've built to convince Hildie to leave?" Thinking about her, sitting in that dorm room by herself, makes me sick. I should have checked in with her today, especially after all she told me.

"It's...part of that," he admits. Wil holds something with both hands inside the box as he concentrates deeply.

"Do you even need these?" I ask, picking up the smallest screwdriver I've ever seen.

"Sometimes. I can manipulate the inner workings of most machines, but I'm not Magneto."

"How does it work? Because...I hate to sound disparaging, but you've been spending all your time in here, and all you've been able to create is a slightly smaller desktop computer?"

Wil raises an eyebrow and looks sceptical. He doesn't tear his concentration from the box.

"What? C'mon Wil. I'm not stupid. Tell me how this thing works. It has to be more than what it looks like."

"Didn't say you were stupid. I just don't think explaining this machine would really help you understand."

"You offering a demonstration?"

"Now you're really getting into dangerous territory."

I set the tool down. "Why did you ask me to come here?"

Normally, Wil is good at hiding his emotions, probably because he spends his life defending his mind from other people's thoughts. A flash of panic crosses his face as he opens his eyes. "I promised you I'd tell you about my secret project when I was ready."

"Right...but what about the experiments? If you want to talk about your secret project, why not call Jia and Misty? Isn't this something we should all hear?"

"You can tell them," he says simply. "And the experiments can wait for now."

Something about this scenario doesn't feel right to me. "Okay, out with it."

Wil blows a long sigh. "I knew it would only be a matter of time before Mrs. Harris showed up. Before any of the parents of the missing students showed up. I had to do something to minimize the damage to our progress here and find a way to set the Collective back permanently.

"When we allowed Laura to take the fall for the protest, you said that it was the wrong thing for us to do. So after the protest failed, I decided that I had to take drastic action, and if that failed, it would be me and me alone that would take the fall. Sacrificing the few so the many can live is the best solution."

I grip the underside of the counter. "Wil...what have you done?"

"Like the Hunger, I've been...collecting information,"

Wil says. "First, all knowledge of the disappearances from any close friends of the missing students. Interviewed them exhaustively about the day their friend disappeared. Recorded the conversation. Stored it on the device I've created." He lands a careful hand on the computer case. "Then, erased all knowledge of the event in their minds and on any nearby cameras. At first, it wasn't easy to walk into a dorm, initiate a conversation, and then erase all knowledge of the event, both in the mind and on the camera. After the first ten, I found myself getting pretty good at it.

"When Mr. and Mrs. Trites arrived, I sensed their intensions, and stopped them before they could confront a professor. I interviewed them, recorded their experiences, and erased all knowledge of them meeting me."

"Why didn't you just make them turn around and leave? Why did they go to Mystic Shadows? Why let them walk into the belly of the beast?"

"Ingrid, let's say you wanted to learn a particular tune on the piano. It's hard. One day, you sit down and manage to master it. I come along, and erase the memory of that day. It's not going to stop you from *wanting* to master the tune. You're going to sit down and try again."

"Can't you erase the desire too?"

"It's... tricky. Too much tinkering leads to permanent damage." I feel like he's speaking from experience, yet he doesn't elaborate. "The Trites saw Shadow's flyer. They were desperate to try anything. If not for the fire scaring them away, they would have stayed and tried again the next day, likely.

"After Mystic Shadows burned, I knew I had to try to gain

evidence of alien involvement. After I left you in the dorm, I went back to the site. Hafelglob were swarming everywhere, trying to control the flames, trying to recapture the Hunger.

"I'm not Misty. I can't subdue a handful of aliens with my hands. I only have the power of mind. But I did manage to lead one away from Mystic Shadows and planted the suggestion that I was on their side. He told me his orders: recapture the Hunger. Clean up the site. Eliminate all people associated with Mystic Shadows. I even managed to get him to transform from his human form to hafelglob form. I captured it on video. Added that to my stash."

My heart pounds. "You said that Shadow was...gone."

"By the time I'd interrogated the hafelglob, convinced them that the site didn't need a thorough clean up, and that recapturing the Hunger was the clean-up crew's top priority..." He shakes his head. "I watched them wrap her body and put it in a truck."

No wonder there were so few hafelglob at the site when I visited the next day. But at such a high cost. "You could have saved them."

"I have a video of a hafelglob. That's more ammunition than some book stolen from an underground library."

Blood rushes to my face. "That book is important. I just...haven't figured out why yet."

"An omnipotent alien is not my concern. You've made it yours, perhaps to your detriment. If he was on our side, he'd be here helping. Although," he says, holding up a finger before I can retort, "there has been more activity around that library ever since we broke in there. Jadore *is* looking for that book. She's obsessed with him almost as much as you are. I was going to return to the library, but I... haven't had a spare moment. I'll leave that mission to you."

My fingernails dig into my palms. I'm so furious I can barely string a sentence together. "Why didn't you tell us about any of this?"

"If all of you knew about the operation before I was taken, it could have destroyed everything I am working towards. Better that only I knew until the right time."

The right time. "Wil... why are you telling me all this now?"

"If the Collective were to ever get a hold of this, it would be disastrous. My project has attracted a lot of attention. Many gaps in camera feeds. And I'm not as good at manipulating alien minds."

It takes a second for his words to sink in. "They know what you're doing."

He takes a long, deep breath. "More or less. My access card has been tampered with. They've limited my access to this building and my dorm."

"They're going to take you soon." A chill runs through me as I speak the words aloud. "Why take this risk, Wil? The four of us are supposed to be a team. We could have figured out a less... aggressive... situation."

He presses his lips together, and he heaves a long sigh, as if he's had this conversation a thousand times. "We've been fighting this like it's a cold war. That's no longer the case. The Collective has been aggressively targeting students who have shown some potential for power, and have taken them. They're ramping up. We have to do the same if we're going to survive. This isn't about keeping secrets anymore. The Collective already knows we're a threat, even if they're unsure of just how much damage we could do to them. Now it's about survival. Ensuring that the progress we've made isn't lost."

I round the counter, seeing the computer case in a whole new light. "We could let our families know the truth."

"I've collected the data and stored it somewhere safe. We can leak it and put the spotlight on the Collective. Whether or not the world believes us...maybe that's less important than actually getting some firepower on our side. If I'd only had more time..." He shakes his head. He looks amused, and a rare smile crosses his face. "My device could have been more advanced. I could have created it to store our memories of what has happened here. Make multiple copies. Send them digitally to our families, our friends, the government, into space via a capsule. Anything so that what we've done here won't be forgotten." Wil fiddles with a tiny circuit board absently. "I've made do with what I've been given."

"If you're so concerned with preserving yourself and preparing for the worst," I say hesitantly, "then maybe you should tell Kimberly how you feel. That's what I would do."

He hesitates, picking up a screwdriver. "It would crush Jia."

"She'll get over it."

"Jia is my friend. Kimberly is...important to me. I don't want to hurt her while I'm gone."

"So you're saying you'd rather date Jia, because it's less of a risk?"

"I'm saying I don't want to date anyone, and that I'm tired of erasing—" He stops himself, but it's too late.

"Wil ... did you ... erase parts of our minds too?" I'm hesitant to even ask.

He pauses too long before answering. "No."

"You're lying."

Wil heaves another sigh. "I suppose it's appropriate to purge all my sins." He closes his eyes briefly and for the first time, I'm afraid of my powerful, mind-manipulating friend. "Today, you went for a run with Jia. She told you she's going to ask me out."

"Yeah. But I don't appreciate you looking into my mind to find out that info."

"Sorry. Trying to prove a point. Why do you think, with her feelings as strong as they are, that she hasn't done that already?"

I blink. "Obviously because she doesn't want to ruin your friendship. And like you've made clear. We're in the middle of a ... " I trail off, stunned. "She's already asked you out, hasn't she?"

He closes the flap on his computer case and carefully stows it in a shelf beneath the desk. "A couple of times." He appears embarrassed. "And she's right. I can't stand the thought of ruining our friendship. We need to be able to work together if we're going to defeat the Collective. Romantic attachments will only get in the way, Ingrid."

No. My feelings for Ethan make me stronger. He makes this entire prison worth bearing. My vision blurs. I should have eaten more before I came. I'm exhausted, and dealing with this betrayal is too much for my starved body.

"I can't believe you did that to Jia. And let me guess. You're going to do it to me too, now that I know?"

"No. I need you to be mad at me right now. It'll make this next part easier."

I back away from Wil. I don't know what the hell he means by next part, but I'm not sure if I want to stick around and find out.

"Ingrid, please don't leave. I'm not going to hurt you. I'm sorry I didn't tell you this before. Like I said. I can't kill her desire for me, just like I can't kill your desire to get out of here. That would be inhumane. Just...help me clean up here first. Okay?"

I back against the counter at the front of the room. "How do I know you're not manipulating me right now?"

"You know your own mind. You know when I'm routing around in there—you can feel it, like you can feel a Q-tip when it enters your ear. Hard as I try, it's not easy to disguise that feeling."

With a sinking feeling, I know he's not making me stay. It's my own curiosity, my admiration for my friend, and my desire to save him that keeps my feet planted firmly on the checkered tile floor. "What do we need to clean up?"

"Just wipe down my counter space. Could you grab us some paper towel?"

There's a paper towel roll on the counter behind me. I rip off a piece for him, and one for me. The thought of running crosses my mind. I could tell Jia the truth. I could patch things up with Misty—she knew Wil was dangerous, why didn't I listen to her? Conflicted, I pass the paper towels to Wil. He strides down the room to the sink at the back, wets them, and returns to his station. I could have run within that time. Wil passes me one of the wet towels and we proceed to wipe down his counter space. His clean-up process is calm and methodical, despite not making much of a mess in the first place. I wipe down the area next to him to keep my hands busy.

"Thanks for staying with me, Ingrid. I appreciate it," he says. "And I'm glad you were able to come even though I changed the time. I was going to reach out telepathically had you not shown up."

"Yeah." There's little point in speaking to him. He knows what I'm thinking. He knows what he did is wrong—I think. All I know is that Jia deserves to know the truth.

"If that's what you want to do," Wil says softly. "It will break her heart."

"Then you break her heart. Don't cover it up. You do that, and you're no better than the Hunger."

He stops wiping the counter and stares thoughtfully out the window. It's pitch black; the only thing we can see are our reflections and a mirror image of the lab around us. He stiffens suddenly. His fingers dig into the wet towel, squeezing dirty water around his hand.

I'll always be there for you, Ingrid, he says.

I glance between our reflections and Wil. "Uh huh…"

You know I'm trying to help you and the others, right?

"Yeah, in your own twisted way." Now I'm getting worried.

Wil has gone from in control to tense as a deer before it crosses the road. "Are you okay, Wil?"

The thing about friendship, he says, walking closer to the windows, away from me. *You'll get it from us, regardless of what you feel you deserve. And you need us more than ever—just as I need you now. I hope you can feel the same.*

"You've done a terrible thing and now you've made me part of it. I don't know if it makes you or me undeserving of friendship. I'm too angry at you to think about that right now."

My comment jolts him from contemplation as he spins around. "That's why you have to listen to me, Ingrid. I need you to get in that cupboard, and stay there."

"Uh..." I take a step back. Wil isn't joking. He points to the large, locked storage cupboard behind me against the wall. "What do you know that I don't, Wil?"

"A great deal. And yes to your next question. Someone *is* coming. You need to hide, or they'll take you too."

I draw a sharp breath in and rush toward him. "No, no, no. I'm not letting them take you. I know what they do to kidnapped students, I saw Tilly die, and I know that—"

Wil catches wind of what I refuse to speak out loud, and it throws him off for a second. The knowledge of Joseph Campbell's prophecy, his vision of the future, blooms in his dark eyes. "If you try to teleport me away, we could end up who knows where."

"It's worth a try. Don't you want to *try?*"

"No. I'm done with that. I've set things in motion that can't be undone. Get in the cupboard, Ingrid."

"I'm not going anywhere!"

"Yes, you are."

He grabs me and walks me backward. I nearly trip with the force of him against me but he holds me fast. I grab the nearby long lab table and attempt to wrench from his grip as he throws open the cupboard door. For a brief second, his grasp slips. I'm free. Surprised, I fall backward, one hand gripping the end of the lab...

...and then I am suspended in mid-air.

I'm trying to help you. You are making this harder than it has to be.

"Wil. Don't do this." Tears well in my eyes. He could let me go at any moment, and I would crash to the ground. Though I'm maybe two feet from the ground, I'd still probably suffer a terrible head injury.

I trusted him. Wil is supposed to be my friend.

We are at war, Ingrid, he says, not unkindly. *We have to do what is necessary to defeat the enemy. We all have to do our part.*

Whatever part of my brain acquiescing to Wil's command loosens—a feeling similar to a relaxing a muscle. Not completely, though. He gently guides my body to the floor with his mind, setting me down on the tile with all the grace of a feather drifting to the ground.

When did he learn to do this?

Into the cupboard. You'll be safe in there. His expression is one of desperation and pain.

Despite my instinct to run, it is with a heavy heart that I step into the empty cupboard. There are supports for shelves; they have been removed. Wil has been planning this. Perhaps for some time. The cupboard is just tall enough for me to stand in; I turn and face him, hands by my side, hoping against hope that he will hear reason.

"Teleport out if you can," he says. "But I doubt you have the power. It would be easier if you just listened."

"Wil, I—"

He slams the cupboard shut, and I can hear the click of a metal lock and the toss of a key. I bang against the door. It won't budge. Now I'm terrified.

"Wil!"

If you don't be quiet, they'll take you too, and then we'll all be lost.

I stop banging on the door, even though every instinct in my body wants to scream. I shift my position and lean against the back wall. "How long do I have to be in here?"

For as long as this room is compromised. Now listen. There are three pieces, he tells me. *They fit together. They look like this.*

An unescapable image appears before my mind's eye: three pieces of silver, nearly identical. The three pieces slide together and form a USB drive.

You and Jia and Misty have to find them. Destroy them as a last resort, but they contain all the evidence we need to prove the harm the Collective is doing to Earth.

"Evidence," I whisper. "Where are they?"

If I told you their locations, it would destroy the work I've put into protecting them. You were right to suspect the computer on the counter. It's a decoy. There are several in the lab, in my dorm, one is buried in the quad. This is to buy you all some time. The real information is stored on three USB pieces. Fit them together and you'll have everything you need to prove to the authorities of Earth that we are being invaded. To find them, figure out the clues I've placed around campus. Now be quiet. And stay quiet until you're positive no one is around. Cameras in this room are off—they've been off for some time now, ever since they dispatched hafelglob and others to this location. A pause, and then: *I have to fight them to make my struggle legitimate—to prove I didn't know they were coming. No matter what you hear, don't come out.*

Wil. No. Don't let them take you.

I have to. My powers are putting the rest of you in danger. Use what I've created to help. Protect the others.

I place my hand on the door. You don't have to sacrifice yourself, Wil. You don't have to die now. We need you.

Glass breaks, and the sounds of struggle hide my gasps. I bite down on my finger and close my eyes, but my body feels too heavy to leave the cupboard by means of teleportation. Each sound keeps me grounded in reality. The squishing of the hafelglob. Wil's cries for help. The sounds of gunfire. Someone collapsing to the ground. Then a faint *zap*.

Then, only the sounds of the building, the heating system, and my intermittent, terrified breathing.

PART THREE

If she learns the why, she will learn the how.

—J.G.C., *Campbell's Multiple Verses*

CHAPTER 13

I wait in the darkness for some time, my adrenaline buzz eventually leaving me exhausted. I doze off, and it's only when I jolt awake several hours later, trying desperately to recall why I'd choose such a cramped space as a bed, that I remember that I have a phone.

It's eight a.m. No doubt Wil's lab mates or a clean-up crew will be in here soon, if they aren't out there already. Shifting to my knees, I press against the door. It rattles back in protest. Right. I'm locked in here.

I close my eyes. *Ethan. Think of Ethan. And not the fact that my friend locked me in here, betrayed my trust, and has tasked me with finding his project.*

Sighing, I whip out my phone. Now isn't the time for experimentation, not now that his life is at stake. I've already spent several hours sleeping. Who knows how many more hours I could waste in teleportation. I text Misty and Jia our secret code number for trouble and my location. Hopefully Wil was kind enough to leave the key handy. Hopefully Misty and Jia are able to make it into Conrod Building—everyone's key card is coded differently, depending on their residence and their majors.

I wait urgently for a response. Each noise sends new panic searing into my stomach, distracting me from my hunger. I try to picture the scene just a few feet in front of me. I imagine the cupboard doors opening and coming face to face with Ohz, and being whisked away to Agailya's lab.

Stop it, I tell myself. *I'm going to get out of here. My friends are on the way now.*

Moments later, the door clicks open. I hold my breath.

"Jesus Christ," Misty says, and emits a low whistle as the door shuts again. "What the hell happened in here?"

"The blood...!" Jia exclaims.

"In here!" I call, tapping on the cupboard door.

"Where's the key?" Jia asks. I hear her scurry towards me.

"Don't know. Must be somewhere."

Misty curses under her breath and the two of them quickly the search the area. After several minutes, Jia finds the key. She pops it into the lock and I hear a joyous click.

I don't know if I've ever been more pleased to see Misty and Jia.

"Thank god," I say, leaning against Jia for support.

Misty stands back, arms folded. She doesn't appear unhappy to see me—she's still not talking to me—but she does look relieved that I'm not hurt.

"I dampened the cameras as soon as I came in," she says, pointing at her wrist. "We had to wait for someone to enter the building to get in."

"Wil said he disabled the cameras in this room, but probably a good call." Who knows how fast they can be repaired, and if they can be fixed remotely. The red light, in any case, is still on.

"So. What the hell happened here? Where's Wil?" Misty demands.

I swallow hard. This is the most she's said to me in nearly a week. "Wil's...gone."

"Gone?" Jia echoes.

"The Collective took him."

The story tumbles out of me. I'm interrupted several times as Misty demands clarification and scoffs at Wil's hypocrisy. Jia's expression becomes more emotional as I go on, her usual calm and collected presence broken down by the lengths Wil has gone to *protect* us. I don't dare tell her that he manipulated her mind.

The computer Wil was working on is gone. Scattered pieces of blank pages litter the floor. The entire lab has been ransacked and all of Wil's research, stolen. A cursory glance around the rest of the room, it appears that the rest of the projects and gadgets stored in this room have not been touched. Only Wil's stuff.

Wil knew they were coming for him. He had prepared this. Even a night in the cupboard hasn't dulled that fact.

By the windows, where the glass has been broken in, there's a trail of blood, stark against the white tile, leading around the island lab table. It forms a sizable, messy pool.

"Oh goodness," Jia says, covering her mouth in alarm.

Misty lets out a string of swears. "That's too much. Too much blood. He's—"

"No. Don't say it. He can't be," Jia says firmly. "I won't accept his death."

"All this time. I knew he was up to no good. That bastard!" Misty hurls a ball of ice at the cupboard, slamming the doors shut and freezing them in place.

"He said...he did this to protect us. So that we'd have something to take to the authorities to mount a real resistance!"

"Don't you get it?" Misty says. "The three of us in this room are the resistance. We're the only ones who can stop the Collective now. Sure, Wil collected us a ton of evidence—but who the hell are we supposed to give it to? The prime minister? The minister of defense, or whoever is in control of the military in this goddamn country? Yeah, have fun trying to get to Ottawa unless Dorothy Goody-Two-Shoes here clicks her feet together and transports us there. That would be convenient."

"Yeah. Real helpful," I retort. "As soon as I can control myself, I will do exactly that. But first we need to find those drive pieces."

"He should have just told us where they are," Misty mutters, pacing the room.

"Better to make it hard to find than have them fall into the Collective's hands."

"USB drive pieces that small could literally be anywhere!" Misty sneers at Jia. "You're always defending him. Doesn't this prove to you that he's a terrible person? How many awful, questionably moral things does he have to do before you can see that your trust in him is misplaced?"

Jia's lip quivers. Her determined gaze befalls mine. I don't feel like I deserve her friendship right now. Instead, I speak to Misty. "Wil didn't ask us to find him. He asked us to find the evidence he collected. Don't you see that he's sacrificing himself so that we can be free?"

Misty listlessly roams the lab, picking up stray beakers and computer parts. "Bastard tells us not to write things down, and gives us a hard time when we break the rules. Now when he decides to bend the rules in the name of the greater good, we have to spend time cleaning up his mess, and following his orders from beyond the grave."

"He can't be dead," Jia insists.

My stomach curls with guilt.

"Even if he's not, how do we know the Collective aren't forcing him to use his power against us?" Misty argues. "They have an all-powerful cloud that can take and give memories to people. Combine that with Wil's power? Yeah. We are not in good shape right now. This is the endgame."

The image of the Hunger fogging up the glass prison in Agailya's lab makes me shudder. "All the more reason to find what Wil has hidden so we can use it against the Collective," I say. "Let's just see what we can find before a clean-up crew comes."

Misty sighs but doesn't argue any further.

Jia picks up every single scattered piece of paper on the floor and sorts them. Misty tries the desktops in the room, swearing as she fails to guess the passwords. Once she's punched two of the monitors in frustration, she moves on to the shelves and cupboards lining the walls. I check in every cubby and shelf beneath the lab desks.

All five rows of counters are exactly identical, except for one. On the bottom left-hand corner of the desk at the back of the room, there's something wedged on the bottom, seemingly propping up the desk. At first, it appears to be a block of wood to even out the wobbly desk. Upon closer inspection, however, it appears to be a tightly folded piece of paper, not unlike the other scattered paper that Jia sorts at Wil's station.

Thankfully, my fingernails are just long enough to be useful. I pry it out, nearly bending my nails in the process. It could be nothing—could be a forgotten love note for Wil, from Wil, or some other Sparkstone student. Or it really could just be a lazy form of support. The desk doesn't appear unstabilized by this action, and the place where the paper was seems perfectly cut out and smooth—as if someone placed this in there on purpose.

"Found something," I say, bringing it back to Wil's station.

Misty joins us at the desk and Jia nervously taps her fingers on the countertop as I carefully unfold the note. It's been folded more than eight times, and tightly packed, as if done by a machine.

"You sure this is ... " Misty begins, but as soon as she sees the red ink on the paper, her eyes go round. "Oh. Holy ... "

The scrawl is written in blaring red pen: a collection of random numbers and letters, as well as a dollar sign in the middle. It appears to be nonsense, although Misty snatches it from my hand.

"That's ... " She steels her gaze. "That's last night's configuration."

Jia frowns. "That isn't any of our codes."

"Not our group codes. It's..." She briefly glances at me before returning her gaze to the scrap paper longingly. "Remember when I told you I write messages in code to Sunni sometimes, on my phone?"

Right. "Wil must have read your mind and used it to send a message."

"Can you translate it?" Jia asks.

"Yeah. Pen?"

We find her a pen, and she begins to decrypt the message. There are fourteen characters on the piece of paper, and Misty pairs them off, attributing a letter to each pair. It takes her less than thirty seconds before we are left with a new puzzle.

Mikdinf

"A password?" I say, squinting. "Seems too simple for someone like Wil."

"Yeah, especially considering he can just charm computers into giving him whatever information he wants," Misty remarks. After another second, she scoffs. "Oh, c'mon. That's too easy. Mikdinf? It's *Find Kim* backwards."

"Kimberly?" Jia says hesitantly. "Why would he want us to do that? What does she have to do with all this?"

Other than his feelings for her? God, the things just keep piling up. We don't have time to quibble over relationships. I let that slip, everything else will follow, and then we will truly be doomed. "I guess she's one of the clues. Or she has one of the pieces."

Misty shoves the piece of paper into her pocket. "He'd

entrust a bunch of evidence against the Collective to a random ditz, but not one of his own?"

"Moreover, what would he have done if we hadn't found this slip of paper?" Jia says under her breath.

"I suppose we would have run into her eventually," I say.

Jia purses her lips. "We don't have time for eventually."

"Agreed. I might have her number." I scroll through my phone.

"We should get out of here anyway," Misty says, glancing at the broken glass on the floor. "Sooner or later, a clean-up crew is going to be in here. I'm surprised one didn't come already."

That is also troubling. "The Collective is going to watch our every move." Especially if they've already dissected Wil and found a way to use his powers against us. "We should hurry."

As Jia, Misty, and I invisibly escape the Conrod Building, I phone Kimberly. Somehow I'm not surprised when it goes directly to voicemail.

"Hey, it's Kimberly here, leave it after the beep! Oh, and by it, you know I mean name and number and stuff...I mean...you probably know that. Though, if you are calling me and intend to leave a message, I probably already know who you are. Even so, I'd really appreciate it if you left your name so—"

BEEP!

"Uh...hey, Kimberly. It's Ingrid. Ingrid Stanley. Call me as soon as you get this. Otherwise, I'll just come to your dorm. It's important."

"We should head there anyway," Jia suggests. "She might be painting and not checking her messages."

"Good point."

"We probably shouldn't stay invisible too long, in case we spot Kimberly," Misty says.

We duck behind Conrod Building, in one of the building's blind spots, and emerge from Jia's invisible world. The three of us fan out. The quad isn't too busy at nearly nine in the morning, besides some runners and a couple of maintenance men across the quad. I realize with a sinking feeling that Kimberly might still be in bed.

"Jia's right. Let's just go back to the dorms," I say. My stomach rumbles. It's been too long since I've eaten. I could get some breakfast on the way.

My phone buzzes—a call from Kimberly. I answer it immediately. "Hey! I just called you."

"Yeah! What's up?"

"I'm just outside Rita House. Want to come outside for a minute?"

"Sure, I'm heading outside anyway."

"Okay. See you soon."

Kimberly exits Rita House a few minutes later. She has white earphones in, attached to her phone, which she holds tightly in one hand. She rocks out silently to her music, mouthing along to the lyrics.

"Hey, Kimberly!" I say, waving to get her attention.

She pulls out her earphones and seems a little overwhelmed as Jia, Misty, and I surround her.

"Hey, Ingrid! Haven't heard from you in a while. And...Jia...and Misty, right?" She smiles at each of us. "What's up? Have you seen Wil? He isn't answering my texts."

I blink. "I haven't seen him since last night. Are you...expecting him?"

"Yeah, I was supposed to meet Wil. For coffee. At the bakery? Did he leave his dorm? I guess you might not know that. It's so early in the morning! Bleh!"

"Nope," Misty and I reply, while Jia asks, "Coffee?"

Kimberly picks up on Jia's question. "Yeah. I know, I'm trying to cut back on caffeine and focus on using only my natural energy! It's really hard though." She wags her hands in the air and dances on the spot. "But he's been working so much on his project recently, and I'm the worst at sitting down and working. Procrastination, am I right?"

She looks to Misty for affirmation, and receives only an icy stare.

"Ookay," Kimberly says, realizing that Misty is a lost cause. "Well, I texted him, and got no reply. And he usually replies within like ten minutes? So...yeah. Kinda worried." Her gaze drops to her shoes. "You guys haven't seen him, have you?"

"No," Jia says quietly. Her voice wavers the tiniest amount, picked up by my sensitive, musical ears. "You'll tell us if you see him?"

"Yes. Definitely. You're...looking for him too?" Kimberly seems mildly confused by this. "I mean it's right now we are supposed to meet for coffee. He said he'd be free, right?" She has a sudden brainwave. "Oh. OH. His lab. *Duh-doi*. He's probably so engrossed in whatever he's doing in there that he forgot. Have you guys checked—"

"Don't go in there," Jia says just as Misty says, "We already tried that."

"Whoa, *ookay*. You couldn't get into the lab, or you know for sure he's not in there?"

"He's not in there," Misty says, casting Jia and me threatening gazes. She takes charge of our fiction. "Maybe his room?"

"Mmm. Yeah. I'll see if Ethan is around." She grips the top of her head suddenly and furiously starts scratching. "Itchy! Maybe he'll let me into the guys' dorms. Yeah?" She winks at me, still trying to relieve the itch. "Word is you got in easy enough."

She takes out her phone and her thumb flies across the screen while her other hand works on her head.

I frown. "Uh, Kimberly, I don't want to get too personal here, but—"

"Hmm?" She stops texting and scratching and peers up at me.

"Are you using different shampoo? Maybe it would help you with that itch."

"Itch! What itch? Oh." She laughs nervously. "It's weird, it was so itchy, but it's fine now. Yeah, I guess I should switch shampoos. If only we had variety here, right? I mean, the drug store barely has enough tampons, and always during my time of the month, it's like, ladies are we all bleeding at the same time? Why is there never enough? Do I have to be in charge of ordering? So sometimes, I just go into the store and buy enough to satisfy an army of Amazons. Get what I'm saying? I have to take, like, four bags, and my bag is—ugh, goddamnit, this ITCH!"

"Let's go visit Ethan," Misty says, backing away slowly.

"Oh Ethan! Right! Sorry, let me finish this—" Kimberly lets out a string of swears as she drops her phone. Both hands are busy trying to relieve her scalp of the random itches.

"Wait a minute," I say. "Kimberly, let's talk about Wil for sec."

Like magic, she stops scratching. "Sure! He's supposed to meet me for coffee this afternoon. Have you seen him? He's probably in his lab. Have you checked?"

The three of us exchange worried glances. "He's not in here."

"Oh. Hmm. Oh, that's weird, my phone is on the ground. I'm so clumsy." She bends to pick it up, and wipes the stray grass from the screen. It reveals the text she was sending Ethan. "Right. I was texting Ethan... ugh no, not again, stupid *SKULL!*"

Kimberly releases her phone and Jia catches it with uncanny reflexes. Before she can hurt herself, I grab Kimberly's hands. "Stop it." They continue to shake and dig as I pull them away from her head, but she doesn't resist.

"What is going on here?" Misty asks hesitantly.

"I think I have an idea," I mutter. Looks like Jia's mind isn't the only one that he has tampered with. "Kimberly, tell me where you're going today."

She looks confused. "I think I already did, right? To meet

Wil?" She glances up at my hands holding hers above her head. "Is this a thing we're doing now? Holding hands? Did you know in some cultures, best friends hold hands?" Her eyes grow wide. "Ingrid, I admire you so much. I'd love to be best friends with you. I think we have a lot in common and later maybe you should come to coffee with me and—"

"Sure, later. Hey, would you do me a favour and tell me who you were texting just then on your phone?"

"My phone. Oh. Jia has it, I dropped it again, right? I was texting... Ethan... oh, so itchy, Ingrid, please let me scratch... "

I hold her hands steady as she struggles. "Okay, let's think about something else. The drug store, you said, sometimes you go there?"

Immediately her hands still. "Uh... sure... when I need to, you know, buy stuff. Is it weird that we're holding hands still, above my head?"

"Yes," Misty says. She sighs. "You think this is Wil's doing, Ingrid?"

"Has to be," I agree. I gently guide her hands down by her side but keep them firmly in mind. "Sorry for being weird, Kimberly. I'm running a little psych experiment, but if I tell you why I'm doing it, it could taint the outcome. You're going to meet Wil for coffee today. Is this something you do often?"

"Well, yeah!" She seems surprised that I don't know this. "Especially the past week or so? Every day. He's so sweet. I mean, I know I prattle on and on and on. I know I can be annoying. But he just... listens, you know? Even when I send him little *emails*, he always—" She struggles against my grip.

"What do you talk about with Wil?" Jia interrupts, trying to distract her.

"Uh ... anything. I mostly talk. He's kinda quiet. Distracted. Just says he's working on this big project in the lab, can't talk about it, you know, *Wil stuff.*" She grins excitedly. Jia seems unnerved that he would want to spend this much time with her.

"Okay," I say slowly. "Tell me again about going to the drug store, Kimberly, and how you have trouble getting tampons."

She repeats the story in her typical longwinded fashion, but when she gets around to talking about fitting things in her bag, the frantic urge to itch her scalp resurfaces.

"Bag," Misty says insistently.

"Ughh, you're only making it worse!" Kimberly shouts.

A couple of people walk by, giving us weird stares.

"Grass. Wall. Sunset." I say random words as I glance around campus, trying to refocus her.

It works. She sighs in relief, and appears genuinely concerned. "Is there something *wrong* with me?"

"None of this is your fault," Jia assures her. "You're not going crazy."

"I didn't think I was," Kimberly replies. "Not any more than normal. Where we talking about something just now?"

"Yeah. You stuffing stuff into your bag," Misty says.

Jia says something in broken Mandarin to Misty as she protests, and Kimberly's hands fight me violently. Her bag, swinging on her shoulder and banging against her body, appears mostly empty.

As I try to keep her under control, Misty goes for Kimberly's shoulder bag. After digging around for a few moments, she pulls out a mess of keys on three connected keyrings with a million keys attached. Among the confusing mass of metal, however, is a small piece of silver attached by a chain to one of the keyrings.

"That's it," I say.

The silver piece of metal is no bigger than my thumbnail. It looks like a tiny USB drive, but without the plug. It has two square end holes, presumably to attach the other pieces.

"Three pieces. Like he said. Get it unhooked from that... collection," I tell Misty.

"Like who said what now?" Kimberly asks, smiling like a person who really wants in on the inside joke. "Hey, how did you get my bag? I don't remember giving that to you. Give it back!"

"Did Wil give you this?" Jia asks, briefly snatching the keyrings and holding up the silver piece of the USB drive by the keychain for Kimberly to see.

Her eyes grow wide. "Yeah. Wil gave that to me as a gift about a week ago."

Jia purses her lips. "Why?"

"Said that it was some piece of technology to help me be more organized. I don't really know what that means. Sometimes when Wil talks all I hear is *blah blah blah*, especially if he happens to talk about his work—you know? Do you know what it is? I just attached to my keys. Thought stupidly it would maybe make them seem less messy. I guess that's too many keys for one person to have, right?"

"Yes. It is," Jia agrees, as Misty says, "Who even has that many locks?"

"I just like keys. They're fun to draw sometimes," Kimberly says, beaming. "But is there some reason you care about my organization thingy?"

"Can we borrow it?" I ask. I carefully let go of her hands, and take Kimberly's bag, handing it back absently to her. If I keep her focus on the USB drive, she won't think about her bag, and how thinking about it causes her to melt down.

"I...guess so. You didn't have to route through all my stuff to get it though." She slings the bag over her shoulder. "Here, let me get it off."

Reluctantly, Jia hands over the mess of keys and within two seconds, Kimberly has maneuvered the keychain and coaxed the silver USB piece from the prison of keys. She drops it into Jia's palm. "I want it back when you're done with it. Having it makes me feel a little more organized. I know, it's kind of a totem, it's my belief in the thing that makes it what it is, but still. Wil doesn't really seem to be the kind of person who gives gifts for no reason, right?"

"Right," Jia replies, curling her fingers around it protectively. "We'll keep it safe. I promise."

"Good." She turns back to me, slightly confused. "So...Ingrid...is that good? We done with this experiment? That's what we were doing, right?"

"Maybe you should lie down and rest," I say. "We'll tell Wil if we see him that you're not feeling well."

"I...guess that's a good idea. I should switch shampoos. And try not to think about *those three things*..." Immediately she starts scratching again. "*Those three things. Those three things*..."

"Bag...we know that one. Ethan maybe? What was the other one?" Misty asks. Jia looks mortified and Misty shrugs, a little shamefully. "Three pieces. Three trigger words."

I frown, remembering her mutterings from days ago outside the cafeteria. I catch Kimberly as she goes to town on her scalp. I don't want to put her in any more pain. I just want to get this over with. "Just think about painting. Or your favourite TV show. Napping. Sweetheart." I sweat a little at that. "Wil. Computers. Meeting. Coffee. Texting. Emails..."

She whimpers and struggles against my tight grip on her wrists.

"Okay. Kimberly? I think you should have a nap," I tell her as I carefully release her.

Dazed, Kimberly looks out towards the collection of shops and houses in Sparkstone Town. "But...I thought I was supposed to...were you just saying random words to me?"

"Just part of a little experiment. Wil will text you when he wants to reschedule for your coffee."

"Oh." She purses her lips, frowning. "Okay. That's weird he isn't here to tell me that himself, but we're all busy. I guess I'll go take a nap. Right. Well. See you ladies later!"

She spins on her heels and waves an excited goodbye as she hurries back towards Rita House. As she goes, she digs out her phone, half skipping and half running as she mutters to herself.

"This is part of Wil's puzzle, isn't it," Jia says quietly. "He manipulated her mind."

"Yeah." Misty nods. "That's messed up."

"He must have been so desperate," Jia muses. "He was willing to do anything to protect his project. He's always been willing to do whatever it took to fight the Collective."

I turn away from Kimberly. Despite his feelings for her, he put them aside to make her part of this. Or perhaps because of his feelings, he felt that by making her part of this, it justified his spending time with her. Either way, my stomach churns at the thought.

"Sorry," I say to Misty, looking her squarely in the eye.

She frowns. "Why? What you do this time?"

"All this time, I thought you were the most dangerous of all of us. But Wil could have manipulated any of us at any time if he thought it would further our mission to defeat the Collective."

Misty nods slowly at my words, and averts her gaze. I don't know if it's the right apology for what I said to her that night we were searching for the Hunger, but it's the right apology for this moment, in these new circumstances.

"Yeah. Uh...thanks." She shoves her hands in her pockets. "Let's just solve this damn puzzle and rescue Wil so I can punch him in the face, okay?"

"Don't—" Jia stops short when she sees Misty smirking, though it's hard to tell if my impulsive friend is joking. "Okay. Three pieces. Three trigger words. Ethan. Emails. And Kimberly's bag. Which we've already solved. We got this."

I wish I could feel Misty's confidence. "I guess I should be the one to see Ethan."

"We're doing all this together. No splitting up," Jia insists.

"Ethan first. Searching our emails might take some time."

"Yeah. Agreed," Misty says reluctantly, crossing her arms.

I smile a little, though my brief elation over my breakthrough with Misty is short-lived as I remember how much Ethan hates me right now. "Okay. Ethan's probably in his dorm. He rarely leaves unless it's meal time." Or unless he has an appointment with Ms. Agailya. I shudder. "Wil knew I'd do anything to protect him. That must have been why he made him part of this mess."

"His heart's in the right place," Jia says defensively. Her voice cracks. She takes a deep breath, trying to calm herself, and clasps my shoulder. "I can get us all in there."

Sneaking into the guy's dorm building is the usual awkward affair. Instead of opening the door while invisible and having the guard waiting at the desk become suspicious, we wait outside the building for ten minutes for someone to come along. Misty and I use our free hands to search through our phones, which are slow as usual. We both have new emails, but nothing that contains anything remotely clue-like. A young man finally exits the building and we hold the door long enough to slip inside, and then quietly scurry up the stairs to Ethan's floor.

Once up there, Misty activates her dampening device to make the hallway cameras malfunction while we come up with a plan. "You have any idea where Wil may have hidden the next piece? Like, where in his room, I mean?" She seems to be getting into the hunt now.

"Don't know. If it's anything like this one, it could be anywhere. It's so small."

"Maybe he did the same thing to Ethan as he did Kimberly," Jia muses. "We'll have to keep him talking. See if it triggers an unusual physical reaction."

Butterflies dance in my stomach. He better not have done such a thing. Ethan's mind is already a fragile place, tainted by Ms. Agailya. "I'll talk to him," I say, taking a deep, fearful breath. "Alone."

"And what, we're just going to wait out here like invisible idiots?" Misty demands.

"It's fine," Jia says, tilting her head and giving Misty a look. "I'm sure there are subjects that Ethan will talk about with Ingrid that he wouldn't with us."

Misty blows a raspberry and leans against the wall. "They're probably watching him. Use your dampener. We'll keep at our emails. If you're not out in ten minutes, we're coming in."

If Ethan will even talk to me for more than a minute with all I've done to him, that will be a miracle. "I won't be that long."

I break from Jia's grip and rematerialize in the land of the visible. It takes extra encouragement from my brain to move my feet towards Ethan's dorm. He is going to think I'm insane. I mean, what can I even talk about with him? *Hi Ethan, our friend Wil is sending us on a scavenger hunt to find some real damning evidence on the alien group that controls this school—do you know anything about that? Oh, you're an experiment subject yourself? Cool, I definitely did not witness an innocent person die at the hands of a desperate scientist who is also experimenting on you and I am definitely not feeling survivor's guilt.*

I pause before the paint-fingerprinted door with my eyes closed, trying to wash away Tilly's face. I promise I'll get to the bottom of this, Tilly, so no one like you has to die again. Please, stop haunting my waking thoughts. I beg of you.

I knock on the door. "Ethan?" I hear him muttering softly. I knock a little louder. "Ethan? Can I come in?"

"Ingrid?"

After some awkward stumbling, the door opens cautiously, wide enough for him to peer out and evaluate whether I'm worthy enough to enter.

"Hey," I say, playing with my long braid. "Look, I think we should talk."

"Now's not really the best time." He gestures down at his paint-stained clothes.

"It's important."

"So is my schoolwork."

I can't win this argument, not without giving up more than I'm willing to. "Fine. I just wanted to ... say ... I'm sorry for the way I've been ... acting lately. You don't deserve that. And this person I've been ... it's not really who I am. I just wanted you to know that." I glance down the hallway to where I think Misty and Jia are silently hiding. Maybe we should just focus on the emails clue. This one is just too hard. "Okay. See you later. Text me when you are less busy."

Ethan breathes a heavy sigh. He starts to close the door, holding my gaze desperately, and then swings it open fully. "All right. Let's talk. Five minutes. Then I really have to finish this painting. Yeah?"

"Yeah. Okay."

In the past couple of days since I stayed over, his room has become a disaster zone caused by frenzied creativity. On the left side of the room toward the window, ten canvases of various sizes lay against the wall, drying. About four of them are abstract blends of bright turquoises and dark navies in no particular shape, yet looking at the four of them together is oddly calming. The other six are more detailed character and object paintings. One of a sword, long and silver, detailed with strange markings. Another: a stack of books on a night table, lit by a yellow-light lamp. The back of a dark-haired girl's head as she paints something abstract—Kimberly, likely. A lake with a red rowboat. Detailed, lovingly painted hands gripping the hilt of a sword. The last is a series of ripples echoing outward from a single finger punctuating the otherwise calm, still waters.

The finished paintings surround a large easel covered in a dark, paint-stained bedsheet.

On the other side of the room, the bed has been pushed to the far side of the wall and is covered in empty canvases, painting supplies, and dirty laundry.

"You've definitely been busy."

"Yeah. Sometimes I'm just hit with an urge. You know?" A smile breaks out on his face as he gestures to his work proudly, and then fades as he looks at me, as if remembering he's supposed to be angry.

"These must have taken you a long time." I crouch, admiring the one with the ripples in the water.

"A day or two."

"A day or two? These ten?"

"Yeah I...haven't really been sleeping that well."

"Me either." I turn to face him. "I'm really sorry, Ethan. I don't want to be one of those girls who treats their boyfriend like he's disposable and will forgive every crappy thing they do."

"I know," he says quietly. He wipes his hands on his jeans. They're stained with various blues. "I just think if you tell me why you hate Ms. Agailya so much, I'll be able to understand. Then we don't have to do this song and dance. Communication is...important."

I nod, thinking about Wil in the hands of the Collective. He could be in one of Agailya's experiment rooms. Needles poking into his arms. The Hunger surrounding him, tempting him with fantasies while draining him of his life energy...

"Ingrid? You said you were here to talk. Not stare at my unveiled painting."

"Right." I try to shake the horrifying images away.

"You look pale. Did you eat today?"

"Yeah. I'm...doing better at that."

"That's a lie."

I cross my arms. "I'm...trying to be better at it." As much as I want to meet his intense gaze, my attention is pulled to the covered easel. Attempting to change the subject, I say, "What are you working on now?"

Unhappy that I'm avoiding his line of inquiry, Ethan grimaces before carefully removing the bedsheet. "Usually I don't show my art until I'm completely satisfied with it… but…"

I am drawn to the large canvas as soon as the bedsheet hits the floor. It's a painting of ripples from the top down; it has to be at least twenty inches tall. The acrylic paint is thick but deliberately applied; the water is deceptively real. Like the other painting, a pair of hands seems to be the cause of the painting, but they look like they are emerging from the center of the ripples, as if the water is a solid structure that can be gripped.

"Hands are the hardest to get right." He lines up his fingers with the painted fingertips.

Except Ethan's hands don't *entirely* match the painting. The hands in the painting are smaller, and the fingers are shorter. I follow the hands deeper into the center of the painting… and then I'm truly seeing the image for the first time.

The shadow of a face lies beneath the surface of the rippled pool. As I draw closer to the painting, the clearer the image beneath the water becomes. Bright green eyes with highly detailed irises and murky white pupils stare back at me, imploring me to…

…to open a door.

"Hey, whoa, don't touch that, it's not one hundred percent dry." Ethan grips me gently by the shoulders and steers me away from the pull of the mysterious painting. My hand reaches for the image of Sunni beneath the water—I don't consciously remember moving.

There's something else about this painting. Sunni looks exactly how I remember her in my dreams and in real life, but her eyes—there's something eerie about them. The detail is hyper realistic: streaks of a snowy off-white blue deepen into turquoise and light green as they stretch from the inky depths of the pupil, like billowing smoke. In that space between pupil and iris, tiny black dots twist into random shapes, as if Ethan's hand was unsteady as he filled in the iris. Yet with the immaculate attention he paid the rest of the painting, this seems more of an artistic choice than a mistake. It's not just one eye, either. It's both, and the tiny black dots are different on each eye.

Ethan must have spent hours on this. But why? They're not the first thing I noticed about the painting. I only noticed when my sightline was drawn to the center of the painting by Ethan's hand.

"This is... extraordinary," I say, unable to take my gaze from it. "The eyes..."

"The eyes?" Ethan frowns. "I... guess. I mean, I think the hands are more impressive, no? And the ripples. So much paint overlaid over more paint."

"Overlaid? Why?"

"Uh... well... I didn't quite get it how I wanted it the first time. So I painted over it. Now this version is a lot better."

"So there's another version of this painting, underneath this one."

"Well... in a manner of speaking. It's more of a rough, charcoal outline not fit for human consumption. In my artistic opinion."

"This hidden painting...does it cover the whole canvas, or just a specific part?"

"Hidden painting?" He scoffs. "C'mon now, you're making it sound like it's some kind of conspiracy."

"The eyes, Ethan. It's almost as if..." It's hard to curb my enthusiasm and interest. The painting's call is strong, like my dreams. "You must have spent hours getting all that detail in there."

"Um...I guess."

"Did you paint over the eyes?"

"Possibly."

Determined, I lean in again to get a better look. I raise a single finger toward the left eye. "I want to know what's behind there."

"Don't—" He shoves a hand between my finger and the painting protectively. "You're right. I spent hours on this. That's why I don't want you to touch it. There's a line between weird and cute, and you're crossing it."

"Sorry. I just think this painting is important."

"It is. To my schoolwork."

"More than that, Ethan. It could—" It could save you. All of us. It's one of Wil's clues. I feel it. "I feel like every time I open my mouth I'm spouting craziness."

"That's okay! As long as it's the truth."

Then I can't save you. Or anyone. "When did you paint this?" I ask.

"Middle of the night when I couldn't sleep until now. Just finished. Why?"

"Were you ... extremely inspired ... to paint it?"

"Well ... yes. I was."

"More than usual?"

"I'd say so, yes. I knew I wouldn't be able to sleep without finishing it. I didn't even have coffee or an energy drink or anything." He rubs his chin thoughtfully. "I like it a lot, actually. I think it's good enough to display in the art show I have coming up. The one down in Calgary I was telling you about?"

Oh. "That ... complicates things."

"Why? Do you want it? I mean, you can have it, if you like. After the show. Look." He takes me by the arms, gently turning me to face him. "I'm flattered that you're interested in my paintings, but I feel like you're dodging the subject of us, here."

"I need to ask you to do something for me," I blurt out. "I know I'm being insensitive. I wouldn't be if it weren't important. And time sensitive."

He exhales forcefully. "Out with it then."

I steel myself. "I need to borrow ... and maybe destroy ... this painting."

CHAPTER 14

Ethan blinks, stunned, and for a moment, seems like he's searching for something reasonable to say. "Now that's probably the most out-there thing you've said yet."

"I know. But I wouldn't ask you to do this if it wasn't important."

"Perhaps you'd ask me to do it if you thought I was some kind of lovesick fool, who believes my art is not worth pursuing."

Frustrated, I pace the room. "I don't think that. This is important."

"Yes, well, this is my art. And Ingrid, I like you. I like you a lot. But I'm not sure I like you enough to destroy hours of work just on your word. Or…*lend* it to you, whatever that may entail. You're going to have to give me more than that."

Someone knocks on the door. My time must almost be up. Or Misty has gotten impatient. Likely the latter.

Frustrated, Ethan calls, "Who is it?"

"I'm going to open this door whether or not you actually want me to come in," Misty says.

Ethan glances at me and gestures at the door. “Real polite, that one. You’re going to bring your friends into this? Are they your emotional backup?”

“Yeah. I’m just trying to—”

“You run away from me. You refuse to see me. You insult me, you blow me off, more than once. And now you come into my room—”

Misty swings open the door, glances between us indifferently, and then becomes fixated by the painting. “Whoa. Nice. Is that what we’re looking for?”

Jia daintily steps in the room and peers around Misty. “Ooh. Very nice work, Ethan.”

The unexpected compliment throws Ethan off. “Uh thanks. Do you know why Ingrid wants to *borrow* it?”

While Misty drifts closer to the painting, Jia draws a deep breath and surveys the state of Ethan’s living conditions. “It contains a clue that will lead us to the next…piece?”

“What? Are you playing some kind of game that I’m not aware of?” Ethan demands. Noticing Misty’s dangerous proximity to the painting, he grabs her by the arm. Startled out of her trance-like attraction to the painting, Misty’s face twists into a snarl as she recoils from Ethan’s touch.

“Don’t—” She stumbles backward and raises her hands defensively.

I can smell the smoke from the imminent fire beneath the surface of her skin before it takes form. As the fireball and the ice bolt leave Misty’s hands for Ethan, I grab him and pull him sharply towards the bed. We collapse in a heap.

Unfortunately, the damage is done. The portable, flimsy easel wobbles in the face of Misty's firepower and is thrown back. The painting tumbles to the floor. Fire rips and burns the wood black: ice freezes the easel and causes it to shatter upon impact with the wall. The chaos of the destruction also hits Ethan's palette and jar of murky water housing the paintbrushes: it falls to the floor as well.

Misty pushes back into the nearest wall beside the bathroom, shocked at her reaction. Her hands tremble as she regards the destruction she has wrought. "Sorry," she mutters. "I…just don't like being touched."

"Evidently," Ethan replies dryly as he climbs to his feet. He holds my hand tightly, and gives me the once over. A rush of our previous night together in this bed returns to me. "Are you all right? How did you—?"

He follows the path of the fireball and the ice bolt and realizes the fate of his easel—and the painting.

Sweating, he releases me and sifts through the pieces of his broken easel to find his painting. He holds it up. Half of the girl's face completely covered in blue, acrylic paint.

"It's…ruined." The paint drips from the left corner of the acrylic onto the hardwood floor. He looks up at me with such pain. "Is this what you wanted?"

"No. Misty, why—?"

"I didn't mean to, all right? I was just trying to get a better look—"

"I…I don't know how this happened. But all of you, leave. Now," Ethan says.

Jia nods. She gestures to me and heads for the door. Misty follows her. I don't move. I can't begin to make this up to Ethan. He truly thinks I don't support his art, the passion we both share. Apologies don't cut it. He isn't even curious about how Misty destroyed his painting; he only sees something he's created has been destroyed. He deserves more than this.

"The school is run by aliens and we all have superpowers."

The words don't sound like mine. I spill the truth like I'm vomiting, getting rid of something foul. It stops Misty and Jia in their tracks. Ethan lowers the painting like he's about to sheath a weapon.

"Superpowers." He shoves his free hand in his pocket and stares at me in disbelief, despite what he's just witnessed. Misty and Jia are just as shocked.

"She doesn't know what she's saying," Misty says, just as Jia interjects, "You nearly died once."

My gaze doesn't leave his. "I made a promise to tell you what was wrong the moment I was ready. I'm not ready now, but…now seemed a good time."

His eyes flash with recognition. He steps protectively towards me, as if suddenly I'm the only one in the room. "Superpowers. And…cameras everywhere. I remember you telling me that. And…aliens? That was what you wanted to tell me, but couldn't."

"Yeah." I feel sheepish. Why would I have ever thought I couldn't tell him those things? He's my…boyfriend. I should be able to tell him anything. "Misty…obviously she can shoot fire and ice from her hands. Especially when she feels threatened."

Misty rolls her eyes but doesn't protest.

"Jia can turn invisible," I continue. Ethan's gaze snaps to her to see if she's still there—she is, she just smiles wanly at him. He's still holding the painting, but it is momentarily forgotten. "And me…I…can sometimes…teleport places."

"Like when we were on the bed, and you looked like you were only half there."

"I don't know how to control it very well. Right now our friend Wil is in trouble. He's left us messages. We think one of those messages is in your painting."

Ethan frowns. "How? I just painted it. No one was here but me."

"Superpowers. He can influence people's minds from afar," Misty says.

"That sounds…evil." He holds up the painting and looks at it again as if for the first time. The blue is starting to dry, yet it still drips intermittently at his feet. "He made me paint this? Is this…even my work?" Rubbing his forehead and leaving a blue streak of paint there, he holds it out to me, lost. "I…I remember painting this. Vividly. Yet I remember it like someone remembers a fever dream. Vivid, but…patchy."

"Do you know what message Wil might have been trying to convey?" Jia asks.

Ethan shakes his head. "I only made the charcoal outline, and then painted, and painted over it again, when I made mistakes. I mean…do you really need to take it with you? Can't you just stay here and…we can figure this out?"

"No. If we stay we might attract unwanted attention," I reply. More than we probably already have.

Jia opens the door and holds out a hand to Misty. "We'll be outside."

"Right." I take the painting from his outstretched hands. "Sorry, Ethan."

"Uh... okay, but you owe me a new easel," he says, pointing to Misty.

"Uh huh," she says as she slips from the room with Jia.

For a long minute, neither of us say anything to the other. I'd come up here expecting to find a piece of silver USB. While it's been my secret fantasy to draw Ethan into our small resistance movement, in the cold light of the fading day, I'm not sure if he's any safer from Agailya's grasp.

"You should probably pack a bag or something," I say finally.

"Why? Am I target now?"

"You've always been a target." I take his hand briefly and squeeze it.

"Why would your having superpowers endanger me? Because of our relationship? Do you have equally powerful villains chasing you around campus?"

"Aliens. Yeah."

"So... when you say aliens. You mean... " He purses his lips. "Ms. Agailya."

I draw in a deep breath. "Yeah."

"That's why you don't want me to go near her. Because you think she's from another planet. Is that so bad?"

"It is. This is Cybermen and Daleks bad, Ethan. And what she's doing here—to you, and to others—that's why I need you to stay away. If she ever did to you what she did to Tilly…"

There's a pregnant pause. "What did she do to Tilly?"

I play him the video and show him the pictures. Agailya's cold voice through my phone's awful speakers fills the room. I wish I could block my ears. I close my eyes and I'm back in that stuffy vent, watching her torture Tilly for the greater good of her people. It could be Ethan next.

When it finishes, he seems to be at a loss for words. I pocket my phone again and head for the door.

"Look. I don't really expect you to believe me. I know this is a lot." I gesture around the room. "I should have told you earlier because I think your life is especially in danger. And I wish I had more time right now to sit down and talk about this. But if we don't find all of Wil's secrets, they will fall into the wrong hands, and then none of us will be safe ever again. So…maybe later. Okay?"

He parts his lips to reply and nothing comes out. Although genuine concern seems to arrest his voice, he nods, and that's enough to assure me. For now.

It is nearing noon, though it feels so much later. Hunger rips at my stomach, but I can't stop. Misty and Jia, pale-faced and determined, seem to share the same sentiment. We silently exit Morris House into the brisk air. From our invisible world, we watch from a safe distance as several janitors busy themselves in a major clean-up in Conrod Building. Yellow caution tape surrounds the outside, and two security guards man the door. An approaching student is denied entry, protests, and turns away, frustrated.

"It's taking them a while, whatever they're doing in there," Misty mutters.

"No hafelglob in Morris House. Maybe they already cleaned his dorm," Jia says, trying to keep her voice level. "We'll find him. We'll find his clues and we'll find him."

Neither Misty nor I try to dissuade her from this idea. When we don't acknowledge her, she glances at me. "Ethan seems like a sensible person. He'll be all right. Of course, Wil isn't here to tell us if someone is safe or not." The nervous edge to her voice breaks her concentration; the normally blue tint to the invisible world flickers.

If I tell her about Wil—both what he did to her, and his inevitable fate—her powers will fail us when we need them most. I don't want to be responsible for that.

I also don't want to be the friend that lies.

We're far enough into the quad that we're pretty sure the cameras on the surrounding buildings can't capture us. Even though it's sunny, it's briskly cold, so most people are in the library or in their dorms studying. The students that are outside stick to the sidewalks along Sparkstone Boulevard. The nearest maple tree sheds its red and yellow leaves, and we shed our invisibility behind it.

Jia wipes her hands on her yoga pants. She's been holding our sweaty palms all day. I know I could use a shower. She and Misty take a minute to check their phones. While Misty taps away, Jia makes a surprised noise.

"I just got another email from Paige. No, wait, two emails. Huh. That's weird." Jia looks concerned. "We email and text all the time. Email is usually easier because she usually has a lot to say. She's going through some ... stressful times at school. Anyway. This first new email seems normal. This second one is titled PS." She shows us her screen. The email reads:

Nags Yipus came to visit again today. I know more about the silver Buddha than I did before.

Misty snaps her fingers. "Emails!"

Jia's eyes widen. "Of course ... "

"The silver Buddha? Is that ... a thing?" I ask cautiously.

"Mostly in Tibetan Buddhism, there are colour associations you can meditate on. But silver, to my knowledge, isn't one of those colours. You can buy silver Buddha statues. I have one."

"What about Nags Yipus? Who is that?"

"Not ... sure." She frowns. "It does look familiar ... "

"Has she sent you other emails with the subject line *PS?*"

She searches her phone. "Yes. Two in the past few days." Pulling them up, she makes a contented noise. "Hmm. Always four minutes after her regular long email."

Another one reads:

That guy NaGS YiPuS gave me no trouble. You're right. I should listen to the Buddha's wisdom more.

"Is it the nineties? What's up with the weird capitalization?" Misty asks.

"Another scrambled word, like before?" I suggest.

"Now I know what it is," Jia says confidently. "That *name* isn't scrambled. It's an acronym, sort of. *Namo Gwan Shi Yin Pu Sa.*" She says the words quickly under her breath. Immediately her shoulders relax. "It's a common mantra that I find effective...for me. But Paige doesn't know my mantra. No one does. No one except...well, probably Wil."

Of course he does. "Does it mean anything?"

"Yes. Though the meaning behind a mantra is less important than quieting the mind." She closes her eyes and moves her lips, presumably whispering the words. "Any time I say them, I feel calmer. Oh." She opens her eyes and grins. "Oh, I think I know where the piece is. I usually meditate in the dorm. I have a small Buddha statue there." She trails off, staring up at Rita House. "But how would he get the USB in there?"

I wait, hoping she'll connect the dots. How many times, Wil? She blushes and shakes her head.

"I guess we must have been in there at some point. Or he snuck in there when I was in the lab. That's a huge risk he took...for me..."

I clear my throat. "Jia, there's—"

"Right, right. There's no time. I'll go to my dorm, because I know exactly where it is. You two stay here. I'll just be one second."

"We don't have to split up, it's not safe," Misty says quickly, as I say, "Maybe too big of a risk."

"Figure out the painting clue," Jia says as she runs away, grinning wildly.

"Check on Hildie!" Misty shouts after her. She blows out a

massive sigh, glances at me, and then after Jia. "Maybe I'll just go check on her. For a minute."

Scrubbing my face in frustration, I reply, "I don't think it's possible to only stay with her for one minute."

She shrugs, looks up towards Rita House, and then seems to think better of it. She slumps in front of the thick trunk of the tree, arms on her knees as she chews on her lips.

This is the first I've been alone with Misty since our fight. This whole day, we've managed to set aside our differences and work together to save Wil's project and the entire school. Yet, now that we're alone, we can barely look at each other. Or more accurately, I can't bring myself to look at her, because I'm too embarrassed.

Holding the painting like a shield, I give her a wide berth and sit down a foot away. The leaves are crunchy beneath my jeans. I scoop some up and throw them lazily. "We... should probably figure out if there's something going on with this painting," I say quietly.

She nods, tapping her fingers on her bare arms.

Jia will be back soon. I check my phone. She's been gone a minute.

I prop the painting against my knees. Even with the damage, the girl arrests my attention each time I look at her, as if seeing her anew each time. I catch Misty staring at her.

"It's Sunni," she says with the utmost certainty. "You can tell. In the eyes. Or... eye, now."

Ethereal Sunni, watching over us from a ghostly otherworld, trying to communicate Wil's message to us. Or perhaps, she has a message of her own. As usual, her messages are vague and interrupted.

Misty flexes her fingers, examining her chipped black nail polish carefully. She avoids my gaze like the plague.

You could have hurt Ethan. It's on the tip of my tongue. *But you didn't because I saved him. How am I supposed to—*

I draw in a sharp breath. How am I supposed to *control* her when she's not in control of herself, is where I almost went.

That's not the person I want to be.

"You asked me not to apologize until I knew what I was apologizing for. I saw you as someone who needed help. And while I'm not convinced that you don't…we all need help…I do know that you're capable of handling yourself. You're smart and I don't give you enough credit. It was wrong of me to stereotype you, fit you into some box or label just for the sake of making me feel more comfortable. I'm…sorry. For real."

For a long time, Misty picks at the nail polish on her fingernails and doesn't say anything. Clouds gather above us. "I…appreciate that." She hesitates. "I know you're tryin'." She draws in a long, deep breath, takes out a pack of gum, and then seems to think better of it. "And…I'm sorry too. For…almost hitting you with a fireball. And your boyfriend, today. I…could have killed him."

"I would have teleported us out of there if it came to that."

We share a nervous laugh, both knowing that's not true.

"You weren't totally wrong about me. I don't always have control over my powers. I get real angry and sometimes I overreact." She glances at the painting. "I'm not my anger, though."

"I know. I think you feel very deeply." I lay a hand on the painting, tracing the outline of Sunni's curly hair beneath the rippling waters. "All this is very new to me. All this being... being around people that are different than me." I scoff. "Okay, now I'm making it sound like I'm blaming my upbringing for my behaviour. I guess I am."

"I get it. You said all that already. Just stop talking, and listen."

"Okay."

Misty says nothing and stares at me expectantly.

"Um," I say, "were you going to ... say something?"

"No. I'm trying to prove a point. All you have to do just listen. If you're not sure, say nothing. I don't need you to check up on me—I'll tell you if I need something."

"Will you?"

Misty gives me a look. "Yeah. I'll also tell you when your privilege is showing. C'mon. A little trust here?"

My gaze falls to her scarred wrists. "Fine. I'll...do better."

"Good. That's all I wanted." She scoots closer, peering at the painting. "She's beautiful. It kills me that I did this to her."

"You aren't responsible for her death. This is just a painting of her." I pause. "You were drawn to the painting, like I was before you came in. What was it you noticed?"

"The eyes. I looked at her, and it was like she was alive. Callin' me closer." Misty looks uncomfortable. "They're ... so lifelike. Highly detailed. Almost like ... "

"Like there's something under there," I finish.

"Yeah. I wonder if I can scratch away the paint."

"I don't think so. You may ruin all the layers."

"There's definitely something there." She takes out her phone and uses the camera to zoom in extremely close on the eye that isn't covered in blue paint. Once the camera finally focuses on the iris, Misty squints at the details. "I'm not sure but...does that look like letters to you?"

Misty passes me her phone. The camera refocuses. Tiny yellow details that I had thought were part of the bright green iris seem impossibly intricate. They encircle the pupil. From far away, they appear innocuous and act as a natural blending mechanism for Sunni's eyes. Up close, it appears to be tiny random numbers, letters, and symbols.

"Maybe. Can we check my phone's zoom, see if it's better?"

"Sure."

I take it out. It's marginally better. I pass it to Misty so she can have a closer look. She scoffs and shakes her head. "This is...this is the language that Sunni and I made up. Again. That bastard."

"It looks completely different from before," I note.

"It's always different. I change the symbols all the time, especially since...it's only me now." She swallows audibly. "If we ever see him again, I'm going to murder him."

Goosebumps appear in a wave of fear on my arms. We may never see Wil again. What will happen has already happened. "Can you read it?"

"Well. Sort of. I think we only have half the sequence, with only one eye. Sometimes we would jumble the letters across the entire message. This...is weirdly specific and doesn't use a lot of letters. D&DC%B&BBAG%BC%D..."

I gasp. "That's a tune. It's music. Notes, I mean. To...one of my favourite tunes. *If Ever You Were Mine*. Is that all of it?"

"No, it continues around the eye. There's some symbols in there. Those aren't notes, are they?"

"They probably indicate rests, inflections, and sharps. Key of G, though, so, not many sharps," I smile, but she doesn't get it. I move on. "That's the beginning of the second part of the tune. I bet the left eye had the beginning of the first half. So that would be, D-E-G-natural, E-D, B-B-A-G-natural...and so on. It's a slow air. Is there something to the name? Maybe—"

"Maybe we're thinking about this too literally," Misty interrupts me, waving her hand. "That's your favourite song, or whatever. A love song, I guess, by the title? So..."

"Oh. So...maybe he wants me to go to the music room."

"Yeah. Probably. Let me look at this again."

She recites the letters and I tap my feet in time. Just hearing them, even in Misty's monotone recitation, I feel the tune clearly in my mind, and I'm filled with a sense of peace. I remember Ethan and I freestyling at the piano late one night, him kissing me, him telling me how he can't remember, me leaving him...

"I think it has to be the music room," I say quietly when Misty is done reading.

Jia materializes suddenly before us and squats in the leaves. Between her thumb and forefinger she holds a silver piece of the USB. "Got it. It was wedged inside the Buddha. Sorry it took me so long. Had to pry it out. It looked like he drilled a hole in the bottom to make it fit. I… had to almost smash the Buddha to get it out. Where did he found the time? Anyway. Do we know what the painting is about?"

I have a sickening feeling exactly when and how he found the time. I'm about to reply when Misty interjects, "Yeah. A whole painting and a bunch of symbols just to tell us that it's probably the music room."

"Probably is better than nothing," I say, standing. "If it's not there, we'll check my room." The Collective did smash my instruments. I still have the pieces. Maybe Wil was able to sneak the silver piece inside the keyboard. I shudder at the thought of smashing my instruments just to find what we need… but so far we've destroyed something from Ethan and Jia and even Kimberly to move forward. It feels like Wil is sending me a sinister message there, and it's not one I want to dwell on.

"Can I see?" I ask Jia.

She passes me the piece. It is exactly the same as the one we got from Kimberly. I hold one in each hand, and like magnets, they snap together seamlessly.

"Whoa," Misty says. "Did you check on Hildie?"

"Oh. Shoot. I forgot. After, I will," Jia replies.

Misty fumes. She considers taking the painting with her, but instead buries it underneath the fallen autumn leaves at the foot of the tree. "Later… I'll come back for that. It's so huge. Anyone who steals it will be in major trouble. Let's get going, we'll hit Hildie's room if and/or when we go back to Ingrid's room."

Jia nods emphatically. "So far he's chosen people and places that are important to us. Especially to you, Ingrid. Kimberly is one of Ethan's best friends."

"Yeah..." Now isn't the time to go there. Later. I'll tell her later. That's my mantra. I put the connected pieces of silver in my pocket with my phone. "Let's just get this last piece so we can carry out Wil's wishes."

"We could always try flying a spaceship again if needs be, to make a quick getaway. Remember when we did that?" Misty asks dryly. We both take Jia's hand and disappear into her watery world, heading for the music trailer.

"We don't know if he's on the mother ship. He could still be here on campus."

"I wish I could sense him," Jia mutters. "I'm just trying to think good thoughts for him, so he doesn't lose hope."

That's not what Wil wanted. "Jia, there's probably something I should tell you about that..."

"Yes?" She lifts her thin, light brows. We've arrived at the music trailer and we're climbing the stairs.

"Well...a couple of things actually. First..." I fish out my key card and press it against the scanner. It beeps green. "It's something that Joseph G. Campbell told me..."

"Ugh. Don't tell me. He's come to you in a dream and told you all of our futures," Misty remarks.

We swing the door open and pile into the tiny entryway as I swipe the second scanner and open the second door. Inside, the music room is eerily dark and quiet. I feel for the lights. My finger brushes the switch and flips it up. My heart sinks into my stomach. It's easy to forget in Jia's invisible world that sound is not covered.

"Show yourselves," Jadore says with a twisted smile. "I know you're there. In fact, we were wondering when you'd finally arrive."

CHAPTER 15

Surprised, Jia releases us and brings her hands to her mouth. We pop into reality. Misty raises her hand and readies a fireball inches from my face. Jia grips Misty's arm tightly. Four hafelglob and two fishmen flanking Jadore take slick, futuristic guns from their belts and take aim at Misty. The hafelglob are in human form and wear security uniforms. I don't see Ohz among them—the only hafelglob that has shown an ounce of sympathy towards our cause. The fishmen don't appear to have the same privileges as the hafelglob: I've never seen them in human form. Their barbels wave back and forth as they hiss threateningly.

I give Misty a look that says, *we're outnumbered.* She shrugs. Her face says: *I don't give an eff.*

"One of you might have cloaking abilities, but we have infrared cameras on most areas of the campus now. We've been following you all day. We know your friend Wil McBride hid his valuables around campus. We've already found and destroyed much of his hardware." Jadore slides off the piano bench, swinging her cane as if she's about to perform. Her hips swing from side to side as she approaches us. She's boldly walking around in broad daylight in her alien form: skinny jeans and a sports bra show off her green skin. It looks smoother than before, but peering closely, I still see the faint outline of scales. "I heard that there might be something hidden in this room."

The music trailer hasn't been trashed. Either Jadore and her crew just got here, or they haven't been looking very hard. More likely: they don't know what they're really looking for. Misty, Jia, and I are silent.

The fishmen hiss something at Jadore in her native tongue. She scowls. "No. Set up the table. We are going to be in here a while. Prepare those two"—she points at Misty and Jia—"for this afternoon's transport. I'll ensure the others make the usual arrangements for them."

"Don't take them," I say impulsively, just as Misty hurls the fireball in the direction of one of the keyboards. It knocks over the stand and the keyboard crashes into the wall before tumbling to the floor.

"Do that again," Jadore says coldly, "and I'll chop off your hands. Then we'll see just how deep that power runs."

Jia closes her eyes. I see her struggling to revert to invisibility. Her skin becomes noticeably transparent, but not enough to be effective. Of course—she can't become invisible if she's not completely calm.

Fascinated, Jadore flicks her tongue and stalks around Jia. She fully solidifies.

"You both have done well to hide from me," she hisses. "No more." Jadore flicks her wrist at the fishmen. "Take them. Go."

They hiss compliantly and grab my two friends. The hafelglob keep their distance but hold their weapons steady. Jia offers very little resistance, shooting me a worried look. Misty kicks and screams and shoots ice in every direction, managing to freeze the fishmen's feet in place. Scrambling, Misty frees herself.

I rush for her, but so does Jadore—and she has something I don't. A weapon.

Like before in the tutorial room, a blade flicks from the tip of her cane. One of the hafelglobs grabs Misty's arm. She spins around, readying a fireball. Just as I leap for Jadore, she slices Misty across the back, which breaks through her clothes and leaves a long red mark.

Jadore doesn't expect my weight and I crash against her into the wall. Misty wrenches from the fishmen's grip—yet this time, no one stops her. She readies another fireball for the fishman holding Jia and hurries for the door.

Misty makes it two steps and collapses. The fireball flickers and dies in her palm, blackening the wooden floor where she falls.

Jadore pushes me off and I'm stunned as I stare at Misty's unconscious form, watching for signs of breathing.

"Poison," Jadore says simply. The blade in her cane slides back into its hiding place. "What little my body produces now. All my blades are coated with it." She gestures to the fishmen. "Get them out of my sight."

The other guards crush the ice holding their fishmen friends captive with their boots, pick up Misty, and escort Jia out the music trailer. Dark clouds have gathered in the sky, though it's barely one in the afternoon. There aren't many people outside, possibly because of the impending storm, but I secretly hope that some enterprising student has their phone at the ready and captures the fishmen dragging two students across the lawn.

Jadore and I are finally alone. She locks the doors with a key card from a bag slung over her shoulder and saunters towards me. I stare out the window, formulating ten different escape plans that would all end with her sticking me with her poison cane. Jadore's eyes in her original form are as endlessly dark as a black hole, and just as inescapable.

I could plead with her. *Don't hurt my friends. I'll give you whatever you want so they can be safe.* A strange calm descends over me. That conversation will go nowhere. What will happen has already happened. Wil has already died. I will be alive in six months—seemingly, my friends will too. I have to trust Misty and Jia will escape their situation alone. I have to have faith in their abilities.

If only I had enough faith in mine to get out of here.

Jadore points her walking stick at me and a blade flicks out. I smell the herbal poison dripping from the tip. From her own body, she'd said. Gross. She smiles, and points at the piano bench—the same one I'd summoned Joseph G. Campbell from over a week ago.

"You know what I want you to do," she says. "Consider it your *final* assignment."

"He might not come," I warn her.

"He will, if he thinks your life is in danger," she replies. I feel the blade millimetres from the back of my neck. "Now." She pushes down on my shoulders, forcing me to sit. "Play."

I am instinctively rebellious. Being forced to play is one of the worst interactions I can have with a person, made hellish when it is my enemy's hands on my shoulders. I grit my teeth but Jadore is persistent, taking my wrists and slamming them into the white keys. The sudden explosion of sounds and colours disables me, and I writhe, the over-stimulation melting my senses, but Jadore has chained me to the keyboard, and her ironclad grip will not allow me mercy.

"You're..." I press into her, blinded by the need to escape. "Stop!"

"Play!" She releases me suddenly, knowing that I can do nothing when in her grasp.

My wrists are sore, and the room spins around me. I lean forward, my hands falling into place on the keys, and out comes something resembling a G chord.

"More," she insists.

Tone deaf, that alien, but I am not, and I can't abide a foul chord, not in my condition. I launch into something slow and brooding, because whether Jadore knows it or not I will express my emotions through my song.

"Play the one you were doing when Campbell showed up in the cafeteria," Jadore barks.

What Ethan and I had performed had been improvised, and I am unable to replicate it note for note. Doubtful that Jadore would know or care about that.

"And what will do you when he gets here? Kill him?" I ask, dwindling my fingers on random keys, pretending I am heeding her request.

"That is not your concern."

"I think it is. You obviously think he has some sort of connection to me."

"He does. And after your display last month, it is safe to assume you are ready."

"Then why wait this long?" I slow my tempo and switch to D minor to underscore my curiosity. "If Campbell really *wanted* me, if you thought I was *ready,* why not harvest me now?"

She makes a hissing noise, first low, then high. Her native language. I try to pay it no mind, but that smell again: an earthy smell, like compost and decay. I risk a glance. She has her back to me, but I catch a glimpse of the cream. The container is white and circular, and doesn't carry a brand name. She applies it liberally all over her face and neck, and it absorbs quickly into her green skin. I whip my head around just as she screws the top back on the cream and tucks it into her shoulder bag. The smell lingers in the air like a bad aftertaste in my mouth.

"What is that?" I ask, running my tongue along the inside of my mouth, eager to dislodge the taste.

"Not your concern."

"It smells awful." I stop playing as I suppress the urge to vomit. My hand presses suddenly on the piano keys, creating a kaleidoscope of spring colours for my sensitive brain, which only sours the earthy mixture surrounding me.

"Don't stop playing!" Jadore screeches, gripping the base of my neck and forcing my head down.

"Stop..." The scent overwhelms me. I feel faint. Stars dance before my vision and my head falls heavily for the keys.

"No!" Jadore pulls me up roughly by my hair. Hissing, she glances between her cream and the piano, and releases me. I'm still dizzy, but as she puts some distance between us, I feel better. I take a breath, cough from the remaining putrid fumes, and tentatively play some random chords.

"What the hell is that stuff?" I ask again. "Part of your human disguise?"

She hisses again, this time more to taunt me than in annoyance. "It does not just keep me humanoid," she says. "It keeps me beautiful."

I almost roll my eyes. "Your organization is capturing and killing people left and right. Does beauty really matter in the greater scheme of things?"

Her nails, painted black or perhaps naturally so, dig into my neck. "It is *everything*." Her tongue flicks from her mouth, tasting the air. "All my life, I had been worrying about the wrong things. The Collective, they showed me with their science. I can be beautiful too. I can be more than what I was born to be."

I recoil from her touch and she releases me, pacing the room once more. As much as this repulses me, I feel like I'm onto something here. I press her further. "Is that why the Collective kills humans? Just to make you beautiful?"

She scoffs, but it is a half-hissing sound. "Scientific advancement is their goal. And once I am in complete control of the Council…" Trailing off, she taps her cane on the ground. "Very good, Ingrid. Trying to get me to reveal my plan. Especially with Campbell nearby. Not that it is a complete secret to anyone who pays close attention. Well, if he wants to know my plan, he can reach into my mind and take it. It does not matter. Once phase four is complete, we will have no further use for you or him."

Phase four. I've heard her say that before, to Ms. Agailya.

"I didn't tell you to stop playing. You're trying too hard to get to know my motivations, when that is pointless. All that matters is the Sparkstone Project, and you bringing Campbell here for me. Do that, and then you will be free."

Right. Free as in dead. I listlessly play a jig in E-minor as I try to formulate a plan.

Two hafelglob return with trays of silver platters. I sneak glances over my shoulder as I continue to play. They remove keyboards from tables and line them up in the middle of the room and place the trays ceremoniously there, as if we're about to have a banquet. The entire building smells like a fast food restaurant, replacing the equally comforting smell of wood and old instruments. Eventually, the arranging and soft hissing subsides, and Jadore ushers the hafelglob away once again.

"You may stop," Jadore commands.

I let my fingers slide from the keys as I turn around to face the spread of delicious smelling food. All of my favourites are here. Creamy tomato-basil soup. Oven-roasted salmon with a hint of lemon. A stack of hamburgers with accompanying condiments. There's even two pies and a chocolate-chip cheesecake. Everything smells like it's just out of the oven or off the pan.

All this food is mine. It's all for me.

My feet have a will of their own and take me to the table.

There's a lone chair and place setting, complete with white napkin, white plate, and a set of silverware. I grip the back of the chair, licking my lips, trying to reason with my body. My stomach is screaming with hunger. There is enough food here to feed twelve to fifteen people, easily.

"So. All this because you intend to keep me here until I summon Campbell for you?"

Jadore twirls her cane. "Everyone must eat. And you rarely eat in the cafeteria, Ingrid. In fact, according to our surveillance, you've barely eaten anything in the past twenty-four hours. That's a long time for a human to go without food."

I swallow the accumulating saliva. "I refuse to eat your garbage."

"No need to insult our chefs. The food is already prepared. Would be a shame to waste it."

"The whole 'starving children in Africa' emotional-manipulation angle feels like a stretch for you, Jadore."

"Sit down and eat, Ingrid," Jadore says curtly. "You'll need your strength."

Despite myself, I sit in the chair. Sitting doesn't mean eating. I'm... tired. I'm tired because I didn't sleep well and I've been running around trying to find hidden information on the Collective and of course because I haven't eaten in ages. I take the napkin and bunch it up in my hands to keep them distracted. Those hamburgers are too close to me. All it would take is to grab one and shove it in my mouth. Jadore is the witch from *Hansel and Gretel*, and I am the tempted young child ready to be fattened before I'm baked into a pie.

"Campbell won't come if you're here." At least, I'm pretty sure that's true. "It's a nice try. But I'd rather starve than help you."

"What do you think starving to death proves?" Jadore hisses. "That you can resist us? That through passive resistance, you can make a statement about human resilience and tenacity?"

"I won't let you poison me and make me weak."

"Poison? Our food will make you *better*." She leans in closer. "Yes, the side effect is lethargy and it does make you easily suggestible, though our scientists have reformulated the balance in this meal specifically. I won't have you falling asleep while you're playing. Eat, Ingrid. Don't you want your powers to develop? Think of what you could do, Ingrid."

My stomach growls fiercely. The food had always made me feel queasy and nauseous. "If I eat the food—my powers will become stronger?"

I'm not sure whether Jadore knows that teleportation is my power; her only reaction is one of pure excitement. "The Collective is here to enhance humanity. And humanity loves to eat. It is the most efficient way to administer the gene-altering drugs. The chef has personally tailored this meal for you, Ingrid. We have been watching your progress. We know that your connection with Campbell is getting stronger organically. We want to speed that and any other developments along."

Enhance humanity for the Collective's personal gain, she means. My fingers press eagerly into the hamburger bun. I hear it calling to me. I wipe away the drool trickling out of my mouth. "What's stopping me from gobbling up this food and winking out of existence?"

"Threatening your family was effective the last time you strayed."

"And once I run out of family members and friends for you to take advantage of?" I ask. I'm holding the hamburger to my lips. It smells like Alberta beef. "Let me guess. You'll chain me in some kind of cell and force me to help you."

Jadore makes a low, amused hissing sound. "Force you to help us? That implies that you have a choice." She twirls her cane playfully. "You and your friends can scurry all over campus and sing songs and rally against the Collective all you like. In fact, many of the Council members take delight in guessing what you'll do next. Which camera will be blacked out when? Will Misty Ellen Carter finally murder all the hafelglob staff in a fiery rage? One Council member has drawn up a special action plan just for that scenario that he's itching to enact. My point, Ingrid, is while you think your actions are noble and worthwhile, they're nothing but entertainment for my friends upstairs." She hisses some more, flicking out her tongue and running her hands down her body, almost seductively. "Although, those fat reptiles sit around all day discussing these matters and favour sloth to true progress." She appears to remember that I'm sitting here and composes herself. "You move, I move, Campbell moves. In the end, your choices here won't matter. Starve to death, be killed by my staff, accidently get fried by my lightning powers. As long as there's enough of you to scrape off the sidewalk, the Sparkstone Project will go forward as planned."

"I will never help you."

Jadore smiles. "I'm not here for the conversation, Ingrid.

I didn't learn your language to interact with lesser-evolved beings."

"Then why did you—?" My lips are around the burger. My resolve is weak. I'm starving. If I don't eat, I'll die, and I'll be of use to no one, and Jadore is right—as soon as I'm unresponsive, she'll fly me up to the mother ship and dissect me. Just like the rest of the missing students.

Campbell had said my choices had been made already. What has happened will happen, and there is nothing I can do to stop them.

"Yes, very good. Give into your hunger."

The food is in my mouth before I can remind myself of the consequences. Hamburger—the beef is juicy and the bun is toasted. Cheesecake? There's no time to cut myself a slice with a fork and knife. Just scoop it out with my free hand and deliver it to my mouth. Chew, chew, chew, swallow—and then it's time to taste that soup. For that, I use the spoon. Some dribbles to the napkin, left haphazardly on my lap.

This is what I am now. A bottomless pit. I tried to prevent Wil from dying, and I couldn't even do that. But I can eat, and I can grow stronger. When I am stronger, I can fight Jadore and anyone else who gets in my way. Or die trying.

Jadore's reaction to me pigging out is not what I expect. She can only watch me binge-eat for a few seconds before she turns away in disgust. "Animals. I'll step outside until you're finished. If you disappear, remember that we are watching. We will find you and we will drag you back here. And we'll kill your friends—etcetera, etcetera."

I shove half a piece of cheesecake in my mouth without breaking eye contact with her.

"Oof, I cannot watch. This is ugly," she says, and hurries out the door.

Once I hear her exit the trailer, I swallow the cheesecake, recognize my slovenliness, and wipe my face with the napkin. I do feel better. That is the most I've eaten in at least a month.

Right. Now is my chance.

I leap from the chair, ripping off pieces of a roll and stuffing them in my mouth as I frantically search the room. One final piece of the puzzle. There are several keyboards in the room, all of them shoved against the wall, each with accompanying stools or benches. There are other instruments in the room: guitars are mounted to the wall, violins tucked in cases shoved beneath benches, cellos displayed upright in the far left corner of the room.

I check the pianos first, beginning with the grand piano. I run my hand along the sides and push it an inch away from the wall and view behind it with a flashlight. Nothing unusual. I inspect the keys: none of them look like they've been tampered with. I move on, quickly handling each of the keyboards. I want to be thorough. I want to find the last piece. But my heart races. Jadore could come back any second and all hope of telling the world what the Collective has done will be lost.

There are thirteen guitars mounted on the walls. Hope sinks into my stomach. I have to try, and if I'm going to be quick, it's going to be messy.

I grab the nearest piano stool, climb on top, and one by one

I grab the guitars from their wall mounts. I check inside the sound box, finger the frets, and shake the instrument viciously. The first six line the left wall, and another six line the right, and there's one hanging on the far wall. Upon first glance, this lone guitar doesn't look any different from the rest—it's a dreadnought, which is slightly larger and less curvy than the other classical guitars on display. After I inspect the first four on the left wall, it dawns on me that the lonesome guitar would be the most obvious hiding place, and it's better to eliminate that possibility first. I leap down from the piano stool and barrel towards the lone guitar.

The piano bench beneath the guitar is more unstable than the last. As soon as I steady myself on it, the doorknob rattles. My legs wobble and the bench with it. I reach for the guitar and it tumbles to the floor, cracking the delicate round wooden body. Swearing, I jump down and scramble towards the food. I hear her voice on the other end. The outermost door to the trailer beeps and opens. The door to the music room beeps and creaks ajar—

—and then slams shut again. She opens the outermost door as she lets out a long string of commands at someone passing by.

I can't turn back now. I scramble for the guitar and shake it.

Nothing comes out.

Damn it Wil. Why are you making me work for this?

Quickly brushing the broken guitar bits out of my way, I'm about to return to the left wall when, on the floor amidst the debris, I spy a glint of silver.

Hand over hand I crawl as fast as I can as Jadore yells at the students passing by, and grab the final piece of the USB puzzle. Finally. Success.

I take out the other two pieces and fit the third into place. It's now as long as my thumb. Immediately, the USB plug slips out, ready to find an appropriate drive.

I take out my phone. Damn. Of course, that's not going to work.

I'm about to replace my phone in my pocket when a smaller-sized plug reappears—perfectly compatible with my phone. Leave it to Wil to somehow make this possible.

No time to contemplate how. I stick the drive in the phone. Within seconds, my phone's OS goes dark and a blue screen takes over. A long string of code zips down the screen, and then a MS-DOS-type interface pops up. I tap on the prompt, and fortunately a keypad appears.

Glancing at the door and hurrying back to my seat, I type in, *show all folders.*

The command screen disappears as it considers my request.

Almost a terabyte of data. More. My phone lags just trying to access it all. He must have interviewed a lot of people to accumulate this much. I shouldn't even be accessing it on my phone. The Collective is probably monitoring all of our devices. If they find out what Wil so meticulously put together, they will destroy it, and gone with it would be our only leverage, and all he sacrificed would be meaningless. I have to be quick.

I scroll quickly through the collection of files. The file names are gibberish. Maybe Misty can make sense of them.

There's only one that isn't nonsensical: there's a folder called SUNNI. I tap it. Inside is a single audio file. Taking a deep breath, I press play.

"Hey, Mama. It's me. I'm havin' a great time in Manila. Just amazin'. Sorry I haven't called. Long story, but I shouldn't have went clubbing with people I didn't know. Lost everythin'. It's fine, though, the school really helped me when I was in a tight spot. Oh, shoot, I'm runnin' out of battery. I'll call you soon! Love ya!" *Click.*

That's not the end of the file. A few seconds later, Sunni's voice returns, and presents a follow-up message. She paints a picture of the college, her new friends, and what new advances in insect psychology have happened in the last month. But of course she has to go once again to "class" and promises to call later. There are six falsified messages in total, and after each one, she presents an excuse for missing her mother's call and one for cutting the message short. At the end of the file, there are some generic responses recorded separately with a few seconds in between.

So amidst his crusade, he actually had the time to make a false Sunni. Not that it would really convince Hildie in the long term.

The outermost door beeps. Jadore's coming back. I remove the flash drive and stuff the devices in my pocket, and then use both hands to shovel a large hamburger in my mouth.

Disgusted that I'm still eating, she slams the music room door behind her and twirls her cane as she moves towards me. I try to focus on the food. It's getting harder to concentrate the more I eat. My brain feels fuzzy. The drugs in the food are kicking in. Despite what Jadore said, the drugs are still affecting me. I chew what's in my mouth and set down the hamburger.

"Now," Jadore says, pointing at the grand piano. "Play for me."

I can't keep doing this forever. How long have I even been here, anyway? What am I in here for?

I have to get out and find a way to release Wil's evidence to the public. It's what he would have wanted. Then, I can tell Jia the truth of what he did to her. To us.

I stand up, wobbling. My stomach protests. I feel like I just rode a wild rollercoaster. Groaning, I make my way to the piano bench, my fingers *splunking* down on the keys with a giant brown roar that rips through my sensitive ears.

"Stop that," Jadore remarks. There's the sound of her blade coming out of her cane again. Yet another sound that doesn't jive with my nausea; it's too turquoise. I cover my ears and try to think of tunes with colours that will rein in my urge to throw up everything I just ate. Red? Ugh no, that's too loud.

"Play!" Jadore yells. She grabs my neck and forces my head down toward the keys like she did before.

This time it's different. Whatever is in the food, I feel the foreign substance swirling inside me like sour milk. Her touch lights up my brain. Goosebumps rip across my arms. I can smell all the earthy and iron layers of her cream and skin and the blood rushing through her veins, and it compounds into a solid feeling of fullness, as if someone has force-fed me a lump of dirt.

Wrenching from her grip, I lean away from the grand piano and vomit all over the floor.

"You *sick animal!*" Jadore exclaims and slaps me across the back.

Just like the first time I ate the Collective's drugged food, I feel much better after purging it everywhere. No longer am I hyperaware of Jadore's smell.

What I am aware of is her strength. She grabs the collar of my shirt and forces me upright. Wobbling like a newborn calf, I manage to stand, but she pushes me against the wall. She points the poisoned staff at my neck and clamps her hand around my neck.

"You did that on purpose," she says, furious.

"Why do you think I don't eat at the cafeteria?" I retort. I glance at the vomit on the floor, much of it still resembling what I just crammed in my body. "The drug you put in the food doesn't agree with me."

She sneers.

"Go ahead," I spit, raising my hands. "Stab me."

Jadore inhales sharply and holds her position. She presses harder on my neck, but not hard enough to choke me like she did before in the tutorial classroom.

"You can't do it, can you?" I lean forward as much as I can towards the tip of her poisoned spear, and she moves backward, loosening her grip on my throat. "You need me."

"Just because I've been advised not to do any lasting physical damage doesn't mean I won't."

Jadore doesn't seem like the kind of person—alien—to take other people's wishes under advisement. "Advised by whom?"

"It doesn't matter." She snarls and reaches into her pocket.

"I'm calling in the Hunger, and we'll extract the information from you directly."

My eyes widen. "No."

"It will happen, one way or another. You can attempt to prolong it, but you cannot escape it."

"Why do you want to talk to him?"

She smiles deviously, as if she's been waiting for me to ask that very question in this very moment. She releases me, and walking backward with her spear still pointed in my direction, she removes a familiar book from her shoulder bag. Campbell's treatise. "Did you really believe that keeping it in your toilet would be enough to hide it from me?"

I reach for it. "Give it—"

She whips the blade inches in front of my face. "No. You're going to summon Campbell so he can translate this mess into sense. He's going to tell me exactly which universes are the best to infiltrate—as described in this volume—and then we'll set the portal accordingly."

The portal. That's where Campbell told me to meet him, in six months or so. So that I could...open the door. Open the portal and let him through to *another universe.*

So that the Collective could take over.

So that he could *save* someone.

"That book was under your nose the entire time, you know," I retort. "In your *secret* underground library. You could've got it at any time. Why now?"

She seems surprised. "He gave it to you. He...teleported it from some other plane. Because he favours *you.* I have been studying him since I've been able to string a sentence together, and yet for some reason, he's attached himself to you. A primitive animal."

Yeah, well, this connection isn't all it's cracked up to be—is exactly the wrong thing to say in this moment. "I read the treatise. It's one of many. And like I said. I'm not going to help you. I don't even know if I want to help *him*."

Jadore sets the book carefully down on the table. With her now-free hand, Jadore pulls a cell phone from her pocket and taps the screen without taking her gaze from me. It rings loudly, there's a click, and then she brings the device to her ear. "Yes, this isn't working. Bring it in. We have to control it. I don't want her damaged." A brief pause. "Well, then, we'll take her to the mother ship!" Another pause. "Why did you come down here in the first place? You know what happened when we brought in down last time. Get in here." She ends the call. "Idiots." Then to me: "Last chance to call him here. The Hunger will be all too happy to feed on you, be it now or later, it makes little difference to me."

I swallow hard. "The Hunger will ruin me."

"Yes, it does have the unfortunate side effect of not knowing when to stop. That's why it's the perfect power source for the portal. It serves other convenient uses in the meantime." Jadore twists her lips into a devilish grin. "The Hunger is coming now for you, because I am too impatient to wait until the portal is complete, and I'm tired of being in this *cramped* wooden space. And so I can smell your fear instead of your vomit. I'm just informing you so you're prepared. Maybe Campbell will notice your demise and come to your rescue."

I think fast. "Okay, okay!" I purse my lips and nod emphatically. "I'll do it. I'll...call Campbell. But you have to turn around."

"I'm not taking my eyes from you."

"You got cameras in this room, don't you?" I point to the ceilings. "Just...I can't do it when I know someone is staring at me, wanting me to do it."

She hesitates. "You have until the Hunger gets here. Do what you will. If you are unsuccessful, the Hunger will extract the information from you."

"Okay. I'm concentrating."

I take a careful step backward. Then another—as I begin to sing. "*There lived a young maiden, she lived all alone. She lived all alone on the shore-o...*"

Jadore spins around. "What do you think you're—"

"Music, Jadore!" I say, frustrated to be interrupted. "Do you want to see Campbell or not?"

Anger clouds her vision and she raises her cane, only to drop it. "Very well. Continue your pathetic ritual, for what little good it will do you."

Sure thing, Jadore. I clear my throat. I'm a fair singer, though my voice is not as honed as my piano playing. I turn casually and saunter towards the table as I continue the song.

"They placed her away in his cabin below.

Let the winds below high, blow low;

She sang to him so sweet, so neat and complete;

She sung captain and sailors to sleep, to sleep.

She sung captain and sailors to sleep...

I grab the half-eaten cheesecake and throw it at her face. "*But she robbed them of silver, she robbed them of gold!*"

Disgusted and surprised, she rears back as the pie tin hits her and smears delicious cheesecake into her eyes, nose, and mouth. I have no broadsword and I have no oar, so I kick it into high gear and run for the exit.

Jadore is right behind me. She hadn't bothered to lock the doors. I stumble down the stairs and trip over myself, landing on the cold grass. Jadore is on my heels, yet she stops short behind me.

I look up, groaning. I am no maiden on the shore—not yet. What lies before me is so chaotic that it takes a moment to realize it isn't normal.

It's as if the sky has fast-forwarded to night, yet storm clouds obscure all stars. No. Not clouds. One cloud. The Hunger. It looms menacingly over three fishmen and another three hafelglob in human form.

At the eye of the cloud stands Wil, motionless, eyes closed, concentrating.

CHAPTER 16

Wil isn't dead. Yet.

Nor does the Hunger seem particularly interested in consuming him. They float idly, two feet in the air behind Wil. He stands before the cloud, bloodied, his shirt ripped, his glasses askew, but otherwise completely calm. His hands are clasped in front of him, eyes closed, concentrating or perhaps meditating deeply.

The six henchmen are also at a standstill. If it weren't for Jadore's laboured breathing beside me, I would have thought the world is standing still.

Wil inhales deeply. The darker clouds within the Hunger ripple. The aliens in human form, three on each side of the Hunger, inhale as well.

He's controlling *all* of them.

Jadore looks furious. She yells at the fishmen and the hafelglob, who appear to be doing nothing to stop the Hunger. "I told you to get him to control it. Not here. Not in the open, where they can see? Where it can escape...!"

Fear settles in. Wil's time is drawing to a close. Campbell said it would be a battle, and Jadore would be there. And he'd be there. I glance around: I don't see him, but that means little. I don't *feel* him here. That could change in an instant.

Without looking up or acknowledging her physically, Wil's voice booms in all our minds. *You underestimated my power, Ja'Dor'Esss.*

Surprised, Jadore glances at me, as if to ask if I heard it too. "I knew your mind was ripe," Jadore replies as she approaches Wil cautiously. "That's why I wanted you for my collection."

To control the Hunger, you mean.

"Yes, that is what I mean." She signals to the hafelglob security guards and the fishmen.

Although his eyes are closed, Wil knows what Jadore's game is. He holds up a hand, and all the hafelglob guards screech to a halt. The fishmen resist more, walking in slow-motion towards Wil, but they soon succumb as if their feet and the ground are covered in superglue.

"I see." Lightning dances between Jadore's long, green fingers. I step away cautiously. "Try that with me, and I'll do to you what I did to your friend Sunni Harris."

I'm unsure if she realizes the breadth of Wil's power. I contemplate grabbing her and attempting to teleport when I hear Wil's voice in my head. *Ingrid. Can you hear me?*

I nod, then realizing he might not be able to see it, I just think in the affirmative.

Good. I can't hold off the Hunger. I can shield them from entering my mind. They cannot be controlled. They are far too powerful. The Hunger must be destroyed. It takes all my strength to—

Jadore waves her hand and everything descends into chaos.

Electricity flies from Jadore's green fingers towards Wil. With the foreknowledge of her strike, he sprints left, between the still-stunned fishmen. Electricity gets Wil in the leg, and because he has broken his concentration, the fishmen aren't so stunned anymore. Hissing, the two nearest him grab his body and press him into the ground, while the third draws his gun and points it at Wil's head.

The hafelglob have bigger issues. And so do we. Now that Wil isn't holding off the Hunger anymore, they are free to choose their victims. Gathering all the stray bits of cloud tendrils, the cloud becomes denser and darker as it envelopes the nearest hafelglob. It screams, both in fear and then in laughter. The other two hafelglob, terrified, run off, flapping their arms and wailing.

"Don't you *DARE* abandon me!" Jadore shrieks, and fires off a warning shot of electricity at the two of them. It hits the grass at their feet, and they stumble, falling face-first. With her non-electricity hand, she removes her phone and presses one button. "More backup! I don't care who sees, we have a major breech of—"

Wil might die today, but I'll be damned if I stood there and did nothing.

"Hey!" I run towards the fishmen, waving my arms. "Hey, look at me! Guess what, I definitely have superpowers too! Remember!"

The fishmen hiss at me. The one with the gun points it at me.

Wil uses the distraction. With a grunt, one of the fishmen releases Wil, stands up straight like a doll who can only bend at the waist, and turns in one swift ninety-degree motion towards the fishmen with the gun.

Run, Ingrid. Release my files. Tell the world. Use this opportunity.

I'm not leaving you to die. But I'm also not staying put. The fishmen with the gun regains control of himself and starts firing. Jadore's electricity joins in—a shot nips at my heels as a warning: *Don't get in my way, we have unfinished business.*

I take off, running towards Rita House. I keep glancing back at the fight, and every time I do, my stride slows. I feel the USB in my pocket. How exactly am I going to release this to the world? On social media? No, I'll send it to one of the larger Calgary newspapers as well as *The Globe and Mail*. Better—I'll put it on social media, and I'll send it to as many media outlets as I can. It'll take some time. But Wil is giving me that time. I'll need my laptop, though I could do some of the uploading on my phone ...?

Blowing out a sigh, I'm barely twenty feet away from Wil, Jadore, and the Hunger when I hear footsteps to my right. I look. No one there. My heightened senses tingle. Murmurs, not unlike the whispers of the Hunger, invade my mind, and I have the distinct feeling I'm being watched.

"Jia?" I call.

No. She was taken. It can't be her.

The murmurs stop. A huge blast of electricity hurls overhead. I'm not as far away as I'd hoped from Jadore's dangerous lightning. It lands a foot in front of me. The smell of burning grass haunts my nostrils, sending me to my knees in a flurry of dark, deceptive green-blacks. I'd thought I was safe.

Three shapes materialize from nothing. One lights up her hand, grinning in greeting. "Ingrid!"

"Misty!" I crawl closer. "Put out the light, it'll—"

Another shot of electricity. This time it lands half a foot behind me. Misty's light flickers out, and I hear an unfamiliar, older woman scream. Jia, stares into the distance at the fight, and a bewildered Hildie grips Misty's arm. She gasps for air, clutching her chest at the shock of the blast. She glances around, her gaze falling upon me as if I am a rescue buoy.

"Oh...my stars. My head...are we in the middle of a war zone?"

I don't have time to worry about how they got here. I'm just thankful to have them by my side. Jia removes herself from Hildie's tight grasp clinically and strides up to me.

"Did you find the last—?"

"Yes. Wil asked me to go upload it to the world."

Her eyes flash with something—anger? She mutters something under her breath as her gaze settles on Wil as he singlehandedly takes on Jadore. Wil uses the fishmen and the hafelglob as meat shields, taking control of them and throwing them in Jadore's path. She doesn't seem to want to damage her assets, yet she isn't going easy on them either. The smell of fresh rain surrounds us.

"He's going to die, isn't he? That's what Joseph G. Campbell told you."

Jia's voice startles me. "Now isn't really the time..."

She grabs my arm. "Yes, it is. Tell me."

I purse my lips. All I can do is nod. Misty is right beside us, but she's busy listening to Hildie's complaints, and I don't know if she hears.

"Here, today?"

"I don't know."

She shakes her head, closing her eyes. "No. The answer is, not today. Not as long as I am here to protect him."

"Jia, no—"

She blinks out of existence before I can retort. Hildie, startled, takes Misty suddenly by the arm. "Now, don't you go leaving me. I want an explanation. You drag me out here in the cold, through hell-water. You of all people, Misty, I thought I could trust."

The guilt trip is not lost on Misty, though she shrugs her arm from Hildie's grasp. She itches to get into the fight: I can see it in her eyes.

"Hildie, you can come with me. I'll tell you everything on the way," I say, drawing near to her, as if I can do anything to physically protect her.

Misty pats Hildie on the hand. "It'll be all right, now, Hildie. You can trust Ingrid. She won't put you in the hell-water like we did."

"That was atrocious. You gave me some kind of *drug.*"

"Hildie..." Misty is torn between explaining Jia's invisibility powers and joining the fray.

"Go!" I yell at Misty.

Relieved that Hildie is in someone else's care, she turns. The long tear in the back of her sweater is still there. "Go with Ingrid, Hildie. Promise me you'll be safe!"

"I don't know what is going on—"

"Wait, are you okay to fight? Weren't you poisoned?!" I shout after her.

Despite herself, she grins. "Yeah. It burns. Less talk, more fighting! Protect Hildie!"

Protecting Hildie—that's useful. Something I can do. I lead her away from the fight, fast-walking, giving the Hunger a wide berth. I don't touch her; I want her to come of her own free will so she'll trust me. Perturbed, she follows, but she glances at the ensuing fight like she's watching a public display of affection.

"Is that ... fog?" she asks.

"Sort of. Look, Hildie, we need to get out of here. Come with me."

I manage to get her a few feet away from the action when she suddenly stops. "Is that woman over there Professor Jadore? What on Earth ... ?"

Her green skin sticks out like a sore thumb, even at over twelve feet away. She throws electricity at her former minions, reducing their bodies to burning cinders.

I grab Hildie roughly and spin her around to face me. The look on her face—the surprise at my rudeness, the firmness of my grasp—is enough of a reprimand, though I press on. "We have to leave. Jadore is not someone to mess with. She killed your daughter."

She blinks, horrified, as she processes this. "No, no, no ... "

"It's true, Hildie. You know Sunni was special, and—"

Her eyes glaze over as she glances toward the fray once more. I know this look.

Like a predator catching a whiff of a new, easy prey, the Hunger heads right for us and its next victim: Svanhild Harris.

All of the fishmen lay on the grass, dead, and the hafelglob seem to have vanished. Misty throws ice bolt after ice bolt at the Hunger. She's as close as you can get without being inside the fog. As the Hunger drifts closer to us, Hildie pushes me away and runs towards the approaching cloud. I hear snippets of its temptations of fame, fortune, and love. Wil is locked in a fierce battle of wits with Jadore—she resists his mind control and attacks, and falters as Wil gets inside her head a little further each time. Jia plays defense between Wil and Misty, ready to snatch either one and pull them into her world should they need the advantage. One of Misty's ice bolts whizzes by Hildie, and she screams, tripping and falling on the cold grass.

Hildie isn't elderly. She is cautious on her feet. She mutters to herself as she pushes herself up, taking the time to wipe off her good Sunday skirt, muttering about grass stains. The Hunger closes in, and the closer I get to Hildie, the louder and more tempting the Hunger becomes for me.

YOU CAN SEE THEM AGAIN. JUST COME A LITTLE CLOSER. SUNNI IS HERE.

"Don't listen to it, Hildie!" I shout. Hildie glances back at me for a moment, but the Hunger's whispers are so insidious that her head slowly turns back to face the slowly approaching cloud. I skid to a stop a few feet away, panting, staring at the back of Hildie's head as she looks up in wonder at the massive collection of sentient fog, and wanders closer.

A light *dings* in my brain. I shove the flash drive into the phone and dodge the Hunger's wispy, outstretched tendrils and Misty's attacks as she wildly spews fire everywhere. I've lost track of Wil and Jadore and Jia. I think they're still fighting. Lightning strikes out of the corner of my eye. I bring up the audio file of the false Sunni and turn it up to full volume.

"Hey, Mama. It's me. I'm havin' a great time in Manila. Just amazin'. Sorry I haven't called..."

Hildie stops her zombie shuffle towards the Hunger, and as if waking from a daze, she turns in my direction. "Sunni...?"

Noting the distraction, the Hunger moves in faster until several tendrils wrap around Hildie's body. Misty fires off another few ice bolts, but she looks pale. She can't keep up this kind of assault, and now that the Hunger hovers above her best friend's mother, she risks killing her too.

The Hunger is eager to give Hildie what she seeks. *SHE IS HOME NOW. JUST LIKE YOU.*

"Sunni."

"I'm sorry, Mrs. Harris," I whisper. "It's not really her."

"Sunni," she exhales the name again as tears stream down her face. Bits of smoke wisp from her mouth as she speaks, joining the cloud. "You came home. Your father...he's home. You came back. I knew...I always knew..."

"It's not real, Hildie. I'm sorry, I wish I could bring her back..."

"She's not dead, Ingrid," Hildie says, her voice increasingly heavy. Her eyes droop with the urge to lie down and give up her worries.

I refuse to let her waste away. "You can't do this to her!" I shout as I grab Hildie and pull her away from the Hunger's tendrils. I don't get that far as Hildie is still partially in the Hunger's control; her body is heavy and she pulls me to the grass with a painful *thump*. My left arm aches but I ignore it. "Hildie, are you okay?"

Patiently, the Hunger approaches us. I have given them another dinner: me.

Hildie sits up, dazed. Her gaze darts from the approaching cloud to me, as if she'd forgotten where she was. "What…no…no…take me back. Please." She reaches for the cloud, not in mercy, but with desperation. "Don't go…"

"That's death, Hildie. Don't you get it?"

"They're here. I've been waiting for them, yet they never left me at all," she says, smiling through her tears. She breathes in the Hunger cloud as its tendrils tousle her grey-blonde curls. "Please."

The Hunger is happy to oblige. Like a tender lover, the Hunger settles on Hildie, wrapping and swaddling her with their cloudy body. I scoot away, coughing, concentrating on the grass beneath my fingernails, my aching left arm, and the sound of Misty's futile shouts.

"Hildie! Hildie!" She throws a fireball off the topside of the Hunger, hoping to draw them away from Hildie, yet the cloud is too smitten with its willing victim.

Anything I can say is too slow to process my horror. She volunteered to be silenced, because it will give her peace. She wanted them to come home. She wanted...she wanted...

Several feet in front of me and mostly obscured by the thick body of the Hunger, Jadore appears to have found a way to resist Wil's mind attacks. They have been silently dancing: Jadore, her arms entangled with electricity, tries to advance on my powerful friend. Wil holds out his hand, closes his eyes, and slows her down. Like he told me earlier, alien brains are a challenge for him. Likely Jadore's genetically manipulated brain doesn't make things any easier, as she is truly the only one of her kind.

As I run towards them, Misty grabs me and stops me. Her eyes are starkly blue amidst her pale, sweaty complexion. "Don't interfere with them. We have to help Hildie."

"She's dead, Misty. Don't make the same mistake."

"I'm not lettin' her body be beamed into space like they did to Sunni. Help me draw the cloud away."

As Misty readies an ice bolt and attacks the Hunger, Wil's voice booms in my mind. *She's called back-up. It'll be here—*

Jia materializes to Wil's right, just a few feet away. "Ingrid and I will deal with—"

Jadore knows when to seize an opportunity. The swirling electricity on her right arm builds and breaks away from her form, hurling towards Wil.

Wil can control Jadore, but he cannot control pure electricity surging through the air.

"Wil! Move!" I shout.

Yet it's not me he looks at. Wil's head turns, his eyes betraying his foreknowledge of Jia's intent.

In his shocked state, she is faster.

Propelled by a sense of duty, or perhaps by her untamed feelings for Wil, Jia does not cry out as she surrenders her body, allowing it to be a living shield. The blow hits the left side of her body and electricity dances across her skin. Her arm disappears and then reappears. Her invisibility doesn't grant protection from bodily harm. As her concentration wavers, she flickers in and out of sight, until her body finally decides it belongs in this wavelength. She collapses onto the grass. The stench of burning meat fills the air as she twitches involuntarily.

"Why would you do something so...?" Perhaps Wil realizes he's speaking aloud and trails off into incomprehensible muttering as he cradles Jia in his arms. She groans.

Misty forgets the Hunger entirely and charges for Jadore. Jadore readies more electricity in both hands and meets Misty's challenge, but she's not ready for Misty's brutality. A string of profanity in every language tears from her mouth as she hurls ice and fire at Jadore. Even when she's at the point of collapse, Misty doesn't hold back. Jadore stumbles, unable to avoid Misty's unrelenting attacks. The fire burns her delicate green skin, and the ice engulfs her right hand and her left leg, holding her awkwardly in place on the grass. The Hunger notices they have another vulnerable victim and slowly floats towards the battle. Jadore's black eyes widen in terror as she falls, trying to pull herself free from her ice prison.

"You killed her. Now, I kill you," Misty says.

Shouts and gunfire rain down on us from the direction of Conrod Building. A team of hafelglob mobilize on the quad and run toward us in their awkward, human forms.

We need to get Jia out of here, Wil says.

"Misty..." Jia croaks. Half of her face is burnt badly.

Laser-fire whizzes by my left ear, singing some of my hair. I crouch down with Wil and Jia. "Can't you control them, shooting at us?"

Wil glances at me, presses his lips together, and closes his eyes. Blood runs down his nose. Behind me, their approach slows, but one or two continue firing at the Hunger as it descends on Misty.

You have to choose, Ingrid, Wil says. *Save Misty. Or save us. I can hold them off for a minute or two... but...*

"I don't... I can't teleport..."

"Now isn't the time for *can't,*" Wil says through gritted teeth. "Do it. Or die with us with dignity."

I stand, nodding continuously as I shake in my boots. I don't know what to do. I feel like this is a test I should have been studying for all semester, yet now that I'm faced with the question, my mind comes up blank. I trust in my body, and ignore my instincts, and run towards Misty.

The Hunger wraps its smoky tendrils around Misty's head. Misty tortures Jadore incessantly, slapping Jadore with her fire-infused hand, screaming at her about Sunni and revenge and love and hate. Jadore bears it, though as the Hunger descends upon them both, the hazy look of surrender clouds her vision, and she grins with a terrible evilness knowing that her death means Misty's too.

Snapping either of them out of their trances will do no good. I must walk into the belly of the beast and stab it at its core. I have one power—one shot. The Hunger's whispers invade my mind as I approach the densest side—the side nearest Misty. Grey-white tendril arms sprout and invite me into the fantasy.

The battlefield fades away like a bad dream, replaced by another reality, where I'm in the music room, playing the piano. All that aliens running the university stuff was just a story. I am practicing for a concert with Ethan later.

A concert at Sparkstone? I already performed for them. We were trying to fight the drugs in the food.

No, wait, that wasn't real, that's from the story. What's real is the ivory beneath my fingers as I play a melancholy slow air. The music flows through me like warm tea on a cold day. I could sit here all day and play. Forever.

Yet something isn't quite right. The music sounds real, yet the connection deep in my stomach, the butterflies I feel when I play a haunting minor—it's not there. Colours that intertwine with the story of the music, creating texture and life—they're gone too. That pull within me, that strange, ever-present anchor that connects me to—whom? An alien? Gone. No, that was part of the story. That was—

I open my eyes wide, inhaling sharply, trying to suck up the wisps of smoke that I've already lost. No, this battle is real. And so is my part in it.

"Come with me, now," I command the Hunger. I stick my hand into the foggy depths. The sensation is strange, like touching ice on the side of a freezer. I don't dare recoil. I close my eyes, and reach deep within myself to where my powers must live.

I can do this. My friends have made sacrifices tonight. It's my turn.

The Hunger slips inside my mind further—I feel them digging deeper, trying to distract me with enticing promises they can never fulfill. *YOU ARE CAPABLE OF MUCH MORE. LET ME SHOW YOU.*

Somehow, this only makes me feel lighter. The idea that I can play at Carnegie Hall or marry the man of my dreams lifts my spirits, and erases the barriers between my body and the surrounding air.

I want to go far from here. To a place where the Hunger cannot escape from.

HOW—?

I suck in a breath of air as I shut my eyes. The world swims around me and an undeniable force pulls me through space and time. It's as if a giant vacuum sucks away all my surroundings and the air because when I open my eyes, I'm tumbling through cold, dark space.

No air to breathe. Nothing to hold onto. Oh, except that passing asteroid. It whizzes by me like an at-capacity bus in the middle of a busy city. Other bits of dust and ice and rock surround me like mosquitos and I try to bat them away. An undeniably strong force pulls on the entire right side of my body.

The question of how our galaxy formed is subject to some debate, and more so, what is at the center of it. As I stare at the collection of light and nebulous gas spiraling towards the black nothingness at the center of the Milky Way Galaxy, I see the Hunger soaring towards the supermassive black hole. Its cloudy form mixes with the other light and gas until they're almost indistinguishable. Unfortunately, the Hunger is not the only one to be swept away. Due to the sheer force of its gravity, Sagittarius A, the supermassive black hole at the center of the Milky Way Galaxy, pulls me into its orbit. Before me, the event horizon, the point of no return on a black hole, from which there is no escape.

CHAPTER 17

I have maybe fifteen seconds until I asphyxiate.

Less than that until I'm past the event horizon, and my body becomes spaghettified.

The black hole is not alive like the Hunger is. It doesn't discriminate in its attraction. It's just heavyset in the fabric of space-time, and everything rolls towards it. I brought this upon myself. Chunks of rock and ice whizz by. My fingers freeze around one the size of my palm.

I hear the telepathic cries of the gaseous beast as it falls into eternal, inescapable orbit of the black hole.

YOU WILL CEASE TO BE.

So will you, I try to say, but my lips have frozen shut.

I try to concentrate on teleporting back to Earth. *Ethan. Ethan.* I bring his face to mind, allowing it to fill me with fuzzy warmth, the only kind I'll ever feel again. I just want to go *home.*

My tongue feels like it's boiling. I've already expelled all my air. I can think of several ways I'd rather die than be slowly stretched out by a black hole over millions of years as time whizzes by around me. It's dark, though that could be because I'm staring into the depths of space and not because I've lost my vision. The black hole pulls gradually on my body. It's way more powerful than I am. It's just best to let it stretch me out until the end of time. It's easier to let that happen, than for me to even try to escape.

I don't want to die here. I refuse to die this way.

There has to be something worth living for. My friends back on Earth, fighting Jadore and the Collective. My family. Ethan. Understanding my superpower and using it to help others.

Bringing Sunni, Tilly, and the others who died at the Collective's hands to justice. Finally escaping Sparkstone for real. Helping everyone else escape. Booting the Collective off our little rock and ensuring no one else in the universe will suffer at their hand again.

Each thought makes me feel lighter. It could be I'm completely numb to the feeling of the black hole's influence on my body. Yet even the thought of being trapped forever in space seems unlikely in my current mindset. I'm going to make it home. I choose life.

I *choose*...

I blink. The fact that I can do that at all is surprising. Tears line my eyelids. Beneath me is soft solid ground, smelling richly of earth and recent rain. There's something familiar about lying on the grass, staring up at Wil and Misty as they stare back, extremely concerned at my well-being.

Oh Right. I teleported.

Wait. I teleported…from space…?

Oh no. The battle!

I attempt to stand, groan, and lay back on the soft grass. I feel like a stiff board that's been packed into a freezer.

Misty stands above me, concerned but determined. She flames up her hand and holds it at a safe distance. The heat washes over my frozen skin. The pain of going from one extreme to another is considerable. My tears fall freely, warming my cheeks. Misty moves her hands over my arms and legs, and above my chest, careful not to burn off my frozen clothes. As the ice begins to melt, my shirt feels uncomfortably heavy. My fingers twitch—the space rock is still in my hands.

There's some murmuring around me, yet it's at a distance. Wil also stands above me. While Misty attempts to save me from hypothermia, Wil examines the stray piece of space rock in my grasp.

"Brought you a present," I mutter.

"Oh thanks," he says dryly. My arm is too heavy to lift, so he gently pries the rock from my palm. "Where the hell did you go?"

"S-s-s-space." I can't shut my eyes without seeing the black hole, and feeling the undeniable, body-stretching power of its gravitational pull. I could curl into a ball just thinking about it, if I had the strength.

"Uh... the Hunger is just a bunch of mist," Misty says. "Can't it fly through space?"

I'm too busy gasping for air to explain the intricacies of gravity and space travel. "It's gone to a place where even light can't escape."

Wil lays a steady hand on my forehead. "But... the images in your mind... they're... real?" He looks incredulous.

I nod; my throat is sore. I've talked too much already.

"Hmm." Wil looks uncomfortable. He glances around his shoulder. The murmuring gets louder, and people are shouting behind him, and behind me. He kneels and seems to wage an internal war with his words.

I raise my eyebrows.

"Well," he says eventually, acquiescing, "a black hole's gravitational pull is strong. Especially the closer you are to it. It's difficult, if not impossible, to escape."

I wasn't at the event horizon, I don't think.

"No, you weren't, at least you seem sure of that. Yet we're talking about a force that, once you're caught in its rotation, you can't escape."

But I did. I teleported back. That's my superpower.

"Yes..." He looks up again, and it occurs to me that I haven't seen Jia. I try to follow his gaze. I don't see her. In fact, I don't see Hildie's body, or the bodies of any of the fallen aliens.

"They took Jia—she's in the infirmary. The others, the morgue. Not without attracting a crowd first," Wil says quickly to my sudden concern. "But Ingrid. You must have exerted more gravitational force than a supermassive black hole to create that kind of escape velocity."

"Supermassive black hole?" Misty asks. She glances up from her work warming my body and sees the space rock. "Jesus Christ, Ingrid."

I think the feast Jadore fed me must have supercharged my powers, despite the nausea.

"Ingrid, not even light escapes a black hole. *The speed of light*, the fastest thing in the universe, can't outrun a black hole. I don't think teleportation accurately describes what you just did. You bent space-time, and accelerated from nothing to faster-than-known speeds to arrive at your intended destination." Sweat beads on Wil's forehead. "Ingrid, you must be..."

"I'm very tired, is what I am," I whisper groggily.

"Yeah. I'll say. Can she stand now?"

"If we help her," Misty replies. "What are we going to do with the crowd?"

As my brain becomes more in tune with my surroundings, I realize that we are surrounded by Sparkstone students. At least fifty of them have gathered around us to see the display—that's many more than were here before. Panic surges through me. I see faces I recognize, even in the dark afternoon. Laura, the girl we framed for the protest. Kimberly, finally shocked into silence as she holds up her phone, presumably recording. She's not the only one. About three-fourths of the students have their phones out and are capturing my weakness, while the other fourth are texting quickly.

The same questions fly through the air.

"What was that cloud?"

"O-M-G, Professor Jadore is being carried away on a stretcher! But…I didn't hear sirens…who called 9-1-1?"

"Man, is it just me, or was Professor Jadore looking really weird?"

I try to turn and see this very sight, but Wil and Misty obscure it as they help me up. Wil holds me by one shoulder, but my feet are pins and needles. I slump to one side—

—and Misty catches me, her hands two extremes; the pain is manageable compared to the embarrassment of appearing weak in front of my classmates and peers.

I'll tell them there was a confrontation, we got into a fight with Jadore, Wil says telepathically.

I frown and shake my head. "We don't know what they've seen. Can't…erase memories forever."

"I don't want to lie anymore," Misty adds quietly. "Isn't that what you wanted?"

Exposing them was part of my plan, Wil admits. *But not like this.*

My gaze sweeps the many inquiring faces, and one face stands out above the rest. Ethan bursts through the crowd and approaches me fearlessly. Misty steps in front of him, ready to fend him off, but I manage to make a sound that she interprets correctly for her to back away.

Ethan cups my face with his paint-stained hands but immediately recoils. "Oh my god, you're freezing!"

"I did try to warm her up," Misty mutters.

His caring gaze melts me just as much as Misty's fire did. My eyelids droop. I could fall asleep at his touch right here, right now. Yet I can't. Not yet. "It's all true, Ethan."

He shakes his head, not in disbelief, but in relief. "I just want to know that you're all right. You...appeared from nowhere...and that cloud thing...what on Earth *was* that...?"

"I'm okay," I reply feebly. "Just...need rest."

We'll take her back to her room, Wil says telepathically.

Ethan appears taken aback at Wil's style of communication. "Yeah...yeah, sure. I'll go with you."

"Okay," is all I can say.

"Um...by the way, Wil, about that painting I did..."

I slump over with exhaustion in the strong grip of my friends. I'm vaguely aware of people crowding around us, and Wil and Misty muscling them out of the way, and Ethan's comforting voice as they guide me to the relative safety of Rita House. As they place me gently on the bed, I feel him next to me, stroking my hair, telling me that everything will be okay. All I want to do is believe him.

I sleep until late the next morning. When I wake, Ethan is no longer at my side. Misty informs me that Jia is still in intensive care in the infirmary, and then shoves a white piece of paper in my face.

Still groggy, I sit up and take the paper in my grasp. The notice has small authoritative print, and its message is curt and to the point.

Dear Sparkstone Student,

A strange weather phenomenon that staff had been tracking for some time passed over Sparkstone University late last evening. Trace amounts of 3-Quinuclidinyl benzilate were found in the phenomenon. There is not enough to be dangerous, however, several students reported auditory and visual hallucinations to senior staff. This is an unprecedented discovery as until now, this substance was not thought to be naturally occurring. Until the area is tested by our on-site lab scientists, staff has suspended all classes. Students are encouraged to stay in their dorms until the area is deemed safe.

Students studying this weather phenomenon independent of their major will be excited to hear that university staff plans to publish the full data on the university website within the next several days. Some students suffered minor injuries from the phenomenon and are currently being treated on campus.

Those with questions or concerns should contact Ms. Grace Agailya.

-Sparkstone Staff

"They can't expect everyone to believe this, can they? A *ton* of people saw the Hunger and your powers and me appearing out of nowhere with their own eyes!"

"Don't know. People always believe the easiest explanation. Plus, they have drugs in the food."

"The drugs don't make everyone forget. They just make us too lazy to care." I crumple the note and throw it off the bed. "Where's Ethan?"

"He had to eat. He was here all night," Misty replies. "And

yeah, I tried telling him about the food, but he's got nothing else to eat. And frankly, neither do we. But more importantly, I was guarding Jia's room all night. And since you're the one who got sleep, I'm going to say it's your turn to do that now while I get a few hours. 'K?"

The guilt of harbouring Wil's secrets from Jia comes rushing back at me. "Okay."

For the next two days, we split our time between our dorm and the infirmary in Rogers Hall. The Collective restricts access to Jia's assigned room, but Misty and I take turns sitting in the hallway beside the door. Sometimes Ethan joins me, when he's able to escape Morris House. There's more security than ever trying to keep the students inside and under control. I upload everything on the flash drive to multiple cloud storage accounts, and Misty does the same. We take turns guarding the small piece of hardware. Neither of us see Wil during that time, and even though we text him and think his name, he doesn't join us in our vigil.

When the nurses slip in and out of Jia's room, we grill them relentlessly on her status. None of them acknowledge our presence, nor do they shoo us away. Finally, at the end of the second day, one of the nurses finally shakes me awake. I must have dozed off. I quickly climb to my feet and glance at the door. It's ajar. The nurse before me is tall, slender, and impatient. "You may see her now. She's awake. We've treated her for the pain, but everything else will have to heal in its own time."

"Everything else?" I ask, but the nurse hurries away.

I put a hand to Jia's door to open it further, surprised to hear voices from within.

“It was foolish,” Wil remarks.

“I’d do it again,” Jia replies. Her voice is croaky and weak. She probably hasn’t spoken in days. “I would. Even if Ingrid hadn’t have told me what Campbell knows. I’m not going to let you—”

“Don’t.” His voice is quiet. And then, he’s silent for a long minute. He probably knows I’m at the door and has switched to telepathy. There’s no point eavesdropping on telepathy.

I steel myself for the worst as I enter the infirmary. I open the door wide and step gingerly into the room, steeling myself for Jia’s injuries. Wil sits in a chair beside the bed, hands clasped as he leans over her. He turns his head as I enter, but doesn’t get up. Jia’s expression lifts in surprise. Her left eyebrow is gone, as well as half her right eyebrow. Second degree burns mar the left side of her face, neck, and the underside of both her arms where she attempted to negate Jadore’s blow. They have not been covered in bandages; they glisten, likely covered in some sort of cream. I can’t take my gaze from them, and not because they are grotesque: quite the opposite. The burn marks are shaped like tree roots winding and twisting around her body.

“Ingrid,” she says. She grimaces as she talks. It must be painful.

“I’m glad you’re awake,” I say, sauntering closer. “Misty and I were taking turns guarding the door, but I guess Wil slipped by as I was taking a nap.”

Wil stands, ignoring my attempt to lighten the mood. “I’ll leave you two alone.”

Jia doesn't protest his leaving, though her gaze follows his form as he exits.

I approach her bed warily. "I didn't mean to interrupt."

"It's all right. Probably...for the best."

I shift my weight awkwardly from side to side. "I'll admit it. I don't really know what to say right now. I owe you a thousand apologies and I don't know where to begin. How...are you? Feeling pretty terrible, I bet?"

She manages a smile. "I think they gave me something for the pain. Everything...itches. They say it will get better. I don't know what to believe."

"And your powers?"

"They work," she says simply, and does not elaborate further.

"If you don't want Wil to come visit you—tell me. I mean, I'm sure you can tell him yourself, but, you know, if you need us to continue guarding the door—"

"I...appreciate that. I don't know if guarding is necessary anymore. But...my emotions are too strong when it comes to Wil." She looks, unabashed, up at me. "How do you do it? For Ethan? Not worry that the Collective will...take him?"

"Knowing that I'm protecting him—it fuels me."

She nods slowly, and then clutches her face in pain. She lays back into the pillow and stares at the TV screen in front of her. It's not on. "Our fuel is different from each other."

"Yeah." I take this as an invitation to sit down where Wil had been only minutes before. Did Wil tell her everything? Can I tell her what he has truly done to her mind? Am I a terrible person if I just want to spare her that terrible truth? I sink my teeth into my sensitive, chapped lips. "What are you going to do about him? Did he... say anything?"

I regret the question and I'm about to walk it back when her lip trembles, possessed by emotion. "I know that I should focus on things that will improve my strength so I can stay in the invisible realm longer. Mastering control over my emotions and living simply, according to the doctrines I have embraced. If I don't do this, then I put my family at risk. Paige is smart. She will become a target. They already have me here. It's not a stretch to assume the Collective will also want my sister too. I'm not sure, but she may possess abilities too.

"Yet when I see Wil, part of me freezes. All I want to do is ask him to be with me and I'm constantly afraid of what feels like inevitable rejection. I act on instinct without considering the consequences when I'm with him. I... I can't do that if I'm going to be a useful member of this team." She moves her gaze to mine, and after a long while, she adds, "He doesn't want to be with me. But I still don't want him to die, Ingrid."

"I'm going to try to prevent his death." So he didn't tell her. I take her least injured hand. "I'm here for you. We're stronger together."

She squeezes my hand, even though it causes her pain. "That's my favourite mantra."

I keep Jia company for another half hour until she falls asleep. Quietly, I leave the room, relieved that she's alive. Her burns will become scars, and I can't imagine how she's going to explain that away to her parents, but Wil's words echo in my mind: we're at war. We all have to make sacrifices. Some of us more than others.

Just as I exit Jia's room, I spot Agailya gliding down the hallway towards me. I freeze in place. Misty should be here soon to relieve me since I've been standing guard here for several hours, but there's no way that I'm letting a known alien experimenter be alone with my vulnerable friend.

Her gaze captures mine and she smiles politely as she approaches the door. "Ingrid."

"What are you doing here?" I ask cautiously. Knowing that she holds Ethan's life in her alien hands is reason to not upset her; worse, is knowing she stood on the sidelines while the rest of us fought without her.

"The same as you," she replies, nodding slowly at the closed door to Jia's room.

I barricade the entrance with my body. She's not getting Jia. She's not getting any more of us.

"You have nothing to worry about, Ingrid. I'm not interested in Jia on a scientific level. Only as a resident here at Sparkstone."

I cross my arms. "They're one and the same, aren't they?"

Agailya readjusts her stance, clasps her hands, and digs her short, rounded nails into her fingers. "I take it she will recover."

"Eventually."

"I've read her file. Severe burns. Scarring is inevitable. The Collective could extend a hand. She does not have to live with disfigurement."

I wonder if they've already made this offer to Jia. "Yeah, and what would they want in return?"

"The same thing we always want. Scientific betterment for all member species."

"Member species. Betterment for some at the expense of others. Right?" Emboldened by lack of sleep, and my fear for Ethan's life, I advance on her. She is immoveable, but her large, round eyes regard me cautiously. "I know you think we're just animals. But you know we're intelligent. And yet you still do experiments with us. Take our DNA and use it in…in…whatever you want. Like we're lab rats."

"This isn't about the rights of sentient species. This is about survival."

"One and the same again."

"To you. You haven't lost anyone."

"I've lost Sunni. You've threatened my—" I shake my head, smiling in disbelief. "No, I don't have to justify my feelings to you. I saw what you did to Tilly. I *saw*…" It's too horrible to say. The memory of her convulsing within her animal cage stills my tongue.

"Her mutation was unstable. Our attempts to enhance it were…unsuccessful."

"You made her worse. She could have lived if it weren't for you!"

"She did not die in vain!" Her voice, normally calm, raises and intensifies. "You were observing; I thought as much. Then you must have also gleaned *why* I do what I do. Tilly's unique condition allowed me to collect samples that could potentially save millions of lives."

"And those fishmen you tortured? The Hunger ate them up and you just stood there and watched."

"As did you," Agailya remarks without sympathy. She takes a deep breath. "The Hunger was not my project. Jadore is furious at its destruction. She is unkind when she is angry."

"I know."

"No, you don't." She breathes in deeply, and lets out a long, drawn out sigh that's barely audible. "You have made everything worse." Her pale lips quirk upwards, but there is no malice in her smile. Sadness—yes, but strangely, opportunity.

I shouldn't care about Agailya's well-being. Yet part of me, deep down, is moved by her steadfast reaction to the threat of Jadore's wrath. "I haven't seen Jadore around campus."

"For the failure of the Hunger Project, Jadore has been recalled for the time being," Agailya says evenly. "Consider this the eye of the storm, Ingrid. I suggest you think carefully about your next move. You are mere minnows to the shark. The Collective is a large beast, but it does learn from its mistakes."

"Hildie didn't have to die," I say quietly. "You could have sent her away."

"I agree. It was your involvement that tipped the scale. Though her death was quick. A pinprick of pain followed by overwhelming comfort and peace as the new memories filled her. She probably lived a lifetime in the space of a few minutes."

I press my forehead against the cold wall. It hurts, and that's good, because I need something to drown out the emotional monsoon in my stomach.

"Ingrid, I think it would be best if—"

"Don't." My teeth sink into my lips. "Just...don't. Haven't you done enough?"

The soles of her flats scrape on the floor as she turns and faces the door to Jia's room. "For what it is worth...I agree. She should have lived with her pain. She had found beauty in it."

I frown and push myself away from the wall. "Why would you say something so... morbid?"

She looks insulted. "You would think as I do, if you lived as my people have. Half, Ingrid. That's how many live past adolescence if they do not die of the vitaphage." Her lips press white, determined. "It becomes a part of you and it is easier to love and accept the darkness than to spend energy hating it. To end your suffering prematurely, to take away someone else's..." She shakes her head slightly, like she's said too much already.

"Is that why you find it so easy to make us suffer these experiments?" I whisper, as loud as I dare, fearing the answer. "Your... *experiment*?"

"As I have said, the Collective is a scientific organization first. We do whatever it takes to find the answers we require. And sometimes that means there are sacrifices that must be made. But"—she holds up a silencing hand before I can protest—"it is better that a few hundred die to save hundreds of thousands. That is not a question. It is true. It is the truth that I must accept as a scientist, as a researcher, as a..." She trails off again. Her sadness morphs into contempt. "You are concerned about Ethan, and you need not be. His genetic makeup is the key to curing my people."

"And you would take him away from me? Just like that?

Wipe him off the face of the Earth, for thousands of aliens he's never met on a planet in a galaxy far, far away?" I'm screaming now, close to tears. I gasp for air. My throat is tight with fear.

She grits her teeth. "It is a noble sacrifice, and he will go willingly. His death means salvation for my people. He will be *remembered.*" She looks me up and down. "Which, unfortunately, Ingrid, is more than I can say for what the Collective has planned for you."

I cross my arms. My turn to be contemptuous. "I thought my presence here was critical to the portal project. The Sparkstone Project."

"Yes. It is, very much so. Your abilities are greatly sought after, and when they manifest fully, you will be harvested. But the Collective does not plan to memorialize you. Your name will not be whispered by people across the galaxy. Your sacrifice will be meaningless to Campbell and the Collective, because nothing means more to him than the end. He will use you to get what he wants, and on that day, you will realize what it means to be unimportant in the grand scheme of things."

"But I am important," I reply. "I am important to me. And my friends. To Ethan. What I do here is important to the survival of—"

"You may tell yourself that," Agailya interrupts, not unkindly. "Every girl will tell herself that to fuel her purpose in her brief existence. But I have seen Campbell's mind. Glimpsed its glory, only for a speck of a moment, for that is all I can handle. You are a combination of circumstance and DNA to him. Do not fall into his charm. You will fulfill his mission, and you will perish, and your name will be forgotten. No matter what you will do for him, or what he does for you now."

"Ethan will remember me," I say meekly.

"He will be gone before that, I am afraid."

"I won't let you take him," I say again.

Ms. Agailya shrugs, and for a moment I am almost convinced that she is human. She regards me as though I am a mouse who has declared war on an army of cats. "Try if you think you must. If you succeed, then you will condemn my race to extinction."

Then perhaps you are meant to die. The horrible sentiment surprises even me. I am not a murderer. We have hurt and maimed many aliens in our private war against the Collective, but I have never actually planned and executed a murder. An entire race, dead, because I'm unable to let go of someone who means a lot to me. I cannot fathom thousands of deaths, because the death of one is far more potent.

She takes my silence with a farewell nod, and treads back down the hallway from where she came. "We will send Mrs. Harris's remains to be buried in her community burial lot. The Collective will handle the arrangements and her death will be labeled a suicide."

I want to argue this verdict but Svanhild did volunteer to die.

Taking one last furtive glance at the doorway to Jia's room, Agailya turns and heads down the hallway.

She stands in the very spot she died.

"I opened a door," I tell her, unable to hide some pride in my voice.

Sunni nods, but she still looks worried. "It's not the last."

"I know."

She stares down at Earth, deep in thought. I have a sharp moment of clarity, gazing upon my home planet with my dead friend. I know this is a dream. Yet I'm strongly aware of the heaviness of Sunni's presence next to me. She is not an apparition. She is as real as the bed my body is sleeping in.

"Is Campbell trustworthy?" I ask her.

She turns her pools of glistening green up to me, and in them, I see the answer isn't that simple. Instead, I feel myself drifting backward, her image frozen in time until it blurs and fades. No nasty Jadore this time. No insistent pleas about doors. Just confusion and sadness.

I feel the mattress and the comforting warmth of my blankets first, yet my mind remains in a floating, malleable state. A dark, heavy weight exerts its own warmth a foot above me. It has its own gravity, yet it's not strong like the black hole was. It does not really exist in the physical realm—yet when I open my eyes, my brain still half in the dream world, I see it clearly. A whirlpool of dark blue hovering from the ceiling, watery, but dry; soothing, but thunderous in appearance and scope. Something floats in the center of the vortex, swirling round and round.

My hand is drawn to it; my brain insists the anomaly real, but I cannot trust it, for I am still half asleep.

Like the young King Arthur, I pull the treasured object from the swirling pool, grazing an ethereal hand as the item emerges and becomes real. My Lady of the Lake has a face drawn in greyscale with shining bright eyes, the faint hint of a nose, and lips full and parted, ready to sing, surrounded in a mess of curls that become the whirlpool.

Sunni?

It is Ethan's painting, made real.

My mouth is heavy with sleep and I cannot call out to her, nor does dream communication seem to function in this limbo between waking and slumber.

I grab the item from the pool—

—and then I wake up in bed.

In my hand, I grasp Sunni's journal.

And yet, it's not the same book. The binding is different. More worn. The edges appear burnt and are fragile to the touch. Black soot stains my palms and fingers. It has travelled a long way to get here.

Not to mention, Sunni's journal was destroyed in the underground library weeks ago. Did I pull this out of a…dream? Or from the past, moments before the book was destroyed?

Or does she still exist in spirit form in this world, and this gesture is to assure me that I am not alone?

I open the tome gingerly, shy but eager to discover its secrets. From what I can tell, everything inside is the same.

I look up at the ceiling and see the white paint and the light fixture. I wonder how much of this they caught on tape.

I climb out of bed to head to the bathroom and then think better of hiding Sunni's journal in the toilet. Jadore still found

Campbell's treatise there. Who knows what secrets she's been able to uncover from it—assuming she's well enough to do anything at all. No, I have to keep this on my person at all times if I truly want to keep it from Jadore's clutches. And if I have to teleport at the last minute...well, I guess I'd better start practicing.

Switching off the light in the bathroom, my steps falter as everything that has happened in the past forty-eight hours slams into me, the weight of the force almost equal to the black hole that nearly sucked away my life.

We struck a major blow to the Collective. And now that the Hunger is gone, they can't use it to alter people's memories. If Tilly has proven anything, it's that their drugs aren't effective on everyone. Jia saved Wil. He didn't die—at least, not today. Misty nearly defeated Jadore.

Ethan knows my secret. Ethan finally knows.

Now, I can save him from Agailya's experiment.

Goosebumps ripple up my arms with a wave of euphoria. For a brief moment, I'm unaware of the boundaries that separate my body and the floor and the wall and the air. I feel at one with the universe.

The absurdity of the thought brings me back; my knees wobble to support my weight as they remember how to hold me up.

Did I almost teleport? Again?

I slump against the wall as I catch my breath, clutching Sunni's journal close to my chest.

Almost all of my successful teleportation attempts have

all been when I was close to death. First, on the mother ship, before it broke apart. Second, in the underground library during the Collective's attack. And then there was that time I went to the centre of the galaxy to dispose of an intelligent cloud... a few days ago.

For the longest time, I'd thought that Ethan was my trigger. That somehow, my intense attraction for him was the key to unlocking my power. I scoff in the dark, climbing to my feet as I pace silently around the room. Now I realize how silly that sounds. Why would someone I happened to meet in this prison be the key to unlocking the mysteries in *my* DNA?

My friends' powers don't rely on external factors. So why would mine? Misty's fire and ice surfaces most powerfully when she's angry. Jia, when she's calm. Wil... well, I don't know about his feelings, but likely intense focus and practice has honed his connection to intelligent minds and technology everywhere.

Love, then. I'm in love with Ethan.

I rush to the window. The promising light blues and reds of sunrise are in the distance. Yes, Ethan: the thought of seeing him twists my stomach into knots. He's one good in a sea of bad. Even thinking of seeing him later, of finally explaining the truth in full, makes my body lighter with joy, and the familiar sensation of losing awareness in my body rushes through me.

No, no. It's the middle of the night and I'm half dressed.

I breathe in suddenly, feeling the cold wood of the floor beneath my soles. Sunni's journal is on the floor.

It's not Ethan that triggers my power. It's what I feel when I'm with him that triggers my power.

Love?

No. A deeper feeling, and far less flimsy than the ups and downs of romantic attraction; a manic euphoria that trumps reason and reality. This is the very enemy of the Collective that uses fear and deception to control us and the sole driver of our resistance from the beginning.

Fear makes me heavy. Hope carries me away.

Hope is stronger than fear.

CHAPTER 18

That morning, I'm up early. I'm on a mission. Collective quarantine be damned. It takes some time and hafelglob security evasion, but after a half-day of asking around and knocking on the wrong doors around the girl residences, I've finally arrived at the correct location. Basement floor, Raylene House. I raise my tired knuckles and put them warily to the wooden door of the dorm, hoping the sound would wrestle away my doubts. My phone feels heavy in my sweater pocket.

After the fourth knock, I hear a young man muttering from the other side. He swings the door open and fixes me with the most annoyed look I've ever seen. He's tall, has terrible posture, and wears his flannel shirt half-unbuttoned. He's barefooted. "We're in the middle of a project. Who the hell are you?"

"Uh…" I clear my throat. "Are you Greg? You help Tilly run the *Don't Read Zine?*"

Greg looks nervous but maintains his aggressive stance. "Yeah. We do. So? You liked our issues? We haven't started selling subscriptions yet. And we don't have a system for reporting spelling or factual errors, and we're *not* taking submissions."

"Good thing I don't want to do any of those things. Can I come in?"

Taken aback, Greg glances behind him. The room is dimly lit. Faint rustling and low conversation indicates he's not alone in there. "Why?"

"I know what happened to Tilly."

For a brief moment, Greg's eyes flash with concern. "Don't touch anything. We're in the middle of a *huge* crafting session."

He opens the door all the way and I step across the threshold. Greg slams the door behind me just as quickly. The room is similar to mine but with a bigger square footage. Large bedroom area, with a bathroom off to the left. Directly to the right of the door is a double-door closet. The queen-sized bed has been shoved to the far left corner of the room to make space for a large table, filled with plastic boxes, paper, and crafting supplies.

Two people sit at the table—one, a larger young black woman with thick glasses painstakingly hand-lettering headlines on a large broadsheet. The other, a young Caucasian woman with gaunt, freckly features hunches over a laptop. I recognize them from the zine Tilly gave me: Elisha and Lynn respectively.

There's probably a camera in the light above us. I consider disrupting it with my bracelet and wonder if there's really any point. My hoodie hides my telltale hair, but that was mostly to avoid awkward questions about the incident on the quad. I was almost sucked into a black hole, and no, I don't want to talk about it with my fellow students. There is only one reason I'm here.

"Do you want to *really* know what happened to Tilly?" I ask.

The two women look up from their activities hesitantly. Greg shifts his weight and holds his head up defensively. "What do you mean by that?"

"Jadore said she got sick. And then was transferred to a different school in Nova Scotia," adds Elisha. There's a touch of uncertainty to her voice. "Why? What do you know?"

"Elisha!" Greg hisses.

"Oh, c'mon Greg. Cut the bull and let the girl talk. Don't you know she's the one who organized that big protest? Tilly's been going on about Ingrid Stanley for weeks. Said that she knew what was *really* going down at this school."

"You're Ingrid Stanley?" Lynn asks. Her voice is high-pitched and quiet, like a mouse. She smiles a little and straightens her posture. She winces—she must have been hunched over that laptop for hours. "I heard you play last month. You were lovely."

"Thanks," I reply.

"Is your friend Jia going to be okay?" Elisha asks. "I heard a girl got seriously hurt out on the quad yesterday, and I tried to ask Ms. Agailya for a comment—"

"Typical Grace. She's just a pawn in this whole conspiracy!" Greg remarks. He's already fuming, and paces the room like a bull in a china shop.

"Funny that you say conspiracy," I say slowly. "Tilly isn't the only student that has been mysteriously transferred this month. She was looking into that too. I—"

"Do you know what's really going on here?" Greg interrupts.

"Yes." His bluntness is infectious. And dangerous. But I'm past being cautious. Now is the time to bring Tilly and the others to justice. I pull out my phone. "I didn't want to deliver this in person, but it's the only way to ensure that it wouldn't be intercepted."

"Intercepted." Lynn's face lights up at the word. "Tilly said that there were cameras everywhere. That we were being monitored..."

"That's only the half of it." My hands shake as I take out my phone and navigate to my pictures. "Jadore said that Tilly was transferred. I can show you the timestamp on this photo—I took this *after* Jadore told us that." I point the phone at them, revealing the picture I took when I was on the mother ship.

"You can barely see anything! Where the hell were you, in a grate?" Greg demands.

I flip through the gallery to a better focussed version. "In a vent, actually. Look closer."

"Is she trapped? Why is she wearing that cat costume?" Elisha looks at me, disgusted. "Is this a prank? 'Cause we are a serious journalism outfit here."

I purse my lips. "Tilly was onto something dangerous. So are me and my friends. It affects all of us. If you stop pursuing it, we might survive until graduation. Tilly and Fahima and Avery and Daniel and Kendra—"

"We are not stopping anything!" Greg retorts. He marches up to me, pointing, getting in my personal space. I try not to flinch or recoil. "You can get out right now—"

"Oh. My. God, Greg, chill out," Elisha says, pushing him away. She rolls her eyes. "Sorry, Ingrid, Greg is kinda intense. Tell us—is this photo real, and why does Tilly look like she's about to attend a comic con?"

I draw in a deep breath and navigate to the video I captured of Agailya, and hit play. As she explains her purpose in dulcet, scientific terms, the three journalists of the *Don't Read Zine* become more focussed and quiet. When the video ends, I scroll through more pictures, including those of Agailya, and the fishmen.

"What are those?" Lynn asks, fascinated.

Elisha is coldly emboldened. "What really happened with Jadore in the quad that night?"

My breath is shaky as I inhale. I've come this far. "I…have more pictures. Videos. But I'm not sure if I want to be—"

"Yes, tell them."

Startled, I turn to see Jia, Wil, and Misty standing behind me. Greg, Elisha, and Lynn stumble backward. Bits of paper and a pair of scissors falls to the floor as Lynn leaps from her chair.

"What are you doing here?" I ask Jia. Part of her neck is bandaged and her lightning scars visibly twist around the left side of her face, still red and raw. "I…thought—"

Jia squeezes my arm. "Like you said, Ingrid. This affects all of us. We are stronger together."

"We don't have to fight a silent war," Wil says. "We don't have to be quiet."

"Yeah. Finally. Fire with fire." Misty lights up her hand with a righteous blaze and grins like the devil.

"Holy sweet God," Elisha says. "Will you teach *me* how to do that?"

"This is so much bigger than we thought," Lynn whispers. "And Tilly ...?"

"If you help us, we can bring her to justice," I say.

They're stunned into silence. I glance at Jia, then at Wil, and at Misty. We share the same thoughts, the same thick tether of strength in adversity, one that we can throw like a lifeline to all that need it. I know exactly what to say.

"We need you to help us spread the word about something."

"You got the candles?"

Jia nods, and produces a bag of tea lights. "For meditation. Thank goodness I brought a whole bunch when I first came here. The rest have already been passed around."

"We should get out there," Misty says.

Instinctively, I reach for Jia as we exit Rita House, before realizing that we have chosen not to hide tonight. Wil, Jia, Misty, and I emerge from the building. Misty torches a finger and lights our candles one by one. Other students are behind us, holding their lights. We use ours to light theirs in turn. I smile at Kimberly, glad that she is here.

"So, Tilly, huh? What happened to her? People are saying that Ms. Agailya murdered her. Is that true, Ingrid?"

"Yeah." It is surprisingly easy to say. "Let's go to the quad, we'll explain what's going on."

"Wish it wasn't so darn cold. At least Ethan is going to be there, right?" She nudges me in the shoulder. Our breath escapes us in small clouds as we speak, but at least it isn't windy.

"I hope so," I admit quietly, as we begin to walk.

One by one, other students emerge from the dorms, intrigued by the shimmering dots of light in the black endless landscape. Like slow, deliberate moths to the flame, they surround us with the warmth of their determination. We all know someone who has been lost, and in the coming together, we find them again. By the time we hit the gritty, perfect pavement of Sparkstone Boulevard, we are twenty-five strong, and upon crossing the road into the section of the quad near the greenhouse, we are almost fifty.

Twenty feet away, toward Rogers Hall and further in the distance towards Conrod Building, I see the human forms of the hafelglob standing sentry. They carry no weapons, and they make no move against us. Neither Jadore nor Agailya nor Ohz or any other member of the Sparkstone faculty has hinted to us that there would be any form of opposition, though that means nothing in the kind of war we are waging. To them, this might be part of the experiment.

Misty eyes the fake janitors with disdain. "Why don't they *do* something? Instead of just...staring?"

Will throws them a quick glance. *Because they know we can't stop them alone.*

"Not yet, we can't," I say. "We'll figure out a way. Just not tonight."

"We are making a stand, in our own way," Jia says calmly. "They might be able to cover up one or two student's disappearances. But they can't explain away fifty, not all at once."

I can see it on Wil's face. Not yet, they can't. Not tonight.

Tilly's team, with our help, had mobilized quickly. They printed a flyer with Tilly's photo, captured "RIP Tilly. Memorial service for Tilly Newman and other victims tonight, seven p.m., in the quad." Greg wanted something more sensationalistic, but anything more would be encroaching on pulp-sci-fi territory and undermine the truth.

From the direction of Morris House, Ethan, lit by the warm glow of his tea light, hurries towards us. My heart lightens at the sight of him. He approaches our group, saying his hellos, and slips a hand in mine.

"Are you—?"

"You don't have to keep asking." I smile up at him. "I'm okay. Really."

"This ..." He nods up at all the students marching towards the quad. "This is something."

I blow out a sigh. The tiny flame in my hand ripples. "I hope so."

At the edge of the quad, near the greenhouse, a large bonfire blazes. Wood and items to burn are scarce, but we managed to convince the woodworking department to donate some wood to the cause. Misty generously donated her old essays and most of her notes ("I know thirteen languages fluently, you think I need notes?"). Greg and

Elisha stand guard with their backs to the flame, handing out their zine and chatting up interested students. Lynn, shier than the other two, circles the fire with a piece of wood in her hand, as if ready to strike the first person who dares tell her that she must put it out.

A small crowd gathers around the fire. I feel the heat from several feet away, and my smile widened. I should be terrified. We're breaking one of the school's rules. The Collective is watching us.

All I feel is warmth, and...safety.

"Is this for Remembrance Day?" I hear someone ask as we draw closer. "It's not for a few weeks and we didn't even have a ceremony last year..."

"So these pictures that that guy Greg just showed me? They're probably photoshopped. First of all. The blur around the edges? Amateur way of blending different elements—"

"—I heard that the school is run by the government, and they're using some kind of mind-altering drug on us? That's why I came."

Ethan and I exchange glances. He squeezes my hand. "You can do this."

I blush. "Thanks."

He brushes my hair out of my face and kisses me softly. Then I join Misty, Jia, and Wil, who have gathered with Greg and Elisha before the fire. I stare out at the faces. All these people came here tonight because of our quick work. It's not the drug-eyed audience in the cafeteria—these people are here because our flyers and the events of the past few days have sparked their curiosity. Our tutorial mates—Cheng, Todd, and Emily—wave from afar solemnly as they grieve with the reflection of the fire in their eyes.

Wil glances between the three of us. *Who wants to start?*

I clear my throat and raise my eyebrows in question. Jia and Misty nod; they look a little relieved.

"I know it's early for Remembrance Day," I say slowly, raising my voice so I can be heard over the flames and the friendly chatter. People fall silent as I continue. "We invited you here tonight because I think we need a night of remembrance. I'm going to say six names. Hopefully in the next ten minutes, you'll know why it's important you commit them to memory.

"Tilly Newman. Fahima Osmond. Daniel Chomber. Avery Trites. Sunniva Harris. Kendra Aguirre." I take a deep breath. "They all have one thing in common. Their fate is a lie. You were told they were transferred from this university. That is a lie. What they have in common is…they're all dead."

Misty's lips twitch, but she does not protest.

There are things I can't change. I don't know if I can stop Ms. Agailya from experimenting on my people for the sake of hers. The Collective is always going to be stronger. Better equipped. One step ahead. But we will give as good as we get.

I cup the tea light, encouraging its warmth, as our unsure voices gain confidence with each new sentence. Misty's forearm brushes against mine on my left and Jia's reassuring smile beams on my right. Wil holds up his phone and amplifies its power to send pertinent videos and pictures to everyone in attendance, and seems to be in his element as we take turns telling our story.

There will be consequences for this tomorrow. But I will do what I can to keep our fires burning bright until we are sniffed out. Agailya was right that I may not matter in the larger scheme of the universe—but that doesn't mean I can't make a difference in the here and now. It is better to burn brightly and briefly, than not at all.

Ingrid, Wil, Misty, Jia, Ethan, and many more return to openly oppose the Collective as they advance their agenda in:

BOOK FOUR
THE SPARKSTONE SAGA

Acknowledgements

The Acknowledgement Faery devised a scheme to exact revenge on the publishers. One night, she snuck into a large warehouse, and with the wave of her wand, turned the pages in all the books into heartfelt acknowledgements! Bookstores were outraged and returned stock immediately to the publishers. People were angry and disappointed that their anticipated new release was just a bunch of thank-yous!

Sir Copy Right thought the Acknowledgements Faery was taking this too far. The publishing world was on the brink of war. He was conflicted. As he was about to confront her, he came up with the perfect solution. Or so he thought...

What will Sir Copy Right's grand plan be? Tune in to the next Sparkstone Saga book to find out!

Champions of the Acknowledgements Page:

Thank you to Mum, Dad, Jessie, Marie & Joe Farrell and family for all their support and help. And Winnie too! =^.^=

Jessica Corra, for your patience!

Chadwick Ginther, for your friendship and fun times.

Kate Larking, for all your help in the past year at conventions large and small!

S. M. Beiko, or as I know her, Sam. It's rare to find a best friend who grew up on the other side of the country yet understands everything about you and drops everything to tell you about exciting business opportunities or the latest gossip. TWINS! Best friends 5eva.

And Dave, always, for his unwavering devotion.

About the Author

Photo Credit: Terence Yung

CLARE C. MARSHALL grew up in rural Nova Scotia with very little television and dial-up internet, and yet she turned out okay. Her YA sci-fi novel *Dreams In Her Head* was nominated for the 2014 Creation of Stories award. She is a full-time freelance editor, book designer, and web manager. If there's time left in the day, she devotes it to Faery Ink Press, her publishing imprint. When she's not writing or fiddling up a storm, she enjoys computer games and making silly noises at cats.

Website: FaeryInkPress.com

Facebook: Facebook.com/faeryinkpress

Twitter: @ClareMarshall13

If you enjoyed this book, please consider writing a review on Amazon or on Goodreads. Thank you!